M000078676

The Merry Maids

Stefanie Contreras

Copyright © 2019 Stefanie Contreras

All rights reserved.

ISBN: 9781079186062

WITH LOVE

This book is dedicated to JoAnn Coronado.

CONTENTS

1

I was upside down when they walked into the gym, and about to drop from twenty feet. I always knew when Stryker was nearby, but I didn't risk a glance at the doorway. A circle of classmates had formed around the mat below me. They called up a mix of encouragement and warnings to be careful that I ignored.

One deep breath in, and hold. A bead of sweat traveled from my forehead down into my hairline.

I shifted my weight and let gravity pull me over the ledge. As soon as my weight left my arms, I tucked my legs into a ball so I could make a clean rotation. I plummeted to the ground. Someone screamed. I used a shallow burst of telekinetic energy to slow down and then popped my arms and legs open wide as I landed on my feet and took a couple steps to stop my forward motion.

"I think you've got the hang of it," Reggie said over the sound of our classmates clapping for me. His blue eyes were smiling but he shook his head at me.

I unwrapped the tape from my hands and let some of the guys clap my shoulders in respect.

"Don't tell Cutter, but I'm going up to the roof next," I said to him quietly.

Reggie's eyes got wide and his mouth popped open. He angrily stepped toward me.

"Oh hell n-," he started to say but his voice cut off when he saw Stryker at the edge of my mat with two men whom I'd never seen before.

"Tippin, do Serasoma number twelve," Stryker commanded, naming a difficult routine he'd taught me last year.

I dropped my wrist guards and turned to face him. His wrinkled face was uncharacteristically void of expression. I met his chocolate brown eyes

1

and saw a twinkle there that was meant only for me. I felt my lips move into a small smile when I saw it.

Why do you want me to show you a Serasoma routine, I wanted to ask. But he was with the strangers, two men with well-worn faces. Generals most likely, or some other form of top brass. They both looked me over with unreadable expressions. Stryker looked odd beside them. He was short and wore the robes of a Master. The strangers were tall and wore the space-ready suits of travelers.

I couldn't question Stryker, and embarrass him in front of strangers. So I simply asked in a clear voice, "fast or slow?"

Stryker raised an eyebrow at the strangers, to let them decide.

"Fast," one of them said with the easy authority of a leader. Definitely a general. Reggie cleared my things and got off my mat.

I ignored the looks we were getting from the other students around us and fell into my starting position immediately. I bowed once, then began the routine. Fast, as requested, and true. I whipped around the mat the way Stryker had taught me: ducking, spinning, rolling and tumbling. My muscles flexed with every movement, and I reveled in the way it felt to execute each and every step in the routine the way it was supposed to be executed. The tape on my feet protested and stretched taught against my skin as I twirled and pointed my toes.

Just a little more.

I did two one-armed flips backward followed by an aerial backflip and shouted, "sa!"

I bowed. My Serasoma was flawless, and I knew it.

Stryker knew it too. When I straightened from the bow, I saw his pride. Our eyes met across the mat and he nodded. I was sweating and breathing hard but I had done what he asked of me. It made me want to grin.

I don't know why, but making him proud was always more satisfying than doing routines well and winning competitions.

The two strangers drew together for a muted talk. I tried to capture Stryker's attention but he was ignoring me now. All his focus was on the men he'd brought to the gym. So I waited in silence, and slowly realized that I had the entire gym's attention. Apparently everyone had noticed the strangers. My cheeks grew warm as I glanced around and saw a sea of faces. It was unnaturally quiet. Usually there were people talking or yelling over the noise of the machines and the sounds of sparring. Right now there was restless whispering and no one moved.

"Good," one of the strangers said finally, drawing my attention back. His partner nodded in agreement, and Stryker grinned. "Thank you, Miss Tippin."

Then they left. Stryker went with them before I could get an explanation. He opened the doors and waited while the men exited the gym.

When he glanced back at me one last time, Stryker looked proud but maybe a little sad. I didn't understand it, and I stepped forward to go to his side. Before I could get across the mat, he dropped his gaze and left.

As the gym's door closed behind him, the room suddenly buzzed back into motion. It was like someone had flipped a switch and everyone surged forward. They all wanted to know what had just happened, but I was as clueless as they were.

"They were scouts," Reggie said from my side. "Stryker brought you scouts, Tip."

My mouth hung open. Scouts? Had those strangers really been scouts? And if they were, had I done well enough for them to give me an assignment? Was I going to get the chance to go shipboard based on my Serasoma routine?

"They said you did 'good,'" I heard someone else say with unsuppressed jealousy. "You lucky bitch, you're going shipboard."

I sucked in a breath.

I didn't know what to say, so I whirled back to the edge of my mat and snagged my jacket and water. I heard more questions called out as I made my way to the back of the gym. Some of my classmates gave me high-fives. Others pounded my back companionably as I passed them. In a daze, I somehow made it back to the student quarters without a clue as to how I'd gotten there. I just kept playing it back in my mind — the strangers and the looks on their faces after I'd finished the routine.

"What happened?"

I was in Cutter's doorway. He was my oldest friend at the Academy, and the only person I knew better than Stryker. He always left his door open so people could holler hello as they passed his room. Everyone knew and liked Cutter. He had a ton of acquaintances but I was one of his only true friends.

"I think I was just scouted," I blurted. My eyes focused on his face.

Cutter was tall. He jumped up from his desk and took a half step across the length of the room (a half step that equaled four of my steps) until he grabbed me by the shoulders. He leaned down so we were eye to eye.

"Lyvvie, are you serious? What happened?"

He dragged me inside and kicked the door shut. I giggled at the intense look in his eyes. I wasn't used to being on this side of that stare. Cutter has dark eyes, darker than night, to match his dark hair and skin. When we first met I couldn't figure out how to read him, but his intensity became part of his charm. I knew it came from a driving need to succeed and make something of himself.

That intensity had propelled him to his ranking as number one in our graduating class. I was proud of him. Really proud of him. That pride reminded me of the way Stryker had looked at me in the gym today.

"I was working out with Reggie in the gym," I said. "Stryker came in with two men I assumed were generals, and he ordered me to perform Serasoma number twelve. So I did it. Fast."

I lifted my eyes to catch his reaction. He blinked at me.

"Fast," Cutter repeated. "You did Serasoma twelve, fast, for scouts."

A slow smile burned across his entire face.

"I think so," I said. I didn't know for sure. No one had said so before they left. "Why are you saying it like that?"

"Like what?"

"Like, I just told you a present."

"I'm excited!" Cutter said, and laughed throatily. He gave me a little shake. "This is great news! I can't believe the old man did it. He's a genius."

Stryker really was a genius. If I was honest, I could admit that performing Serasoma twelve was a brilliant way to show off in front of scouts. It was the most elite routine I knew—extremely difficult, but beautiful, and I now knew it like the back of my hand thanks to months of practice with Stryker. It would give scouts a fairly reliable summary of my qualifications and potential if they were looking for someone with movement skills.

Stryker had told me a few weeks ago that he was going to recommend me for shipboard work, but I hadn't really believed him. At the Academy, only the elite got to go shipboard right after graduation. The top five people in the graduating class are guaranteed positions. Everyone else had to wait and start earthside instead.

On the other hand, I had done really well in the Tests.

Seven silvers, a bronze and two golds meant I'd ranked in every event, finishing in second place for females and eighth overall. My golds made Stryker especially proud, because I broke school records in those events— my specialties—telekinesis and movement. But since I'd ranked eighth, I wasn't part of the top five like Cutter who immediately got shipboard positions. I assumed I would have to wait for a spot to open up on a ship somewhere, and get in if I could. It didn't bother me much – I didn't mind sticking around and learning more from Stryker.

Stryker obviously had other ideas, though.

"You're excited but I don't even know what for," I reminded Cutter. The smile ebbed from my face. The bubble of excitement slowly turned to anxiousness. What if the men with Stryker didn't like my routine, and that's why they didn't stay and chat?

Cutter squashed me in a huge hug, and pressed me against his chest until I couldn't breathe.

"If you aren't accepted by these scouts, they're crazy," he assured me. "You should just go and pack your bags now to get it over with. They're probably on their way over to snatch you up and send you on assignment."

I laughed.

"Cutter, we're doing it," I breathed, feeling the world expand around me. "We're seriously doing what we've been dreaming about since day one."

"Weird, isn't it?"

I nodded.

Cutter got a sudden mischievous look that I recognized immediately. He let go of me and turned to rummage under his bed.

"We're going to get blitzed tonight in celebration," he announced. "I didn't want to before because I was stressed that you weren't going to get a shipboard position but now everything is happening the way it's supposed to."

"You were really worried about me?" I asked.

I took a seat on his bed and started to pull the tape from my bare feet. Cutter's room was always flawlessly immaculate. Everything had its place, even me, and my spot was perched on the end of his bed while he sat at his desk. He didn't answer my question. Cutter doesn't like conversations that have the potential for getting emotional. It's the control freak in him.

Which reminded me...

"Oh by the way, if Reggie tells you any weird stories about me being on the roof don't believe him," I said as casually as possible as I tossed my tape into his wastebasket.

"What?" Cutter's muffled voice under the bed made me laugh.

"A-ha," he said triumphantly a moment later. I looked at the bottle he presented and felt my eyes go wide.

"Tequila?"

Cutter laughed.

"We're celebrating old-school tonight, baby girl," he said. "You're going to be out of your mind when I'm through with you."

My stomach lurched because it believed him.

If I had known the scouts would come for me that night, I obviously would have protested when Cutter brought out the hard liquor. He was in such a good mood, it was easy for me to give in and join the fun. I vaguely remembered finishing the bottle with him and immediately puking it all up into his sink less than an hour later. Cutter took care of me and helped walk me to my bed in the other side of the wing without teasing me at all. In truth, he was the person most responsible for finishing the tequila. I did my share, though, and he had to give me credit for that.

"See you tomorrow," he whispered. I felt him kiss my forehead after he helped me get into my pajamas.

"Stay out of trouble, big brother," I mumbled automatically. Then I climbed into my bed and passed out before he'd even left the room.

Nevertheless, I was awake immediately when they came for me. I heard the knock at the door and stumbled from my bed to open it. There had been something authoritative to that knock that I knew was not normal. When my door swung open, I saw the two men whom I'd done my routine for earlier.

Stryker was not with them.

"It's time," one of the men said. "You've been selected to join a ship."

"Get up and pack quickly," the other one said. "Leave whatever you don't need."

I nodded.

I turned and rubbed my eyes until I could focus them, but I was also using the time to get my thoughts in order. There were actually very few things in my room that I needed. Clothes and bedding could all be supplied later from standard issue. Besides those things I had only a few personal belongings. I grabbed my duffel bag from my closet and started packing. A hairbrush, an image album, a music player, a jewelry box, my make-up stash and my coat. A battered journal tied shut with pieces of leather. That was it. My bag looked pretty empty when I was finished, so I went ahead and tossed some clothes and shoes in to fill it up. Then I turned to face my scouts and told them I was ready to go.

It was still early, much too early for students, as we passed through empty and silent halls. We didn't go down the hall past Cutter's door, or I would have tried to say goodbye. Instead, we turned the opposite direction and kept walking. I was tired and hungover, much too uncomfortable to try and be charming, so I didn't bother to start a conversation. My scouts led the way out to the Academy's docking station, and I was content to simply follow.

I eventually found myself aboard a small passenger ship. Without much to-do the scouts prepped the ship for launch. I laid myself in the hold where they pointed and immediately drifted off into sleep.

I'm not sure if the tequila or the lack of sleep had anything to do with it, but I was unconcerned about the fact that I hadn't been given the chance to say goodbye to Cutter or Stryker. Stryker probably knew what was happening to me, and wouldn't be too upset. Cutter would hunt down Stryker until he had an answer about my disappearance. Then Cutter would be happy that I was already on assignment, and he would appreciate the fact that he didn't have to suffer through an emotional goodbye with me. There wasn't anyone else I cared about more than those two. Lulled by the hum of the ship's engines, I fell asleep with their faces in my mind.

A hand shook me awake. I opened my eyes and looked up at the scout who hovered near me.

"Hungry?"

My stomach flip-flopped.

"Sure," I forced myself to say, and sat up. The scout handed me a sandwich and sat down to join me for breakfast.

"Miss Tippin, how much do you know about the Merry Maids?" he asked without preamble.

I took a hesitant bite out of my sandwich and considered his question.

"The Merry Maids?" I glanced at him, and saw that he watched me from narrowed eyes. "I've heard of them, but no one really knows what they do or where they go."

The scout seemed satisfied with my answer.

"From what I understand," I continued, "you have to be pretty special to be a Merry Maid. Since they are so elite, and no one knows what they do, it's assumed they do black ops."

"I invoke Alpha clearance," the scout said, meaning I was bound to intergalactic codes of confidentiality. "What I tell you now is information for you alone to know. You may not share it with anyone else."

I lowered my sandwich. Its smell was making my stomach roil, and I was glad for the chance to stop pretending I wanted to eat it.

"Understood, sir," I said immediately, as was expected.

He nodded in approval that I understood.

"We are taking you to join a ship that is already in the field," he said. "You are going to be the newest member of the Gamma Squadron. Your gold medals in the Tests are exactly the skills needed to complete the team. They recently lost one of their members and need a replacement. You are that replacement."

"*Lost* one of their members?"

"To civilian life," he clarified. "She wanted to start a family. That's just not possible for the type of work the Gamma Squadron has to do, so she decided to leave."

Interesting, I thought. I filed this piece of information away for later.

"The Gamma Squadron is the official name for the Merry Maids," the scout said. "Their purpose is to unofficially clean up official messes. This usually means extractions. After you're aboard their ship, you'll immediately be taken on your first mission with them. They're waiting for you somewhat impatiently. Otherwise my partner and I would have waited for a more reasonable time to bring you."

I nodded my understanding, feeling a flush of excitement. If only Cutter could see me now, I thought. He would be stoked for me.

But I guess he would never really know, I realized. Not if I was going to uphold my agreement to the Alpha clearance. Any adventures I might have with the Merry Maids would have to stay between me and the Merry Maids.

Cutter would never know. Neither would Stryker, for that matter. If I ever returned to his gym, I wouldn't be able to share anything about what I'd done.

"So I will be using my skill with body movement and telekinesis," I said, since he'd mentioned my golds.

"Yes, you are the new Courier for the Merry Maids. Every time your team is sent on a mission, you will be on the front lines."

I nodded. We had studied ship roles at the Academy. I had never practiced a Courier's duties but I generally understood what was expected of them. Couriers were often the go-between on diplomatic missions – they carried messages between parties. They were expected to be representatives for the diplomats who employed them. I had never actually considered diplomat work, so I didn't know if it was going to be a good fit for me, but hopefully these scouts knew what they were doing.

"And what do the others do?" I asked.

"The Captain usually stays on the ship during assignments unless she is absolutely needed," he said. "Her name is Lira Orvobedes, and she's one of the most brilliant tacticians to graduate from a training Academy. You'll learn a lot from her.

"The Medic is AJ Cason. He is the youngest Medical scientist to graduate from the Academy. He'll be there in case anyone gets hurt, or if you find others who need Medical attention during a mission.

"The Pilot always stays on the ship during missions," the scout said. "The Merry Maids Pilot is Marco McNarry. He's the oldest member of the team and another one who will teach you a great deal."

"Then there is Gig Freeley, the team's Gunner. He'll operate the ship's defense systems during flight combat and provide weapons protection during missions. Gig is a bit rough around the edges, but you need to get on his good side since the two of you will most likely be sent on missions together."

Flight combat? I took this all in, and found myself extremely curious about what was expected of me. I counted names silently.

"This is only a five-person team?" I asked, amazed.

"Yes," he said. "Small but sufficient."

"Do you have any vids or case histories of past missions?" I asked.

"No," he said flatly. "No evidence of the Merry Maids is kept. If anything should happen to the team, you will all be replaced, and knowledge of you disavowed. You don't exist above ground."

I put my sandwich aside, and tried to decide if I was okay with this. If I died, no one would know what had happened to me, or have any proof that I'd ever existed. I was going on the first shipboard assignment of my life, and it wasn't at all the way I'd expected it to be.

The scout seemed to sense my conflict. He patted my shoulder and stood up to leave. Before he went, he looked down at me with respect in his eyes.

"Miss Tippin, I envy you," he said.

I looked up at him to see if he was joking.

He wasn't.

"The work you do with the Merry Maids will be the most important work done for our Order of Planets. Without you, many men and women would die needlessly and without a hero to go in and save them where others cannot. Without you, we would all be in danger. Because of you, I will be able to put my kids in bed tonight and know they are safe. I envy you for the work you will do. I hope you understand how vital you are to our way of life."

I sank low in my chair, and thought about what he'd just said.

2

I peered out the window as we approached the ship that carried the Gamma Squadron; I was feeling pretty impressed. Most ships were hulking behemoths that all looked the same. By comparison, the Gamma Squadron's ship looked lightweight and modern. It was obviously built for speed. Sleek.

My scouts piloted their passenger ship up beside the Gamma Squadron's and opened a comm link.

"Scout to Gamma, we are ready for transfer," one of the scouts said.

"Gamma here," said a woman's voice. "Proceed with transfer."

The scout I'd spoken with earlier got up from the co-pilot's chair and came to the back where I was waiting.

"Put this on," he instructed me. He pulled a dark blue space ready suit from an overhead bin and handed it to me. I took the suit from him and did as he instructed. It was thin but he promised it would protect me while I crossed from one ship to the other. I pulled it on quickly, eager to find out where life was taking me. The scout took my duffel and dropped it in a transport container that would go with me. Then he turned and led the way to the bay doors.

"You'll pass through these doors into the containment room," he said. "Once these doors close behind you, open the outer containment doors and wait for Gig to come get you."

I nodded my understanding.

"Thanks," I said.

The Scout handed me my helmet with a nod.

"Good luck, kid," he said, tapping the panel beside him. The access doors opened wide. I pulled on my helmet and grabbed the case that held my duffel before walking inside. I watched as he closed the door behind me.

10

Alone in the containment room, I looked around. My helmet muffled all sound. On the far wall was the touchpad I needed. I went to it and keyed it up, then opened the doors to space.

I've seen it many times from my quarters at the Academy, and on the handful of trips I'd taken with Cutter or Stryker to other planets. Those trips had always been interplanetary travel, with no starwalks. This time was different, and when I saw the stars yawning before me I was awed by the beauty of it. I smiled to myself and let the vision soak into memory.

The Gamma Squadron's ship shifted into view, blocking most of the stars from sight. I looked at it, and saw that a door was opening in the ship's hull. A man stood on the other side, dressed in a suit just like mine. He waited for the ship to shift closer, then leapt across to fetch me.

"Ready?" he asked, taking my case in his left hand and my arm in his right. His voice was deep and rumbly, even through his helmet comm.

"Let's go," I said, trying to sound casual through my excitement. I turned to face the opposite ship, ready for the jump.

His grip tightened around my arm and he held me in place.

"Hold on, girl," he grumbled. "You have to latch yourself to me."

I looked down at his waist and saw that he was tethered to his ship with a line. A second waistlength waited for me.

"Oh," I said. I took the line, clipped it to my midsection and secured it to his. I looked up when I was done and grinned. "Now?"

He pulled me to the lip of the ship, then in one fluid motion we leapt across the expanse of space to the Gamma Squadron. I watched the stars disappear as the door closed behind us, shutting me in with my new shipmates.

As the door sealed shut I felt a tug at my waist. I looked down and saw that I was being helped from my tether. I pulled off my helmet and let my hair fall back around my shoulders.

"Hi," I said, "I'm Alyvia Tippin."

"Gig," he said, shaking my hand briskly. He pulled off his own helmet, giving me my first good look at him. A shiver of attraction fluttered through my chest but I pressed it away.

Gig looked the way I'd come to expect all Gunners to look. He was extremely muscular and had a certain roguish look that matched my expectations for Gunners. His midnight black hair fell in his inky dark eyes and his deep tan was a startling contrast to the whiteness of his teeth as he tried to hide his sneering at me.

"First time working shipboard?" he asked.

I nodded, zipping myself out of my space suit. "That obvious?"

He turned away from me to open the containment doors, but I caught him rolling his eyes as he did it. Embarrassed, I decided to make a better impression on the rest of the team.

As the doors opened I saw the inside of the Gamma Squadron's ship for the first time. Vid screens and computer faces blinked lazily. The chairs around them hovered off the ground with red padded pillows for comfort. Instead of cold metal there were vibrantly colored rugs and carpeting. In the center of the room we were entering, the ship's commissary, there was a wide rectangular table with seating for five. Something caught my eye about the dining chairs that hovered near the table. I stepped closer and saw that the red cushioning on the chair headrests were emblazoned with names: Orvobedes, McNarry, Cason, Freeley and, best of all, Tippin. I ran my fingers over my name and looked at the chairs on either side of me: Freeley and Cason. I would be sitting between Gig, who had rolled his eyes at me, and AJ Cason. Wasn't he the Medic? Directly across from us sat Orvobedes, the Captain, and McNarry the Pilot. I tried to picture myself sitting at this table for a meal, surrounded by the team.

"Captain's waiting for us upstairs," Gig said, leading the way from the room without looking back.

I fell in behind him, trying to see everything at once. We left the commissary and took a short flight of carpeted stairs up to the next deck. I stopped at the top of the stairs and looked around.

To my right was the Pilot's deck, encased by clear windows. On the other side of the window, I could see a man in the Pilot's chair with a woman standing at his back.

To my left was a spacious planning room with a map table in the center, and doors that led off to more parts of the ship.

Gig went to the Pilot's deck and rapped on the window. The woman standing inside glanced back and spotted me by the stairwell. I watched as she grinned and said something to the Pilot. Then she looked at Gig and tapped her wrist. Gig nodded and turned away.

"We're going to fly straight to our assignment," he told me. "The Captain will come find you when she's ready to greet you. For now, why don't I show you to your quarters?"

"You got all that from her tapping her wrist?" I asked, following him across the room to the doors at the back.

Gig didn't say anything.

The doors slid open silently and he led the way into the corridor beyond. Doors lined both sides of the hallway, which curved in a circle around and slightly below the Pilot's deck and computer room we had just left. Gig named the rooms as we passed, "This is a guest quarter in case we take on important company, here's my room, here's Marco's room, this is AJ's room, this is your room. Down that way is the Captain's room and around the corner is the Medic's lab."

We stopped in front of the door to my quarters and Gig touched the keypad. The door slid open and Gig led the way in. I followed slowly, and looked around.

The entire far wall of my room was a window that looked out into space. It was the first thing I saw, and I gasped.

Gig glanced at me quickly and saw my mouth open wide.

"Better than the student quarters, isn't it?" he said.

I nodded dumbly, trying to dampen my awe. I looked at where Gig had placed my stuff and saw that my new bed was twice the size of the bed I used to sleep in. It sat against the left wall framed by cherry wood. To my right was a lounge area with a couch, armchairs, a desk and vid screens. There was also a short hallway that doubled as a closet. The hallway led to my own private bathroom and shower.

"Are you sure this is for me?" I asked.

Gig stepped closer and took my arm.

"This is your room," he assured me. "Get used to it. It's the Order's way of keeping us happy. What we do is dangerous so we are compensated for it. You will probably see more on your first assignment than any of your friends will see in their first year."

He led me into the hallway and showed me the closet.

"We have clothes here for you already," he said. "Take a shower and find something regulation to wear. Then come back and meet up with the Captain on the main deck."

I watched him leave, vaguely noticing the way his back muscles rippled under his shirt as he walked.

"Do I smell that bad?" I joked.

"You smell like alcohol," he assured me. Then he exited my room without looking back.

I felt my face burn and immediately turned toward the shower. How embarrassing, I had definitely not made a good first impression on Gig.

Showered and (hopefully) clean of the smell of alcohol, I changed into my regulation shipwear: black pants, tall boots and a sleeveless blue tunic. I braided my wet hair and tied it with black elastic. When I looked at myself in the mirror, I realized how pale my face was. It was a side effect of the tequila, I knew, so I grabbed my makeup from my duffel and added some color to my eyes and cheeks. Feeling better that I looked presentable, I took a deep breath and left my quarters for the main deck.

When I entered from the back of the room, I saw that everyone was there: all four of my new squad turned to greet me.

"Welcome, I'm Lira," said the Captain.

I studied her like Stryker had taught me. She was probably in her early fifties and had her hair tied up into a bun that was dark hair like mine, but a short length of it fell into her hazel eyes. The Captain was tall and slim, and carried herself with authority. She had strong cheekbones, thin lips and a barely visible scar next to her nose on her right cheek.

I smiled at her and shook her hand firmly, and saw that she grinned at me. She looked beautiful when that happened.

"This is our Pilot, Marco," the Captain said and gestured to a man at her right.

Marco stepped forward and clapped my shoulder.

"Nice to meet you, Alyvia," he said. "Welcome to our team."

I thanked him and studied him, even as he studied me. He was near the Captain's age, I thought, and had a few streaks of gray in his military-style sandy blond hair. Blue eyes and a slightly crooked nose were framed by a square jaw. He was thick in his arms and legs but not fat by any means. His hands were big too; he could probably palm my head. He seemed fit for work as a mechanic, not toggling controls as a Pilot, but I could tell by the way he politely stepped back behind the Captain that he was not really aware of his dominating presence.

"You've already met Gig," the Captain said. "So this is AJ."

My eyes found Gig's. He just nodded at me.

The other person, AJ, came forward and took my hand in his. He stepped a little too close into my personal space.

"Alyvia, we are very glad to have you," he said, as he peered down at me. I wanted to take a step back and have my own space back, but he still held my hand. I looked up at him and took in the perfectly straight teeth, the handsome face, pale blue eyes and white-blond hair. AJ was sort of thin. He didn't have the muscle of Marco or Gig but he did seem to know how his presence affected others, and he was trying to affect me.

"Nice to meet you, AJ," I said, disinterested. If Cutter were here I could have signaled him by scratching my shoulder and he would have cut in with some made-up excuse. Unfortunately, Cutter wasn't here, so I had to extract my own hand and politely step away.

"Take this," the Captain said, and held out a bracelet. I took it from her and studied it closely. It was heavy silver with five links.

"That is a tracking bracelet that you will need to wear at all times," the Captain said. "Each link represents someone on the team. You can use it to find your teammates if you ever get separated on assignment. Or they can use it to find you."

I fastened it around my wrist and jiggled it to get used to its weight.

"Did the last girl wear this before me?" I asked.

"Maddy," the Captain said. "No, she didn't. This one is brand new."

"You have some big shoes to fill," Gig added.

I looked over the Captain's left shoulder at him. Gig stood apart with arms crossed across his muscled chest.

"I'll give it everything I have," I tried to assure him.

"Hopefully that's good enough," he replied. My heart dropped as I watched him turn away and retreat down the stairs to the commissary.

"Don't mind him," Marco assured me. "He didn't take Maddy's departure well."

"He doesn't take anything well," AJ said, obviously bored. "Alyvia, come see me in the Medic lab when you have a minute. I need to create a file on you."

"Sure," I said, even though I wasn't looking forward to it. AJ reminded me of those cocky guys who drove me nuts at school. I usually did my best to avoid them whenever possible, but on such a small ship this was going to be hard.

"Let's go through a brief," the Captain said. "I need to prep you for your first mission since we're headed straight there."

"I'll be in my lair," Marco announced, heading back to the Pilot's chair.

The Captain led the way from the computer room and back out into the hallway. We passed the empty rooms, my room, and headed further down the hall to the Captain's room.

When I first saw my quarters, I'd marveled at the luxury I would be living in but the Captain's quarters were even more breathtaking. Three times the size of my own room, she had a much larger lounge area complete with a table and full kitchen in case she didn't want to eat in the commissary.

"Come sit with me," she said, and led the way to her couches. I sat down next to her and waited expectantly while she grabbed a tablet from her coffee table and read it over.

"You received a strong recommendation from your mentor," she said. "How long have you trained with Stryker?"

"From the first week I arrived at the Academy," I said. She must be reading my file, I realized. "We hit it off right away and he's been coaching me ever since."

"Stryker is a name with weight in the Order," the Captain said. "He only takes on the best students and trains them to become Couriers. If he took you on your first week, then you must be the best. We accepted you onto our team before the scouts even saw you in action."

That explained why they already had my last name on the chair in the commissary. I tried not to let my mouth hang open in surprise, but it was hard. The Captain saw my wide eyes though and nodded seriously.

"That's why youth is so great," she said. "You kids are clueless."

She said it with a sympathetic smile that took the sting out of her words but I had to take a moment to collect myself.

"Whoa, hold on a second," I said. "You're telling me that Stryker took me on because he purposely wanted to train me as a Courier?"

The Captain said yes.

"I seriously thought he just felt sorry for me," I said. I was monumentally stupid. "I thought I lucked out to have such a good mentor! He didn't tell me that he'd scouted me."

"Stryker is a man of few words, and fewer emotions," the Captain said.

"You know him?" I asked. I softened a little as I smiled at her description.

"Yeah, he's a good guy," the Captain said. "I heard he was training a Courier and I had to have her. Your performance in the Tests was very impressive. The whole team agreed that you would be an excellent asset for us."

"Thanks," I said. "But I feel like an idiot for not knowing sooner. Why didn't he just tell me?"

"I guess that is a question you'll have to ask him," the Captain said. "I'm sure he had a reason."

In the Academy, we could study a specific focus where our skills would intersect. Other teles had taken up engineering, and almost all of my movement teammates had either taken up combat or espionage. Stryker had encouraged me to study a little of everything, and not commit to a specific focus.

I never asked him why.

The Captain set my file on her coffee table and shifted to face me.

"Let's go over your first mission," she said. "We are on our way to Galaxin 7 in unapproved territory. A ship from the Order crash landed there a few days ago. There is no word on how many survivors remain, if any, because there have been zero communications with anyone on board. You will go with AJ and Gig to scout the area and bring back any survivors, although the odds of survivors is doubtful. Then you will destroy the ship to remove evidence it was there. Aye?"

"Aye Aye, Captain," I said.

She nodded and reached out a hand. I took it and shook it firmly.

"The full report is on your desk in your quarters," she said. "Go brief yourself and get some rest. We will arrive at Galaxin 7 in fourteen hours."

I removed myself from her quarters and found my own after counting the doors. On my desk, just as she had said, was a tablet with the full brief of my first mission on Galaxin 7. I grabbed it and flopped on my bed to read it over, eager to learn every line in preparation.

3

A little over an hour later, I felt as prepared as I could be considering we didn't have much information to work with. The Captain had said the chances of finding survivors was unlikely. That wasn't something I necessarily wanted to see, but I was going to do my best not to embarrass myself. The report detailed the layout schematic of the downed ship, and gave some specifics on the territory that Galaxin 7 fell in – a colony of planets that operated outside the Order and had a rivalrous relationship with the Order that was currently peaceful but could negatively impact the Order's shipping routes from that region if threatened.

I lay down on my bed and napped. Yes, I still had some alcohol to sleep off, but I was also feeling pretty nervous about my first mission. Galaxin 7 was going to be the starting point of my career. It would set the bar for all the future missions I took on with the Merry Maids.

I would be lying if I said I wasn't daunted but Stryker had always told me that success was when preparation met opportunity. I was as prepared as possible for this mission, minus the stretching and limbering I would do before we went to ground. My opportunity was aboard the crashed ship. I had to make it count for me. I tried not to anxiously think up ways I might mess up the mission. It was difficult but I eventually pushed the negative thoughts out of my head and eventually was able to relax.

I slept for a few hours. I could have slept longer but a chime sounded at my door. I rolled over and stared at it before comprehending what it was.

"Who is it?" I called out sleepily.

"It's me," came a reply.

I sighed and got up to answer the door. Before I did, I tried to wipe at my eyes and smooth my hair.

"Am I disturbing you?" the Medic, AJ, asked when I got the door open. He stood in the hallway with hands behind his back.

"Not at all," I said politely. "What can I do for you?"

"I'm here to drag you into the Medic's lab," he said. He shifted to extend a hand toward me. "I need to start a file on you before the mission."

I looked down at his hand and wondered how I could get out of letting him touch me, but it was too early in our relationship to be rude. So I put my hand in his and let him lead me down the hall.

"Are you excited to go on your first mission?" he asked. He pulled me into the lab and led me to an examining table. I pulled my hand from his and helped myself up.

"Yes," I said with confidence. "This is what I've been training for."

I watched him closely as he pulled a tray over and took an instrument from it.

"Put this in your mouth," he instructed, handing me a soft red cube. "Don't swallow it, just let it dissolve."

I took it from him and did as he said. A computer screen across from me immediately lit up and started showing numbers. AJ turned his head to see what the initial numbers showed: temperature, blood pressure, muscle mass, etc. The cube was flavored to taste like strawberry cheesecake. I was tempted to bite into it, but Medics hate it when their numbers are incomplete.

AJ turned back to his tray and pulled on a half glove that covered all of his fingers but didn't extend to his wrist. Using his fingertips only, he pressed them to all of the parts of my body where vital organs were, starting with my head. I sat silently and tried not to squirm.

"Looks like you are in perfect shape," he said at one point, his lips a little too close to my ear. I tried not to flinch away from him.

"Well," he amended, "except for your alcohol count. You must have been at a party when they were scouting you."

I blushed, ruing the day I'd let Cutter break out the tequila.

I could tell AJ was grinning behind my back. I turned my head to look at his face, and realized with a start that Gig had come in.

He stood at the door to the Medic's lab with an inscrutable expression on his face.

AJ seemed to notice Gig just then too.

"What do you want?" he asked Gig. There was a lack of warmth in his voice that made me do a double take between them.

Gig's gaze shifted from me to AJ and grew perceptibly colder.

"The Captain asked me to bring you and Tippin to dinner," he said. Then he turned and left.

"What a gorilla," AJ said when the door slid shut behind Gig. "He'll make some primate a happy husband one day."

I rolled my eyes and sighed, wishing the cube in my mouth was gone.

AJ pulled off his glove and came around in front of me again. He watched the numbers scroll on the computer screen until the cube dissolved completely and the numbers dwindled to an end. Then he leaned closer with a lopsided smile and put his hand on my knee.

"All done," he said. "Can I take you to dinner?"

I swallowed and pushed his hand away. Then I slid off the table and strode quickly away from him toward the door.

"Let's go," I said over my shoulder. I didn't wait for him to catch up. I found my own way to the stairwell that led down to the commissary. Gig, Marco and the Captain were already there setting the table.

"Hi," Marco said pleasantly. "We're almost ready. We decided to do the formal dinner thing tonight to welcome you."

I smiled.

"Great," I said. "I love family bonding time."

Marco chuckled at my lame joke but the Captain and Gig looked like they hadn't heard it. They moved their heat dishes from the counter to the center of the table and arranged serving spoons and forks around the meal.

AJ entered the commissary behind me and placed a hand at the small of my back.

"Sit next to me," he said, guiding me to the chair with my last name stitched on it. I took my seat and watched while everyone sat around me— Gig on my right, AJ on my left. Marco sat down across from Gig and the Captain sat down across from AJ.

Just like that, I was part of the team.

"Alyvia, did you ever study with Master Cotón?" Marco asked. He pushed one of the heat dishes toward me so I could serve myself.

"Yes, I did!" I said. "I refused to take my theory classes from any other teacher."

"She and I went to school together," he replied. "Although back then you never would have known she'd become a respected theory teacher."

"Really?" I perked up, eager for dirt. At the Academy, I had found that the lines between teacher and friend melted away fairly quickly as you improved in your studies. But Master Cotón had never let down her walls between teachers and students. In the end she was one of the least loved but most respected of all the masters.

Marco and I launched into a full discussion of her background and teaching methods while we served ourselves and started eating. I was vaguely aware that the Captain and AJ were having a discussion too. I glanced at them and caught the Captain smiling at me.

Startled, I smiled back.

"Alyvia," the Captain said, "tell us more about you than what your file says. Where did you grow up, do you have a big family, why did you come to the Academy?"

I paused before answering. This was too soon.

"Oh, I don't think you guys want to hear my boring story," I said, and laughed self-deprecatingly. "I came to the Academy as a stupid little girl looking for adventure. Little did I know there would be *work* involved."

Everyone laughed with me (except Gig I noticed). They obviously sympathized with this feeling in some way. I tried to think of a way to deflect the question without sounding like a weirdo.

"When I was a kid I had these Academy comics, you know—the typical propaganda they send out?"

Everyone nodded.

"There was one with this heroine named 'Ace' and I wanted to be her so bad," I said. I could still picture the detailed drawing of Ace with flowing black hair pleated in rows down her back. Her space suit was the kind that hugged all of her womanly curves and was seductively zipped low in the front. And, my favorite, she had the craziest, loudest make-up. I wasn't allowed to read Ace's comics, or anything from the Academy, but my brother had shared his collection with me before he ran away, and I had managed to keep the secret from our parents.

"I remember those Ace comics," the Captain said. "Wow, I'm really feeling my age."

"I know," Marco agreed, looking at me. "I bet you've never even heard of The Drawer."

"What drawer?" I asked, which seemed to confirm his thought.

"Ugh," Marco said. He laughed and threw his arms up in defeat. "I'm old enough to be your father. We're going to have to do some more training with you so that we don't feel so old."

"I don't think teaching her about The Drawer is going to make you feel younger, Old Man," AJ said.

Marco sighed in defeat.

"It's worth a try," the Captain said kindly. "Age is in the eye of the beholder."

"Said by someone with all the trappings of youth," Marco grumbled good-naturedly.

"Oh come on, you're not that much older than I am," she retorted.

I listened to them bicker back and forth with a mixture of happiness and longing. It was obvious that they were longtime friends—and I missed Cutter.

Pleasantly well-fed and becoming drowsy, I tried to stifle my yawns as we sat around the table in languid conversation. Mostly I listened, but Marco seemed intent on finding out more about me. Luckily, he asked no more questions about my background before the Academy, but it seemed like only a matter of time before he brought it up again.

In the middle of stifling another insistent yawn, AJ leaned closer and placed a hand on my knee again. I tensed and leaned away from him.

"Let me take you back to your room," he said. "I'm sure you're exhausted from all the excitement."

I pushed his hand off my knee and frowned at him.

"Oh yes, it's best if you get all the rest you can," Marco agreed. "I've got to get back to my chair."

"I have some more reports to read," the Captain said. Everyone started gathering their plates and cups and got up. Marco grabbed my setting despite my insistence that I could do it.

"Next time," he assured me. "Go on and get some rest."

"OK," I said. I stood up and saw AJ stand too, determined to walk me to my room so he could hit on me some more.

I reached out and put a hand on his arm.

"Thanks, I can find my own way," I assured him.

AJ grinned and shrugged, but he backed off. I left him behind and quickly found my bed, surprised by my sudden tiredness.

I was asleep before my head hit the pillow.

I dreamed of a hot simmering desert where everything was brown and dry. A city sprawled below me in a valley surrounded on all sides by mountains. I could name each of the mountains...and each of the little communities that had grown up nestled in their embrace. The signature beauty of a red, purple and blue sunset cast an angelic glow over everything I saw. It was all so familiar, and yet foreign at the same time. It had been a long time since I had been here—and yet, not long enough.

I found the ship silent when I woke. Only Marco was around, sitting in his Pilot's chair assessing his readings and maps. The soft blips of his console were the only noise in the room.

"Hey," I said when I came in.

Marco looked up, slightly startled, until he recognized me.

"Oh, hey," he said back. "I haven't learned your voice yet."

"No problem," I said. "May I join you?"

"Of course," he said, "Tired of sleeping?"

I nodded. I settled myself in the co-pilot's chair and drew my knees up to my chest.

"What did you study at the Academy besides flight?" I asked.

"Technology and theory," he said. "I've always had a head for machines and numbers. When I was young my mother let me tinker with all of the systems in our house. I would take things apart just to put them together again."

"Sounds messy," I said with a smile, as I pictured what he described.

"Only when I ended up with more parts than I started with," he replied.

I laughed and studied Marco's face again. He had laugh lines around his eyes and mouth that creased as he grinned at me. He wasn't as old as Stryker but I guessed he was probably ten or so years from retirement.

"We're about two hours from your first mission," he said. "Are you excited?"

"Yeah, a little bit," I said. "It's what I've been training for. It's hard to believe it's actually here now."

"You'll be great," he assured me.

"Have you ever had to go on a mission?"

"No," he said. "I don't leave the ship unless we're in dock. I've never had to join the team on a mission. My first duty is to the ship."

"Have you ever had to fly in for a daring rescue mission?"

"Yes, that I have done," he said. "There was this one mission where Maddy was sent to take readings on a volcanic planet in Sector Four. I'd had to drop her off over this desert of ash so she could hike up the side of a mountainous volcano. Then I circled our ship nearby. When she was about halfway up, I started sensing activity from the volcano that were not good. I warned Maddy, but she either didn't believe me, or she was stubborn enough to believe she could finish her mission. The Captain warned her to make it quick and AJ and Gig told her to get out of there, but she refused."

"Wait," I interrupted. "I thought the Courier was always accompanied by the Gunner?"

"Not always," Marco said. "In this instance, there was no chance of Maddy encountering human or animal life, so she went by herself."

"Oh," I said. That made sense.

"Well, of course, Maddy got the reading she wanted, and started her hike back down," he said, "but the volcano spiked its readings on my panels. We heard her shout for extraction at about the time we saw the volcano start to erupt from our viewers. I flew the ship low and tried to match her pace so Gig and AJ could hoist a line from the dock. We managed to get Maddy up right before the lava touched her sneakers, and we were pulling her up the line even as the ship was being tossed around from the heat of the lava. Whew it was close!"

"Wow," I said, dutifully impressed. Was I going to have to dodge lava in this job? What a weird life to come into after so many years at the Academy. I had been safe and sound in my tiny bunk while the Merry Maids were trying to outrun volcanos, and no one was the wiser what they were up to.

"Marco, what was she like?" I asked. "It feels like Maddy is still a shadow here."

"She only left us a few weeks ago," he said. "But it was pretty sudden.

We were all stunned, especially Gig."

"Was there something between her and Gig?"

"I don't know," he said. "They never held hands or kissed in front of us on the ship. But when you're in the field and you're in tough situations where your life is on the line...you would *have* to become close with the person you are sharing that with. Don't you think?"

"Makes sense to me," I said.

"I think Gig loved her, but either she didn't know it or she didn't feel the same. Knowing her she probably didn't even think too much about it. Maddy was not exactly a sensitive person. I always found her rather aloof."

"How long was she on the team?"

"Four years," Marco said. "The Captain and I started this team first. We worked with three others who were probably closer in age to us than you kids."

I grinned. Marco was *not* that old. But what I said was "what happened to them?"

He shrugged.

"They have families now, or they moved up the chain," he said. "We took on Gig first and then Maddy. AJ was the last one to join us before you, and he came to us about two years ago."

I felt dislike ripple through me.

"What's AJ's story?" I asked. "Is he a sleaze to everyone, or is it just because I'm new?"

Marco grinned.

"I noticed he was trying hard with you," he said. "He did the same to Maddy but she gave it right back to him. They drove Gig crazy when we were shipboard for too long."

I wrinkled my nose.

"That would be really annoying to me too," I said. "Why would she put up with it?"

"She liked the attention," Marco said simply. "She's the type who had to have a new man at every dock. That's why her leaving didn't surprise me as much as Gig. It made sense after I really thought about it."

"Hmm," I said. I knew a lot of girls at the Academy who sounded very similar. Cutter had dated some of them.

Marco slid a small container of nuts across the dash.

"Have some," he offered.

I reached out and took a handful. They were honey roasted cashews and they tasted delicious. I helped myself to half the container before he realized what I was doing and slid it away from me again.

We drifted into companionable silence. I stared off into space for a while, savoring the view. Marco told me some more stories about professors at the Academy whom I knew, while I laughed in disbelief.

"What's up with the Merry Maids?" I asked. "Where did that name come from?"

Marco grinned.

"We gave it to ourselves after *another* round of cleaning up the Order's bullshit," he said. His cheeks turned an extravagant shade of red. "I'm sorry I said that."

I lifted an eyebrow and gave him a funny look.

"The word bullshit?" I clarified.

"Yeah, sorry," he said.

I laughed.

"Yeah, how dare you," I teased him. "My innocent ears! They've never been near a Constantine Stryker."

He paused and sucked in a breath as he turned to look at me with wide eyes.

"I forgot about Stryker's mouth!"

Marco laughed the loudest belly laugh I've ever heard. He bent over in his chair and laughed his ass off while I laughed at how hard he was laughing.

We went on that way for quite some time. Marco slowly quieted and then whispered stories of Stryker's legendary mouth. Some of the stories I'd heard but some were new, and I held those stories close to my heart. Marco, as it turned out, was very nice. He made me feel comfortable in his presence, and I didn't mind when he occasionally reached out and touched my hand or arm to emphasize a point. I didn't have to worry about him hitting on me like AJ. He was willing to talk and mentor the way Stryker had, and I felt like he probably was someone I could trust.

When the Captain came in a while later, Marco and I were already friends.

"You should start putting together your gear," the Captain said.

"Yes, Captain," I said. I unfolded myself from the chair and left immediately. I went to my room and looked for the items I wanted: a small pack that would fit close to my body in case I had to crawl in a tight space; a dual video flashlight; a length of line; a toolkit; a tube of water; and a few bars of space food.

With everything put together, I re-braided my hair and tucked my trousers into my boots. Then I examined myself in the mirror and nodded in approval. I looked like I was ready for anything, even if I was having a small hiccup of self-doubt.

I shoved that feeling away though, because really—what were the chances that I would see any lava on Galaxin 7?

I took a deep breath and started my stretching and limbering exercises.

24

4

"This is what I've been training for," I told the Captain when she asked if I was nervous. I stood beside Gig on the dock and watched him prepare a land cruiser for travel. He and I and (shudder) AJ were going to use it to take us closer to the downed ship. Marco would only be able to get us so far. Apparently the ship was in a sea of forest.

"You'll do just fine," the Captain assured me.

I simply nodded. Glancing at her from the corner of my eye, I could see she was grinning.

"I remember when I went on my first mission," she said. "I was older than you, though. We went to this planet where all of the tribes were constantly in war. When the locals saw me with my crew of shipmates, who were all men, they wanted to give me my own land. That was when we realized it was a matriarchal society."

I burst into laughter and shook my head.

"So where is your land?" I said.

The Captain winked at me.

"We're entering range," Marco's voice said from the comm unit. I glanced out the dock windows and saw forest looming on the other side. "Prepare for drop."

"Alright, this is it," the Captain said, with a clap on my shoulder. "Obey Gig and AJ."

I nodded and mounted the landcruiser, then settled myself in the seat behind Gig's. AJ entered the dock, slung his pack beside me and sat next to Gig. We watched as the ship settled low to the ground. The Captain opened the bay doors for us from the doorway. Gig maneuvered the landcruiser backward, down the ramp and onto land. We pulled away from the ship. I watched it loom away from us as Marco steered it back into the atmosphere. Then Gig turned us the direction we needed to go, and we were off.

The landcruiser was a bulky way to travel. It had no top and jostled us back and forth as we crawled over felled trees and brush. But I liked the fresh woodsy air and the taste of adventure. This was it, my first mission. The first of many I would take with Gig and AJ as a team.

AJ turned his head to grin at me, as if he sensed I was thinking about him. I was in such a good mood I grinned back, but then he winked so I had to look away. His wink was different than the Captain's and I didn't want to encourage him.

We drove so far into the woods, the canopy of trees blocked the sunlight from ever touching the ground. These were the huge trees that were wider than three men lying across them.

"It's chilly without the sun," AJ said to no one in particular. "But if there are survivors aboard ship they would be able to use the wood for fires."

That thought finally reminded me of what the Captain said.

"What do you think the chances are that we'll find nothing but bodies?" I asked grimly. I tried not to picture the scene we were about to walk into.

AJ shrugged.

"In reality," he said, "our scans show the ship is mostly intact. Besides impact, which should have been softened by the release of emergency air pockets, there is a chance that people from the ship are alive and just waiting for rescue. They're probably grilling a barbecue right now, just waiting for us."

Gig glanced at AJ but didn't contradict him.

"How many people are logged on the ship?" I asked.

"About 25," Gig said in his rumbly voice. "It was only a skeleton crew returning the ship to be re-outfitted and to drop off some miscellaneous passengers."

"Where are we going to put 25 people if they're alive?" I asked.

"In the gym and the med lab and in the dock if we need to, plus our extra rooms," AJ said. "If you see anyone you like, you can let them stay in your room. Or maybe we could bunk together and let someone have my room?"

I rolled my eyes.

"Don't count on it," I said, so that we were clear. I am definitely not like Maddy.

"Just a thought," he said. He sounded amused.

"Cut the chatter," the Captain's voice said in my ear. "You're nearing the ship."

I touched the commlink that was hooked around my ear and raised the volume a little louder.

Sure enough, we saw a clearing ahead made by a propelled ship as it crashed. Gig drove closer as we surveyed the damage.

"It looks mostly in one piece," AJ said. "Except for the left engine and part of the left lower deck."

I've never seen anything more wrong-looking than a space ship leaning on its side on land, instead of hovering at a dock. It took me a minute to get over the feeling of wrongness before I could take in the rest of the damage.

This ship was probably about three times bigger than the Merry Maids ship, but it was made mostly out of windows, which meant it was used mostly for surveying. Rich families could post on as passengers along for the ride as the number crunchers explored and tested new places.

One of Cutter's older friends had been posted on one of these ships as the flight crew. He had been bored out of his mind piloting the ship for what he described as "weasels and wimps."

"Thank God I don't have to worry about that," Cutter had often said. He would be working on an emissary ship using his brains and charm to their full advantage.

I wondered what the chances where that Cutter's friend could be on this ship. I hadn't noticed any crew reports in the files I'd studied.

"I'm opening the hatch," the Captain said. A few seconds later we heard the sound of decompressed air as the hatch of the downed ship began to yawn open. Gig revved the landcruiser right up to the lip and inside the cold metallic air of the hatch. We parked near the unused survey cruisers and dismounted quickly.

I slipped my pack onto my shoulders and secured it at my waist while Gig and AJ did the same with their own belongings. Gig opened a box on the bed of the cruiser and pulled out three satchels. He handed one to me and the other to AJ.

"Explosives," he said. "Deposit them throughout the ship, timed to detonate from the trigger."

We nodded and made our way to the access doors. Gig touched the panel that should have opened the doors, but nothing happened.

"Captain, can you open the doors into the main part of the ship?"

"No," she said after a moment. "You'll have to do that on-site."

AJ and Gig both turned to look at me.

"You're up, Kid," AJ said. "Ever hot-wired a ship before?"

I grinned.

"I think that's a yes," he said to Gig.

I scanned the room for a control panel, and found the access ladder that would lead to the circuit boards. I climbed up swiftly to the main panel, pulled my toolkit from my pack and undid three of the four panel screws so it could be pushed aside. Then I climbed up into the cramped access cave and let the panel swinging.

I used a new tool to snip some wires and reconnect them in different places. In order for the door to open I would need a power source, so I re-routed a portion of power from the main computer and used it to stir the door to life.

"She got it," I heard AJ say.

The power was weak but if it shut down the door would still remain open. I tied off my work happily, put my toolkit away and clambered back down to the dock.

"Well done, Tippin," the Captain said.

I peered through the gaping darkness on the other side of the doorway and said the obvious.

"It looks like no one is home."

"No lights, no people," Gig confirmed. "Let's go. Stay behind me."

He cautiously led the way into the ship, with his flashlight to show the way. I followed with AJ close on my heels.

Together, we peered inside every room we passed, looking for signs of life. These must have been the study labs where earth and water samples were tested and examined. Every room on the dock level was empty.

"We're going higher," Gig said.

He stopped where an elevator stood open in invitation.

"There's no power in this thing to take us up," he said.

"I guess we're climbing the ladder in the shaft," AJ agreed.

Gig looked up at the ceiling of the elevator where the standard panel could be slid aside. His gaze raked over me and AJ.

"AJ, I'll give you a boost," he said. "Then you can pull up Tippin when I boost her, and both of you should be able to pull me up."

I wanted to protest that there was no reason why he should believe AJ could pull himself up and I couldn't. In other circumstances I would have roasted him for this assumption, but I kept my mouth shut. This was my first mission and I didn't want to argue with my teammates; plus Gig already had his reservations about me as it was. I wanted to show him I was a team player.

So I waited while Gig cupped his hands and let AJ put a boot into them. AJ lifted his other boot to Gig's shoulder and stood up high enough to open the ceiling of the elevator and climb up on top. He disappeared from view for a second and we saw his flashlight do a quick sweep around him. Then AJ reappeared and leaned over the lip of the ceiling and stretched his arms toward me. I went to Gig and braced a hand on his shoulder, then I put my own boot in his cupped hands and held my body straight while he hoisted me right into AJ's hands.

AJ held me around my upper torso until I got a handhold and pulled the rest of my body up onto the roof beside him. In the shaft the light was nonexistent. I couldn't see much of AJ even though he was right beside me. Together, we leaned down and braced ourselves to take Gig's weight.

First he tossed up his flashlight, which AJ caught and set aside. Then he disappeared from the elevator for a second so he could back up and get a running start. He ran into the elevator and kicked off the wall, which launched him up and into our hands. His weight made me grunt, but I strained and pulled until Gig's head was even with the top of the elevator car and he could pull himself up.

I noticed AJ was panting too. All those Gig-muscles were heavy.

"Alright, we're in the elevator shaft," Gig said for the Captain's benefit.

"Excellent, keep going," the Captain said in our earpieces.

AJ shone the flashlight upward. I followed the light and saw the ladder leading up to the next floor of rooms, continuing up for three more floors.

"All those doors are closed," I said. "If there is no power to the elevator, and we are still assuming there are survivors, how are they getting about the ship?"

AJ and Gig didn't respond. I turned to look at their faces in the glow of the flashlight and saw plenty of doubt.

"The engineer could have been injured, and unable to explain how to re-route power," AJ offered. "Maybe they are all using crawl spaces."

"This is a ship full of scientists," I argued. "Are you telling me not one of them knows how to operate the computers?"

AJ was silent. He looked at Gig.

"It doesn't look good," Gig admitted. "We need to prepare ourselves for what we might find."

I noticed that Gig looked at me when he said that last part, which insinuated that I wouldn't know what to do if I saw a dead body. I glared at him.

"I had a feeling it would be this way," I said. "We might as well go take a look."

Gig led the way up the ladder first. I watched him climb halfway up before I moved to follow.

"Let me help you," AJ offered. He put his hands on my waist as if bracing me up the ladder.

"Not necessary," I said quickly. AJ's hands slipped lower and he gave my bottom a push for good measure.

I considered kicking him in the face.

At the doors to the second level, Gig was fiddling with some wires he had exposed in a side panel. I waited as he clipped a small device in place, and the doors opened immediately.

Cool air breezed into the elevator shaft. I saw Gig climb up onto the lip of the landing. He waited for me to get closer, and then leaned down and lifted me by my underarms up onto the landing beside him. I guess my weight was easier for him to bear than his was for me.

"Thanks," I said.

Gig only nodded and turned to wait for AJ. I pulled my flashlight from my pack and turned it to face the pitch-black hallway. My light showed me that we were looking at a long corridor of rooms. This must be where the crew's quarters were.

"What have we here," AJ said. He came up close beside me so he was practically breathing in my ear. I stepped away from him.

"What is it?" the Captain asked.

"A whole deck of bedrooms to check," AJ answered.

"Split up," Gig said. "Holler if you find something."

He went to the first door on the left of the hallway and touched the entrance panel. The door slid open laboriously, straining on the small amount of power it could find. I took my flashlight and went to the nearest door on the right.

"Holler if you want me to give you a hand," AJ whispered in my ear. I pulled away and glared at him, but he kept walking down the hall to find a new set of doors.

This was getting really old. I glanced behind me and saw Gig watching me closely. I turned away from him and walked into the room I was supposed to inspect with an irritated sigh.

Cutter had once told me that the only way to put off a guy who was not getting the point was with a well-placed knee. Unfortunately, I'd never had to do that to someone who was on a small team with me. Not to mention, he would be responsible for my Medical health. There's nothing dumber than pissing off the person who could keep you alive.

OK, so I needed a new plan. I considered the possibilities as I cast the light of my flashlight around to search the room's closets and bathing area. There were clothes on the floor, books by the bed and pictures on the walls. There were some vid screens in the corner, at the desk. I tapped the displays but there was no backup power to get them active. No one was here.

"Empty," I said, after looking everywhere.

"Empty," Gig agreed from his own room.

We checked every room on the floor, but found no one and nothing to say what had happened to them. It was time to go up another floor.

Gig led the way to the stairs and we did the whole thing again on the second floor. It was weird going through and looking at other people's possessions. Everything had its place and was set aside just waiting until their owners came back. But the fine layers of dust that covered the surfaces in each of the rooms told a different story. I did not think the owners were coming back.

In one room I searched, I found children's trinkets like toys and clothing.

"Oh no," I mumbled to myself.

"What is it Tippin?" the Captain immediately asked in my ear. I'd almost forgotten I wasn't alone.

"There must be a baby on board this ship," I told her. "Or there was."

A figure darkened the doorway of the room. I looked up and saw Gig enter silently. He came to where I knelt by a bassinet and shone his light over the things I'd found.

A sudden feeling of urgency filled me. I just knew we weren't going to find anything else on this floor, it was all abandoned.

"We need to go up," I told him firmly. "Now."

Gig's face was unreadable in the shadows but he nodded.

"AJ, finish searching the rooms on this level," he said. "Tippin and I are going to start on the next floor."

"No way," came AJ's reply in my earpiece, "you're not leaving me here by myself. Besides, I'm done. This floor is clear."

"Then let's go," Gig said. He moved to the door quickly. I followed on his heels as we made our way back to the elevator.

AJ joined us before we started climbing the ladder.

"I'm not really in the mood to see a dead baby," he announced. "Let's get a move on, shall we?"

I shivered with dread and clasped my arms over my chest while I waited for Gig to get to the next level. I don't know how I got up the ladder to join him. I was on autopilot. We were going to see something horrific, I feared.

I had seen some horrific things in my life, but that didn't mean I wanted to see more.

From the light of our flashlights, we could see that this was the main level where the engineering room met the Captain's deck. Unlike the rows of hallways and networks of rooms below, this floor was mostly one cavernous room with only two doors on opposite ends leading to smaller sections. One was the Captain's conference room, the other was the engineering room.

"Tippin, see if you can get this deck online," Gig said. His voice echoed strangely in this room. "We can't search the ship's records without power."

I went straight to the main computer terminal and tapped out the standard start-up sequence. It has enough standby power to initialize my codes, but the "Invalid" warning flashed on the screen.

I tried a second time, but again it read, "Invalid."

I twisted a knob clockwise on my flashlight so that it would pick up a visual feed, and pointed it straight at the console.

"Marco, how do I bypass security?" I asked aloud.

"Tilt your light down a little," he said in my ear.

I tilted the flashlight so that he and the Captain could get a better view.

"Did you already try Pass A?" Marco asked.

"Yep."

"Try it again."

I tapped out the start-up sequence so that he could watch me do it, but of course the "Invalid" screen lit up. Before he could ask me to, I also tried Pass B, but that didn't work either.

"Alright, let's try something else," Marco said. I concentrated while he walked me through a complicated series of commands and controls. When I hit enter, instead of "Invalid" the screen read "Initializing."

"You're a genius," I said, grinning.

"I know," Marco said pleasantly.

"Good work," I heard the Captain tell him.

Now that security was loosened, I gave the entire ship full power. Nearby, the elevator suddenly hummed to life. The room's lighting burst into full glow, and filled the room with bright white light that blinded me for a moment until I got used to it. I squinted and blinked rapidly, and could hear AJ and Gig groan in discomfort.

"Sorry," I said. I toggled a lever quickly. The room dimmed slightly to a more bearable wattage.

Gig shook his head.

"Scan the ship's logs to find the last records they kept," he said. "AJ, go check the engine room and plant explosives if you don't find anything. I'll check the conference room."

I turned off my flashlight and stuffed it in my pack while AJ and Gig crossed to opposite sides of the room. I didn't have time to do more than that before Gig opened the door to the conference room and recoiled. He coughed and covered his face like he was about to vomit.

"What is it?" AJ said. He went to check what Gig was reacting to but stopped before he even got to Gig and covered his face too.

A second later the stench found me where I was rooted to the spot. I clamped my hands over my nose and mouth, but I started choking in disgust. Bile rose in my throat and my eyes watered.

"Well, I guess we found them," AJ said, moving closer to the door to peer inside. He sounded defeated.

From my vantage point I couldn't see any part of the room.

"Is it the crew?" I asked.

"Their bodies," Gig replied.

"All of them?"

"I don't know," he said. "We need a crew log to check."

I turned back to my computer and typed in a search command for the most recent crew log.

"Access denied," I read aloud. I pounded the computer's face in annoyance.

"The log probably exists in the Medic's lab," AJ said.

"Did we find the Medic's lab?"

"I searched it downstairs," he said. "It's just one floor down on the starboard side if you want to go look for it."

"Okay," I said gratefully. I hailed the elevator and jumped inside quickly, eager to leave the Captain's deck behind.

"Leave your comms on," Gig said before the elevator doors closed.

I sucked in a lungful of fresh air when he was out of sight and tried to stop trembling.

Now that everything was lit, the floor below looked entirely different than the one we had just searched not that long ago. I strode the hallway leading to the starboard side of the ship like I was seeing everything for the first time.

The Medic's lab was right where AJ had said it was. I walked in and made a beeline for the side office where the Medic's personal computer would be.

"Alright, I'm here," I said, grabbing a chair and pulling it over so I could sit at the terminal. In my ear, I could hear AJ and Gig talking in low voices as they searched the conference room upstairs.

"Why are they all in their dress uniforms?" I heard Gig ask.

"Show us a feed," the Captain ordered.

There was a short pause before AJ started narrating what he was showing them. I tuned out as I typed in my search parameters for the most recent crew logs and manifests. Watching the screen, I saw hundreds of file listings pop up in descending order. I accessed the first file on the list and read the date of revision. It was a crew log from three years ago that listed forty-five crew and seven passengers, but that was too long ago. I needed to keep looking.

I scanned the files again, and selected one that was dated six days ago. I pinged it to Marco so he could help Gig and AJ start the ID process.

Suddenly the hairs on the back of my neck stood up, and my scalp started tingling. I froze, and listened intently. It felt like there was another presence in the room, or someone was watching me.

I turned my head to scan the room but nothing seemed to be different.

"Who's there?" I called out, thinking it must be AJ. It would be just like him to try and sneak up on me while I was alone.

If he tried to scare me, I was going to knee him between the legs.

I got up and went into the main lab where rows of low beds lined the walls.

"Hello?"

I scanned the entire room for clues to why I was feeling so strange. The only thing that caught my eye was an odd shadow in the far corner. I silently stepped toward it, practically tip-toeing in the too-quiet room. Something metallic smelling wafted toward my nose.

"Tippin?" I heard the Captain ask.

I felt, more than heard, a whisper of sound behind me, back the way I'd come. I started to turn and look, but something tackled me bodily from behind and my side suddenly burned like fire. Gasping in pain, I hit the ground hard and tried to roll away from my attacker but I was too slow. A sharp kick to my belly knocked all the air from my lungs, and my vision went fuzzy.

A shadow passed over me. Crazed, dark eyes came close as a man I did not know screamed in my face, "You are TRESPASSING!"

I tried to suck in ragged breaths and gather my strength to fling him away from me with my tele but my body wasn't obeying the frantic panic of my mind. I thought I could hear shouting in my ear, but comprehending the words was impossible in that moment.

A heavy weight settled on my chest and thick hands wrapped around my throat. I bucked and struggled feebly. I tried to strike out at the face and arms of the man on top of me. My mind splintered. I was in too much pain to construct a thought of self-defense. My mind evaporated. I was defenseless and lost. The lack of oxygen, the red in my vision, the choking sounds I made—I was dimly aware of them but the only thing I truly felt was the fire that ate through my side. Pinned to the ground and dying, I fell into the blessed oblivion of unconsciousness.

5

"She's burning up."

I felt something soft touch my lips before I gasped oxygen back into my system.

"We need to get her back to the ship."

Hands touched my skin near where it burned, and I flinched instinctively. I tried to push the hands away so I could die in peace.

"Hold her still."

I was being gripped, pinned to the ground again, and I remembered how that ended last time. Panicked, I tried to fight again. Dammit if I didn't have to keep doing this.

"Sssh, sssh," someone whispered gently in my ear. They caressed my cheek. I tried to pull away but I recognized something familiar in that voice.

Confusion blurred into nothingness.

I was uncomfortable. Very uncomfortable, but I didn't have the energy to move. I was hot and aching. I was tossed aside on a wave of pain that rose up and carried me away.

Something peeled my skin and muscle away from my bones. I screamed, and writhed in agony, and then shivered. I reached out to grope for a lifeline, but found nothing.

Someone held me up while I puked. It must be Cutter, I thought. Only he would have the patience to stay with me while I was sick. Tears stung my eyes and dripped down my cheeks.

"Thank you," I tried to tell Cutter. "You're a good friend."

It sounded like a hoarse moan. What had I done?

Cutter didn't respond. Despair dragged me down.

I gave in to the weakness and slept.

At some point (was it before the puking or after?) I reached out and felt a hand in mine. My face, chest, arms, and legs were cooled with a wet rag. I sensed that I was getting stronger and feeling better but I was asleep again before I thought much more about it. My last thought was, *what did I do?* A man's enraged face chased me into the darkness of my dreams.

"Alyvia."

I stirred.

"Alyvia, open your eyes."

I did as he said. The light of AJ's Medic lab was dim but it still hurt. Tears filled my eyes quickly. They overflowed down my cheeks and dropped on the pillow by my ears. I tried to lift a hand to wipe them away, but even that simple movement required more strength than I had.

I groaned.

A soft cloth touched my cheeks, removing the moisture there. I blinked his face into focus.

"AJ," I whispered. "What happened?"

AJ propped his hands on the edge of the table where I lay and leaned over me.

"You had a rough few days," he said. "Your body was fighting the poisons that were contaminating your blood stream. You look like you've been through hell."

"I feel like I've been through hell," I said in a haggard voice that sounded alien to me. My throat felt raw, like I'd been screaming for days.

I frowned at him.

"Have I been screaming?"

He nodded in sympathy.

I shut my eyes and tried to shift a little on the table. A dim memory wafted up from my subconscious. I sorted through a hazy memory of panic and pain.

"Someone attacked me," I said. My eyes flew open. I stared into AJ's pale blue eyes, and remembered a fire along the right side of my body. I lifted a heavy hand, shifting the light blanket that covered me, and realized I was naked except for a gauzy bandage wrapped around my mid-torso.

AJ adjusted the disturbed blanket to keep my nakedness covered. I looked up at him in surprise. I half-expected him to say something sleazy.

"Are you thirsty?" he asked instead.

I said yes immediately. AJ picked up a short glass of water with a straw in it and held it close so I could take the straw in my mouth and drink from it. I had only swallowed a few mouthfuls when a weight of sleepiness settled over me again. I sighed and my eyes drifted shut on their own.

"Go ahead and rest," AJ said softly. "I'll be back to check on you soon. I'm going to go and give the Captain an update on your condition."

I fell asleep wondering what condition I was in.

"Cason, what are you doing?"

Gig's voice was low and dangerous. It resembled the rumbling purr of a speedbike. The intensity caught my attention and brought me out of nonsensical dreams, back to the reality of a Medic's lab and an uncomfortable examining table.

I had to twist my head to the left and up to see the person standing in the doorway. Gig looked ominous, and he was staring in my direction.

The weight of a warm hand lifted from my chest, and my blanket was flipped back in place to cover me.

"What are you talking about?" AJ asked above me. I shifted to look up at him hovering over me and saw the frown on his face as he glared back at Gig.

"It looks like you're taking advantage of one of your patients," Gig said. He stepped into the lab to let the door slide shut behind him.

Something sparked in AJ's eyes, and his handsome face darkened.

"I'm checking her heart, meathead," he said. He held up a hand that was partially covered by a sensor glove. "Have I ever taken advantage of a patient?"

Gig didn't reply. He rounded the table where I lay and peered down at me with more than a little concern on his face.

"You all right?" he asked.

"Yeah," my voice scratched out. "I think I'm whole."

"Well, you look better than when we found you," he said.

I frowned.

"What do you mean?" I asked. "Who attacked me?"

"Apparently we missed him hiding on that level," Gig said. "We found out he was one of the crew, and completely deranged."

An icy shiver stole down my spine.

"He was," I agreed. "I remember his eyes."

They loomed up in my memory like a ghost, both terrifying and intense.

"Tell me the rest," I said quickly, as I tried to shove the memory away.

Gig shifted, folding his arms across his chest. He recited the situation like a field report.

"We heard a commotion over the comm link," Gig said. "When you didn't respond we came to find you. By the time we arrived you were already unconscious and the attacker had his hands around your throat. I lasered him and tied him up while AJ checked on you. At that point we discovered a knife protruding from your right midsection. AJ removed the knife and staunched the flow of blood while I worked to resuscitate you. After that, we brought you back to the ship, where AJ has been nursing you back to health."

Gig glanced over at AJ. Some of his earlier malice seemed to have faded.

"So I was stabbed," I said, mostly to myself. I had been in so much pain, I hadn't realized what was causing the fire in my side. AJ and Gig had come to find me, and discovered the crewman doing his best to strangle me.

"The knife was laced with an unknown chemical from the planet," AJ said. "It worked like a poison in your bloodstream, but I've managed to neutralize it using a combination of antidotes."

Thank the stars that AJ was smart. I was impressed that he was able to come up with something that worked.

"We discovered that most of the dead crew had stab wounds as well," Gig said. "Which means they didn't die in the crash; they were murdered."

I was trembling now. Gig reached out and clasped my hand in a surprising show of comfort.

"The baby," I said. It came out as a whisper. Gig nodded.

My stomach roiled. I closed my eyes and tried to collect myself before my brain started to think of a different time and place.

"Where is he now?" I asked. I could only guess at the confusion and fear the crew must have felt from being hunted and murdered by one of their own. I opened my eyes and looked up at Gig.

"Dead," Gig said. "He didn't survive my laser blast."

I breathed a small sigh of relief, glad I wouldn't have to share a small ship with a killer. Gig had to kill him for me.

I vaguely wondered if he thought I was a liability.

"Sorry," I said.

He shook his head.

"And the mission?" I asked before he could say whatever he was opening his mouth to say. "Did you destroy the ship?"

There was a pause as Gig squinted at me in a measuring way.

I heard AJ chuckle.

"She's all business," he said to Gig. "Single minded, just like her predecessor."

"Must be a mark of the trade," Gig said, his face impassive now. He looked at me. "Yes, I completed the mission, as ordered."

"Just wondering," I said quickly. I had the feeling like I had erred somehow.

Gig stepped away and headed toward the door.

"Glad you're recovering," he said as he left.

I heard the door slide shut behind him. My face was heated in embarrassment. Gig didn't really need more reasons to dislike me, but I seemed to be finding them. It was obvious that any mention of Maddy rankled with Gig. As long as I reminded him of Maddy, Gig would continue to distance himself from me, I knew it. Unfortunately, out of all the people on the team, the Courier and the Gunner worked together the most. They had to trust each other to work together, because they each had the other's life in their hands.

I had to find a way to show Gig that he could trust me.

"AJ, I feel awful," I said pathetically. "That poison really clobbered me."

There was a pause as AJ's eyes focused on mine.

"The poison, but not the knife wound?" he said. "I saw that you've been cut before."

His finger snaked out and traced a line along my right shoulder. My skin felt like it burned where he touched me. An old, familiar feeling of shame clenched at my insides.

"When can I get out of here?" I asked, instead of answering his question.

"Why would you want to go?" he asked back.

"One, I want to be in my own bed, not on this rock," I said. I rapped my knuckles on the bed beside me to prove my point. There was no padding or anything to make it more comfortable. "Two, I need to get up and move around. If I stay like this my muscles will all go to mush. Third, I really hate Medic's labs. No offense."

"Well, you've been on that table for about a week now," he said. "As soon as you have the strength to stand and walk out of this lab on your own, you are free to go."

"Good," I said. I gathered my strength and pushed myself up onto my elbows. AJ crossed his arms and stepped back from the table to watch.

The room shifted lower, and my head suddenly felt like it weighed a hundred pounds. Dizzily, I decided to lay down again and wait until later.

"That's what I thought," AJ said smugly.

I glared at him.

"That was just my first attempt," I said. "Give me a minute."

AJ rolled his eyes.

"Can I have more water?" I asked.

He grabbed my cup and held it close so I could drink a little more.

"Not too much or you'll be sick again," he said.

A vague memory of someone helping me be sick washed over me.

"Was I throwing up a lot?" I asked.

"I'm never going to get the smell out of my lab," he confirmed.

I ignored him and closed my eyes to nap but a new thought hit me and I found myself staring at him again.

"What happened to my clothes?"

I could practically hear his eye roll.

"Your clothes were contaminated," he said, "so I cut them off you."

"Can you please find me something new to wear so I'm not hanging tits out in your lab all day today?"

He sighed like I was being a pain in his ass but he told me to hang on a minute while he went to find something. Excessively pleased with myself, I finally closed my eyes again and was able to nap.

6

I dreamed of two balls of fire. Eyes filled with hatred seared my skin and stole my breath. I struggled against that gaze, even as my blood started to boil and my skin started to steam. Crying out, I flailed, trying to divert the deadly eyes from my face but I wasn't strong enough and I knew with certainty that I was going to die.

Marco looked up from his flight panel as I settled into the co-pilot's chair. When he realized it was me he stared in surprise, but said nothing. I drew my legs up and wrapped myself with the blanket I'd brought from my bed.

"I didn't know you were released from the lab," he said finally.

I spied cashews in his hand and reached my hand out for some. Marco shook a handful into my palm from his container.

"I had to get out of there," I said. I leaned my head against the head rest. I was out of breath and shaking, but I felt better than I had in days. I'd wakened from a nightmare, slick with sweat and had determined it was time to get up. I had forced myself into a sitting position on the Medic's table, and paused for a long time, trying to hang on to my balance and strength. Then I had half-stumbled, half-dragged myself to my room, not caring if anyone saw me. It must have been late, I'd realized, because no one was around. In my room, I'd collapsed on my bed in total weakness and tried to collect my breath. The room spun for several long moments. It didn't really stop spinning until I crawled to the shower. The water had felt cleansing, as if it washed away the last of the poison from my system. On wobbly legs I'd dressed and grabbed the blanket from my bed, using the last of my strength to join Marco on the darkened Pilot's deck.

Now that I was here, I didn't think I could get up again.

I stared out the window, taking in the inky blackness of space and the brilliance of stars. The ship's engines hummed at the edge of my hearing, and Marco's console bleeped softly every now and then. I chewed on my cashews and let my body relax into the cushions of the chair.

I took a deep breath and smiled.

"I love this view," I said. "This is what I needed."

"I know what you mean," Marco sympathized. "I once caught a fever and had to stay in bed for two days. I didn't feel better until I was back in this chair."

"Mmm," I said.

We sat in companionable silence. Marco handed me more cashews which I accepted gratefully.

"Where are we headed?" I asked after a while.

Marco looked at his navigation system. Only his face was visible in the dark, lit by his computer screens.

"Thredenar," he said.

"Never been there."

"I've been there a couple times," Marco said. "Not much to see except the women."

"Well that doesn't do me much good," I said.

Marco chuckled. "I guess not," he said. "But it will be a brief trip either way. We're just collecting some information for the next assignment."

"Good, I could use some more time to rest," I said. "I'm not really up for another assignment just yet."

"That's fine, the Captain wouldn't let you out on another assignment without permission from AJ," Marco said. "It doesn't matter who assigns us a mission, if we're not one hundred percent, the Captain won't do it."

"Oh," I said. I let go of some of my worries.

I had to get over this poisoning so that my body would function the way I'd trained it to. I longed to see Stryker and have him with me right now, even if he just confirmed what AJ had said: that I would be back to normal in no time. In the years that I had trained with him, no one had earned my absolute trust to the degree Stryker had. If he told me my eyes were blue and not brown, I would believe him.

"Hey Marco," I said, "are we allowed to link with other members of the Order? I mean, even if it doesn't relate to a mission?"

"You mean friends of ours?" he asked.

"Yeah," I said.

Marco glanced at me, but I didn't meet his eyes.

"Do you have a boyfriend that you need to check on?"

I shook my head.

"Actually, I want to talk to my mentor," I said.

"Stryker?"

"Yes, I think I'm having withdrawals," I joked. "I'm used to seeing his

face every morning at dawn."

"Poor thing," Marco said sympathetically, but he was grinning. "But to answer your question, we can comm with others if we are on a secure line—which requires business of the Order—or if we are on leave. You can talk to the Captain if you urgently need to speak with Stryker."

"Oh," I said lamely. "That makes sense."

"So, you don't have a boyfriend?" Marco asked.

"No, why?"

Marco shrugged.

"When I was at the Academy, I never let a pretty girl walk by without asking her out," he said. "You probably had your pick of gentlemen at the Academy."

"Not exactly," I said. I cracked a grin that Marco thought I was pretty, but not in a gross AJ-way.

"Why?" he asked curiously.

I sighed and thought about it.

"Well, first of all, if I wasn't training with Stryker I was studying or hanging out with my best friend," I said. "Second, I didn't have a sponsor to the Academy, so the other students didn't think I was important enough to date. And third...well, my work seemed more important."

"So you spent most of your time working instead of socializing," Marco said.

I nodded.

"It sounds like you are more grown than your years," he said.

I made a face.

"I've been told that," I confessed.

Marco laughed.

"I can see it," he said, settling back in his chair like me.

We sat together in silence, and just watched the stars. I started to yawn and it was making my eyes water. I was feeling warm and comfortable in my chair and glad for a companion to share the night with.

My eyes started to droop shut, so I let them, and my breath slowed. I drifted over the edge of consciousness.

I slept deeply, and only woke when Gig came to find me.

"C'mon, girl," he said. "AJ's looking for you."

I mumbled something about being comfortable but Gig slipped his arms around me and picked me up, blanket and all, like a child. I rested my head against him and fell back to sleep. I think I heard Marco say goodnight.

"You found her," I heard AJ say heartbeats later. "Where did she wander off to?"

"She was sitting with Marco," Gig said. "I found her asleep in the co-pilot's chair."

"I guess even the co-pilot's chair is more comfortable than my lab tables. Alright, have it her way. Let's take her to her room."

Gig carried me to my room and carefully laid me down on my bed. I smiled, eyes still closed, rolled onto my left side and let sleep take me again.

"AJ said you're healing well," Gig said a few days later. "Let's go through a light workout."

We stood in the ship's gym among the various machines and sparring mats. Gig had fetched me from my daily perch in the co-pilots chair to ask me to join him. Marco and I had been in the middle of a discussion on our favorite musicians where he was explaining the galactic implications of The Drawer and I was eating all of his cashews. I'd had to promise to come back and listen to a session by The Drawer once Gig and I were done.

"You're learning the hard way," Gig whispered as we left the Pilot's deck. "Don't get him started on The Drawer."

I giggled.

"How was I supposed to know?"

The gym smelled comfortingly familiar when we walked in, which was such a strange thought. But gyms were one thing that stayed the same, whether you were a kid fresh off an intergalactic shuttle bus, or a girl fresh off a poisonous injury.

"Where do you want to start?" I asked eagerly.

"Let's go through some sparring exercises," Gig said. He went to a bench beside the center spar mat and sat down to unlace his boots. I was already barefoot, which was unregulation the Captain had scolded me. She spent most of her time looking through briefing documents and daily reports. I only ever saw her at meals or when she came to join me and Marco on the Pilot's deck. But she didn't *really* seem to care that I left my boots in my room when I padded around the ship, so I left them there.

While I waited for Gig, I did a quick stretching routine. My muscles felt like they had been unused for too long. I was glad at the opportunity to get them back into shape.

"Come on," Gig said.

He led the way onto the mat and turned to face me with a smooth bow that made his muscles ripple. I followed suit, and bowed as low and as gracefully as I could manage.

"Call it out," I said, and fell into my starting position.

"Craymer One," he said immediately.

I did not smile. Craymer One was the very first sparring routine that children learned when they arrived at the Academy. It was short and basic, but I still saw the beauty in the routine even after years of practicing it over and over again.

So we walked through Craymer One, facing each other as was proper and taking our steps and jumps together.

"Craymer Two," he said when we had finished. We bowed and began Craymer Two. I began to see some of Gig's logic.

"Craymer Three," Gig said next.

By Craymer Ten we were in sync, and our motions flowed like mirrors. Gig compensated for his height difference, and I compensated for my lack of breadth. We swept easily from stance to stance, in unison, the way a team should.

"Copper One," Gig said. We advanced to the next level of routines. We bowed and each turned to face the other over our right sides. Then we did the Copper routines together, still in sync.

"Clover One," Gig said when we finished. We bowed and shifted to face each other over our left sides before completing all of the Clover routines.

"How are you feeling?" he asked when we were done.

"Relieved," I said. "Let's go through some of the Darden routines."

"Hang on, why are you relieved?"

I shrugged.

"I just don't like to be off my feet," I said.

Gig nodded.

"Darden Eight?" he suggested.

I bowed and then crouched into starting position, ready to go. Gig had chosen my favorite of the Darden routines. Darden Eight required a nimble body and plenty of speed. It would be a good test to see how much I'd recovered.

Gig crouched and made the first pass. I hopped backward then forward, and extended my right leg in a kick that was choreographed to stop over his left shoulder, just beside his ear. Gig wrapped a hand around my ankle and tugged it backward to execute his portion of the routine. I dropped my weight back so that my arms held me off the ground. A single kick around with my left leg gave me the momentum to flip my body in a tight arc out of Gig's grip, and land on the mat in a roll away from him.

When my body hit the mat I rolled automatically, but my brain registered a prick of pain.

I exhaled and pushed the pain away. I was back up in a crouch a second later and ready to continue the routine, but my peripheral vision saw the door open to the gym. Then AJ walked in.

"What in bloody hell are you two doing?" he asked in a sharp tone.

Gig and I turned to face him, instantly forgetting our stances. AJ strode over in the blink of an eye with a full-blown glare. I sat back on my heels, suddenly feeling like a child in trouble.

"We're just," I began, but AJ made a chopping motion with his hand and silenced me with a hiss.

"I already know," he said. "You two blockheads are trying to drive me insane! Come here."

Gig and I exchanged glances.

"Tippin, come here."

I stood up slowly, feeling the ache in my side re-announce itself. Unable to meet his penetrating gaze, I slowly stepped forward as AJ had commanded.

He came close and tugged up my tunic, baring my midsection and the ugly red scar I'd gained from my knife wound.

"Easy, man," Gig growled at him.

I looked down at my skin. The wound hadn't re-opened, but it looked irritated.

AJ looked at me like I was stupid.

"Look, I can't lay around forever," I said reasonably. "I need to get back into shape. We just did a couple low-impact routines, but we're pretty much done."

"Maybe you could let me be the judge, considering I'm the Medic," AJ said. He included Gig in his glare now.

"Okay," I said quickly, before he could lecture us any further. "You got it."

AJ narrowed his eyes, obviously expecting more of an argument. He crossed his arms over his chest and faced me squarely, unaware that getting out of trouble was my specialty. I had learned early on that acquiescing immediately usually made things easiest.

"You are only allowed to exercise when I am here to monitor your activities," AJ said. "Until I tell you that your injury is no longer a factor. Clear?"

"Yes," I said. I looked him in the eye.

AJ looked like he wanted to say more, but he stayed silent.

Gig stood up from his crouch.

"So can we continue?" he asked.

I looked up at AJ with a pleading look and waited for our answer. Even though my side was not well, I wasn't ready to stop.

AJ rolled his pale blue eyes but gestured for us to continue. He found himself a place on the bench where he could watch our exercises closely.

"Okay, so now what?" I asked Gig.

"We can do more routines tomorrow," he said. "Do you want to spar, or work on individual skills?"

My right side ached.

"Let's hold off on sparring for now," I said. I glanced at AJ surreptitiously. "We could trade off on skill building."

"Okay," Gig said easily. "Where do you want to start?"

I paused to think. "Ohh, telekinesis first," I decided. "What do we have?"

Gig glanced around at the gym equipment.

"Not much," he said, "we've never had a tele on board before. Not one with your ranking anyway. I think our only implements are colored spheres."

Colored spheres.

"Juggling," I said with a sigh. It was one of the most boring exercises for teles, but people seemed to enjoy watching it the most. I'd spent a lot of down time entertaining other students at the Academy by juggling random objects.

Gig pulled out the spheres and handed them to me in a heavy box. I took them to the center of the mats and sat down with crossed legs and the box in front of me.

My tele teacher, Master Flynn, was so advanced in the art that he could move objects simply by willing them with his mind. I had learned how to do it without needing my eyes open and staring at the object I wanted to move. That was an excellent accomplishment for my age, Flynn had assured me. But I still needed to use my hands to motion at the object I wanted to move, whereas Master Flynn's hands stayed tucked in his sleeves.

I focused my mind in preparation, and summoned a sense of mental stillness so I could concentrate. I lifted my right hand from my lap, made a scooping motion in the air and saw that a small blue ball lifted from the box. Using my telekinetic power, I held it aloft above my head and let it spin lazily. I glanced back at the box, made two more gestures and watched as a thick yellow ball and a second small blue ball lifted up.

Now for the entertainment.

I started by making the two small blue balls rotate clockwise while the yellow ball rotated counterclockwise. Then I made the balls juggle in tight arcs as if an invisible person tossed them in the air and caught them quickly.

I sketched patterns in the air: circles, stars, parallel lines. I swirled the balls around my arms and across the room to arc around Gig and AJ. I made the balls stop on a dime and skitter in a different direction. Then I did a trick that Stryker used to call Helter Skelter. I used my telekinesis to shoot every ball in the box into the air to join the three I already held aloft. There were different sizes and different colors, probably 25 balls total. I sent them reeling to opposite points of the room, then made them all dance and bounce in syncopation. The balls in the right corner of the room crisscrossed to the left side of the room and vice versa. Moving almost faster than the eye could see, the balls hurtled toward the opposite wall from where they had been moments before. At the last minute, I released the balls from my hold and let them slam into the walls around the gym, their momentum causing them to bounce back and tumble about the room in a mad dance.

I looked at AJ and Gig, who were grinning at me like little boys. I had to smile back at them. For some reason, men always loved to watch juggling acts.

"She won a gold medal for her telekinesis," AJ told Gig. "This is probably just a small sample of what she can do."

To show him he was right, I used my telekinesis to give a sharp tug. The balls, which were all over the floor leapt into the air one last time, and in graceful arcs dropped back into the box where they belonged.

"Show off," AJ said. "We already knew you were good at handling balls."

I rolled my eyes, catching the innuendo in his words.

"That was stellar," Gig offered. I pocketed his comment as the first compliment I had won from him since coming to the ship. Finally!

I stood up, grabbed the box of balls and carried it to where it belonged.

"Gig, are there any skills you would like to work on now?" I offered as I went.

Gig got up and went to the weapons armored on the back wall.

"We have a shooting sim that I like to use," he said. "We can do it together."

He grabbed two standard-issue blasters from the wall and tossed me one. I caught it easily and checked the cartridge. It was empty except for a computer chip that was tied to the sim.

Gig grabbed two headsets from the wall and synched them so that they shared data.

"Here."

I took the headset he offered and slipped it on over my head where it settled like a mask. Gig led the way to the wall of windows so that we could have an unrestricted vision of the sim. Through my headset I could see a dim vision of the stars on the other side of the window. Then Gig started up the sim and my vision was filled with a shooting gallery-style game.

"Let's see who can hit the most targets," I heard him say.

"Well I hope it would be you since you're the Gunner here," I muttered. I already knew I would lose.

"Not necessarily," he replied, "there's always a chance."

I snorted but said nothing. Raising my gun straight out in front of me, I waited while the game counted down to its opening sequence.

In the sim, there was a one-minute time limit in which you had to destroy as many silver disks as possible for the highest score. The disks varied in size so the smaller the disk, the more points you could earn. The disks moved and hovered around the screen on a background that shifted colors. When the screen turned silver it was almost impossible to differentiate where the disks were.

Time started and I began firing at the disks nearest to me on the screen.

I hit four in the first six seconds of the game, but that was no match for Gig. I watched as he snapped off eight shots that destroyed a perfect eight disks.

I whistled and kept shooting. I aimed for the smaller disks to make up more points. Several times I went to shoot a disk, and it would be destroyed by Gig before my shot ever landed.

The screen went silver then, and the outline of the disks disappeared. I paused, seeing that Gig had paused too. He was waiting for the screen to flip colors again. I squinted my eyes, and stared intently at the screen. I could vaguely make out three disks on the screen that were moving near my field of vision. I fired and took them all.

Shifting my sight a little, I could detect two more disks in my peripheral vision. I missed a few times, but eventually got those disks as well.

"You have good eyes," I heard Gig say. My second compliment!

Then the screen flipped to yellow and the disks were in plain view again. Gig handily finished off almost all of the rest of the disks, making the final score 78 to 42. Pathetic.

I flipped up my mask and looked at Gig.

"Let's do it again," I said. Gig gave me a lopsided grin and started up the next game.

"We'll arrive at Thredenar in two hours," the Captain said.

She had pulled AJ, Gig and me from the gym where we'd been practicing for days and had us join her and Marco in the commissary. We sat in our places around the table and listened to the Captain's briefing.

"AJ, I want you to visit the Medic's Hall there and restock the ship. Marco, you can restock our other supplies," the Captain said. "I'll take Gig and Alyvia with me to my meeting with members of the Order. They want to send us on a top priority mission, and I have a feeling they want to test our team first."

"What do you mean?" Marco asked. "They've never felt the need to test us before."

"By 'us' I mean Alyvia," the Captain said. Her gaze met my own. "This mission will be very important to the Order, and they want to know if you can handle it fresh from the Academy."

I felt everyone's eyes on my face, while I digested this information.

"How do you test someone's ability to handle important missions?" I asked. "And if they decide I'm not good enough, will they replace me or just not give us the mission at all?"

Was my stint with the Merry Maids going to be short-lived?

"They won't give us the mission at all," the Captain confirmed. "There are other squads like ours working out there. But no one has a record like the Merry Maids."

In other words, if we weren't chosen for the mission, the Merry Maids would lose status as one of the top teams in the galaxy. I swallowed. The weight of my team's reputation settled on my shoulders.

"So how will they test me?"

"I do not know," she said.

I breathed out a lungful of air and looked at Gig and AJ.

"She's gotten stronger over the past few days," AJ said. "I've never seen anyone recover so quickly."

"We've also seen some of her routines," Gig said. "She will pass their test."

He said it so confidently that I felt like I should believe him, but I still felt a twinge of nerves at facing the Order. The Order would expect me to know solid routines, and would probably be less impressed than people who rarely see them, like AJ and Gig. It was just today that I had finally shown them the Serasoma routine I'd done for the scouts. They'd obviously been impressed and had asked me a lot of questions about my training.

I didn't think The Order would care as much.

"I wouldn't worry too much about it," Marco said. "The Order knows you're rather untested, but you have a lot of potential. Otherwise you wouldn't be with us—as arrogant as that may sound."

"Nevertheless, whatever happens after the test, we will support you one hundred percent," the Captain said, and everyone nodded. "Now, back to business. Gig, after we meet with the Order, I want you to take Alyvia to some of the armories and find her some lightweight weapons. I'll leave it up to you what you get her, but I want these to be concealable and durable. Something that you can train her to use in case anything should happen like it did in the last mission."

I shifted uncomfortably and lifted a hand to my side. The scar from the knife wound I'd received throbbed as if reminding me it was there.

Gig and AJ sat up straighter too. I guess we were all a little traumatized now.

"Good idea," Gig said. "I know the perfect place on Thredenar."

The Captain nodded.

"After that, you are free for the rest of the night. You can stay in the Order's barracks or come back to the ship, as long as you are here and ready to go in the morning."

The Captain released us from the briefing and told us to prepare the ship for docking. This was one of those annoying things you just had to do, Marco informed me, because everything aboard the ship had to be itemized and reported.

"Come on," he said. "You can help me in the dock."

"I'll be in the Lab," AJ called over his shoulder as he left.

"I'll do our weapons cache and the gym," Gig said, and followed right behind AJ.

"I guess that leaves the Captain's deck for me," the Captain said. She went to a cupboard and grabbed a water before heading up the stairs.

"Let's go," Marco said.

He led the way to the dock and handed me a touchpad with lists of supplies.

"Here," he said. "Take the touchpad and scan everything I pull out for you."

I felt the weight of the touchpad in the palm of my hand and briefly scanned through the list. There were a lot of items.

When we entered the dock, I watched while Marco went straight to the nearest hold and opened it. Inside, I could see various engine parts and machinery, all neatly hung or tucked into drawers side by side.

"This is an easy one," he said. "I'll get the next one started."

He moved off as I set to scanning the merch with my touchpad. I watched the screen catalog and compare every item with the previous list. When I scanned everything, I closed to doors of the hold and moved to the next line of items. Marco had pulled some of the heavier items out from the bottom for easier scanning access. I set to work scanning everything while Marco moved to the next hold.

I was suddenly bored.

"Do we have to do this EVERY time we dock?" I asked.

"Only for the red-flagged ports controlled by the Order," he said. "It's kind of a hassle, but it saves us from fines and being searched by brass."

"That sounds like reason enough," I agreed.

I scanned layer after layer of miscellaneous dock debris, all the time wondering if there was a better way to get through this chore.

I glanced at Marco. There were beads of sweat on his face now but he had given me the easy task.

"How do you feel about cheating?" I asked. He paused and looked at me to see what I was up to.

I smiled and handed him the touchpad.

"Let's switch," I said. Marco took it gamely and waited for my next move. "Come over here."

We stepped away from the holds while I considered how to do this. Then I lifted a hand and started a new juggling game.

Each item flew to Marco then returned to its spot once he scanned it. It took me a few items to get the hang of it, but then I fell into a rhythm and had merch flying around the room in organized chaos.

As I used my tele to flip the last hold closed, I glanced at Marco with a grin.

"That...was STELLAR," he said with enthusiasm. He was looking at me with wide eyes, obviously impressed with my abilities.

"Much faster, and much less boring," I agreed. We looked around, but everything was back in its tidy little place.

"Okay, so I think that just cut off a good 45 minutes from my usual routine in here," Marco said. "I can't believe how easy that was."

"Now what?"

"Well, we could go find the others and offer to help out," he suggested. He didn't sound very enthusiastic.

"Or?"

"Or we could hide in here for an hour and stay out of everyone's way." I laughed.

Our plan worked until the Captain showed up about a half hour later to find us sitting by the bay windows. We had been talking and laughing like schoolgirls.

"Are you two done?" she asked suspiciously.

I glanced at Marco, who looked pretty guilty. *Don't*, I wanted to tell him but he wasn't looking back at me.

"We just finished up," he said. "Were you looking for something?"

The Captain raised an eyebrow.

"Yes, I thought I'd invite you two to come help me when you're done," she said. "We need to scan the commissary."

"Oh, well we can help now," Marco offered quickly. He jumped to his feet. I followed, with my eyes averted from the Captain's. She led the way, with Marco and me behind her.

"Alyvia, have you ever been to Thredenar?" the Captain asked when we came into the commissary. She handed me a touchpad and another to Marco, before taking up a third touchpad for herself.

"No, I haven't been to a lot of places," I said. I keyed up my touchpad and got straight to work with scanning. "Stryker took me to Cirdaxen, Aribel, and Elomagé for competitions. I once went to Allalia with a friend of mine to visit his family. And I guess now I've been to Galaxin 7."

It had seemed like a lot of my teammates at the Academy had been to a new planet all the time when they were younger, especially the ones who grew up shipboard with their parents. Only the poorest students, like myself, didn't have a laundry list of places we'd visited.

"When I was a kid my family had me traveling all over the place," Marco said. "My father was an engineer for the Order, so my mom and I lived on the ship with him and went to ground on the friendly ports they visited."

I wondered if growing up in the stars was more fun than living earthbound.

"What was the first planet you remember visiting?" the Captain asked.

"Serambia," Marco grinned.

"The beach planet? Your parents let you see Serambia as a kid?"

"Yes, but I wasn't much of a kid after that," Marco said. "Every time I turned my head I think I fell in love with a new woman."

I had never been to Serambia, but I'd seen plenty of images. Serambia was mostly populated by visitors who were there to visit the different islands of the planet and relax by the water. The locals were usually naked, from what I understood. I could picture Marco standing on the beach with his head swiveling from one naked woman to another, getting the shock of his childhood.

The Captain and I exchanged grins.

"My parents have always been fairly liberal," Marco said. "I think they wanted me to see that the human body is beautiful in all of its different forms. They were very disappointed to learn that I was taking their lesson to heart and really researching their theory by doing *a lot* of observation. I pitched an ear-splitting fit when they said it was time to leave."

I laughed.

"The first planet I remember visiting was Etro," the Captain said. "This was back when I was fifteen, just before I joined the Order. Etro was in the middle of a major civil war. I'd been reading about it for years, following the battles closely. I don't know what I thought, I was obviously young and stupid. But I thought if I went there, I would somehow be able to help stop the fighting."

Marco gawked at her.

"You're joking," he said. I saw him turn from his work to stare at the Captain. "Lira, you didn't tell me you were such an idealist."

The Captain laughed. She and Marco had known each other for a long time. It must have been fun to still have secrets to share.

"It was short-lived," she said. "I realized how hopeless it was about five minutes after arriving."

"Is that when you decided to come to the Order?"

"Yes," the Captain said. "I knew that as a Captain I could be involved with things like negotiations for peace and other important duties, so I took the tactician and diplomat track in the Academy."

Marco nodded.

"You already know I came to the Academy when I was fifteen too," he said, "so this is more for Alyvia. I was sick of watching my dad at work. I wanted to have a role on a ship too."

"Did you know you wanted to be a Pilot?" I asked.

"It was the only thing I knew for sure," Marco said. "I'd been watching the Pilots on my dad's ship with growing feelings of jealousy. I wanted so bad to be one of them but they wouldn't let me anywhere near the Pilot's chair."

Not like me, I thought. Marco let me sit in the co-pilot's chair whenever I wanted.

"When you started learning how to be a Pilot, was it everything you thought it would be?"

"Absolutely," he said. "I never looked back."

There was a pause in conversation. I had a sinking feeling in my stomach. I was dreading their next question. The Captain glanced my way. I tensed.

"And you, Alyvia?" she asked. "When did you come to the Academy?"

I hesitated. Cleared my throat. Focused on my scanning.

"Oh, I was kind of young," I said casually. "It seems like such a long time ago."

There was another pause. I could feel their eyes on me. Marco was definitely curious and the Captain just waited for me to continue. I drew in a quiet breath.

"You came to the Academy before you were fifteen?" Marco prompted.

I lifted a shoulder.

"I sort of followed in my brother's footsteps," I said, as casually as possible. "He came when he was fifteen. I followed a couple years later when I was eleven."

"Eleven!"

"Well, I was practically almost twelve," I said, which was a stretch but I didn't want them to realize how weird I was.

"The Academy rarely accepts anyone younger than fifteen," Marco said. Well there went that wish. I should have known that Marco and the Captain had been around long enough to know the functions of the Academy

"You have to be pretty special to be accepted at eleven," Marco said. "I've never heard of such a thing."

"I've heard of thirteen and fourteen-year-olds making it in," the Captain offered. "Eleven does seem rather young."

She didn't look at me like she thought I was weird, but she did seemed to find this information about me interesting.

She and Marco stared at me. They were waiting for me to continue. I scratched my head. I didn't want to keep talking about myself but I didn't know how to turn the conversation around.

I gave in and told them.

"The Academy let me in early," I said finally. "My brother was determined that they would accept me. When I came he was seventeen, and well into his training. He had Stryker meet with me, and the rest is history."

"Wow," Marco said.

"That information is not in your file," the Captain said. "I didn't know you have a brother in the Order."

I stopped scanning and glanced at her briefly to make sure she wasn't mad. Her face was sympathetic. I looked away quickly.

"Had," I corrected, staring down at the touchpad in my hands.

Silence.

"I'm sorry," the Captain said softly.

"If it's okay, I don't want to talk about it," I said. I hated the way my voice sounded suddenly tight.

They dropped the topic immediately.

"No problem," Marco said.

We finished scanning the commissary quickly after that. We chatted companionably about lighthearted matters which was a relief. The whole time, the Captain and Marco radiated sympathy in my direction. I hated that I'd dampened the mood in the room, and that they treated me kindly because of what I'd said. But when I talked about Sen it hurt too much, and I just wasn't ready to go through it.

7

Thredenar was a planet run by the Order. As we docked and were led to rooms near our hangar, I felt like I was back at the Academy. Like a higher force was watching everything and nothing escaped scrutiny. At the Academy, it was normal to feel like you had eyes watching over you. Thredenar felt more impersonal, however. It was much larger than the Academy.

"You all will have these rooms during your stay," said our guide, a tall, gangly youth with pale skin and midnight black hair. He looked like he was about my age. I wondered if we'd met somewhere, because I saw that his eyes often returned to mine when he spoke to us. I had been to a lot of competitions, maybe that was it?

The suite we'd been given had six rooms. They fanned out in a semi-circle around the main chamber where tables, couches and vid screens were set up for everyone's use.

"Pick a room and freshen up," the Captain said. She went into the first room on the left and walked inside to inspect her choice.

I saw Marco head for the room to the right of the Captain's. Glancing at AJ and Gig to see what rooms they picked, I realized that they were waiting for me.

"Ladies first," AJ said. He gestured to the rest of the available rooms.

I looked around, and decided I wanted to first room to the right of the exit. As I went over to peek inside, I heard Gig say in a low, warning voice, "where are *you* going?"

I stopped and turned to look back at him in confusion, and realized he was staring at our guide, who was now right behind me.

The kid's face turned an impressive shade of red as his gaze slid from Gig to mine.

"I just thought I'd show you some of the amenities," he said to me.

56

"That's not necessary," Gig said. In a heartbeat he was at the boy's side and resolutely marching him out the door.

Wow, Gig was unwelcoming to anyone new, not just me. I shook my head as I went to check on my room.

In the far corner I found a single-person bed with a utilitarian brown blanked on it. There was also a vid screen, a guest chair and a small sink with a mirror. I went to the sink and washed my face with soap, feeling sticky from Thredenar's humid air. I looked in the mirror, and ran my fingers through my loose hair to comb it out a bit. I remembered that the Order wanted to test me to see if I was fit for their missions. I wondered if they would ask me to show them some routines or spar. If they did, I would need my hair out of my face.

I was in the process of pulling it up into a chignon when Marco tapped at my door.

"Hey," I said to his reflection in the mirror. I watched as he came in and tapped out some commands on my vid screen.

I turned to see what he was up to.

"We have a bit of free time if you want to check in with Stryker," he said. "Watch as I do this."

I went to his side, and watched the special commands he put in.

"There you go," he said. "You're all set up now."

"I can really comm Stryker?" I asked eagerly.

"Go for it, kid," Marco said. "I'll leave you to it."

"Thanks Marco!"

I dialed in Stryker's comm link and waited impatiently for him to be paged. Then the screen lit up, and I stared at a face I'd been missing. He grinned at me, his brown eyes bright.

"There's my girl, you finally remembered me, huh?"

I grinned back, elated to hear his voice again. Happy tears sprang to my eyes.

"Stryker, I linked as soon as I was free," I said. "I've been missing you."

"I know, it's a bit of a shock isn't it? You get used to seeing someone every day...then when they're gone it takes a while to get used to it."

"In other words, you missed me too," I said.

Stryker shrugged but he still smiled.

"Well, how has it been going with the Merry Maids? Was my training useful?"

"You knew they were scouting me for the Merry Maids?" I asked, surprised.

"Of course," he said. "I'm good friends with Lira, so I had you scouted when she told me she'd lost a Courier. That's what we've been training for all this time."

I almost let my jaw fall open but I knew he hated that.

"Stryker, am I an idiot?" I asked. "It didn't even occur to me that you were training me to be a Courier. I can see now that my abilities are tailored for the job, but I thought…well, I don't know what I thought."

Stryker gave me a sympathetic look.

"Tip, you're a good girl and the best student I ever had," he said. "You're also one of the most naïve; partly because I took you on when you were so young and partly because your best friend kept a good watch over you."

He was right about that. From the moment Cutter and I became friends, he'd taken on the role that I used to see from my brother, Sen.

"You followed all of my instructions without question; with full trust," Stryker said. "That's why you did so well; I didn't have to break through your pride to teach you what I needed to teach you. But as you're learning now, that's a habit you need to break if you're going to be a smart Courier."

I nodded. I took his wisdom to heart, the way I always had, but I felt a little deflated that there was something about me Stryker didn't think was perfect.

"I guess that's training I need to give myself," I said slowly.

"You're a smart girl," Stryker said, "and you've made me very proud."

I was suddenly very close to tears again.

"Thank you, Stryker," I said.

"Lira, it's a pleasure to see you again."

My head popped up and I saw the Captain in my doorway. She smiled at Stryker's image.

"Stryker, it's been too long," the Captain said. "Why are you keeping yourself scarce?"

"Well, I *was* training your new Courier," he said. "But now? Well, I'm actually thinking of retiring from the Academy."

I gasped in shock. What was the Academy without Stryker?

"I'm not a youngling anymore," Stryker said. He looked back to me. "I spent the last of what I had to offer with you. Now you're in the field, so my work is done."

I tried to picture the Academy without Stryker, but as I stared at his wrinkled face I realized how old he was getting. As an eleven-year-old little girl I'd seen him as an owlish authority, wise but strong. Ten years later, he was smaller and less spry than I remembered.

"What will you do now?" I asked.

"I heard my daughter was starting a family," he said. "I may find her and see what it's like to be a grandfather."

Stryker rarely talked of his daughter. They weren't close, but I'd always been able to tell he loved her. I'd seen a picture of her once. She was beautiful, but her face had seemed distant. I hoped she was good to Stryker when he found her.

"Good for you," the Captain said. "It will be good for you to get away from the Academy."

I wanted to disagree but I knew I was being selfish.

"I probably won't be able to stay away," he said. "Old habits die hard. Anyway, let me see your team."

The Captain called for Marco, Gig and AJ. I watched as they filed into my room. They waved and nodded to Stryker.

"This is Stryker," I told the group. "Stryker," I said, "this is Marco McNarry, AJ Cason and Gig Freeley."

"The Pilot, Medic and Gunner," Stryker said. He studied them. Quick assessments that I recognized. "I read the scouts' report before they took Tip. You're all first-class teammates, I'm glad she was picked up for you."

"Well, she's definitely earning her stripes," Marco said. "But she's fitting in perfectly around here."

"Good," Stryker said. "I knew she would. I was reading the report from your first mission, though, and I have to say I'm rather disappointed in you, Freeley."

Gig stood up straighter, and his eyebrows pinched together.

I was so startled I stared at Stryker myself, dumbfounded.

"Are you referring to the crewman we overlooked on the ship?" Gig asked.

"Yes," Stryker said. "As the Gunner on the team, it is your duty to protect Tippin from danger. I don't expect that another incident like that will ever happen again."

"No, sir," Gig said seriously. "I can assure you it will not."

"Good," Stryker said. He eyed the rest of the team while my face burned in embarrassment.

He looked at me again, and his face softened.

"I have to go now," he said. "Mind your teachings, do your best, and when you get a chance, comm me every once in a while to let an old man know you're doing well with yourself."

I didn't want to hear him call himself an old man. For the first time, it occurred to me that I might not see Stryker again in person.

"Of course I will, Stryker," I said. "Thank you. For *everything*."

He nodded and cleared his throat. He looked like he was blinking a little too rapidly.

"Take care," he said. "I'm sending you a clip from your buddy. He made me promise to send it as soon as I heard from you."

I grinned. It was probably a message from Cutter.

"Okay," I said. "Take care of yourself too."

When Stryker signed off I immediately accessed the file he sent me without waiting to see if my shipmates had left the room. I was vaguely aware that they had exited and were talking to one another as they went, but

I was dead set on seeing my message.

Just like that, Cutter was on the screen. My chest expanded as soon as I saw his face. His message played out without me having to advance it.

"Hey, baby girl," he said with a lopsided grin. "You took off without saying goodbye but Stryker told me you're in good hands so I asked him to send you this message. I'll be heading off to my own ship soon, so we may not get the chance to talk right away. When you can, try to comm me and let me know you're doing okay. They posted me to the Guardian."

I whistled to myself. Everyone knew the Guardian. It was the most coveted ship to get assigned and most newbies from the Academy had to work years before posting on with them.

Cutter shifted and put his hands in his pockets, which meant he had something important he wanted to tell me.

"Listen to me, Lyv," he said seriously, "I want you to take care of yourself. I've been watching out for you since the day we met. Not that you always wanted or needed me to but I was there for you and I'm concerned that wherever you go, you might not find someone to do that for you. I hope you do. If I find out that no one is keeping an eye on you, I might have to come transfer to wherever you are or something, I don't know. I guess I just want to know that you are safe and doing okay."

It was so like Cutter to be concerned for me. He'd been like a protective older brother since the day we'd met, the security blanket that I couldn't—and didn't want to—shake. Tears welled in my eyes and spilled over my cheeks as I thought of what a great friend he'd been to me. I reached out a hand and touched the screen where his face was. I wished I could thank him for everything he'd done for me. I was really lucky to have his friendship.

"So like I said, comm me," Cutter continued. He looked down like he was thinking what to say next. He grinned again and looked back up, "I hope you weren't too sick when those scouts picked you up. They probably had to hose you down to get the smell of tequila off."

I choked on a laugh.

"Bye, Lyvvie. Love you."

The screen went black as Cutter cut the feed. I ended the link, and wiped at my eyes. My heart was full again; I had just seen the two people who meant the most to me in this world. I knew they were concerned for me and, maybe after my first mission I understood why.

It was nice to have people who cared for me, though. When I was little, before I came to the Academy, I only really had Sen.

"Is that a boyfriend of yours?"

I jumped out of my skin before I realized that Gig had hung back and was still in my room.

"You scared the stars out of me!" I accused him, embarrassed.

"Sorry," he said automatically. "I wanted to talk with you, though."

"About what?"

"Stryker," he said, his dark eyes got darker. Gig stalked over to the guest chair and sat down. I made a seat on the edge of my bed and waited for him to explain. "He was right about Galaxin 7. I've been wanting to talk to you about it but I...didn't know where to start."

"Gig, Galaxin 7 wasn't your fault," I said. "I'm sorry about Stryker. He's overprotective. He doesn't realize that we all missed signs of that—" I struggled for the right word, and eventually settled for "guy. I was just the stupid one who walked into his knife."

"No," Gig said firmly. "What happened was unacceptable. I should have been absolutely certain every deck was safe before I let you go unprotected. I failed you and I failed the team, and you could have died for that mistake."

He ran his hands through his hair, and leaned forward so his elbows were propped up on his knees.

"I offered my resignation to the Captain," he said.

"What!"

"She didn't accept it," Gig said. "She dressed me down but she wouldn't let me resign. I've been trying to think how I can make up to you the mistake that I made. If you had died on that mission, I would have quit and there is nothing that would have stopped me."

I thought about how disappointed Stryker would have been if I had died on my first mission out. He would have blamed himself for not teaching me any sense. Cutter would have blamed himself for not being there to protect me.

I'm glad he didn't know.

Gig must have picked up on my thoughts of Cutter.

"It's like your boyfriend said, about protecting you."

"He's not my boyfriend," I corrected. "Cutter is my best friend and a brother, just without blood ties. Like Stryker, he also was very overprotective of me. They both made it their job to keep an eye on me when I was at the Academy."

Gig nodded.

"It makes sense they were looking out for you," Gig said. "You're a vulnerable girl."

"I'm not vulnerable," I argued, feeling my face flush. "I don't need protectors. I need to learn how to make better choices. I need to learn to be more aware so I can spot when crazed murderers are about to attack me."

"So do I," Gig said. "I need to be more aware but I don't make the same mistakes twice."

I looked into his serious eyes and saw determination there. Something about the way he stared at me reminded me of Cutter. I wasn't sure if that was a good thing but it made me soften a little.

"Okay," I said. "Neither do I."

Gig stood up to leave, obviously satisfied that he'd made the amends he needed to. I watched him go, and secretly admired the way he carried himself. His body insinuated power and strength. I wondered how you acquired that look but Gunners tended to have it in spades. It must be something you were either born with, or you weren't.

"What is your friend's name? Cutter?"

I met Gig's eyes and nodded.

"When you talk with him," Gig said, "tell him I've promised to keep an eye on you. He seemed like he was really worried about you."

"He was," I agreed. "That will probably make him feel better. Thanks."

Gig closed the door behind him. It was the longest conversation I think we'd ever had.

I lay back on the bed. I felt tired but fulfilled at the same time. In the space of a few moments I had seen both of my family again, the way I'd hoped but Stryker was potentially about to leave the Academy, and Cutter was shipboard seeing new things without me. I had started a new life with four strangers. How could things change so quickly? It was strange to think that life was completely different this time last year. Now I was living out a dream wilder than anything I'd ever imagined as a child, when the most adventure I'd thought of was getting out of the house and swimming in the nearby lake.

Life amazed me.

The Council of the Order sat arranged in a semi-circle before us. There were ten masters, one to represent each discipline in the Order. Gig and I stood deferentially behind the Captain. We waited for them to speak. There was a low hum of white noise that the Captain had explained was meant to divert spies. We had been led here to this dark hall, where everything was in shadows except the center where the Council sat in dim light. I glanced into the darkness surrounding us and wondered if guards or servants stood nearby, ready to protect the Council, if necessary.

"Captain Orvobedes, thank you for meeting with us today," said the woman at the center seat of the table. She was fair haired and light eyed, with a thin upturned nose and pursed lips.

"Master Maranda, it is my pleasure," the Captain said. "Please allow me to introduce two of my crew: Gig Freeley and Alyvia Tippin."

"We acknowledge your crew," Master Maranda said, her voice sugared. "In fact, they are of great interest to us."

She motioned to the others seated on either side of her. I didn't dare to look at each master separately. I kept my attention on Master Maranda, the person who addressed us.

Stewards wearing gray robes came forward from the walls with chairs for us to sit on. I perched, straight-backed on the chair that was brought for me. I felt like ten pairs of eyes watched my every move. A quick glance at Gig showed me that he sat with a straight back as well. He stared at the wall in front of him with no expression on his face.

"How can we serve the Order?" the Captain asked, once seated.

"That is what we are here to find out," Master Maranda said. She looked down at a viewscreen in front of her and said, "What do you know of Master Ignoracius?"

There was a brief pause.

"Hector Ignoracius?"

"Yes," Master Maranda said. Her sugared voice grated on my nerves. "It seems he's been asking for you."

I glanced at the Captain quickly. Her face hadn't changed expression but she radiated surprise.

"We were classmates at the Academy," the Captain said. "We were good friends, but I haven't heard much from him in the past few years."

Master Maranda raised an eyebrow at the Captain.

"Then you know what he did."

"Yes, I believe I know what you are referring to," the Captain said. "I read the report on his Starkiller mission."

"Did he ever talk to you about that mission?"

"No," the Captain said. "And to be truthful, I never asked him of it. Ignoracius always had reasons for making his decisions, and I never had reason to question them. I'm certain his decisions during the Starkiller mission were equally reasoned."

"Then you place a lot of trust in Master Ignoracius."

"Yes I do," the Captain said. "Despite his unpopularity among the Order."

That sounded like a challenge to the people in this room.

Master Maranda did not speak for a moment. She simply gazed at the Captain like a fish on a hook. The Captain returned her gaze without flinching; cool as ice.

"Well it seems he places a lot of trust in you too," Master Maranda said finally, as if the words were pulled from her at great cost. "He knows you are a member of the Gamma Squadron, and he wants to talk to you and your crew."

"My crew?" the Captain said. "What for?"

"He has decided to give up his knowledge," Master Maranda said. "Starkiller."

The Captain frowned now, and considered what this meant. I looked at Gig to see if he knew what was going on, but he gave me an imperceptible shake of his head. I guessed he didn't know either.

"When?" the Captain wanted to know. "How?"

"As soon as possible," Master Maranda said. "We will give you and your crew the coordinates to him and you will leave immediately, Orvobedes. But first..."

It took me a moment to realize Master Maranda stared at me now. I felt a jolt of surprise as her eyes bored into mine, like she looked for something in my expression.

"Captain, take your Gunner and return to your rooms," Master Maranda said. "We wish to have a short conference with your Courier."

The Captain sat up straighter, obviously as surprised by this request as I was. Even Gig looked startled.

"If you don't mind, I would prefer to stay with my crewman," the Captain said.

"That is not necessary," Master Maranda said dismissively. "Leave now."

There was nothing left for the Captain to do but get up and usher Gig from the room. I stared at her with wide eyes but she only nodded at me. As they left I sat stiffly in my chair, and tried to look nonchalant. I heard the Captain and Gig leave. Their footsteps echoed in the silent room.

When we were alone, I sat under the weight of the Council's regard, covered in a thin sheen of sweat.

"Miss Tippin," Master Maranda said, "welcome to our Council. We have some questions we would like you to answer before we send you off on your mission."

"It is my duty to answer your questions to the best of my ability," I said clearly, thankful that my nerves didn't show in my voice.

"Very good," Master Maranda said with an approving tone. "Then we invoke Alpha clearance. What we discuss with you now is information for you alone to know. You may not share it with anyone else, including your team."

"Understood," I said immediately. I didn't. I didn't understand why they would want to invoke Alpha clearance with me.

"Do you know of Master Ignoracius?"

"No, Master Maranda," I said. "I had not heard his name until you first mentioned him to my Captain."

"Master Ignoracius was once the Captain of a Squadron like yours," said the man to Master Maranda's left. He was a waspy man with a squinty face and a sour voice. "On his last mission, he discovered a planet where the inhabitants had built a device called the Starkiller. Master Ignoracius and his crew watched as these people destroyed a star in their galaxy without a moment's hesitation. A very dangerous people indeed."

"That is right, Master Omin," Master Maranda said. "Master Ignoracius quickly acquired the device from the people and dismantled it. He then alerted the Order to these people and disappeared while the Order sent units to contain the planet."

"Master Ignoracius disappeared, and hid pieces of the device in locations which he refused to divulge. Even to the Order."

The way Master Maranda said it, I could tell how ridiculous she thought Master Ignoracius was.

"Despite our attempts, he has not divulged the locations of these pieces," she said.

Until now, I guessed.

"Which is why we are permitting him to tell your Captain where he is," she said. "Though we do not understand why he does not trust the Order."

He probably wanted to tell the Captain because they were friends. He trusted Captain Orvobedes to find the device. I looked at her sharp, unfriendly, face and kept my mouth shut. If she were the Master he'd met, I could understand why Master Ignoracius preferred someone else.

"We generally trust the Gamma Squadron," Master Maranda said, "but we need assurances that Captain Orvobedes won't go the same way Master Ignoracius did. That is why you are here at the moment."

I frowned.

"Captain Orvobedes has been a loyal member of the Order for decades," I said. I remembered the stories she'd been telling earlier in the commissary. "Do you really think you can't trust her?"

I was outraged on the Captain's behalf. I couldn't understand how they could look at her and think she could be disloyal. The Captain and the Merry Maids risked their lives for the Order on every mission they took. *Every* mission. How could that service on behalf of the Order be questioned, and why were they sharing this information with me—a rookie on the team?

"It remains to be seen how the Captain will respond after meeting Master Ignoracius and hearing his account of the Starkiller mission," Master Maranda said. "We are not interested in losing the device a second time."

"We will keep a close eye on your team, to make sure you are working in the interest of the Order," Master Omin said. "But we need eyes within the team to make sure our requests are met."

He stared at me while I took this in. My eyes looked from him to Master Maranda, and then to each face on the Council as I realized how very serious they were.

"We know it is much to ask of someone so new to active duty," Master Maranda said, her voice like sugar again. "We can see by your face that you think we are asking you to do something disloyal. May we remind you that you are in the service of the Order, and everything that is asked of you is for the good of the Order."

"You want me to spy on my own Captain," I said, unable to hide the accusation in calm tones. "What is the point of letting her lead a team if you don't even trust her?"

"That is a very naïve thing to say Miss Tippin," Master Omin said.

"We want you to be our eyes and ears during this mission, and report to us if you think the Captain, or anyone on your team, should try to keep the Starkiller device from the Order," Master Maranda said. "That should not be difficult for a member of the Order. Are you a member of the Order, Miss Tippin?"

Rebellion flared in my heart at what they asked me to do for them, but there was no other answer for me to say. I took a deep breath and nodded.

"Yes, I am," I said.

I felt the wind go out of me and sat back in my chair. How did it come to this? Anger bloomed in my belly; I was furious with myself.

"Return to your team then," Master Maranda said. "And expect to be contacted by us again."

And with that, I was dismissed. I felt like I'd just been pummeled.

A steward escorted me from the Council's chamber and told me how to find my rooms again. As soon as I stepped back into the hall and left the hum of white noise in the Council's chambers behind, the sudden onslaught of noise and activity jarred me in an uncomfortable way. There was a rail in front of me where I could stand and look over the edge to see hundreds of stories fanned out below in circular chambers. Everything on Thredenar seemed to be this way, I'd learned. Thredens loved the symmetry of arcs. They built around and up, to create cities of tall domes. The Council's building, where I stood, was the tallest of them all. It fit ships on the lower levels, and visitors on the middle levels. The upper levels, where I was, all belonged to the offices and chambers of the Council and their representatives. To get back to the Merry Maids I had to go down about two hundred levels.

Instead, I stood at the rail, and looked down. I felt very small.

I blew out a breath and tried to process what had just happened. I replayed the conversation over again in my mind. The more I dwelled on it, the more my shoulders slumped until I felt like the rail was all that kept me on my feet.

"I see you have not gone very far," said a voice beside me. I looked up and saw Master Omin, with his squinty face turned toward mine. "I had a few more words which I wanted to say in private."

My heart sank even lower. The Council already asked me to spy on my team, what other disloyal things could they ask me to do?

I straightened and turned to face Master Omin. Up close, he was taller than me but his body hunched over so much that his face was close to mine. He smelled like cigars, and his teeth were yellowed. I shifted away from him but he shuffled closer.

"Alyvia Tippin," he said. "Have you spoken with your father lately?"

My heart stopped beating for a moment as I stared at him in surprise. I shuddered.

"Yes, I know all about you, girl," Master Omin said. "I know where you come from and who your family is, in fact. I read all the ambassador accounts of your journey to the Academy. If it weren't for those files and details, you would have been contacted earlier. How wise for Stryker to keep your information confidential."

I felt an invisible hand clutch at my heart and squeeze. It robbed me of my strength and breath.

"What do you mean?" I whispered.

"Cayberra has become very unpopular," Master Omin said sourly. "It was always the most backward of planets in the Order, but lately they have been working to separate themselves from us. The Order is actively seeking out our members from Cayberra and weighing their loyalty."

I swallowed.

"If you read my file, then you *know* where I stand," I said, suddenly angry. He was playing games with me, and I didn't appreciate it. "You would also know that I have no loyalties toward Cayberra whatsoever."

His lip curled.

"I don't blame you," Master Omin said. He turned to peer over the railing. After a moment of trying to control my temper, I turned to mirror his stance and looked down at the activity below. "It seems as if things were better for you when you left Cayberra and came to the Order."

I nodded.

I remembered that time very clearly. It was such an awful period of darkness and depression, fear and anxiety. But the one bright point was the Academy, which became my safe haven. I had been a disaster when I arrived at the Academy but it had become my home.

"It would be awful for you to go back to life on Cayberra, wouldn't it," Master Omin said, with no question in his statement.

I nodded my head, unsure if words would come if I tried to speak. Just thinking about it made my heart drop. In the back of my mind, a dark tidal wave was suddenly rising in the distance.

"Does the Captain know? Does anyone on your team know where you came from?"

I shook my head no. The tidal wave was crashing over me now. I stood beside Master Omin, but I felt like I was drowning. My heart was pounding erratically in my chest. I stared out ahead of me, but saw nothing. My thoughts jumped from idea to idea with no logic as I tried to figure out why Master Omin was saying these things to me, and why I was feeling the way I felt. Afraid. About how the team would react if they only knew. If they only knew what I was. Where I'd come from.

What I'd done.

I couldn't breathe. I sucked in short gasps of air but my vision was going hazy.

"It would be a shame if they found out and started to distrust you," Master Omin said, like a mirror of my thoughts. "Luckily, the Order trusts you. We know you will serve us faithfully, as you have since the day you came to us. Right?"

I nodded my head slowly. The movement was difficult. I was being bandied around by unknown currents and it wouldn't be long before I drowned.

"I thought so," Master Omin said, satisfied. "As long as you are a trusted member of the Order, there is no reason for you to return to Cayberra, or to affiliate with them at all. The Order will watch over and protect you..."

I waited for him to say more. I forced myself to focus on what was happening. I looked up and realized Omin was looking at something nearby. Turning my wobbly head, I saw Gig approaching us on the balcony, his unreadable gaze focused on Master Omin. I nearly cried out in relief at seeing his face. The feeling of being suffocated lifted. Master Omin's hand lifted from the back of my bare neck, where I had not realized he'd been touching me.

He stepped away from me, and said, "remember who you serve."

Then he was gone. He nodded to Gig and returned to the Council's chamber.

I stared at the door he'd stepped through. It was a massive effort to stay on my feet.

"Are you okay?" Gig asked when he arrived a moment later. "You're shaking."

I looked up into his searching eyes, and meant to say I was fine, but when I opened my mouth I burst into tears instead. I covered my face in embarrassment and tried to choke the crying, but I couldn't stop. Gig clutched my arm and pulled me away from the railing. I let him lead me from the Council's deck into the nearest empty lift. As it started to move, I dropped to the corner with my knees drawn up to my chest, and tried to suck in calming breaths. My eyes were leaking hot tears all over my face, and I realized Gig was right about my shaking but I couldn't stop it. I heard myself sobbing and wondered why I sounded like that but couldn't make myself stop.

Gig crouched next to me and touched my shoulder.

"What the hell happened up there?" he asked. So gently.

I shook my head and looked away. I struggled with myself, and wished the tears would stop but I knew I couldn't control them. I started to dry heave, and felt Gig rub his hands on my back. His rough hands collected my hair out of the way in case I did throw up but fortunately I didn't have anything in my stomach.

The tide of emotion finally seeped out of me until I felt like a used husk of flesh. I sucked in lungfuls of air. When I wiped at my nose, I felt a piece of cloth get pushed into my hand. I took Gig's handkerchief gratefully and used it to dry my face. I sucked in more lungfuls of air to try and quiet the roiling in my gut.

Still sniffling a little, I sat up and lay my head back against the wall, and tried to clear my vision.

"Alright now?" Gig asked.

I nodded, still unable to look him in the eye. With his help, I pushed myself to my feet, smoothed my hair, and said, "I need to wash my face."

I could tell Gig watched me closely, but he got up too and hit a button on the lift's touchscreen. The doors opened and he led the way to a small washroom for general use. I washed my face quickly, then stared at it in the mirror, and wondered how I could make the red go away. Gig stood behind me. His reflection silently stared at mine. It was comforting to have him there but I started to feel embarrassed.

"I look like I've been crying," I said softly. The words perversely cued another tide of emotion that threatened to start the tears all over again. I fought it, angry that my body—the tool I had trained at the Academy to obey me at all times—was suddenly out of control.

I sighed in frustration. I turned away from the mirror and crossed my arms over my chest, taking deep breaths as I paced the room to clear my head. I kept replaying my conversations with the Council and Master Omin over and over again, wondering how they could have happened. This was not at all what I'd expected. I'd been waiting, through both of the excruciating conversations, for someone to finally ask me to do a routine or to test me in some way, the way I'd been tested at the Academy. I'd assumed, foolishly, that when the Captain said the Order wanted to test me for the mission, that the test would involve my skills, not my ability to spy and deceive.

And Master Omin, who had brought up my past and threatened to send me back to Cayberra if I didn't obey the Council. What was that? The Order couldn't do such a thing. Banishment to Cayberra was the supreme punishment for me, and Master Omin must have known that. I was scared by what he'd said, but disappointed too. In all the things I'd learned at the Academy, being wary of other members—Masters no less—was not a lesson I'd thought to study.

I really wished Stryker were here to discuss this with me. I wondered if I had enough time to comm him again.

Then I reconsidered.

The Council could tap my commlink to see if I broke Alpha clearance. Stryker would come under scrutiny then, which I did not want. I had to maintain Alpha clearance, despite all of my objections to doing so, because that was my duty.

I stopped suddenly and turned to face Gig squarely. He'd been watching as I paced, waiting me out. I forced my shoulders to relax and stood up straight.

"I'm done," I said. I lifted his handkerchief to give it back to him but he waved it away, for me to keep it. "I'm ready to go."

Gig didn't question me, for which I was grateful. He nodded and led the way from the washroom. I followed and we walked side-by-side back to our team. I felt his eyes constantly returning to me, but I resolutely stared straight ahead and replayed the conversations with the Order one more time.

Back in our quarters, three heads turned to look as I walked in with Gig. Marco and AJ were talking quietly with the Captain at the kitchen table.

I stopped a few steps into the room, and clutched the back of the sofa.

"Well?" Marco asked. "What happened?"

I looked down at the floor, unable to meet their eyes.

"I cannot tell you," I said apologetically. "They invoked Alpha clearance."

"Alpha clearance?" the Captain said, clearly startled.

"Why would they invoke Alpha clearance?" AJ asked. "Was it about you, or about us?"

I felt an invisible wall go up, that divided me from the rest of the team. I considered how to respond.

"It doesn't matter," Gig said, from behind me. "Her, us, we're the same team."

"I didn't say we weren't on the same team," AJ argued. "I just want to know if the Council talked to her about the existing team before she joined us."

"What does it matter?" Gig asked.

"It matters," AJ said. "She's new to active duty, they don't have much concern with her except for whether she's ready for the job. It doesn't seem to me like they would invoke Alpha clearance about that."

"So you're worried they talked to her about the rest of us?" Gig asked. "Are you worried because you're guilty of something?"

"There's no reason for us to speculate on this," the Captain said. "The Council invoked Alpha clearance, and that is all we need to know. We do not need to question Alyvia about this further. What we need to do is look over these maps and set our flight plan."

"How long until we're back up?" Gig asked.

"We leave at dawn," the Captain said. She turned back to Marco and began discussing plans again.

Gig placed a gentle hand on my arm and murmured something I didn't catch. I turned toward him. His hand was extremely warm against my skin.

"What did you say?" I asked.

"Go lie down," he repeated. "I'll grab you when I'm ready to take you to the armory."

I nodded and did as he said. I went into my room and quietly closed the door.

In the main room, I heard the Captain's voice stop. Someone asked a soft question, and Gig replied. I wanted to lie down but I had to hear what they were saying about me. I pressed my ear to the door and listened carefully.

"...she was outside the Council chamber...Master Omin," Gig said softly. "Looked like he was doing some damage...her tied up in *knots*. Omin ..."

The Captain interrupted with a question about Omin that sounded like "terror?"

"Yes," Gig answered, "maybe..."

"What could they have on her?" AJ asked clearly, and was shushed.

"Maybe they have something on us," Marco replied.

I heard someone sigh.

"Talk...later," the Captain mumbled.

There was a pause as the meeting to discuss me broke up. I turned and quietly climbed onto the little bed without kicking off my shoes. Using a throw blanket as a cover, I curled up on my side and let hot tears slide down my cheeks. I never cry, and now I was doing it twice in the same day. This time I was upset to find myself becoming an outcast on a tight-knit team where no one felt about me the way they did one another.

I pressed Gig's handkerchief against my face. The tears of self-pity waned as I drifted to sleep. Thankfully I had no dreams.

I woke to a knock at my door. I rolled over and watched as the Captain stepped inside and closed the door behind her. I sat up and wiped at my eyes to clear them of sleep. The Captain sat down on the edge of my bed with a tablet in her hand.

"Hi," she said. "I just wanted to let you know that I received word from the Council."

My heart immediately sank. What more did the Council want with me? Wasn't there a limit to how much they could inflict on me in one day?

"Basically, it is a reminder that everything they discussed with you today is confidential due to their invocation of Alpha clearance," the Captain said. "You are forbidden to discuss any of it with the rest of the team or anyone else except the Council. Out of respect, I've already notified the team that we are not to even bother questioning you about it. As curious as we are about finding out what happened up there, we will never know."

I met the Captain's eyes sadly.

"I cannot tell you what was discussed," I said, "but I wish I could."

The Captain nodded.

"Actually, I wish it had never happened at all," I said.

I looked down at my hands, which were clenched together in my lap.

"Sometimes it is difficult for us to understand what motivates the Council," the Captain said. "They know things that we do not, and have a different perspective that we cannot guess at, but what they do, they do for the good of the Order, and we have to trust in that."

Part of me wondered if she would say that so confidently if she knew that the Council did not trust her the way they should. Another part of me wondered, for a moment, if the Council wasn't right to suspect her. Perhaps I was being young and stupid in putting my faith in the Captain. She seemed to be an honorable person, but what did I know? I'd only met her a couple weeks ago. That wasn't enough time to truly *know* someone.

"So, we have our coordinates and mission details?" I asked.

"Yes," the Captain said. "That's why I came to wake you. We have about an hour before we need to head out, so I want you and Gig to hurry and do the task I assigned you."

I nodded.

"You wanted Gig to take me to an armory where I could be outfitted with some weapons," I said.

"That's right," the Captain said. "Marco and AJ have already completed their tasks, so they will help me with final prep for the ship. I want you and Gig to finish your task and meet us in time for launch. Whatever he gets you, it has to be something he can train you to use, so don't let him buy anything too fancy, all right? He's like a kid in a candy store when it comes to armories."

I gave her a half-smile and got up to smooth my hair and clothes. I went to the mirror and glanced at my reflection. I looked surprisingly fine, if not a little sleepy. The Captain took her tablet and left my room. I followed her out into the common room, where I saw Gig waited for us by the door.

"Ready?" he asked. I said yes and followed him from our suite.

The landing outside our rooms was busy with people. They seemed to have multiplied since the last time we'd been out here.

"A passenger ship just arrived," Gig explained. "Good thing we're leaving soon."

I didn't pay attention to any of their faces. I walked through and around them without seeing them, intent only on staying right behind Gig. A few times people passed between us and I had to go around them to get through. They let Gig through easily; he was tall and built enough to catch their attention. In comparison, I was much smaller than Gig and less imposing, so I was jostled out of the way. When I tried to barrel through to see if they would move for me the way they moved for Gig, it didn't work and I ended up getting bounced off a passenger's arm or chest. They were decidedly *not* moving for me.

Every time Gig noticed I'd fallen back, he stopped to wait for me to catch up. After he had to do this several times, he gave up and grabbed my arm so he could pull me along beside him.

"You need to tell people to move out of your way," he said as we went.

"Why should they listen to me? I'm not tall and muscled like you," I replied.

"You don't need muscles for people to pay attention to you," he said.

"Easy for you to say."

Gig didn't respond. He ushered me onto a crowded lift, and shifted his hold from my arm to my shoulder. The people on the lift shifted a little bit to make room, but we were still tightly crowded together. When the doors closed and the lift began to move, no one spoke. They kept their eyes focused on the number readout, waiting for their floor to appear.

We stopped on a new level, and someone said they were exiting. Everyone shifted out of the way to let three people pass. They jostled into me and Gig. When the three had left, four people made their way onto the lift.

"Awfully crowded, hey?" one of them said as he walked on the lift.

I looked up at Gig.

"What level are we going to?" I asked Gig.

Gig glanced at the readout.

"We have two more stops in between," he said. He steadied me as someone pushed into my back and I almost bounced into him.

"Is there another way up there?" I asked. Dozens of eyes focus on me.

"We're almost there," Gig assured me.

I sighed inaudibly and didn't complain. I tried to focus on the fact that we were almost to the armory instead of all the people who were pressed close to us.

Someone jostled me into Gig again.

I watched as Gig ignored their complaints, and firmly pushed the bodies pressing against me a half-step away so I could breathe. Then he turned me away from facing him so that my back was pressed against his hard chest, and he held me close with a hand around my waist.

Glancing at the people who'd been moved, I saw some of them glared at me in annoyance. I avoided their eyes and looked back to the readout.

At the next stop, more people exited, carefully avoiding us, and only two came on. The second stop was much the same, as more people exited than entered.

Finally we were at our stop and Gig guided me forward off the lift. No one followed off the lift, and our landing was almost empty of people.

"No one comes to the armories?" I asked, looking around.

"We're not on the armory level," Gig said. "We're right below it."

Confused, I followed Gig as he led the way again. We passed several doors on the left as we made our way around the level's ring.

"Where are we going?" I asked.

"To the best armor on Thredenar," he said.

The door Gig led me to opened immediately, and an old man appeared in the entrance.

"I heard you were here," the man said to Gig. "I knew you couldn't leave without coming to see me."

"How could I not come to see you?" Gig said. He stepped into the man's waiting embrace. They did that back-slap thing that men seemed to like.

The old man's eyes focused on my face over Gig's shoulder.

"Well hello," he said, and let Gig go. "What did you bring me?"

Gig grabbed my arm and pulled me inside. His friend closed the door behind us, and smiled at me curiously.

"This is Tippin," Gig said as introduction. "She's the new Courier for the Merry Maids and she needs a weapon."

The old man sighed.

"Tippin," he repeated. "Is that her first name?"

"Alyvia," I said. "I don't think he knows my first name."

The man laughed.

"My son is a little thick-headed sometimes," he said.

My eyes riveted to Gig's in surprise. I looked from Gig to his father, and started to spot resemblances. The two men had the same darkness of features: dark hair, dark eyes, dark tan. I saw in his father the same tilted smirk that was supposed to be a smile. Gig was more muscular and lethal-looking, but they were both very *male*.

"My name's Onri," his father said.

"You didn't tell me we were coming to see your father," I said. I stepped forward and shook Onri's hand politely. "He told me we were seeing an armor."

"Well, I am an armor," Onri said. "Gig comes to me whenever he needs something. So, what kind of a weapon do you need?"

"I don't know," I said. I looked to Gig for help.

"She needs something small," Gig said. "I'm thinking one of your patented knives might work."

"A knife?"

Onri looked at me in a very calculating way.

I waited, letting him look me over carefully. After some consideration, Onri looked at his son again.

"Why does she need a knife, isn't that what you're for?"

Gig shifted.

"I can't be everywhere at once," he said. "When we're in the middle of it, I need her to be able to defend herself if she has to."

"Mmhmm," Onri said. "Come here, girl."

I went to Onri, and let him lead me by the hand from the entranceway into his quarters. We passed through spartan rooms where nothing was out of place, everything economically decorated in precise lines.

In the back, the room Onri pulled me into was covered from wall to wall with weapons of different sizes and types. I tried to see them all at once, but it was impossible. There were knives ranging from picks the size of my little finger to wicked curves of steel taller than a man. I saw blasters and guns, staffs and batons, and even weapons I couldn't name. It was a Gunner's wet dream.

"Look around and take what you like," Onri said. He released my hand and smiled at me pleasantly. "I'm going to talk to my son for a second."

"OK," I said. I walked fully into the room. Onri turned back and motioned Gig after him. I began my search of the weapons, and hoped one would catch my attention. In the other room, I could vaguely hear Onri and Gig's voices. They whispered but Onri's rooms were small enough that I could still make out what they were talking about.

"She's a pretty one," Onri said. "Sort of reminds me of your mom. Pouty lips and doe eyes."

"Dad," Gig said. He sounded like a teenager in that moment.

"I'm just saying, kiddo," Onri said. "Girl like that could make a man think some thoughts...What? Don't tell me you have to leave?"

"We're supposed to be back on the ship in five minutes," Gig said.

I turned back to the weapons and pretended I was examining them closely. I hoped my face wasn't too pink. I felt like grinning at Onri as he and Gig came back into the room, but I kept myself under control and reached out at random to touch something on the wall.

"That one's special," Onri said. He came up next to me and grabbed the object I'd touched to show it to me properly. I looked at it in his open hand and realized it was a thin black ring made of two connecting bands. "See if it fits one of your fingers."

I took it from him and tried the ring on. It fit perfectly on the middle finger of my right hand.

"This would be perfect for you," Onri said. "Good choice!"

"I don't know what I chose," I said honestly. I examined the ring closely but all I could tell about it was that it was pretty.

"It's a Pulsar Ring," he explained. "You twist the two sections of the ring in opposite directions, and it emits an intense burst of energy that will stun anyone you touch. If you don't twist it closed again, it will continue to pulse, and each pulse will grow stronger and stronger in energy until you cook your enemies alive."

"Won't it harm the person who uses the ring too?" I asked.

"Not if you have the ring around your finger," he said. "The ring recognizes the DNA of its wearer and shields you. But if you were to twist the ring open and then take it off, you wouldn't be able to pick it up again without burning your fingers. You would have to wear a protective suit."

"I like it," I said. It would be an unassuming weapon that I could use my tele to activate.

"Of course you do," Onri said. "All girls like rings."

I made a face at him. Girls who liked rings were living a different life than mine but I didn't correct him. For some reason his statement made me feel feminine, which I didn't mind in that moment. Usually the Order kept us all looking gender neutral, and if we were running drills, I had to tie up my hair in a hat.

"That ring won't do you any good if someone is attacking you with a weapon," Gig pointed out. "You would have to get inside their defenses to use the ring, and by then you could be dead."

"Well that's a pleasant thought," Onri said sarcastically. "Thanks, Gig."

Gig ignored his father.

"I told you, she needs some of your patented knives," he said.

"Fine," Onri said to his son. To me, he said, "but you can keep the ring too."

I smiled at him.

Onri smiled back.

"Well, if you're a Courier with the Merry Maids, you need a small and concealable knife," Onri said, almost to himself as he considered his collection. "It would need to be something durable, but unobtrusive for when you are in tight spaces…"

He bent over and pulled a kit from near the floor of one wall.

"This would be good," he said. "Check it out."

He showed me a small sheathed knife with a pearl-encrusted grip. Computer etchings lined the blade as Onri pulled it out and set it in my hand.

"It's very light," I said. I tried to feel what it would be like to possess the knife and use it as part of my world.

"This knife is special, because it has camouflage built into it," Onri said. He took the sheathed knife from me and pressed it against my bare forearm. As he pulled his hand away, I saw that the knife sheath had adhered to my arm and was fading from sight.

I reached out and touched the invisible knife hilt in wonder.

"That's amazing," I said. "I've never seen anything like it."

"It's an old design," Onri said modestly. "But it's yours now."

"Thank you very much," I said. I pulled the knife away from my skin and watched as it shifted back into sight.

"You could strap that to your back, or your hip," Onri said. "Well, anywhere really. I have a different one that you can strap to your leg."

He glanced around the room until he found it, and handed it to me. This sheath wasn't flat; it had straps that I could slide my leg through.

"So she's all set," Gig said in approval of my weaponry. "We need to get back to the ship."

"Onri, thank you," I said again.

"Any time, darling," Onri said. He motioned for me to follow Gig back to the exit. As we walked back to the door, Onri reached out and held my forearm gently to stall me a little.

"You'll be working closely with my boy," he whispered in my ear. "Will you keep an eye out for him? He's not invincible."

I saw the worry in Onri's eyes and felt sympathy for him.

"I'll do my best," I whispered back.

"What are you whispering about?" Gig asked, he turned at the door to look at us.

I stayed silent.

"I was just inviting your friend to come back and visit me sometime," Onri said. "She's lovely."

Gig looked at him suspiciously but didn't argue.

"Take care of yourself, old man," he said to his father.

Onri grunted in reply. The two gave each other bear hugs, then Onri pulled me into his arms and gave me a bear hug too. As we left, I glanced over my shoulder and grinned. Onri was leaning out his doorway to watch us leave.

I saw him give a small wave and disappear inside before Gig turned and saw him.

"Your dad is sweet," I told Gig.

"I'll tell him you said so," Gig replied.

We hustled back to where the ship was docked, and saw the Captain waiting impatiently by the bay doors. As we approached she crossed her arms over her chest and frowned at us.

Gig led the way aboard, and didn't say anything to the Captain. I followed his lead. When I glanced at the Captain sideways I thought I saw a slight upturn to her lips, and knew we weren't in trouble.

"We're all aboard," the Captain said into a comm link.

"Initiating take-off sequence," Marco's voice replied.

I was in my room by the time we left Thredenar behind. I felt a rush of freedom, and stared out my window as the planet fell away. The bindings of the Council loosened from around my throat so that I could breathe again.

I turned my back on the view, and went to find my seat in the co-pilot's chair.

8

"Have you ever thought about starting a family?" I asked.

Marco looked at the stars before us and considered the question.

"It was never really a major focus," he answered at last. "When I'm around families with young kids I think about it pretty seriously. But at this point, it's impossible for me to find someone that I might start a family with. I only leave the ship when we're on leave, and we're only on leave for short amounts of time. You can't find a life partner like that."

I considered this.

"Maddy did it," I said.

"Yes but Maddy is different," Marco said. "She has a different way of doing everything."

I glanced at him in the darkness of the Pilot's deck. I was sitting with my bare feet tucked up on the chair and a blanket wrapped around me. For some reason the co-pilot's chair was just so much more comfortable than any other chair on the ship. I'd taken to sitting with Marco every night before I went to bed.

When I fell asleep there, Marco left me alone until he switched the ship to autopilot and retired to his own bed. He would shake me a little and help me up so I could stumble to my bed.

"Marco, did you even like Maddy?" I asked.

"No," he said bluntly. "She was very immature. Very selfish, and very immature."

"Not exactly the type of person who should start a family," I joked.

Marco shrugged.

"You never know," he said. "She could have some kids and find out that this galaxy wasn't made to revolve around her. At least I hope that's what happens."

I leaned my head back against my chair and thought about what it would be like to start a family and have kids. I shuddered.

"I think I would be pretty useless as a mother," I said. "I don't think I want children."

Marco smiled softly.

"My sister told me you learn quickly," he said. "It was like a culture shock the first time I met her kids. Everything is a zoo when they're little."

"You have nieces and nephews?" I asked. I tried to picture little Marcos.

"A niece and two nephews," Marco said. "My niece decided I was great fun and attached herself to me the entire time I was visiting. If I ever have kids I definitely want a girl."

"Life is easier for boys though," I said.

Marco looked at me sideways.

"Where did you grow up?" he asked.

"Why?" I asked in response.

"It sounds like you grew up somewhere not very girl friendly," he said.

"Oh," I said. "I guess you're right."

"You and your brother?" he prompted. "Is that it? You were treated differently than your brother?"

"Absolutely," I said, like this was the understatement of a century.

"Well you obviously didn't let that stop you," Marco said. "I mean, you followed your brother to the Academy at a very young age."

I didn't have much choice, I wanted to say, but stayed silent and nodded.

Marco sat back in his chair, and stretched his arms over his head before settling back.

"How long ago did your brother die?" he ventured.

I sat up straighter and clutched my blanket more closely around me.

"Actually, I should get to bed," I said.

Marco sat up too and put his hand on my shoulder.

"No, I'm sorry," he said. "I'm being very nosy."

"No, it's fine," I lied. "No big deal."

Gig materialized out of nowhere.

"What's no big deal?" he asked. Marco and I both jumped in surprise. We hadn't heard him.

"I'm just being an ass," Marco told Gig. "Prying where I shouldn't. Tell her to stay."

It was difficult to see much of Gig's face, but I could feel his eyes settle on me.

"Stay," he said.

He grabbed a utility chair, pulled it between our seats and sat. Then he propped up his feet on the console and leaned back comfortably.

I settled back into my chair, not wanting to get up and leave anymore.

"Anything interesting tonight?" Gig asked Marco.

The two compared notes on their favorite space anomalies while I listened in companionable silence.

"How long until we arrive?" Gig asked after a while.

Marco looked at his readouts carefully.

"We'll be there in a few days," he said. "The Captain wants us to get there with NTW, so it'll be a harder pace than usual."

Gig nodded.

"What's NTW?" I asked.

"No Time Wasted," Marco said. "It means haste is our top priority."

"Oh," I said, interested. "What other acronyms do you use?"

"AO," Gig said immediately. "Always on. We use that when we're on a mission and the Captain wants to have our comms going at all times, so they can monitor what we're saying and doing."

"We were AO on Galaxin 7," I said.

"Yep," Gig said. "There is DOS: destroy on sight. AMI: Abort mission immediately."

"BVR," Marco added. "Beyond visual range. BSR: Beyond sensor range."

"CT," Gig said. "Cut transfer. That means destroy your comm unit and wait to be contacted in an alternate medium."

"ECO," Marco said. "Emergency comms only; or don't use your comm unless you are dying or in extreme agony."

I looked at him and saw by his expression that he was being overdramatic. We exchanged smiles.

"We should make up some of our own acronyms," I suggested.

"Like what?" Marco asked.

"Like..." I thought about it. "IATFB. It's almost time for bed."

Marco laughed.

"ITOFTST," he offered. "I'm tired of flying the ship tonight."

"YBAESTE," Gig said. "You both are extremely simple to entertain."

We laughed at how lame our conversation had become.

"I guess it's time for bed if we're getting this slap happy," Gig said. He got up and left without saying good night.

Marco glanced over his shoulder to watch Gig leave.

"He's never come to sit with me before," he said.

"He's been missing out," I said. I gathered my blankets around me. "Night."

I padded back to my room and crawled into my bed, eager to fade out.

I dreamed of Sen. He sat across from me in the paddle boat, out in the middle of the lake. It was long past sundown and the world slept around us. We floated on stars, and I laughed. Sen gave me a funny look, and then his face lit with wonder. Because we really were floating, but it wasn't the water.

It was me.

When I woke the next morning I stayed in bed, feeling somber. Curled comfortably under my blanket I just lay there and thought of Sen.

The night on the lake wasn't a dream, it was a memory; the last happy memory I had until I was at the Academy. It hurt to see his face in my mind and think of growing up so closely with him. It hadn't mattered to him that I was six years younger than him, or that I was a female. Of the seven children my parents had I was the youngest, and the most likely to be kept at home to care for the house.

Sen changed all that.

A bleep sounded at my door, and a second later Gig stepped in. He looked around the darkened room. Then he saw me still in bed and frowned at me.

"Are you sick?"

"No," I said. "I'm up."

I sat up and shoved the covers aside.

"Breakfast is ready," he said.

"OK."

As soon as he left I got up and dressed, and pulled my hair into a knot so it was out of my way. Then I went to join the others for breakfast.

"Morning," everyone said when I came in. I slumped into my chair and said good morning. Everyone was eating a mixture of fruit and croissant except Gig, who had a plate of eggs. I reached for the fruit and juice in the center of the table.

"Did you sleep well?" Marco asked.

"Mmhmm," I mumbled. I tried to push aside the memories of my dreams.

"Well now that we're all here, let's have a meeting," the Captain said, as she did each morning. "Gig, will you begin your combat lessons with Alyvia today?"

"Yes," Gig said around a mouthful of egg.

"Good," the Captain said. "I'll join you. I haven't had time to get in a good workout in quite some time."

I looked up at the Captain in surprise, and tried to picture working with her in the gym. She spent most of her time at her desk, sorting through files and communicating with other members of the Order. We hadn't been in much proximity before today.

"Marco, when will we be arriving?"

"Three days from now," Marco said.

"Good," the Captain said. "When we arrive you can take the ship into the atmosphere. From what I've been told, the planet is uninhabited except for Master Ignoracius."

"He must have really angered the Order for them to hold him in seclusion," Marco said.

"They're definitely not happy with him," the Captain said. "I'm not sure what to expect out of this mission, so I want you and AJ to go through extra training sessions with Gig too."

They nodded.

"Alright," the Captain said. "Finish breakfast and let's meet up again at dinner."

I swallowed the last of my fruit and got rid of my plate and cup.

"Lyv?"

Marco's voice stopped me. He got up from the table, and came over to where I stood.

"Are you alright?" he asked. "You're awfully quiet and unsmiling this morning."

"Am I?" I asked. I was impatient to leave but I forced myself to be still. I could see the concern in his eyes.

"Yes, are you okay?"

"I'm fine, Marco," I said. I gave him a hug and a half smile. Marco's hug was brotherly and warm. I told him I would see him later, and then beat a hasty retreat.

I went back to my room, and felt a little guilty for blowing him off. I changed into my workout clothes, still feeling disjointed, and went straight to the gym. When I walked in, I saw Gig and the Captain sparring in the far corner. I chose a workout mat as far from them as possible and sat down to tape up my hands and feet. When I was done, I crossed my legs beneath me for some quick meditation. When I closed my eyes, I tried to focus my mind and concentrate only on the here and now.

My dreams of Sen still haunted me. I saw his face in my memory. He smiled and looked sad at the same time. Left to focus only on my thoughts now, a flare of fury threatened to rise up and swallow me. I pushed it down anxiously, but part of me welcomed it. Longed for its release.

I jumped to my feet and began working at the Tricino series of movements, the dances of the Masters. Stryker had begun teaching them to me early in my training, knowing that as my talent progressed, I would eventually improve at the Tricinos. I was still far from being in Master form, but the series was so hard and exhausting, it had always helped me get through days like today.

The first series alone had more than two-hundred and fifty spins, kicks, flips and postures. I whirled through it with determination, and immediately felt the gratifying flex and lengthening of muscles as I tossed myself around the mat, oblivious to everything but the dance and the pounding of my heart.

When I was done with the first series, I launched into the second. Slightly more complicated, and with a different combination of movements, I focused my mind, and pushed all hints of Sen far away.

I was halfway through the third series when I collapsed on the mat, out of breath and shaking with fatigue. I rolled onto my back and stared at the ceiling while I gasped for air.

Gig stepped into my field of vision. I looked at him without saying anything. His dark eyes roamed my face. I thought I saw sympathy in his expression.

After a long pause, he said, "That's not the way to work out a problem."

I shook my head, and looked away. How would Gig know? He didn't understand that there *was* no way to face my problems. I would be haunted by them for the rest of my life.

"When you get your air back, can we get started with your knife training?"

I forced myself to sit up and ran a hand through my hair. It had come loose in a tumble down my back and was slick with sweat. I combed it with my fingers and tied it back up into a knot. Then I got up and silently left the gym.

When I returned, Gig waited for me on a center mat. He saw the knives from his father's wall in my hands and nodded.

"Do you know any knife movements?" he asked.

"Of course," I said.

"Show me one," he said, and got out of my way.

I pulled one of the knives from its sheath and left everything else on one corner of the mat. Bowing to Gig, I concentrated, then began the original knife dance.

"Good," he said, when I'd bowed to him again. "You already know how to hold the knife. Now, let's work on that dance in a one-on-one spar."

Gig held up his arms like he surrendered. With a smooth jerk, a knife flew into both of his hands and he took a step toward me.

That was how three grueling days of knife tutoring began. I would watch Gig demonstrate the correct knife stances, and then I would try them myself. My favorite lessons involved knife throwing.

"Flick!" Gig said.

I made a flicking motion with my wrist, and my knife sailed toward its target. With a dull thud, it landed an inch to the right and below of the bull's-eye. I grinned at Gig.

"You didn't..." he said.

I scoffed.

"I haven't used my tele once in our lessons, give me some credit!"

Gig looked to where my knife still stood buried in the target and shrugged.

"You're getting better," was all he would say.

"Thanks for the encouragement," I said darkly. I went to the target and yanked my knife out. I returned to my spot and aimed again. This time the knife landed a hair apart from the bulls-eye.

I said nothing to Gig as I went and fetched the knife again but my face was probably in full-gloat.

"That was good," he admitted.

I ignored him, returned to my spot, and tried again. The knife flew with a perfect arc as it spun and landed in the exact same position it had before.

I did it again, this time landing a perfect bulls-eye.

I retrieved the knife in satisfaction, and turned to face Gig expectantly with a hand on my hip.

"Lucky shot," he said, but I could tell he was suppressing a grin.

"You're trying to piss me off, aren't you," I said.

"No, but it's working isn't it?"

Gig left me by myself, and said we could come back to it after dinner. I watched him go with my jaw set.

We would just see!

I went back to the invisible line and began again. Perfect bulls-eye. Lucky shot my ass, I thought. Then I did it again.

I threw fifteen perfect bulls-eyes in a row. Then I switched to my left hand, which was much more difficult. My first shot went past the target and clanged on the floor. I was glad no one was around, this could be dangerous.

I tried again, and again. It wasn't until my fifth throw that I actually hit the target. That was a good start. I threw and threw until my wrists ached and felt swollen. I refused to quit until I could throw a perfect bulls-eye with my left hand.

"Have you been practicing all this time?"

I paused mid-throw and looked up. Gig was in the doorway, eyes wide. He came closer, and stared at me like I was nuts.

"Have you been practicing all this time?" he repeated.

I dropped my arm.

"Yes," I said.

"Do you know how long I've been gone?"

I looked around, and shrugged. I had no clue.

Gig put his hands to his face and closed his eyes like he had a headache.

"You can't become a master armsman in one day," he said slowly, like I was an idiot. "You realize that right?"

"I have no intention of becoming a master armsman," I said. "But you'd better believe I can throw bulls-eyes with both hands."

Gig opened his eyes and stared at me.

"What?"

I grinned and demonstrated. I flicked with my right and then my left hand. Two knives sliced through the air, one right after the other, and landed with equal thuds in the red bulls-eye of the target, side by side.

Gig stared at the twin knives for a long time.

"You're nuts," he said. "I can't believe you stood here all night until you mastered a skill."

He turned his gaze back to me.

"I'm impressed."

I paused, uncertain if I'd heard him correctly. But the way he looked at me was undeniable. He was grudgingly impressed.

I smiled.

"Thanks," I said. I went to the target and pulled my knives from the bulls-eye with some effort.

"Do you want to work on sparring?" he offered.

"Nope, I'm done for the night," I said airily. I saluted him with one of my knives and exited the gym quickly.

I made an immediate beeline for the Medic, happy to see AJ there reading something. No one else was in the lab. He looked up when I walked in. I went straight to a table and hopped up on it. Realizing I was there for a health reason, he put on his serious face and came over.

"What's wrong?" he asked.

I set my knives to the side and held out my hands for him to look. He stared at my swollen wrists and raw fingers, and rolled his eyes.

"Was it worth it?" he wanted to know.

I thought of the look on Gig's face when he saw where my knives had landed on the target, and grinned.

"You're almost as bad as him," AJ said with a shake of his head. He went and grabbed a sensor, and began working on my right wrist.

Marco noticed that my mood improved after that awful morning. He asked me about it over the next few days. Just a little out of it from bad dreams, I told him. He wasn't sure if he should buy it, but he didn't know me well enough to call me a liar.

He also tried to ask me about Sen, and about what life was like as a kid before I came to the Academy, but I was becoming very good at shrugging him off.

"It just doesn't seem right," he said one night. "At some point you're going to have to trust someone and talk about it. We're not just shipmates, I consider you a friend, Lyv."

I hated the way my stomach turned. I refused to look at him.

"I'm not trying to be a bad friend," I said. "I just don't want to get into it. I don't like who I am when I open that door. It's better shut away, where I don't have to deal with it because it hurts just as bad every time. I'm sorry."

"You can't shut it away forever, Alyvia," he said. He reached out to palm the top of my head. I gave him a weary smile. We stared out at the stars from our comfortable chairs and were silent.

There were several times during my knife fight training when I wanted to quit. On more than one occasion I accidentally nicked myself, or Gig. Each incident sent AJ into a fit, but the Captain refused to stop us.

"This is how they do it at the Academy," she told AJ. "Just bandage them up as best you can. If they lose a finger, they lose a finger."

Gig and I snickered, but AJ was not amused. He sulked nearby as we continued our lessons.

"All right, my turn with the boy. I want to do a few sparring routines," the Captain said after a while. I bowed to Gig, sheathed my knives and went to sit by AJ to watch.

I watched with great interest as Gig and the Captain sparred together. The Captain moved like she'd sparred her entire life. There was something well-practiced about her technique that told me she would be very good in a true fight.

"I much prefer this to your knife lessons," AJ said beside me.

"Well you're going to have to get used to them," I said.

AJ sighed.

"It's just pointless," he said. "Why can't you learn to use a blaster? I've already seen you use one of those, and you have a sharp eye."

"A blaster won't help me in tight spaces," I reminded him. "Like Galaxin. That guy attacked me when I wasn't looking, but if I'd had a knife..."

"Or if we'd caught him before you ran into him," AJ said. "Or if Gig had sent me with you, or if you'd scanned the room before going in. Those are all ifs."

"Yes," I said, annoyed, "and if it happens again I will be able to defend myself."

"For all the good that will do," he muttered under his breath.

I rounded on him.

"What?"

AJ glanced at me and shook his head. He wanted me to drop it but I was at the end of my rope.

"What, you don't think I can defend myself?" I asked.

"I didn't say that," he said.

"You're thinking it. Go ahead and say it."

"Well, think about it," AJ said when he had to give in, "if someone looked at, say, *Gig*, and then looked at *you*. Well…you're the easy target."

I glared at him.

"Say that again" I said with my teeth clenched.

AJ looked me in the eye.

"You're an easy target," he said. "Think about it, will you? You're small. You don't have a mean face, your muscles aren't bigger than your neck compared to Gig, and you don't come up to anyone's waist, let alone their eye level. You're just not that formidable."

He said it so dismissively. My jaw dropped.

"I'm almost taller than you, you idiot. And I'm probably stronger than you. My muscles may not be bulging, but at least I have some."

AJ sat back lazily and shrugged. I realized then that he'd gotten what he wanted—a reaction from me.

"It's just my opinion," he said in his most nonchalant tone. "Sorry if that upsets you but…"

I didn't hear anything he said after that. I stood up and faced him.

"Come spar me then, AJ," I said. "Let's just test your theory that I'm an easy target."

AJ looked up at me appraisingly.

"Yes, please feel free to spar her," Gig said from behind me. "You have to back up your words."

AJ glanced at him and gave another careless shrug.

"I will," he said, "but I don't feel like it just now."

I pictured myself punching him in the face just then. I had never disliked someone so much. He smirked at me and looked pretty pleased with himself.

"You're an idiot," I said.

With a suppressed flicker of my mind, I sent him and his chair tumbling over backward across the room. He yelled in anger as he went, and ended up sprawled against the far wall. I stormed from the gym and ignored the calls that followed me.

As soon as I walked back into my quarters, I threw the knives in my hands at the table and kicked over one of my chairs.

I pictured my father, who laughed at me cruelly as he sold me away. Like I was a silly girl.

I put my hands on my hips like I was winded and closed my eyes to picture something else, but my father wouldn't have any of it. He laughed at me in my memory, and mocked me with words that echoed AJ's.

What can you do? Females don't have talents.

A bleep sounded at my door. I turned to see Gig walk in, his face dark.

"I won't apologize," I said immediately.

Gig let the door close behind him.

"I didn't come to make you apologize," he said. "I came to find out what happened back there."

I saw him glance around the room before he looked back at me. I knew he saw my overturned desk chair. It probably looked like I'd come here to have a temper tantrum.

"Oh," I said. I deflated a little. I had just picked a fight with AJ in front of Gig and the Captain. It was not my best side and I was embarrassed.

I turned my back to Gig and went to the window. I crossed my arms and took a minute to focus my mind as I stared out at the stars. I took several deep breaths until my tension level came back to normal.

"I don't know what happened," I admitted when I felt calmer. I pressed my forehead to the window. "I must be going nuts."

"I don't think you're going nuts," Gig said. "You're just royally pissed off."

I glanced back at him with a frown.

"I *am* pissed off," I said. "AJ wanted a reaction from me, and he figured out how to get it."

I sighed.

"I'm not like this though," I said. "I wasn't like this at the Academy. Well, at first maybe, but not for long."

I tried to remember those first few months and turned back to staring at the stars.

"Maybe that's it," I said to myself. "At the Academy I felt safe. I had safety nets that I could fall back on with Cutter and Stryker. Here...it's different."

"You don't feel safe here?"

"I don't feel safe...from myself," I tried to explain. "At the Academy I could turn to Stryker or Cutter when I needed to talk or work through something. Sometimes I just needed their validation that my emotions were okay."

"You talk to Marco."

"Marco is different," I said. "He can analyze, and he can empathize, but he doesn't really know me. He wouldn't understand."

"Well, what about the Captain?" Gig asked. "Or me?"

I sighed.

"I wish I didn't need it," I admitted. "I wish I could just rely on myself."

"You can't keep everything inside," Gig said. "You can't work out your troubles on a gym mat. You need to open yourself to the people around you."

"What if they don't like what they find?" I asked. That statement made me feel like a raw, open wound. I forced myself to look back and meet his eyes.

Gig clenched his fists but his eyes were kind.

"I don't think that's possible, Tippin," he said softly. "Let go of some of your burdens."

I thought about it for a moment, and couldn't suppress a sudden grin.

"I let go of some of my burdens on AJ," I said.

The corners of Gig's mouth turned up slowly, like he didn't want to encourage me by smiling but he liked what I'd done.

"I'd like to try that sometime too," he admitted. "It was quite impressive."

"Thanks," I said with a sudden smile. I looked down at my feet. "Thanks for coming to check on me."

"Any time," he said.

At dinner that night, AJ refused to speak to me, which suited me just fine. I saw Gig and Marco try to suppress their enjoyment of this turn of events, but they didn't do a very good job. I realized they were on my side. I'm sure someone had filled in Marco about what had happened. If he knew and wasn't fazed by my outburst, maybe I *could* trust him not to abandon me. When I glanced at the Captain, she seemed unperturbed as well. I wondered if I should offer her an apology for my behavior. I was more embarrassed and less angry now that some time had passed and I had cooled down.

I glanced at AJ when the Captain talked to him, and saw that he looked pretty surly. He answered all questions with *yes*, *no*, or *I don't know* answers. His pinched face didn't earn any sympathy from me. I ignored his conversation and chatted with Marco and Gig instead.

9

"This is it," Marco said.

We sat side by side, and stared out at the endless expanse of beach that led to an ocean spread out before us. I knew that the Order watched every movement on this planet from their surveillance satellites but if you ignored that part, the view was stunning.

"It's lovely," I said. "There could be worse places to live in exile."

"No joke," Marco said, obviously awed. "This is amazing."

We went and collected the rest of the team and exited the ship quickly, eager to be outside. The smell of saltwater wafted over to us, carried by a cool breeze that caressed our faces. It danced through my loose hair and made me smile.

I peered at the hut in the distance that was anchored over the water. A bridge twice the length of our starship accessed the hut from the beach. As the Captain led the way to the bridge, I edged closer to her and asked, "how long are we staying?"

The Captain glanced at me, her lips turned up in the corners.

"Like what you see, do you?"

I shrugged, and then grinned at her.

"I really don't know," she said. "It depends on what information Hector tells us."

We walked on in silence. I inhaled the tropical scents like I might not have long to enjoy them. As we started to make our way across the bridge, I saw the door to the hut open all the way. Gig edged to the front of the group, with his hand on the weapon strapped to his side. His bulky shoulders blocked my view of the person standing in the hut.

"Did you bring what I asked for?" a querulous voice called out.

"That depends," the Captain called back. "Did you ask for an old friend?"

There was a pause.

"Lira?"

"The one and only," the Captain replied.

"What took you so long, woman?"

As we neared the figure in the doorway, I could see that he was still a handsome man but obviously weak and fatigued. Dull, pale hair framed his thin face, and his loose clothes sagged over his gaunt body.

"Hector," the Captain said breathlessly, "what is happening to you?"

Master Ignoracius held out an arm, and tucked the Captain into a hug when she stepped into it. I saw the Captain wrap her arms around his waist as he dropped his face into her hair.

"Didn't they tell you?" he asked. "I'm dying."

The Captain sucked in a breath and pulled away from him to look into his face.

"No," she said, as if that could stop his sickness.

He shrugged.

"Bring your crew inside so I can see them properly," he said.

I followed the Captain into the hut, with AJ, Gig and Marco following close behind. Master Ignoracius' furnishings were oversized and comfortable looking. A bed was tucked in the corner, next to a sliding door that led out to a porch. A couch and a couple lounge chairs formed a ring in the center of the hut, near a blazing fire that kept the chilly sea winds at bay.

By the light of the flickering fire, Master Ignoracius surveyed us shrewdly.

"This is my Courier, Alyvia Tippin," the Captain said, gesturing to me.

Master Ignoracius came forward with a hand out. I reached out my own hand to shake his, but he took it and kissed my knuckles. His fingers were like icicles. His eyes searched mine. They looked bright, like beacons. I tried to meet his gaze without letting him see that I felt sorry to hear he was dying. I don't know what he saw when his gaze met mine but he smiled at me sweetly.

"This is our Medic, AJ Cason," the Captain continued. "Our Gunner, Gig Freeley, and you remember Marco."

Master Ignoracius nodded to each of the guys in turn, and even gave Marco a quick side hug, but still stayed with me, my hand clasped in his. Everyone seemed to eye our joined hands but no one said anything. This was the Captain's friend. I relaxed and allowed it.

For now.

"Lovely to meet you all," Master Ignoracius said. He gazed down at me again with a small smile on his face. The longer I looked at him, the more I was able to discern that his eyes were slightly unfocused. When he breathed out close to me I finally knew why. He smelled strongly of alcohol.

I tried to let go of his hand and pull away, but he held it tight and put a finger to his lips for silence. I frowned at him now but he shook his head and waved Gig away, who had stepped forward to intervene on my behalf.

"Everyone, please sit," Master Ignoracius said with a falsely cheery voice, "make yourselves comfortable! And Lira, please, tell me how you've been since last I saw you."

He glanced quickly at the Captain and made a gesture that encouraged her to humor him and start talking. Then he pulled me slowly forward.

I glanced at the Captain and saw her frown, but she nodded her head in permission for me to go along with Master Ignoracius. She found a chair and sat in it, and motioned for Marco, Gig and AJ to do the same. I could hear them comply as I followed Master Ignoracius close to his fire. My hand was still gripped tightly in his, like he knew I would pull away the second I had the chance.

"Well, it's been an awfully long time," the Captain began. "As you can see I have a crew of my own, and they've been top notch…"

As the Captain spoke, Master Ignoracius leaned down and whispered in my ear.

"You're the Courier, so I need you to fetch something for me," he said softly. "I don't want the Order to know I have it. They're probably monitoring your visit, so you'll have to be quick. Can you do it?"

Understanding finally dawned, and I nodded my head. Master Ignoracius was holding on to me because he wanted the Captain's Courier to do him a favor. My mission had already begun.

"Good," Master Ignoracius whispered. "There's a place below my feet where the floor comes up. You'll have to get in the water and dive straight down. You'll see a case anchored by rocks to the ocean floor. Open it, and pull out the box inside. When you come back, just tug on the rope and I'll pull you back up. Do you understand?"

I nodded again.

"Good, then let's get started," he whispered. "You'll need to look dry when you leave here, so I suggest you undress."

I had no intention of diving into the ocean in my shipwear. While I watched Master Ignoracius silently pull up the floor to reveal dark water below, and the Captain talked on calmly, I began to disrobe. As I kicked off my shoes and socks, and then pulled off my pants and tunic, I could hear the Captain's voice falter.

Master Ignoracius and I both looked up at her quickly. Master Ignoracius made a circular motion to encourage the Captain to keep talking. She glanced at Marco, Gig and AJ and made a quelling motion with her hand. I glanced at the boys, and saw that their eyes were all on me. Marco was bright red. He turned away to protect my modesty. AJ leered at me. I couldn't read Gig's expression. He was on his feet again, and seemed…possibly infuriated? I hoped if that was the case that it was on my behalf but I had agreed to this.

Master Ignoracius took my hand again to get my attention. I faced him and looked down into the water. He pointed at the lip of the opening, and motioned for me to stay quiet. I nodded and sat down on the ledge of the floor with my legs dangling over the side. My feet could almost touch the water but not quite. Master Ignoracius handed me a breather and a pair of goggles.

There was movement behind me. I paused, on the brink of sliding through the opening, and glanced around. Gig came forward with his face in a stony expression, and knelt next to Master Ignoracius. He put a hand on Master Ignoracius' arm, and nodded at him. Master Ignoracius let go of my hand and sat back. He watched as Gig reached out to me and took my hands. I slid forward so that my butt was no longer on the floor. I let Gig hold on to me and slowly, quietly, lower me into the water.

When he let go I put the breather in my mouth and then pulled the goggles over my head. I tread water as silently as possible while I adjusted the goggles to fit properly. Finally, I switched them on, and my view went from normal to infrared. I glanced up and saw two green figures peering down at me. I gave them the thumbs up, then sank under the water until I was far enough to kick myself around and dive lower without disturbing the water at the surface.

Alone under the water, the only sound I could hear was the sound I made as I swam down, down, down. My whole body had pricked with numbness the second I touched the water. As I swam through the chilly ocean, I shivered over and over again, and my lips trembled around the breather.

The infrared goggles finally showed me the ocean floor coming closer. I tried to reduce the pressure mounting in my head by clearing my ears but I was more eager to get this task done and return to the surface. Just as Master Ignoracius had described, there was a case anchored directly beneath me. I kicked harder, eager to get this mission over with.

The cold roughness of the case scraped against my fingers when I touched it. I could tell it had been beaten up by the water for several years. I thought of what life must have been like for Master Ignoracius when he came here. He lived in solitude for what I could only guess was years, and was paranoid enough of his captors to keep whatever this was a secret. I hoped that the box he'd sent me for was something useful, and not just a pack of cigarettes or something that he couldn't dive down to get himself now that he was sick.

I unlatched and opened the case slowly, and peered inside. There, nestled at the bottom was a small box that fit easily into the palm of my hand. When I took it from the case, it was surprisingly heavy. I did a quick double check to make sure nothing else was in the case but that was it.

I closed the case and then used it to kick myself back toward the surface. I clutched the box and slowed myself before I reached the surface so that my head slowly slid above the water. Looking up, I could see the darkness of the hut looming over me.

As soon as I lifted my arm out of the water, it broke out in goose bumps. I tugged at the rope Master Ignoracius had left near his floor opening and fought the shivers that were racking my body. Almost immediately, the trap door opened, and Gig was there to reach down for me. I handed up the box I'd fetched, along with my breather and the goggles I'd pulled from my head. These were taken and handed to someone behind him. Then Gig was back for me. He pulled me by my arms, and then silently shifted his grip to my underarms so he could slowly lift me from the water like a child. I clung to his shoulders, and my shivering tripled the moment my half-frozen body hit the air. As soon I was pulled through the floor, Master Ignoracius wrapped warm towels and blankets around me and began to rub my arms and back through them to help dry and warm me. Gig closed the trapdoor and then helped rub my legs through the wraps. I clutched the blankets around me, up to my ears and nose as I shivered uncontrollably, and leaned against Master Ignoracius' couch. I didn't make a sound.

Amazingly, the Captain talked on, as if she were in a perfectly normal conversation. I closed my eyes and listened to her voice float over me.

Something warm touched my cheek. I opened my eyes and saw AJ kneeling next to me. He had a hot bowl in his hand and pressed it to my lips. I opened my mouth and sipped down the broth he fed me. It flowed down my throat and straight to my belly. I quietly drank all of it down. I felt it warm me from the inside all the way down to my toes. AJ handed the bowl back to Master Ignoracius and pressed his fingertips to my throat, checking my pulse. I looked at his face in the dimness of the fire glow and realized how different his face was when he was in work mode. He was serious, with a slightly furrowed brow. It was a definite contrast to when he wasn't on the job. *That* AJ was prone to leering looks, with hooded eyes and a slightly lifted eyebrow.

I preferred the Medic AJ.

He made a hand motion to Gig and Master Ignoracius. I watched as Master Ignoracius got up and moved pillows from a spot on the couch. Then Gig moved closer and wrapped his arms around me. He picked me up and quietly sat me on the couch. As soon as I was settled, I pulled up my feet and tucked them close to my body. Then I took some of my blankets and tugged them over my head, like a cocoon. My shivering was mostly gone, except for a few tremors now and then. I rested my head on the arm of the couch with my eyes closed, and enjoyed being warm.

The Captain talked on.

"So, that's how we ended up with Alyvia as our Courier," she said. "Only an idiot would pass up one of Stryker's protégés."

"Isn't that the truth," Master Ignoracius agreed. "I'm sure she's proven to be a capable player on your team."

I felt a weight settle beside me on the couch.

"Yes, she has," the Captain said.

There was a pause.

"Well, I'm glad you came to see me, and that I could meet your team," Master Ignoracius said from beside me. "But I know there was another reason for your visit, no?"

"The Order said you'd requested my visit," the Captain said. "I had to come and see what my old friend wanted."

"I wanted to see someone I trust," Master Ignoracius said. "Lira, I want to die with some piece of mind."

"How can I give you that?" the Captain asked.

"I want you to collect all the pieces of Starkiller, and have it destroyed," Master Ignoracius said.

I heard the Captain murmur something in response, but I faded out. I yawned under my blankets, and let myself drift on voices and warmth.

A hand pulled away the covers from my head.

"I guess I've put your crew to sleep with my rambling," Master Ignoracius said.

I stirred, and opened my eyes to see AJ bent over me. He held his hand to my forehead and then checked my pulse again. I saw him give the Captain a thumbs-up. The Captain, I realized, stood beside Master Ignoracius.

"Time to return to the ship," she said.

I lifted my head from the couch and looked around. AJ went to the fire and crouched there, ladling more broth into a canteen from a pot there. Marco came forward with my clothing. He and Gig helped me stand and pull off my blankets. My limbs felt stiff, like I'd been in the same position for too long and couldn't stretch them out. Then the three of us did our best to dress me. This was going to be embarrassing when I thought about it later, I figured. I lifted my hands over my head so Marco could pull on my tunic, then held on to Gig's shoulders so I could step into my trousers. I slightly wobbled at this part but Marco steadied me. I sat down again so Gig and Marco could pull on my socks and shoes, while I buttoned my pants and zipped my tunic. Then I took their hands again and let them pull me back up to my feet. It was disorienting to be treated like a toddler but I was grateful for their help. My hair was still damp but I managed to twist it into a clean braid.

"Are we all set?" the Captain asked.

I nodded and made my way to the door. I felt like my body was made of wobbly goop.

"Marco, Gig, AJ, Alyvia," Master Ignoracius said, "it was a great pleasure to see you. I wish you luck on your future missions."

Marco opened the door and stepped out onto the bridge back to the beach. Gig and AJ followed. Before I left, Master Ignoracius took my hand and kissed it again. I saw the guys pause and turn back but Master Ignoracius gently tugged me closer.

"You did very well," he whispered in my ear. "I trust you to find the rest of Starkiller. Find it, and destroy it."

My eyes widened. Master Ignoracius kissed my cheek and pulled away. I looked up into his sad eyes and felt sorry for him. It must be miserable to know you were going to die alone.

I tried to wipe the stunned look from my face and gave him a little smile. Master Ignoracius pressed something into my hand before he let it go. It was the size and weight of the box I'd rescued from under his hut. I didn't look down at it or acknowledge its presence in my hand. Master Ignoracius winked at me, and then I walked out onto the bridge to let him and the Captain say their goodbyes.

"Lean on me," Marco said. He put his arm around my shoulders and walked with me back down the bridge. AJ and Gig followed. I hooked my arm around his waist and did as he suggested. I felt sluggish but I tried to press on. I also tried not to sneeze on him. My nose was starting run, and I wished I had brought the handkerchief Gig gave me so I could wipe it.

When we reached the place where the bridge met the beach, we waited for the Captain to join us. I stared out over the water, and appreciated the sight of the moon hovering over us as an ocean breeze rifled through our hair and clothing.

The breeze felt good, but it was still chilly, and I shivered again. Marco noticed my trembling under his arm.

"Do you want some of AJ's broth?" he asked. He gave me a squeeze and ran his hand up and down my arm quickly.

AJ, who stood a short distance away, immediately came over and handed me the canteen.

"Drink it," he said.

I took the canteen and sipped from it gratefully.

The warmth seeped into my bones.

"Would anyone else like some?" I offered. The others said no and ordered me to finish it. I sipped a little more from it, then capped the lid back on. I yawned so loud my jaw cracked.

"Here she comes," Gig said after a moment.

We saw the Captain cross the bridge toward us. She wiped at her eyes a few times but sucked it up when she saw we watched her.

"Let's get back to the ship quickly," she said, with an eye on me. "It looks like Alyvia's going to catch a cold."

"Not if I give her something when we get back," AJ said.

"Well then, let's get back," the Captain said. She never paused her stride across the beach toward the ship. "I'll race you."

She took off at an impressive sprint. I'd never seen her move so fast. I grinned and set off after her – I was not going to be left out of a challenge. A heartbeat later, I could hear the others following close behind.

A cough started to build in my chest. I stumbled to a halt, and coughed up some phlegm.

"Come on, Tippin," Gig said, "you can't lose a footrace to Marco and AJ."

I turned to grin at him and choked for air. He grabbed me and tossed me over a shoulder and began running again, his powerful legs pumping across the sand. I squealed in laughter, and watched upside down as he passed AJ and Marco, who labored behind us. It caused me to cough over and over again, but I laughed all the way to the ship. In the last few lengths before we reached it, Gig had even passed the Captain. She grinned and stopped beside us, breathing hard and sweating as Gig tapped some controls to open the bay door.

"Hey, you should have tossed me on your other shoulder," she joked.

"It's not too late," Gig said. He whirled and had the Captain over his other shoulder in a heartbeat. I laughed hysterically as she protested being treated like a sack of potatoes. She reached out and nabbed my wrist for balance.

Gig carried us into the mess hall and crouched low so we could get our feet under us. The Captain fanned her face.

"That was fun," she admitted. "If I'd known, I would have had you do that from the bridge."

I coughed into the crook of my arm and tried to stop the laughter. I still clutched the canteen and the box Master Ignoracius had given me. The Captain and Gig saw it in my hand and straightened.

"Show off," Marco said when he arrive with AJ right behind him. They were both sweaty and breathing heavily, Marco more than AJ. "I'm so out of shape."

They came up to where we stood and saw what we did.

"What is it?" AJ asked.

"She hasn't opened it yet," the Captain said. She nodded at me.

I glanced at her and back at the box.

"I guess I should," I said.

There was a little clasp in the center of the box. I had to grip it tightly as I forced it open, because it had rusted shut. As the box opened, it revealed two things: an intricate tubing of metal and a piece of yellowed parchment.

I picked up the parchment and handed it to the Captain. As she unfolded it and began to read, I lifted the heavy piece of metal in my hand and held it up so we could all examine it.

"If you are reading this, I am dead or dying and the Order has sent you to search for Starkiller," the Captain read. "In your hands is the ignition key that will turn on the device. Without it, Starkiller is just another contraption of metal. Guard this key with all your power, and if you decide to use it, may God have mercy on your soul. Signed, H.I."

We all stared at the ignition key.

"Where are we going to put this?" I asked.

I looked from AJ to Gig to Marco, then to the Captain.

"He gave it to you," the Captain said. "I'm sure you'll find a place for it."

I hadn't expected her to leave it in my hands. Responsibility settled over my shoulders as I put the device back into the box and closed the latch. The Captain handed me Master Ignoracius' handwritten note as well.

"Marco, let's say goodbye to this place," she said. "AJ, take Alyvia and get rid of that wheeze. I'm going to comm the Order to let them know we've begun our quest. I will see you all in the morning."

She left, followed by Marco.

"Come on, let's go to the Medlab," AJ said to me. "I should keep you there overnight."

I made a face.

"I'd prefer to sleep in my own bed," I said.

Gig snorted and clapped AJ on the shoulder, then left us to argue about it.

"In the Medic I can monitor your health," AJ said reasonably. "I can't do that as easily from your room."

"Maybe not as easily, but you can do it," I said. "Besides, it's not like I am dying. It's just a cough."

"And a minor case of hypothermia," AJ added, with a frown.

"So, what better place could there be than under my own covers and in my own bed?" I said. "The Medlab is too chilly. And the beds aren't very comfortable, so I won't sleep as deeply as in my own bed. Isn't a proper night's sleep important for recuperation?"

"You're not going to stop arguing with me until you get your way, are you?"

"It's more than likely," I said. "If you give in now, I'll let you win the next argument."

AJ shook his head, but I could tell he was amused.

"Why do I not believe you?"

I went to my room and tucked Master Ignoracius' box under my pillow.

Then I changed out of my shipwear and took a steamy hot shower. When I felt warm at last, I got out and pulled on some nightclothes. As I came into my room, I saw that AJ waited for me, sprawled on the edge of my bed. His blue eyes ran over my face.

"Here, take this," he said when he heard me come in. He sat up and handed me a vial of amber liquid.

"What is it?" I asked.

"A concoction that will clear your lungs and keep you from getting sick," he said. "I'll give you a different version in the morning that'll let you function for the day."

I swallowed all of the liquid and handed the vial back to him.

"Thanks," I said.

"Now get in bed," he said. "Want me to join you?"

And just like that, sleazy AJ was back. I sighed and gave him a look.

"No," I said firmly. "Good night."

AJ stood up and grinned down at me. I looked up into his leering face and glared at him.

"One of these days you're going to wish you'd said yes," he said.

"Not going to happen," I said. I stepped away and folded my arms over my chest.

AJ shrugged and made to leave.

"I'll check back in on you in a few hours," he said. Then he was gone.

Disgusted, I climbed into bed and pulled the covers up under my chin. I felt warmth spread out from my belly to my limbs. The room spun slightly. I closed my eyes and tried to shove the feeling away. Rolling onto my side, I fell asleep quickly, but I had Master Ignoracius constantly on my mind.

AJ came in sometime later. I knew he was there, but I didn't raise myself. I was asleep again almost immediately.

"You slept through the best part," the Captain informed me over breakfast the next day. "Hector set our first course for us on this quest."

"Just the first?" I asked.

"Yes, he wants to remain useful to the Order for a bit longer, so he has agreed to parcel out the locations of the Starkiller pieces one at a time," the Captain said. "As we find a new piece, he will direct us to the next one."

"What if he becomes too ill to finish telling us where the last pieces are?"

The Captain shrugged sadly.

"I don't think that would bother him too much," she said. She pushed around the food on her plate.

"I'm sorry," I said.

The Captain nodded her head.

"I feel awful for him," I said. "He knows he's dying, and that he will die out there in his hut. Does he have any family to grieve for him?"

The Captain shook her head no.

"No, he was like the rest of us," she said. "Focused on the missions, not on building a family."

I thought about that, about what it would be like to die with no one to grieve for you. If I died, Cutter and Stryker would grieve for me. I didn't even want to think about either of them dying.

"I guess for us, your friends are your family," I said. "Master Ignoracius may not have a family, but he has us. Right?"

The Captain stilled, then smiled at me.

"Oh Alyvia, I like you so much," she said.

I blinked at her, taken aback.

"What?"

The Captain shook her head.

"You're a darling," she said. "Now get out of here and go give Gig a workout. I need to plot our course with Marco."

Pleased, I gathered my cup and put it in the washer, then I went to find Gig as the Captain recommended.

Gig was already hard at work, shirt off, when I came into the gym. I sat on a bench near his mat and enjoyed the view. There had been plenty of guys at the Academy who had worked out with shirts off. They could be caught glancing around to see if anyone watched them. Most of those guys had been idiots, and I'd avoided them, preferring to work on my own routines instead of watching theirs.

A few times, guys had come over trying to subtly flex their impressive muscles, and asked if they could share a mat with me because, "the gym was too crowded."

At first I had tried to be polite and share half a mat but as little work actually got done and I had to endure obvious come-ons, it became too annoying. After that, when a male or female came over to share a mat, I would say, "please, have it" and then I would leave.

So why was Gig different?

He didn't invite my attention, first of all. As in I could tell he wasn't purposefully trying to show off. That was nice. If it weren't for the fact that I was so obviously in the room, you would almost think he hadn't noticed me. He didn't glance my way or stop and nod his head at me or anything.

The halfway point of his routine brought Gig close to where I watched. I sat up a little, and tried to pay more attention to his form and not his chest.

Before I could react, Gig leapt sideways—right toward me—and had me by the arms, twisting, so I was pulled from my seat and down onto the mat. I gasped in surprise, and fell over onto my back while Gig pinned my shoulders down. I met his eyes, and saw that he grinned devilishly at me.

"Hey!" I said, "I'm not in this routine."

"You didn't think you were going to get away with just gawking at me, did you?"

I felt my face grow hot.

"I was studying your technique," I said indignantly.

"Oh, is that what you were doing?"

He didn't even pretend like he believed me.

I couldn't help it. My serious face cracked, and I grinned.

"Well, I have eyes don't I?"

Gig seemed surprised to hear me admit as much aloud. I used the opportunity to push him off of me with a contained burst of tele. He sucked in a breath and rolled away automatically. He landed in a crouch a few feet away. I watched him watch me as I got to my feet.

"Do that again," he said.

"What?"

"Do that again," he repeated. "Push me with your power."

I contained the telekinesis in the palm of my right hand, clenching it in a fist.

"Brace yourself," I said. Then I punched him full-on with a sharp slap of telekinetic energy. Gig went flying halfway across the room, and narrowly avoided toppling into some of the stationary equipment. He fell to the floor gracelessly, but was up and back on his feet almost instantly. He regarded me with interest.

"You okay?" I asked.

"Yes," he said, and came back to my mat. "Do it again."

I looked at him like he had a screw loose.

"Is this fun?"

"We haven't worked on this in our training yet," he said patiently. "I want to see what you can do."

"Oh!" I said. "Well, loads of stuff, actually. This was my favorite thing to do with Cutter."

"What do you mean?"

"We did tele exercises out on the lawn," I said. "Cutter would come up with different things for me to do, and then we would work at it until I was good."

"So show me your stuff," he said.

"Okay," I said. I thought back to some of Cutter's favorites. "Well..."

I stretched my arms forward, palms facing him, and slowly pushed upward.

Gig's face betrayed his surprise as he slowly began to lift into the air.

"You're heavy," I said. I strained as his weight settled on my limbs. I could feel my lower back tense under the pressure.

"Well then put me down," he said with a glare.

I slowly lowered him to the ground, and released him when his feet touched the mat.

"That was easier when I was younger," I muttered. I rubbed my lower back to ease the muscles. "I could pick up several men."

"Well if you haven't done it in a while, your muscles aren't used to it," he said. "Don't lift me again, I'm too heavy."

Gig came and stood behind me. He pushed my hand out of the way so he could massage my lower back himself. His fingers gripped me by the waist while his thumbs did all the work. At first I felt myself tense at his touch, uninvited as it was. But I knew Gig, and I was learning to trust him, so I let myself relax and enjoy the attention.

"Feel better?" he asked.

"Umm, my shoulders are kind of sore too," I ventured.

They weren't aching or anything, but you never ever pass up a shoulder massage.

Gig didn't seem to notice my lie. He flicked my hair out of the way and began working on my shoulders. I pulled my loose hair out of his way and let my head fall forward, immensely pleased with myself. My breath automatically slowed and my eyes closed.

"Am I interrupting something?" AJ asked from the doorway.

"Yes," Gig said. His hands stilled.

I opened my eyes and saw that AJ had walked into the gym and stood on the edge of the mat with arms crossed and an eyebrow lifted.

His eyes focused on mine.

"Can I do you next?"

I made a disgusted face at him.

"Did you want something, or are you just trying to be annoying?" I replied.

"Let's get back to our workout," Gig said before AJ could say something else. I turned my back on AJ and tried to focus on Gig's face.

"I'll come back later," AJ said. I glanced back in time to see him head out the door.

"Is he serious?" I wanted to know.

"AJ is a real piece of work," Gig said. "Great Medic but total asshole."

"I cannot stand sleazy jerks that try to push your buttons."

This is exactly what he'd done, of course, because I was still annoyed with him and he wasn't even in the room anymore.

"Well, I can't say it gets better," he said. "AJ is fine when he's working, but if I were you I'd stay out of his way on long leaves."

"Why, is he a bigger perv than usual?"

"You have no idea," Gig agreed.

He turned and walked to the far end of the mat.

"Let's spar," he said.

Taken off guard, I readjusted my focus back to our workout.

"Okay," I agreed. I pulled a band from around my wrist and tied my hair back.

"I'm going to do the attacks, and I want you to defend yourself with your telekinesis," Gig said. "Got it?"

"Sure," I said. "This will be fun."

And it was. Gig did everything he could think of to get to me, but I just kept pushing him away with my tele. He would advance across the mat toward me at full speed, and then hit my wall of tele as he was pushed back to where he started. His feet slid out from under him against his will, or I would turn him away from me and prod him with my telekinesis until he was on the far side of the mat from me.

He was very tired and sweaty, I could see. Finally, he gave up and sat down on the mat to catch his breath. Pushing him away wasn't exactly cake for me either. My muscles had gotten a great workout from the exercise, sort of like weight training. I dropped to the mat too and stretched out on my back.

I stared at the ceiling and tried to imagine what it would be like to live confined to the gym.

"Do you realize that this room is bigger than Master Ignoracius' hut?" I asked. I turned my head to look at Gig. He glanced up at the room too, and took in its space.

"I couldn't do it," he said. "It was beautiful there and everything, but I'd rather be in the stars."

"I'd rather be with friends," I said. "None of his friends will know when he's dead unless the Order decides to tell them."

"That's a shame," Gig agreed. "I would want my friends and family to know."

"I was thinking the same thing," I said. "I would want Stryker and Cutter to know."

"What about your family?"

"They wouldn't care," I said. "For all they know, I could already be dead."

"How many are there?"

"Too many," I said. I got to my feet, and refused to let this conversation continue. "I'm starving, I'm going to go find a snack."

"Come back when you're done," Gig said. "I want to get to some knife work."

I nodded. Knife work sounded like a perfect distraction.

10

"Alyvia, Gig, this mission is for the two of you only," the Captain said as we sat arranged around the table. "Remember that the Order is watching us closely from here on out."

I glanced at Gig and nodded my head. The Captain had no idea how much the Order would be watching us. I was determined to complete this mission with no red flags, so that we could begin to earn some of their trust. There was no telling how many of these missions we would undertake. This could be the first of many, and I wanted to get through it as soon as possible.

"We'll be arriving at Tigenan tomorrow afternoon," Marco said.

"Good," the Captain said. "Hector told us he left a part of Starkiller in one of the cavernous cities there. It's more of a tribal culture, but they are friends to the Order. No one has visited them in quite some time, making it the perfect hiding place for an artifact."

"What exactly is the artifact?" I asked. "What are we looking for?"

"Hector said he left a framework for the hull of Starkiller," the Captain said. "He gave us a sketch."

She passed me a piece of parchment with a scribbled drawing of a cylinder. I held it up and studied it carefully so I could memorize every line.

"This feels like a stupid question," I said, "but where will the hull be when we arrive? Do we just walk up and ask someone for it and that's the end of the mission?"

"That's not a stupid question," the Captain said. "Unfortunately, I don't have much of an answer for you. Hector said the Tigenan artifact is not understood for what it is. The tribes have actually incorporated it into their culture somehow."

"Incorporated it into their culture?" I repeated.

"They value it, apparently," Marco said. "Master Ignoracius told us they were honored to be given custody when he brought it."

"Great," I said. I pictured a tribal war breaking out when I asked for the hull. "That means we have to give them something more important, or we have to steal it from them. They aren't going to just hand it over."

"I'd recommend you find something more important to them," the Captain said. "Remember, they are our allies in the Order and we do not want to start an incident."

I considered the problem while the Captain finished discussing the plans for arrival. While Gig and I located the hull and convinced the Tigenan tribes to give it to us, the rest of the crew would orbit the planet while waiting for us. The Captain wanted us to keep our comms on at all times.

"We'll come fetch you when you're through with this assignment," she said.

"What if we need your negotiation skills?"

"This mission is a priority to the Order," the Captain said. "I'd prefer it if we didn't get to the point where my negotiations are needed. You two are clever enough, I should think you can handle this assignment."

I looked at Gig again, and saw that he looked resigned.

"If you need me, however, then I will come," the Captain finished. "Alright?"

"Sure," I said. "I'd like to get in and get out for this mission anyway."

"Good," the Captain said. "Now, I want you and Gig to relax today and tomorrow. No more big workouts, no more stress. You need to go into this mission fresh, and cohesive. So play some games, hang out on the Pilot's deck, whatever. Okay?"

We nodded our heads in agreement and were dismissed. I sat back in my chair and waited for everyone to file out. The Captain and Marco left to talk about more flight plans, and AJ wandered off to the Medic's Lab. Only Gig stayed behind.

"So, we need to cement our cohesiveness," he said, and swiveled his chair to face me. "What should we do?"

I thought about it.

When I was first getting to know Cutter, we were study buddies because we had the same classes together. We always studied in Cutter's room, on his floor, with our touchpads and food scattered around us. We ate, studied, and talked. That's all we did.

More than once I found myself lying on his floor the next morning where I'd fallen asleep. Cutter somehow always made it to his bed, and he left me wherever I was slept with a blanket over me and a pillow under my head. At some point I smartened up, and realized that if I crawled into his bed when I started to feel sleepy, I could wake up the next day in his bed instead of the floor. Cutter would join me before the night was over and we'd end up cuddled together until morning. I knew it was a strange circumstance for two friends to be in, but sharing a bed on study nights never got awkward between us.

Unlike Gig, I'd never stared at Cutter while he did a shirtless workout. I thought about what it would be like to wake up next to Gig, and felt short of breath for a second.

"Why don't we study recent logs of Tigenan?" I suggested. "That way we can have some idea of what to expect when we arrive."

Gig shrugged.

"Sure," he said. "That's a great idea."

He faced the table and tapped at the touchscreen by his hand so he could access the Order's public logs. There were few, we discovered. Tigenan wasn't a popular hotspot for travelers. In fact, it was quite out of the way and more than a little backward. The logs we read through described a barbaric planet with few amenities for guests.

Gig pulled up visuals on the planet. Everything we looked at was barren and devoid of greenery. The people of Tigenan lived in red rock caves that were surrounded by stony wastelands.

"What's the average rainfall?" I asked.

"Not enough to note," Gig said. He showed me the numbers. "It's warm and sunny the majority of the year. When it does rain, it's violent and destructive because the land isn't prepared to handle it."

"Do you ever wonder how some planets remain populated by people?" I asked. "I mean, why would you want to live in a place like Tigenan when others are more beautiful and easy on life?"

"A person's roots are deeply embedded in their land," Gig said. "You and I are part of the Order, so we obviously feel no deep connections with any one place that we call 'home.' Our home is wherever our stuff is, or in our case, wherever the Merry Maids are. But other people feel a deeper tie with where they live."

I considered this.

The place where I was born would never be a home for me. When I'd left, it was with no intention of ever returning. The Academy had been my home, but I'd always known it was temporary. I wouldn't mind returning there to visit, but Cutter and Stryker were the only people I cared to see, and they were both making their own homes in new places.

"If the Merry Maids were disbanded for a few weeks, where would you go?" I asked. "Back to your dad's?"

"Probably," Gig said. "He'd love to have me work in his shop again.

What about you?"

"I don't know," I said. "I guess I'd try to find Cutter or Stryker if I could. Stay with them for a while."

"You really love them, don't you?" Gig asked.

His serious black eyes studied me closely. I nodded, in response to his question. There was so much I could say on the topic, but essentially, I would not be the person I am today without Cutter and Stryker. I loved them more than I loved myself.

"They are my family," I said. "The family I wish I'd had all along instead of the one that birthed me."

OK, that wasn't fair.

"Well, except for one of my brothers," I said, thinking of Sen.

"How many brothers were there?"

I looked at Gig and tried not to flinch from his gaze.

"Never mind," he turned back to the logs. "You can tell me later."

I felt foolish and bit my lip. Why was it so difficult for me to talk about my family? Cutter and Stryker knew everything about them but I trusted Cutter and Stryker deeply. Gig and the rest of my new team seemed wonderful, but I just didn't know them well enough. At some point I would have to open up and share information about myself. It was just uncomfortable for me to talk about.

On the other hand, the more I put it off, the more my past took on a life of its own. If I continued to hesitate and clam up whenever my family was brought up, then the real story would pale in comparison to what the team probably expected.

I opened my mouth to give in and just share some of my story with Gig. But before the words came out, a vision of Master Omin flashed through my mind, and I closed my mouth again. A sick feeling bloomed in my stomach and I turned back to our research.

I wanted to be brave but it wasn't going to be today.

"So are you ready for this mission?" Marco asked later.

I glanced at him from where I was curled up in the co-pilot's chair, and made a face.

"Are you going to ask me that every time I'm set to go out?" I asked.

"Why, do you not like it?"

"I don't know," I said. "It makes me feel like people are asking me since they really aren't sure if I can handle it or something."

"Because everyone asks you if you're ready?" he guessed.

"Yes!"

"Well, we ask everyone that question before they go out on a mission,"

Marco said. "In fact, I already asked Gig if he was ready."

"Really? What did he say?"

"What does Gig ever say?" Marco replied with a brotherly smile.

I laughed.

"Excuse me?" Gig said from the doorway. I turned my head to watch him pull up a chair and settle himself between Marco's chair and my own.

"I was telling Alyvia that we always ask you guys if you're ready for the next mission," Marco said to Gig. "It's not that we doubt whether you're ready. We're just asking to make sure you're confident about what you're doing."

"You'll get used to it," Gig told me. "Just say 'yep' and they'll leave you alone."

"Good to know," I said with a smile.

"Gig, what brings you to us?" Marco said. "I know you're not here to see me."

I looked at Marco in surprise. Had he just insinuated that Gig had come to hang out with *me*?

"Of course not," Gig said easily. "I'd rather be with Alyvia. But since she's here…"

"I'd rather hang out with Alyvia too," Marco said with a laugh. "She's much better to look at than you."

"She smells better too," Gig said. "And I've spent hours with her in the gym."

"Well, she probably doesn't even sweat in the gym working *you* over."

"Perhaps," Gig said with a crooked smile.

Neither of them glanced at me during this exchange. They stared through the front view monitor at the stars, as if they were having a normal conversation. I just stared at Gig.

"I didn't realize you had a sense of humor," I blurted.

They both looked at me then. Gig glanced at me from the corners of his eyes, as Marco laughed out loud.

"It takes him a while to loosen up to new people," Marco said in a mock whisper. "He's not a fan of change."

Gig rolled his eyes.

"I was not a fan of the situation," Gig said. He turned his attention to Marco. "You know she didn't even talk to me about it before she announced she was leaving."

"Maddy was always the type to make up her mind and then stick to it," Marco said.

"But she wasn't the type to do something without talking to me about it first," Gig said. "I just don't understand what happened."

"Have you tried to contact her?"

"Yes, but I can't find her."

"She said she was going home," Marco said.

"Well, she may have lied," Gig said.

He sat back in his chair and slumped low so he could prop up his feet on the console. I stopped staring and leaned back into my own chair with my head cradled in the headrest.

"Well, you've cooled off since Alyvia first arrived," Marco said. "I'm sure she's forgiven you for welcoming her like a jerk."

I grinned.

"It wasn't you," Gig said to me. "It was the situation."

I nodded my head. I accepted his answer.

"It probably didn't make a good impression to come to work hung over," I admitted.

Gig laughed.

"What!" Marco sat forward and gawked at me in disbelief.

"I didn't know the scouts were coming for me," I defended myself. "Cutter and I were celebrating with tequila, and it doesn't take much to get me drunk."

"That's my kind of girl," AJ said. He stepped into the space behind Gig. His presence made me stiffen. "I think I have some tequila in my bunk, if you want some?"

"Nope," I said. I didn't even look at him. He brought a chair around and sat it to my right. Then he imitated Gig and propped his feet on the console.

"How many times does she have to say 'no' to you before you'll stop asking?" Marco wanted to know.

"I believe one day she'll say yes," AJ replied. "So what are we doing here?"

"Just talking and enjoying the view," Gig said.

"Interesting, interesting," AJ said. "I wondered what you all did in here. So you're talking about getting drunk?"

"We were just talking and spending time together," Marco said. I could tell he was trying to keep the peace. "We all have time to spare right now while we make the last leg of this trip to Tigenan. So we're talking."

"Oh," AJ said. He stayed quiet for three beats before yawning. "Well this was a pleasure, but I've got other things to do."

He stood up and left without another word. I shook my head, grateful that he was gone.

"He is so annoying," I muttered. "Why is he so annoying?"

I could see Gig shrug beside me.

"He's a bit of an odd one," Marco said. "I mostly feel sorry for him. I don't think he knows how to do anything but practice medicine. He was bounced around a lot as a kid with his younger brother, and never really had a family to ground him and knock some sense into him."

"Yeah, didn't he and his brother plow through child home after child home until they ended up at the Academy?" Gig said.

"Yep," Marco said. "For AJ, people are either his patients or else objects of complete mystery to him."

I frowned, and tried to fit the pieces together. I couldn't imagine AJ as a lost kid without a home and without someone to guide him. It would make sense why he had an utter lack of people skills.

"Have you guys met his brother?" I asked.

"Nope," Marco said. "His brother floats around from ship to ship, just like when he was a kid. AJ wanted him to join the Merry Maids, but the Captain couldn't find a use for him."

I felt a very, very small bit sorry for AJ, and I had to put a stop to it.

"Well if he tries to grab me one more time, I'm going to cut his hand off," I announced.

"No need," Gig said. "I had a word with AJ and he promised not to lay a finger on you without your express permission."

I sat up and stared at Gig in surprise.

"What?"

Gig shrugged.

"You're part of our team now," he said. "I don't want you to be uncomfortable just because AJ is an idiot. He promised not to touch you, but I couldn't do anything about the comments."

I was ridiculously touched.

"Thank you," I said.

"Good going," Marco agreed. "I thought I was going to have to do it."

I felt warmth for them both, and knew they were looking out for me.

"I don't deserve you guys," I said softly. I sat back in my chair and relaxed.

"Get used to it," Gig said. "You're a Merry Maid. We look out for each other."

"Even if it's because of other Merry Maids," Marco agreed.

I grinned.

Tigenan was everything my research with Gig had prepared me for: A barren wasteland that somehow reminded me of my home planet. As soon as Gig landed our small cruiser and we stepped out into the night, all of the moisture in my skin seemed to disappear. My bare arms immediately felt dry and cracked.

"It's a good thing we brought packs of water," Gig said when he stepped out beside me. He closed the hatch to the parked cruiser and hoisted one of the packs onto his shoulder. I picked up the other and did the same. We snapped our night vision sighters over our eyes and looked around.

For as far as the eye could see, rocky crevices strained toward the sky. It had been difficult to find a flat enough place to land. As it was, we would have to hike an hour to our destination.

"Maybe we could trade a flight off this rock for that piece of the Starkiller's hull," I suggested.

"Ask them," Gig said. I could hear the smile in his voice.

I let Gig lead the way as we began our hike. He checked the nav on his wrist every now and then to make sure we were heading to the location Master Ignoracius had given us.

"Mark One," he commed to the ship when we were a third of the way through our trip.

"Mark One," I heard the Captain repeat in my ear.

"No locals in your vicinity," Marco reported a few seconds later. He scanned our route from orbit while the Captain monitored the comms. I guessed AJ was in his lab somewhere, completely unaware of the fact that Gig and I had left the ship. He hadn't come to see us launch to ground.

The night sky over Tigenan was crystal clear as we made our way along the route. I could see every star in the sky as if it were only a few lengths above my head. I glanced up every now and then to admire the view as I negotiated the rocky terrain behind Gig and wished I could take a moment to admire it without my night vision. Gig walked slowly, and glanced behind every now and then to make sure I kept up. There was no time for stops.

"Mark Two," he called out a little while later.

"Mark Two," the Captain repeated for us.

A steady breeze kept us cool as we hiked to the Tigenan caves. I'd braided my hair into two lines down my back, but wisps had come free and were floating into my face.

Gig paused just ahead of me. I stopped beside him and followed his gaze. In the path just ahead of where we'd been walking, the terrain dropped off suddenly eight to ten lengths below us. We would have to scale down the rocks to the lower ledge if we wanted to continue.

"This is going to be tricky," he said.

I peered over the ledge and saw that we would need to use outthrust rocks as our hand and footholds down. I tried to picture myself doing it, and realized the weight of my water sack would be much too cumbersome.

I slid it from my shoulder and held it over the ledge. Then I used my tele to lower it gently to the ground below where we could retrieve it. I took

Gig's from him and did the same.

"Report," the Captain's voice said in our ear.

"Steep terrain," Gig replied. "We'll need to climb to the shelf below one-by-one. I'll go first."

Gig sat down with his legs dangling over the edge. He used his upper body strength to hold himself up while he twisted around and reached with his feet for purchase below. I moved closer and adjusted my sighters as he started downward, and hunted for a safe route down.

"Move your foot a bit lower and to your left," I suggested.

Gig did as I suggested and found the foothold. He went slowly, and crept lower and lower down the face of the ledge until he was at the bottom.

"Just do what I did," he called up. "Go slow and wait until you have a solid footing."

I tucked my flashlight back into my pocket and sat down on the edge, just as he'd done. I twisted around and used my upper body strength to hold myself up, I fished for footing with my feet. When I found it, I slowly and painstakingly crept lower. Gig directed me on where to place my feet. His voice floated closer and closer as I made my way down.

"Okay, I got you," he said a few moments later. I felt his hands reach up and pull me down by the waist. He set me down next to him.

"Thanks!" I said, grateful to be down. I swept an arm over my wet forehead and took the water pack that he handed me. I swallowed large mouthfuls while he collected our packs.

"Need a break?" he asked.

"Nah," I said. "Let's get going, we've wasted enough time here."

Gig nodded and slung his pack over his shoulder again. I put away my water and slid my pack over my own mildly sore shoulders. Then we set off again, still intent on our goal.

"Slow down, you two," Marco announced after we'd hiked for some time. "I'm reading a scouting party."

"We're almost to Mark Three," Gig said. "Did they come from there?"

"Looks like it," Marco replied. "You'd better hold and wait for them to come for you."

Gig stopped and glanced at me.

"Here we go," he murmured.

We peered out into the night silently. I scanned the rocks around us, searching for any sign of people approaching. If it weren't for Marco's constant reports that they were encircling us, I never would have known they were there.

"Can you see anyone?" I whispered.

Gig shook his head no, I saw that he was scanning the area too.

And then I felt their eyes on us, and knew they were there. I shifted closer to Gig, and felt his hand on my forearm to hold me still.

A spark and soft popping noise were the only warning we had. A torch suddenly flared up, just steps away. In the sudden light, I blinked and glanced around. I saw them for the first time: the Tigenans.

One stepped forward, the leader. He looked at us, his eyes hidden in shadow. We stared back, silent but wary. The leader appraised us by the light of his torch for several long heartbeats. The only thing we could see was that the hair on his head was long and white. The rest of his face was in shadow.

"Members of the Order?" he asked.

"Yes," Gig said. "We are members of the Order, and friends of Master Ignoracius."

The Tigenan stilled. Then he looked over his shoulder and nodded.

An entire army of torches appeared in a circle around us. They burst into sudden life, and revealed about twenty Tigenans in all as I looked around us. None of their faces were visible, only shadows.

"Hector Ignoracius?" the leader asked.

"Yes," Gig said.

The Tigenan lowered his torch, so that he was illumined by the light and we could see his chiseled face and toothless smile.

"Ahhhh," he said. "I am Koolae. Welcome! Please follow, yes?"

He turned and motioned for his men to light the way. Then he set off. He glanced back at us several times as we followed him, to check if we seemed pleased. Always, he smiled at us. One of his men came forward and took my water pack to relieve me of the weight. I thanked him and smiled, but he said nothing.

We really weren't all that far from their settlement, but the rocky terrain slowed us down. In a few places, we had to drop down from tall boulders to the paths below. At these places, Koolae went first, followed by four or five of his men. Then Gig was allowed to drop to the ground with some assistance from the men who stayed at the top. However, when it was my turn, it became a precise operation. The men who stayed on the ledge with me took my arms and carefully lowered me down, where more men from below came forward and balanced my weight so that they could catch me and safely settle me on the ground. It was infuriating and sweet at the same time.

I thanked them each time we had to go through the steps. I wasn't sure if it would be rude to refuse their assistance. Gig kept a watchful eye over our guides, but he never interfered or tried to help the procession. He was always by my side when we walked straightaways however.

"Mark three," I heard the Captain say.

I looked around but I didn't notice any difference in our surroundings at first. Even as I thought that, I noticed that we approached a circle of huge boulders. The boulders were half as tall as me, but three or four times wider. They must have been monsters to move into a ring.

"Here we are," Koolae said. He scrambled over a boulder and climbed into the center of the ring. As I walked up, I could see by his torchlight that the center was actually a black hole that sloped down into nothingness.

I was lifted up onto a boulder, and Koolae held out his hand. I stepped toward him. I could vaguely make out where his feet stood. I took his hand and let him guide me to his side.

"Down there?" I asked. I pointed into the darkness.

Koolae nodded.

"Stay with me," he said. He shifted my hand to his wrist. I understood that I needed to hold on to him as we climbed down but the rocks were wet under my feet, and I nearly slipped. "Hold on now, young one."

His path steady, Koolae led me down into the dark, dripping cave. The temperature dropped dramatically as we went lower. I felt my face and hands turn to ice. The terrain was difficult. I had to concentrate on every step, and shift my weight low to the ground sometimes to ease myself down. The ground beneath my feet changed from shifting rocks to packed earth, and the descent became easier until we were no longer going down, but straight ahead. I glanced behind me and saw that Gig and the other Tigenans followed slowly behind us. The hole in the earth that lead back up to the surface was far away.

"We could not have gotten here safely without you," I murmured to Koolae. I loosed my grip on him and rubbed my hands together for warmth.

He nodded.

"Why we are always on the look for visitors," he said. "Dangerous otherwise."

When Gig joined us, we continued on. Koolae's torchlight showed us a low ceiling, just breaths above us. The cave stretched wider than ten men in some places before narrowing to where only two could pass side by side. Through these narrow places we went, and Koolae kept me close.

"Almost there," he said to me. "You can warm up by the fires."

"Thank you," I said. The drop in temperature had me shivering. Now that we weren't climbing, I was beginning to freeze. Chills walked up and down my skin from my head to my toes as my body tremored. I felt my muscles constrict tightly as they tried to warm up. It was like being back in the water at Master Ignoracius' hut.

Instead of watching where we headed, I kept my gaze on the ground to keep myself from tripping over stones and outcroppings.

"Your temperatures have dropped off significantly," AJ's voice said in my ear.

I jumped and realized I'd forgotten the crew still monitored us. They seemed so far away now that we were deep in the cave's infrastructure. I'd lost track of time and place.

"It's too cold," Gig said aloud. "Alyvia, come huddle with me."

I automatically paused and turned from Koolae to stop and wait for Gig.

"No, no. Almost there," Koolae said. He took off of his cloak and settled it around my shoulders. He motioned for one of his men to do the same for Gig. Then he took my hand firmly in his and started our walk again.

I let him lead me away, but I glanced back at Gig and saw that he frowned at us. I pulled the cloak tightly around me with my free hand, and felt instantly warmer. The cloak was lined and heavy. It smelled like a male musk and reminded me of my father in a surprisingly un-traumatic way. I clutched it, and kept walking.

Koolae was right. Just a few moments later, the cave began to get lighter until we finally spilled out into an enormous cavern that was lit by so many torches it was impossible to cast shadows.

We paused and looked around. The cavern's ceiling was high, high above us where torches could not reach. The rest of the cavern fell away at our feet, stretching down into the center with almost thirty levels that dipped down below. Each level had caves that tunneled into the walls. I saw Tigenan families coming in and out of these caves and realized they were individual homes. The voices of all the people echoed off the walls of the cavern. I could hear the voices, but not the words. They walked about wearing furry cloaks and furry boots. Only their faces and hands were exposed to the cold. The scent of wood smoke filled my nostrils, and I sucked it in greedily. I remembered camping trips with Cutter when we took breaks from the Academy. I smiled a little and thought of those starry, sleepless nights. The Tigenans were lucky to smell that scent every day. Koolae saw my smile and beamed in pride.

Each level that wrapped around the cave was connected to the level below by thick wooden stairs. Koolae led us to the nearest staircase and had us follow him down. He let go of my hand, and let me walk on my own now that the way was lit. I stayed behind him as we walked down. Whenever I could, I glanced around at the people nearby. They stopped when they saw that Koolae brought them two strangers. Their pale white faces recognized that we were not one of them, and they paused to assess us. Some closed in behind us as we passed. They followed us to see what was happening. The children especially seemed the most excited. They ran down the stairs ahead of Koolae, so that they could already be waiting at the bottom when we arrived.

Tigenans by far were a fair race, with little pigmentation among them. They all had white or white-blond hair and skin the color of snow. In comparison I must have looked quite strange or even ugly to them, with my dark hair and cinnamon-colored skin. Their eyes followed me closely. I tried to smile but I was probably really grimacing at them. It was hard to look non-threatening when your face was frozen from the cold. Still, I felt the ghost of their fingers as the little ones tried to touch my hair.

The floor level of the cavern was populated by dozens of campfires. Some were used for warmth, some for cooking and some for drying. Koolae led us across the floor to the campfire in the very center, which had rows of benches in a ring around it. He motioned for me to sit down on one of these benches, and for Gig to join me. Gig sat down beside me as directed, his borrowed cloak obviously too small for him. He sniffled too, and his nose was red. I wondered if I looked just as out of sorts.

Koolae sat across the fire from us, and his men arranged themselves around him. I felt the warmth of the fire begin to seep into my chilled bones. Huddled next to Gig, I wished we could have this serious conversation when I felt a little less helpless and miserable.

"Friends of Hector Ignoracius; Members of the Order," Koolae said. "Name yourself, please."

I sat up straighter and glanced at Gig. Koolae looked at me expectantly. I thought I saw Gig nod.

"My name is Alyvia Tippin," I said. "This is my shipmate, Gig Freeley."

"Alyvia. Gig," Koolae said. "Welcome to my tribe. You will stay with my family."

"Thank you, Koolae," Gig said. "We appreciate your gesture."

Koolae nodded but looked to me.

"We discuss business now," Koolae said. "What business does the Order have with Tigenan?"

"Master Ignoracius sent us to fetch an item he left with the Tigenans many years ago," I said.

"Believe I know this item," Koolae said. "Brother Ignoracius asked us to keep it safe."

"Brother?" Gig said. He leaned forward. Koolae mirrored him and leaned forward too.

"Brother," Koolae agreed. "We help our brother."

"Will you agree to help us?" Gig asked.

"Always help Members of the Order by bringing them in from the dark and giving them a home while they stay."

"But we've come for Ignoracius' artifact," Gig said. "Will you help us retrieve it?"

Koolae shrugged, his eyes reflecting the light from the fire.

"Ignoracius told us we must keep it among our Brothers and Sisters," he said. "Like to see where we keep it?"

We nodded our heads yes. Koolae stood up and motioned for us to join him. He held out a hand as I came around the fire. I glanced at Gig but took Koolae's hand. Its dry roughness warmed mine as he led me away toward the back of the cavern. Gig followed behind. We crossed the cavern floor, and bypassed several camp fires and curious Tigenans as we went.

In the back, where no fires were set, the chill of the cavern came back. A black nothingness came into view on the floor along the back wall. At first, I thought it was a sinkhole that led deeper into a lower level of caves. Koolae stopped and pointed.

"Brother Ignoracius' gift down there," he said.

I stopped next to him and stared at the darkness. Koolae waited for me to understand. I saw from the tilt of his head that seemed okay if I investigated. I loosed his hand, and took a few more steps toward the lip of the chasm. I knelt along the edge, peered down into the darkness and reached out a hand.

Someone behind me shifted and held their torch over my shoulder. That was when my fingers touched solid coldness and I realized what it was.

"It's frozen," I said. "You have it down there, in a pool of ice?"

I turned my head to look up at Koolae. He smiled down at me, proudly.

"Tigenan brothers and sisters honor Brother Ingoracius' request," he said.

After some insistence from Koolae, Gig agreed we would stay the night. I was escorted by five Tigenan women to the space where I would sleep. They gave me a tour of all Koolae's rooms, and there were many, before they let me stop to wash and relieve myself. Then they brought me to the room that was mine for the evening. I didn't understand their language but they looked up at me from lowered heads and demurely said some of the shared words they did know. I let them examine my hands and finger strands of my hair. One of them cautiously stroked my cheek in a sweet, almost motherly way. When they were done, the women all pointed at the room that was theirs, just down the stone hallway. That's how I realized these were some of Koolae's wives. The rest of the people I saw were their daughters, sons and grandchildren.

The Tigenans built their doorless rooms along the existing walls of the cavern. So when they showed me my bed, I realized it was along a natural shelf in the rock wall. Thick layers of bedding and pillows were piled high on top. Below the bed was a pit of hot embers that warmed the rock shelf, and therefore the bed. I immediately looked forward to bedtime when I could crawl in and get under the covers. My nose was still cold, and every now and then a draft would pass and make me shiver.

When this mission started, I had expected we would arrive, ask for Ignoracius' item and no matter what happened with the Tigenans, still be in my own bed tonight. After the hike and descent underground, I was glad we could stay and try again tomorrow.

A small table with two chairs was set up in the center of the room. On the table sat a meal of meat and potatoes for two people. The aroma of the food filled my nostrils, and made my mouth water and my stomach call out.

The women departed the room when they saw I seemed satisfied. They smiled at me shyly and pointed out their room again, if I needed them.

When they were out, Koolae came in and motioned for me to sit down. Gig came in behind, and was gently urged to sit in the second chair.

"Eat," Koolae said. "Sleep, and talk tomorrow."

He left. I looked at Gig and saw that he already had some potatoes in his mouth.

"He's gone," Gig said.

"Yes," the Captain said in our ear comms. "The rocks of the cavern make it difficult to get a good reading, but we can see faint outlines of where you are."

I pulled my plate closer and used a crude fork to spear some meat and potatoes and put it in my mouth. The meat was tender and flavorful. Definitely better than anything I ever ate at the Academy.

"Yum," I said to Gig.

"We need to discuss strategy," the Captain said. "Where exactly is the artifact?"

"I couldn't see it," I said. "Koolae said it was down where the floor of the cavern falls even further down below but it's all filled with water, and the water turned to ice. If Ignoracius' artifact is down there, its integrity could be compromised."

"Well we need to get it before we can find that out," the Captain said. "Marco has been scanning the area in an attempt to verify if it's even there. In the meantime, you two need to earn Koolae's trust. He may be the key to getting that artifact without any trouble."

I nodded, and noticed that Gig was doing the same. We took bites of our food.

"For now, we're finishing dinner," Gig said. "I've been given a room one-fourth this size, and on the other side of Koolae's spaces, across the pit. I don't like it."

I looked up from my food, and met Gig's eyes. He stared at me seriously, his eyes shadowed.

"Proposal?" the Captain asked.

Gig was silent.

"Why don't you crash in her room?" Marco suggested after a beat. "I don't know if it's just me, but it sounded like Koolae was favoring Alyvia."

"He was," Gig agreed. "I didn't think he was going to let loose of her hand."

I nodded. Koolae had been more interested in me than Gig.

"He has been very kind and accommodating," I said, in an attempt to be fair. "Although, my room appears to be near his wives."

"Well, we don't want him to get any ideas," the Captain said. "Gig, stay in Alyvia's room while you two are there."

"Agreed," Gig said. He looked at me. "Do you have a problem with that?"

"No," I said, and went back to my food. I appreciated that he bothered to ask for permission but it would make me feel better to know he was close by. Koolae and his wives seemed fine but I wasn't used to so much positive attention.

"Good," the Captain said. "Comm us if you need us, especially if you start to bargain with the Tigenans. We're going silent for the night but someone will always be up and monitoring your messages."

"Aye, aye Captain," Gig and I said in unison. The comm link went silent.

I felt Gig's eyes on me when I went back to my food. He looked like he wanted to say something. I waited.

"At the Academy, did you ever come across a guy who *wasn't* kind and accommodating to you?" he ventured.

I tried to read his face to figure out what he meant.

"What do you mean?"

"Just answer the question," he said. The corner of his lip lifted slightly. He was about to tease me.

I thought about it.

"There were a couple jerks here and there," I said, "but most of the people I met at the Academy were very nice to me. Especially if they liked Cutter."

"How many jerks did you date?"

I paused. This was getting personal, and I started to feel a twinge of discomfort.

"Why do you ask?"

"Just curious," he said. "Why do you shy away from personal questions?"

"I'm a very boring person," I said, honestly. "I also have trust issues. I would like to know your intentions before I open my mouth and share with you."

"So, are you saying you don't trust me?"

I realized he was about to lead me into a trap and I was confused by his change of attitude.

"No, I'm not saying that," I said. "I am learning to trust you, but that's a process that takes time. Just like you're learning to trust me."

I said it in a reasonable way but Gig's expression didn't change.

"So until you trust me, you won't tell me any stories about yourself?" he asked. "How am I supposed to learn to trust you, if you don't share stories that help me get to know who you are?"

I opened my mouth to respond, but I really didn't have a good answer for that one.

"Why do I feel like you're picking on me?" I asked. I leaned back in my chair and crossed my arms over my chest while I waited for his response.

Gig leaned forward.

"I just don't like secrets," he said.

My eyebrows knit together. I breathed in but didn't let it out.

"Do you think I'm keeping secrets from you?"

"How would I know?" he asked in exasperation. "You won't even answer the simplest of questions about yourself."

His outburst let me breathe again. I tried to relax my arms and look unconcerned but my skin was prickling.

"Well, what about you?" I wanted to know. "You're not exactly volunteering loads of information. I didn't know I was meeting your dad until he announced himself."

That was a nice touch, I knew. As soon as I said it, Gig closed his eyes and sighed. I watched him lean back in his own chair. He touched a hand to his forehead, like he just realized the headache I gave him.

"Okay, let's start over," he said. "How about this proposition. For every question of *mine* that you answer, I have to answer the question too. And for every question of *yours* I answer, you have to answer likewise. Does that sound fair?"

I thought about it.

"What if it's a question I don't want to answer?" I asked.

"Then you can't ask that question of me," he said. I made a face that acknowledged this sounded fair.

"And the purpose of this is to get to know each other?" I clarified.

"Yes," he said. "You and I will be working together the most. We'll be in situations sometimes where we need to trust each other. Trust that the other person will be loyal, and that the other person will be competent. If we don't have that, we will fail."

I looked down at my food, and thought about it. It made sense. What if one of us was put to a challenge that affected the other? Could I trust Gig to do right by me? I would do right by him, but did he know that and have faith in that?

Probably not.

I loosed a breath.

"Okay, it's a deal," I said. "I agree to your trust-building proposal."

Gig held out his hand, and we shook on it. His hand warmed mine.

"Now," he said. "Tell me about the boyfriends you hung around with."

I grinned.

"I've never had a boyfriend," I said. "So, it's your turn! What girlfriends have *you* had?"

This was fun.

Gig made a face of disbelief.

"Hold on, hold on, hold on," he said. "I don't believe that for one second. You never had a boyfriend? You have got to be kidding me."

"I am one hundred percent serious," I said. "So, perk up and tell me about *your* girls."

I assumed there were many. Gig was a gunner, and I didn't want to be judgmental but if he was anything like the gunners I'd trained with at the Academy, then there was a long history of girls that ended most recently with Maddy.

Gig looked like he thought I'd lied to him. I could tell he wanted to ask more questions but a young boy appeared in our doorway and asked if he could clear our dishes. We said yes, and helped him pile our things together so he could carry them in his scrawny arms. He bent his knees in a semi-curtsy before he left.

Gig stood up.

"I'm going to go wash up," he said. "Do you need to go?"

"No," I said, "I'm good."

Gig nodded.

"I'll be back," he said. "Don't wander off, please."

As soon as he left, I eyed the bed. It was immature of me, but I wanted to go to sleep before Gig could think of more questions to ask me tonight.

I got up from the table and went to the bed to pull back the blankets. I could feel how warm and comfy I would be tonight. It was a relief compared to how cold I'd been all evening. I untied Koolae's cloak and hung it from a hook on the wall. Then I crawled up on the bed, kicked off my shoes, and snuggled under the covers. I left room beside me for Gig. I was used to sharing a bed with Cutter, so I didn't care if Gig and I shared one for the night.

I trusted him.

I rolled over, let the warmth seep into my bones, and sighed.

The only reason I knew I'd fallen asleep was because I woke up, hours later, with the need to relieve myself again. I groaned, disappointed at the idea that I'd have to crawl from the warmth of the bed. I lay still for a moment to try and go back to sleep but after several long moments, I finally admitted to myself there was no way I could go back to sleep unless I went to the bathroom first.

When I opened my eyes, I saw that Gig was asleep beside me. I'd snuggled up close to him. I hadn't left the poor guy any space in the bed to move around. He was on his back, one arm tucked under his head. I held the other arm close to me like he was Cutter.

Embarrassed, I carefully let it go and put some inches between my body and Gig's. I hoped he didn't think I'd pressed myself against him on purpose. I would have to explain my all-over-the-place sleep style later. It had exasperated Cutter to no end when I would toss and turn and accidentally elbow him in the face or knee him in the back. Eventually he had figured out that if he put his arms around me and spooned with me whenever we shared a bed, he could control where the knees and elbows went. I'd been beyond uncomfortable at first, unable to fall asleep. Or if I did fall asleep, it was not a deep sleep. But I'd grown accustomed to the embrace, and even comforted by it. As our friendship grew deeper, it was just one more thing we did. Everyone thought we lied when we told them we were just friends, especially the girls who dated Cutter.

I remember one girlfriend who was particularly hurt after she came to see Cutter and found me cuddled with him in his bed. She threw a book at us and stormed off, furious. The book had been heavy, and hit Cutter solidly on the head. Instead of trying to jump up to chase after her, Cutter had simply groaned and gone back to sleep.

"Another crazy girl," he'd said in exasperation.

I'd seen the pain in her eyes as she'd thrown the book, and felt completely guilty about it. I didn't blame her when she approached me later that day, as I sat outside the Academy with a book.

"If you want to keep him all to yourself, why don't you just let the rest of us know," she said with venom. Her eyes were angry and hurt.

"I don't!" I said. "We fell asleep after studying, I swear! We're just friends."

The girl had snorted in derision.

"Yeah right," she said. "Two *friends* who just happen to share a bed? What else can you do as just friends? Does he kiss you as *just friends*? Does he screw you all night as *just friends*?"

Stunned, I'd shaken my head.

"It's not like that," I tried to say. My voice quavered slightly.

"Oh come *on*," she spat. "Don't start. The vulnerable routine may work on Cutter, but it doesn't work on me."

I wasn't *vulnerable*. I'd opened my mouth to try and explain, but Cutter had appeared just then and taken the girl by the elbow. He led her away from me with a stern look on his face. Some of his friends were with him, but they held back and watched the show.

"Get lost," I heard him say to her. "Take your jealousy out on someone else."

"Oh, good, you're here to the rescue," she said to him through clenched teeth. There were tears in her eyes now. "Go ahead, Cutter. Protect her some more!"

She yanked her arm away from him and walked away as quickly as her legs could carry her.

I watched her go with a tight feeling in my belly. Cutter saw my face as he sat down beside me and told me to forget her. His friends sat down too and congratulated him on how he had handled her.

"Cutter, you liked her," I said loudly. "How can you let her go on thinking what she thinks?"

"It doesn't matter, Lyvvie," he said with a shake of his head. "She can think what she wants. Even if it's not the truth."

I saw then that I couldn't reason with him. I stared at him for a minute while his friends told him he was right, and that his girlfriend was crazy. They gestured at me and said everyone knew that we were like brother and sister. That Cutter looked out for me.

Cutter had nodded but he didn't look happy.

I felt awful inside as I made a decision of my own.

"I don't think we should hang out anymore," I said softly.

Their voices died.

"What?

Cutter sat up away from the tree and turned to face me, obviously shocked. "What are you talking about?"

I looked away and collected my things.

"It's not fair to you," I said. I pushed myself up onto my feet so I could get away. "You're way too good of a friend, and I shouldn't be getting in your way."

I remember turning away from him, because I was anxious to be gone where he couldn't see me shaken. My heart broke and tears jumped into my eyes as I thought about giving up a friend who meant everything to me, but I hadn't taken more than two steps before he'd grabbed me and pulled me back to the tree. It startled me, and I'd instinctively thrown up my arms to protect my face. Cutter had paused, and sucked in a pained breath.

"Whoa," his friend Reggie said, "he wasn't going to hurt you."

"Alyvia," Cutter said softly. "Look at me."

He sounded so sorry and upset, that I dropped my arms immediately and hugged myself tightly. Tears leaked from my eyes and I covered my mouth. Cutter and his friends stared at me in surprise.

"I didn't mean to scare you," Cutter added. He put a hand on my shoulder and gently squeezed. "Alyvia, I'm sorry. Are you hurt?"

I felt so awful and ashamed at my overreaction that I burst into tears.

"I'm sorry, Cutter," I gasped. "I know that. I don't know what happened I just lost it."

He sighed and dragged me into a bear hug against his chest. I tried to push him away in case his girlfriend saw us but he didn't let me. I was embarrassed to be so overdramatic in front of his friends but they gave me sympathetic smiles.

Cutter sat down and gently pulled me down next to him so he could circle an arm around my shoulder. I leaned against him, but I felt pretty upset and miserable.

"Guys, will you give us a few minutes while I knock some sense into my best friend?"

His friends agreed and one of them clapped my knee in solidarity as he got up to leave. I gave him a small smile because I realized he wasn't upset with me. He wanted me and Cutter to be okay.

After a few minutes of waiting for them to get out of earshot, Cutter sat up and turned his body so we were face to face.

"Alyvia, did your family hit you when you were growing up?"

I wasn't surprised by the question. I just nodded and said nothing.

Cutter sighed and his shoulders drooped.

"Well that was wrong," he said. "Where I come from, women are respected and prized, not treated like punching bags. I would never hurt you, and I don't want you to be afraid of me, okay?"

"I'm not," I said. "I just got a little crazy."

"Well knock that shit off," he said. "You don't have to stop being my friend to get me a girlfriend, you know. I just need to wait for the right one."

I felt a wave of relief.

"Then we should stop having sleepovers," I said. "Especially if you're seeing a girl. They just don't understand. I probably wouldn't if it were me."

"Fine," Cutter said quickly. "Whatever you want."

I cracked a smile. Cutter grinned back. We started laughing for absolutely no reason.

And that had been that. We'd shared a bed a few times since then, but never when he had a girlfriend. Cutter's girls just never seemed to last long. It wasn't long after that when Cutter found out the rest of my story. I had been nervous to tell him but he didn't react how I feared.

He was truly my best friend.

The need to pee was now unbearable. I couldn't stay in bed any longer and ignore it. I needed to go find the place where the women had taken me earlier to relieve myself. I sighed and made myself sit up. Gig was between me and the edge of the bed, so I would have to crawl over him. I pushed myself to my hands and knees and tried to quietly shift my weight over Gig without waking him. I glanced at him to make sure his eyes were closed and he was sleeping. I tried to straddle him without touching his body. His eyes flew open right as I had a knee and hand on either side of him. I squeaked in surprise. He grabbed me automatically, his hands clutched tightly at my waist and my arm and he asked what I was doing.

I felt my face turn pink and froze.

"I have to go, sorry to wake you," I whispered. My hair was loose, and formed a curtain on either side of his handsome face. It blocked the firelight and cast him in shifting shadows. His eyes were sleepy and unable to stay open. He glanced down at my body over his and let me go.

"No problem," he said. I shifted the rest of my weight over him and got down from the bed. As I pulled on my shoes, I saw Gig roll over and go back to sleep.

I tiptoed from the room Koolae had given us, and began my search. I'd only taken a few steps when one of Koolae's women saw me and came over. She led me to the room I wanted and bowed to me before she left me to my own devices. I thanked her.

When I'd relieved myself, I stepped out from the network of caves in the wall and looked around the great cavern. It was still very early but the women hustled to and from their caves quickly, like worker bees. Sometimes they had little ones strapped to their back with young ones who followed close behind as they carried laundry and cleaning tools. There were few men or boys moving about, but I did occasionally see them as they climbed up and down the network of ladders that connected upper ledges to the base of the cave below.

I could see Koolae down at the firepits where he'd taken us last night. Had he slept at all? I walked the ring to the wider staircase and followed it straight down to where he sat.

"Alyvia, I see you separating from Gig," Marco said in my ear.

"I'm going to go have a quick chat with Koolae," I said quietly. "Gig is still asleep."

"Don't you think it would be okay to wake him?"

"He looked pretty tired," I said. "I'm just going to talk to Koolae, not go

126

anywhere."

"I'm listening if you need help," he said.

"Thanks, Marco."

Koolae grinned at me toothlessly when he saw me approach. He waved me over. As I came near, I saw him tell a girl on his left to move for me. I took her place and looked around. We were surrounded by women and children of different ages.

"Family," Koolae said. He indicated the group around him.

I'd read somewhere in the texts Gig and I studied that Tigenans were not monogamous. It suddenly occurred to me why Gig acted so funny last night. He probably thought there was a chance Koolae would try to add me to his clan of wives. It made me feel like an idiot for not understanding sooner. I eyed the females, and realized that some of them were eyeing me right back.

"How many wives do you have?" I asked. I hoped that wasn't a rude question.

"Twenty three," he said proudly.

I sucked in a breath.

"How many babies?"

"Sixty five."

"Koolae, how do you have time for anything else?" I teased, astonished.

He laughed and nodded.

A little boy with big eyes toddled over slowly and pulled himself into Koolae's lap.

"Ma ma ma ma," he squeaked and bounced.

"Da," Koolae told him. "Da."

The boy looked over at me and grinned. There was a pocket of drool on his chin. He stepped across Koolae's lap and tried to pitch himself in my direction. Koolae held him upright, but the baby did it again. I instinctively reached out to catch him, and Koolae let him come to me.

"Ma ma ma," the baby said to me with a wet smile. I gripped him under the arms and let him bounce on my legs until he got bored. He smelled powdery and a little milky. He reached out and grabbed some of my hair and sat down on my knee, clutching it in a fist so he could examine it closely. I had to lean over him to keep him from ripping the hair from my scalp. What was he planning to do with my hair?

I glanced up from the baby, and saw Koolae smile at me knowingly.

"Our friend from the Order fits in here," he said to no one in particular.

"What are you doing?" Marco asked in my ear.

I thought of ways I might be able to tactfully say I wasn't interested in fitting in with his family but I got a sudden brainwave, and shifted gears.

"Almost like a brother, or a sister," I suggested.

I bit my lip and thought of what Koolae had told us last night. *Ignoracius told us we must keep it among our Brothers and Sisters.*

"Koolae," I said slowly. "What did Ignoracius do to become your brother?"

Koolae's lips turned up into a smile.

"Ignoracius stayed among us, and was judged worthy," he said.

"What if I want to prove my worthiness?" I asked. "If I become a sister of Tigenan, will you let me take Ignoracius' artifact out of here?"

"You become a sister of Tigenan, and you get artifact," Koolae said slowly. "What does Tigenan get?"

"What do you want?" I asked.

Koolae made one slick motion of his hand. Immediately, everyone around his fire got up and left. The women grabbed their children, including the one in my lap, and dispersed to other nearby fires, or back up the steps to their rooms. When they were all gone, Koolae and I were free to talk.

"The Tigenans would like many things," Koolae said. He stood up and moved closer to the fire. "Our caves are colder this year, and food is harder to find. Our babies are sick and some died. We need help."

I thought of the baby I held and felt sympathy.

"Tell me what I can do," I said. "Perhaps if I were a sister of Tigenan, I could help."

Koolae turned to look at me. I returned his gaze and waited while Koolae remained silent and thought.

"Very few members of the Order come visit us," he said at last. "We need Masters to come and show us how to build warmth into our walls. Show us how to keep our babies alive. Show us how to breed food that will last. When they are done, we want them to take some of our young ones and train them to be Masters at the Order's Academy. We want Tigenan represented in the Order."

His requests were so well thought-out. He must have been waiting quite some time for a member of the Order to visit his lands. I looked at the people by his fire and wondered how they would feel becoming members of the Order.

"The Order is so desperate to have Starkiller, he could have asked for the moon and they would have given it to him," the Captain said in my ear. I hadn't realized she had joined Marco but I was glad she chimed in. "His requests will be accepted if he gives us the hull."

"Koolae," I said, "are you sure you want your people to go to the Academy? It's not easy, and it's not like Tigenan. If your people join the Order, Tigenan will become very different than it is now. A lot of things will change."

Koolae smiled sadly but he nodded his head.

"We must change to survive," he said. "This family will survive."

I saw that my little toddler friend was trying to make his way back to us. Koolae picked him up and held him close. I watched them smile at each other with love. Then Koolae turned to me expectantly.

I saw that it was important to him, and it wasn't my place to refuse him.

"Okay," I said. "If you let me take Ignoracius' artifact, I will help you get what you want."

"Ignoracius' artifact must stay with Tigenan Brothers and Sisters," he said.

"Then let me become a Tigenan Sister, so that I can have the artifact," I said.

"Is this what you want?"

"Yes," I said simply.

"Good," Koolae said. "Follow me."

"Do what you have to do," the Captain urged me, "but don't endanger yourself."

"Okay," I said to Koolae and the Captain.

I got up and followed him. He handed a woman the baby and then led me away from the campfires, and up one level of the staircase. He walked around the outer ring until we came to a tall dark cave on the opposite side.

Koolae paused here.

"This is a sacred Tigenan ritual," he said very seriously. "You may not speak once you enter here, until the very end."

I nodded.

"Alyvia, what are you doing?" I heard Gig's alarmed voice say in my ear.

"I will be a Tigenan Sister," I said aloud, so that Gig could hear me.

Koolae nodded.

"Are you ready?" he asked.

"Yes," I said.

"Then enter," Koolae said. He stepped out of my way. "Go inside and get comfortable. The women will join you."

I looked at the darkness of the cave, took a deep breath, and stepped inside. The light behind me that filtered from the cave floor disappeared almost immediately.

"You don't know what they will require of you," I heard Gig say in my ear. He sounded angry.

"It cannot be harmful," the Captain replied. "Ignoracius did it, and he wouldn't have sent us to do something he could not do."

"Why didn't Ignoracius tell us what we would come against when we arrived here?" Gig demanded. "He had plenty of opportunity to tell us the hull was encased in ice, and that we would have to endear ourselves to the

Tigenans to get it. How do we know he hasn't put Alyvia in danger?"

"He may be exiled, but he is still a Master," the Captain reminded him sharply. "Now stay silent, Gig. Alyvia, we're reading you. Continue if you are comfortable."

I'd walked into the cave, and left Koolae and the lights of the cavern behind. Forty steps later, immersed in darkness, I could see nothing around me any longer. Total dark surrounded me, like a thick blanket covered only my eyes. I forced my breath to stay even, stretched out my arms—palms facing out—and closed my eyes since I couldn't see anyway. I moved forward at an excruciatingly slow pace and toed the path ahead of me before I shifted my weight forward. There was no resistance as I went. Nothing blocked my path or tripped me up. The sounds of talking and singing and laughter grew softer until the Tigenans in the cavern faded from thought and it was only me. In a cave. Alone. And cold.

I kept my mouth shut so that I didn't break the silence Koolae had asked me to keep. I wanted to hear the Captain's voice again, but I said nothing. I simply toed my way forward blindly.

I thought I heard a sound then, and I stopped. My hands dropped to my sides, and I opened my eyes but still saw nothing. I strained to hear, and halted even my breath to listen.

Humming. The sound I heard was humming; a woman's voice. I couldn't tell if it came from ahead or behind so I listened intently. The humming was beautiful, I realized, as a second voice took it up. It was a harmonic tune that slowly played out a somber melody. The humming grew in volume slightly. I thought I could pick out several voices now, and they began to surround me in the darkness.

These were the women Koolae had promised would join me. My skin broke out into goosebumps as they continued to hum. The melody played out for my memory until I knew every note and pause. As they repeated the song, the four voices moved closer and the tune increased in volume again.

Hands touched my arms, touched my hair, my face, my back. I was led forward carefully, with no ability to see my destination. I submitted myself to their lead, and put my trust in them as we took several paces forward. We paused, and one voice stopped humming.

"You must not speak until we ask," the woman's accented voice said ahead of me and to my right. "You are now in our sacred ritual. We must prepare you before you can become a sister of Tigenan. Take off your clothing, you must wear a clean shift."

I felt a piece of cloth pressed against my arm. I kicked off my shoes, and gasped at the coldness of the stone underfoot. It immediately soaked the heat from my feet. I ignored the chilled air as I undid my trousers. When I stepped out of them, hands took them away. Then I pulled off Koolae's cloak and removed my shirt. Unseen hands collected this clothing from me too.

I was helped into the shift they'd brought for me. It was pulled over my head as I put my arms through the sleeves. The shift fell to just above my knees. I rubbed my hands down the front, feeling its softness and lack of adornment. There were no buttons or zippers, and minimal stitching that I could feel. It was very thin material, and trapped no warmth. I shivered.

The women reached out and led me forward a bit further, all four of them taking up their hummed song again. I was grateful when my bare feet stepped onto a rug and the icy cold stone could no longer rob me of body heat. The women wrapped a thick blanket around my shoulders that fell to the floor. I clutched it around my neck, and dragged it behind me. I wished I could thank them wholeheartedly, but I wasn't supposed to speak.

A candleflame suddenly burned into sight before me. Its light hurt my eyes for a moment until they adjusted to the light again. Finally able to see again, I looked at the holder of the candle and then at my surroundings. She was one of Koolae's wives. I recognized her face from last night when I was shown to my room. She was a small woman with hair that fell in pale waves around her shoulders.

"Please sit," she said.

I sank to the carpet and adjusted my shift and the blanket around me so that I could sit with my legs crossed comfortably.

"I am the light of womanhood," she said. "I bring light to my family and use my light to guide. I bring light to you."

She bent and set her candle down on the floor in front of me. I realized, as light flared up, that she was using it to light a fire in a pit before me. It became a small campfire that quickly dispelled the chill around me and lit up the cavern where they'd taken me. I breathed in the scent of woodsmoke and relaxed. I glanced around and saw the three other women who accompanied us. They waited on the edge of the firelight for their turns. We were the only things here, just me and four women on a carpet in front of a fire.

The woman who'd brought me light bowed to me, and then came to sit beside me on my left. A second woman approached me from the sidelines, a bowl in her hand.

"I am the cleansing power of womanhood," she said to me. "I keep my family clean and tidy, and their lives cleansed of trouble. I bring cleansing to you."

She knelt before me, took my hands in hers one by one, and washed them in her bowl. When the lukewarm water touched my skin it gave me goosebumps again that she rubbed away with her towel. Then she washed my feet and dried them too. She stood, bowed to me, and then sat beside

131

me on my right.

A third woman came forward with a plate in her hands.

"I am the sustenance of womanhood," she said. "I keep my family fed with all of the sustenance they need so that they will thrive. I bring sustenance to you."

She knelt before me, took a strip of meat from her plate and fed it to me. She waited while I chewed the deliciously seasoned meat. After I'd swallowed it, she fed me bread, then fruit. When I was done eating, she stood and bowed. Then she went and sat to my left beside the other woman.

The fourth and final woman came forward with a cup in her hands.

"I am the clarity of womanhood," she said. "Like clear fluid, I am the clear mind of my family and am the source of their wisdom. I bring clarity to you."

She knelt before me, and proffered her cup. I lifted my hands to accept it but the women on either side of me clasped my hands with theirs. I understood, and leaned forward as the woman proffered her cup once more. The clay touched my lips and I carefully drank from it until it was empty. I was surprised by how much liquid they wanted me to drink. The crackling fire was behind her. It cast her face into shadows. I stared into the shadows where her eyes were as I drained the last of its contents down my throat. It had a sharp taste to it that I almost choked on but I held my breath and swallowed down the rest.

When she saw that I was finished, she stood and bowed. Then went to sit on my far right.

I took a deep breath, and looked at the fire while I waited for the next part of the ceremony. The women on either side of me began to hum their song again, softly at first. They still held onto my hands. I relaxed even more. I was complacent now that they'd fed me and were keeping me warm. Lulled. A warmth grew in my stomach. It started to circulate through my body. I followed its path with my mind, grateful for the way the warmth erased the chill from my limbs.

My eyes were closed, I realized. I opened them. My breathing was long and slow. I blinked, and looked at the fire, and listened to their song.

"I think she's falling asleep?" someone said in my ear. They sounded amused.

I opened my eyes again, and looked around. Koolae was there. He stood to the side of the fire, and watched me solemnly. I struggled to focus on him, but my eyes refused.

"Relax," he said. His voice sounded far away. "Your drink will bring clarity; do not fight it."

I tried to shout but it came out as an incoherent moan. I'd been drugged. I felt it pulse through my veins with every beat of my heart. It spread a heady warmth and lethargy through my entire body. All of my nerve endings suddenly came to life from my head to my feet, and I was nearly swallowed by the overwhelming feeling. Everything stood out to me. The carpet under my bottom, the shift against my chest, the blanket I clutched around my shoulders. The feeling against my skin was magnified, so that it was both painful and pleasurable to feel them. My lethargy was now complete. I started to lean over, and one of the women helped shift me so that I was on my back next to the fire with my blanket over me. I clutched the blanket and shut my eyes. I started to feel feverish.

The humming continued.

I was in the first stages of this drug, I knew. Ecstasy and pain radiated away from my body, or that's how it felt. I felt like if I reached out and touched something, I could transmit those feelings through my fingertips. I did reach out, and my hand was caught, held and replaced under my blanket.

"In the beginning, there was nothing," Koolae whispered to me. His voice filled up my ear so that his words could crawl into my head and find a home in my thoughts. I pictured a black barren nothingness, like the cave I'd entered some time ago.

"Then my heavenly father asked for a home to rest his head, for he was weary," Koolae said.

I pictured a man who looked tired and lonely, floating in that black nothingness.

"My heavenly mother gave him clarity, and he formed Tigenan. My heavenly mother gave him light, and he added a moon and a sun. He gave Tigenan fire. My heavenly mother cleansed him, and from his own body he made the Tigenan people. My heavenly mother saw what my heavenly father had made, and she gave the Tigenan people sustenance. This was the beginning."

His words washed over me, and I saw all of these things in my imagination.

"My heavenly father and my heavenly mother rested their weary heads on Tigenan, forming the two great mountains of Tigenan. We now live in my heavenly father's weary head. My sister Keelara's people live in my heavenly mother's weary head, a great distance from here. We honor our heavenly mother and our heavenly father every day. We honor them by being their strength as they rest. As a member of the Order, you have great strength. It brings great honor to the heavenly father to welcome you as one of his sisters of Tigenan. A sister of Tigenan the way Hector Ignoracius become a brother of Tigenan. We honor our brothers and sisters, for they honor the heavenly mother and the heavenly father. Will you add your strength to Tigenan, so that our heavenly father can rest? Will you, Alyvia Tippin, friend of the Order, be a sister of Tigenan? Speak now."

I felt a sudden strength of conviction, and a keening sympathy for the heavenly father.

"Yes," I said slurred. "I will be a sister of Tigenan. I will add my strength so the heavenly father can rest."

My eyes flew open, and I saw that Koolae now knelt beside me. I wanted to leap up and lend my strength, but my body had other ideas. It felt like a useless puddle of gel. Koolae touched a hand to my forehead.

"Then you must find your strength," he said.

I nodded. I needed to find my strength.

"I will help you. You will find your strength like a sister of Tigenan."

I smiled in gratefulness. Koolae was going to help me find my strength.

"Close your eyes," he said.

I closed my eyes. My feverishness was growing. The world spun.

"Your strength is buried within you, as great as this mountain we now sit in," he said. "You must tap into it carefully, with control. With clarity. We have given you clarity. To tap into your strength with control, you must go to a peaceful place in your mind, where no one can disturb you. Do you understand?"

I nodded. What he described was like the training I'd received to still my mind before practicing my telekinesis. It was a razor sharp concentration that required total focus.

"Your peaceful place must be like a room in your mind with impenetrable walls. No one can get to you there unless you let them."

I pictured a bare white room with white walls, a white ceiling and a white floor. There were no doors, no windows, and no adornments of any kind. I pictured myself in that room, standing alone, in the white shift Koolae's wives had dressed me in. My skin and hair provided the only color.

"Your peaceful place can be a memory of stillness that you cherish," Koolae continued. "Your peaceful place can be a wish for your future. My peaceful place is lying in bed curled around my sleeping son, holding his little hand on the night he was born. What is your peaceful place, can you see it?"

I looked around my bare white room with no windows or doors and tried to fill it with a memory that I cherished. What memory would serve me best, I wondered? When was the last moment I had where I noticed the stillness?

I thought of the night I'd spent with Cutter a few weeks ago, after the Tests. We'd sat on the steps of the Academy, with the night stars as our light while a party raged in the dorms behind us and many voices shouted and laughed. But where we sat on the steps, it was still. Cutter had sat a few steps behind me and was rubbing my shoulders. I sat with my head resting against the stairwell. Cutter had wanted to take a break from the madness and catch his breath before we went back to the party. Even then I knew it would be the last night when we would be together like that, quiet and at peace.

The last night. Quiet and at peace. Sen.

I shifted gears, and thought of the night Stryker had taken me to an exhibition on Aribel, a planet of nothing but water. After the first night's exhibitions, Stryker and I had set out in search of food on the main ship. As we walked the deck, a salty breeze had whipped through my hair, and Stryker had settled his hat on my head to keep it warm. Grinning at him, I'd impulsively wrapped my arms around him in a big hug. Stryker had hugged me back, and held me a moment longer. Knowing how much he despised showing emotion, I recognized that hug for what it was. A hundred "I love yous" wrapped in two arms.

Quiet love and water.

Sen.

An image of Sen came into my stark white room, so strong and fierce I could not shut him out. I sighed in defeat. My heart swelled with a mix of anguish and an overwhelming love.

"Yes, what do you see?" Koolae's voice asked me urgently.

"Sen," I said. "My brother."

"Now, or in the past?"

"The past," I slurred. I stared at my brother's face. It was Sen at 16 that I would always keep in my mind. "He went to the Academy even though our father told him not to go. When he came back after his first year, I was so happy to see him. He'd left me with Oben and I didn't like it. I was still little, and I wanted him to stay."

I saw myself as a young kid and watched with a tight chest as little me snuck into Sen's room in the attic of our sprawling home.

"I woke him up that night," I whispered, seeing it as I spoke. Little me reached out and shook the lump in Sen's bed. He rolled over quickly and cracked his eyes open blearily.

"Lyvvie?" he asked, half awake.

"Ssh!" I said. "Come with me Sen, there's something I have to show you."

"What is it?" he whispered.

"It's a secret," I said impatiently. "Come on!"

Sen sat up, and the moonlight from his window showed me his rumpled hair and tired face. He was still handsome, though, with his slightly curling hair and big dark eyes. We looked so much alike, I knew. Everyone told us that. He looked at me for a long time in the moonlight. I waited, thinking that he needed a second to wake up. Then he dressed quickly and silently followed me down the creaking stairs and past our parents' bedroom. We went outside to where the landcruiser was parked.

"*I'm* driving," Sen announced. "Where are you taking me?"

"We're going to the lake," I said. "Hurry up, fuzzy legs!"

Sen grinned and started up the cruiser, then drove us away from the house and out into the woods. The lake was off to the side of the road. We parked and waded through the thick grass, our shoes getting stuck in mud, until we found the rowboat I'd left there earlier.

When Sen saw the boat, he paused and said, "Lyvvie?"

"Trust me, Sen," I told him.

We clambered into the boat, and Sen gamely rowed out onto the water. We sat on the water in silence and listened to the sound of wind in the trees, and the callings of the creatures that lived near the lake. The sky was clear of clouds, so that the glittering stars over our head stood out like they were in reaching distance. Their reflection in the black water around us made it seem like we floated on stars.

"I love it here, on the water," I told Sen. My voice sounded so childlike but serious. "I come when no one knows so I can practice where they can't see me."

Sen looked at me with a lifted eyebrow. I loved that, even though I was his baby sister, he took me seriously. I could tell he was very curious what this was all about.

"Practice?" Sen asked.

"Practice my tele," I whispered, confident that Sen could know my secret. "I'm going to be better than you."

Our family all had strong telekinetic powers, but only the men were allowed to use it. It had served Sen well at the Academy. He looked at me funny when a gurgle of delighted laughter escaped my throat.

"I'm doing it right now, and you didn't even notice!" I told him gleefully.

Sen looked around. I watched him mull it over as he tried to figure out what I wanted to tell him. I could see from his face that he didn't notice anything strange at first. Then he heard the sound of wind whistling through the boat, and his face changed. He glanced over the side, and finally realized our boat was floating in mid-air and not on the water. It was me who held it up.

"Alyvia!" he nearly shouted, his voice loud in the quiet.

"I told you I've been practicing; see what I can do? I'm getting strong!" I laughed aloud again.

"You're very strong," he said with pride. He grinned and looked at me.

"You're probably stronger than all of us."

Sen made me add other things to the air like rocks from under the water, and tree branches, until the burden was too heavy for me. As we floated there with debris around us, everything felt magical and timeless.

"That's it!" Koolae's voice interrupted, and I came back to myself. "You found it, right there. Not before, and nothing afterward. Just hold that place in your mind until you can easily find yourself there again at any time."

I focused on the memory, and saw it all again. The debris floating around us while we hovered over the water in a leaky rowboat. Sen's face. The hoot of an owl nearby. The stars above and in the water, and the scent of lake and forest.

"Now that you know how to find your peace, you can tap into the full potential of your strength for our heavenly father," Koolae said. "I will help you."

I felt movement by my head, and then Koolae began to whisper softly in my ear. As he spoke, his women began to hum once more. Whatever he said went into my ear, and sent shivers thrumming along my muscles and joints, but I could not recall the words after they left his lips. He kept whispering, and his whispers guided me.

As I sat in my boat with Sen, I saw the words ripple across the water toward us. They hovered just above the surface and crawled over the side of our boat until they attached themselves to me. I felt a great vastness growing above my head; its bulky shape blocked out the stars and cast a growing shadow over us and the water. I looked up and saw a huge vortex of energy that shimmered above me. It was bigger than a house, and as full as the moon. It simply hovered there like a swollen ball, so large that I could not see its totality though I craned my neck in all directions to stare at it.

Koolae's whispers told me to stand up and grasp the energy. I glanced at my brother. He smiled at me happily. I shifted carefully and got to my feet. My movement rocked the rowboat from side to side as I stood. Then I reached out my hand to touch the ball. I stretched, and my fingers brushed inches past the globe. I'd missed.

I tried again, this time straining my muscles to reach as far as I could while still staying upright in the boat. I missed again.

"This is *your* power," Koolae reminded me. "You are a sister of Tigenan. Call the power to you."

I looked at the ball with a new determination. I lifted my hand and summoned the ball. *It* belonged to *me*, and *I* controlled *it*.

The power that answered my call was stronger than I expected. It surged into my body so swiftly that it awed and frightened me.

"Her readings just went off the charts!" AJ's voice said faintly in my ear.

"Tippin, what's going on?" the Captain wanted to know. She sounded worried.

"I'm going in to find her," Gig said. "This place is being hit by an earthquake."

"I don't think that's an earthquake, Gig," Marco said.

I could only gasp aloud as my power wrapped me in its haze of energy, and my nerve endings sizzled with electricity. It was impossible for me to move, or speak. I could only feel what was building inside of me. I knew I needed to release the power, but I didn't want to right away. I felt abuzz, I felt alive, I felt bigger than myself. Bigger than I'd ever been, and bigger than I ever thought I could be. It was so easy to harness this power; I'd never realized how easily it could be done...

"Alyvia!"

I jumped. Gig's voice echoed in my head and in my ears. I realized he was in the cave, and that Koolae's voice had stopped whispering in my ear.

"This is a sacred place," Koolae said loudly.

"I don't care," Gig said. "This is my teammate. What are you doing to her?"

"Nothing," Koolae said. "She is doing it herself."

"Then make her stop before she brings the whole mountain down, I don't want to be buried down here," Gig said. He called out, "Alyvia. Stop."

I sighed aloud and looked at Sen one last time. He sat on his side of the boat and grinned at me. His shoulders lifted.

"Are you ready to go home?" he asked.

I thought of home, where our mother and father slept, and of all the things that would happen tonight. How our father waited up for us as we drove up in the landcruiser, and how he would stop us as we tiptoed up the porch steps. I thought about all that happened after, and I shook my head as the familiar flare of pain surged in my chest. This was my peaceful place. Koolae had said not to go anywhere before or after. No, I was not ready to go home.

But I could give up for tonight and return to my body, and the cavern where Gig called my name. I released my hold on my power, and let it flow out of me like water through a leaky floorboard. It would be there when I needed it again.

I opened my eyes to the cave, and saw how pale and weary the light was compared to where I'd been. I turned my head and looked at Koolae. He smiled and bowed to me.

"Welcome, sister of Tigenan," he said. "You are reborn."

He kissed my cheek, then grinned and helped me to stand up. I felt wobbly, like it had been days since I last used my legs. With Koolae's help I turned to face Gig.

"What the hell was that?" he wanted to know, his face strange in the firelight.

"That was amazing, whatever it was," I said fuzzily. The drink Koolae's women had given me still worked its way through my pores, so that I felt compliant and lethargic. My nerve endings still tingled with heightened sensitivity, so that Koolae's arm around me and the blanket I clutched felt more significant than they should have. Flushed with warmth, I dropped the blanket as Koolae led me away from the fire. We passed Gig, and the four women fell in around us to guide our way out of the cave with the light of their candles.

As we walked, I hardly noticed the chill of the stone under my bare feet. I felt only the plain shift as it whispered against my skin, and Koolae's hand on my arm. The touches made me feel drowsy and aroused at the same time. It was confusing and wonderful.

We stepped into the light of the cavern, where the Tigenan people were spread out below us like they had been waiting for our arrival. Koolae led me to the edge of the shelf above them and spread his arms.

"The newest sister of Tigenan!" he shouted.

Cheers erupted, and applause from the men and women below. They grinned up at me, a sea of faces that yelled and hooted in congratulations. I grinned at them, and realized these were now my people. I'd been adopted by the Tigenans, a cave dwelling tribe that asked so little of me in return. They did not know how much the Order prized the object I was there to retrieve.

"To gift this new sister, we will allow her to take the artifact Brother Ignoracius left in our care," Koolae announced. "To gift us, Sister Tippin will bring the Order to our people and make us united. We will send our Tigenan children to their Academy, where we will learn to walk with the Order as equals."

The Tigenans cheered louder this time. Their voices echoed in my head in deafening waves. I clutched my hands to my ears and they laughed.

I reconsidered. Perhaps my bargain with the Tigenans was not a small favor at all. To them, it was a great feat.

"Let us celebrate this day!"

The Tigenans moved en masse back toward their ladders and scurried away to their caves to begin the preparations. Koolae took my arm and led me around the ring and back down to the base of the cavern.

"Perhaps we can begin melting this ice for you," he said.

We stopped at the edge of the abyss where Master Ignoracius' hull was buried. There was enough lingering drug in my system that I knew I could get the hull myself.

"I can do it," I said. Then I showed him.

He watched, eyes wide, as the ice swiftly melted into a chasm of water. From the water a grayed hull churned to the surface. It rose up into sight like a ghost from the abyss. It hovered there a second with water dripping from its surface, before it moved and was lain flat on the ground near our feet. Seeing our prize at last gave me a thrill of accomplishment. In my mind's eye, I saw Sen's face as he smiled at me. Then he turned his head to look over the edge of our rowboat.

I blinked and turned to smile in satisfaction at Koolae. Gig caught my eyes over Koolae's shoulder. He stood a few feet away and studied me with curiosity. Koolae tapped my wrist gently. It sent thrums up my arms and down my spine. I stood up straighter and focused on him again.

"You will go with my wives," he said. "They will dress you in the true finery of a Tigenan sister."

"Okay," I said. I sighted the women who waited for me a few steps away. I went to them and followed them back to Koolae's rooms. Before we stepped into our rooms, I glanced back and saw Koolae and Gig by the fire. Gig's eyes met mine and didn't look away. A thrill of desire pooled in me. The women collected me with arms around my waist and directed me back to our rooms. I took a deep breath and tried to collect myself.

That day, I fell in love with the Tigenan people.

Koolae's wives dressed me in some of the most beautiful ceremonial regalia I had ever seen. We feasted on a meal that was the most delicious food I had ever tasted. The Tigenans sang songs of celebration that I didn't understand, and they taught me their traditional dances, which circled the fire in dizzying patterns. I think I danced with every man and child there, except for Gig, who excused himself from the hoopla and simply watched from the sidelines.

I was presented with more gifts than I could count: A beaded necklace, a bone dagger, silken wraps, bolts of yarn, fur-lined boots, miniature rock carvings, unblemished crockery and pretty stones from the children. The rest were packed into carrying bags meant to return with me to the ship.

Each and every Tigenan welcomed me as their sister and embraced me in a firm hug. Hours later, I was weary and ready for a nap. Koolae's wives escorted back to my rooms and helped me undress. When they left, I sleepily crawled into the shelf that held the bed and made a happy sound when the warmth of the pillow touched my cheek. I dropped face first and made myself comfortable.

I heard Gig come in as my eyes drooped closed. I felt him take my arm and slide a shirt sleeve over it.

"You know what was amazing about tonight?" I asked him.

The bed dipped as he leaned over me and pulled a sleeve up my other arm. The fabric of the shirt whispered against my bare back.

"What?" he said quietly.

Sleep overcame me as I lay on my pillow, and I never answered him.

11

"They gave you all of this?" Marco asked, amazed. He sat on my bed and turned over some of the Tigenan gifts I'd laid out.

"I know, can you believe it?" I replied from where I stood beside him. I looked at all of the trinkets and shook my head. "Some of them are so beautiful. They just kept giving me things."

"Wow, I guess they were happy to have you join them."

"I would expect so," I said. "They know that I'm bringing the Order to them."

The morning after my ceremonial adoption by the Tigenans, I sat down with Koolae and had taken a list of all the things he wanted the Order to do for his people. Then the Captain put everything into motion. When I told Koolae an emissary ship was on its way, he clapped my shoulder happily and thanked me several times.

Then the Tigenans had helped me and Gig carry their gifts back to our landcruiser.

"Very soon, Tigenan children will be at the Academy learning alongside other members of the Order," I said to Koolae as we made the trek.

He smiled at me and nodded his head.

"I want to be kept up-to-date on the children," I said. "If they need aid or assistance, I might be able to help them in some small way."

"Of course," Koolae said. "The children will be very happy to report on their progress to you. You are their sponsor, and they love you, Sister Tippin."

"Good," I said.

The Tigenans who'd accompanied us back to the cruiser all said their goodbyes and each person gave me a hug, and Gig a nod. Koolae pressed a kiss to my forehead and bowed deeply to me. I caught Gig staring with a raised eyebrow. I made a face at him like *what do I do?* He just shrugged.

When we finally left them and returned to our ship, I'd had to debrief the Captain. She would debrief the Council while we made our trek back to Thredenar to talk with Master Ignoracius and find out where the next Starkiller artifact could be found.

"Marco, you should have seen them," I said. "The Tigenans all follow Koolae and live like one extended family down in this enormous cave underground. Can you imagine?"

"Well, that's how it feels in the Pilot's chair," he said. "I call it my 'cave.' And we all follow the Captain like a family."

"Does that make her our mom, and you our dad?" I joked.

Marco laughed.

"I prefer 'big brother' although," he said, "I am old enough to be your father."

I tried to picture him as a father. He would make an amazing dad. The type of dad I wish I'd had.

"You know, the Tigenans are just one of the trillions of races you will meet as a Merry Maid," he said. I could tell by the tone of his voice that he was about to tease me. "There are no limits to the different kinds of people you can get to know. This is the first time I've seen someone get adopted by a people, though. You're a real weirdo."

I grinned and looked down at the gifts laid out on my bed again. I picked up one at random – a charcoal sketch of sunset over the Tigenan mountains. I studied the lines closely, trying to see it the way an artist could. Drawing and sketching was a gift I admired in people—mostly because I couldn't do it. I took the drawing and set it on the night table beside my bed.

"I'm going to frame this," I said.

"It's beautiful," Marco agreed.

I looked at him, and plopped myself down at the head of the bed with my back against the wall.

"Can I tell you something, Marc?" I asked.

"Yeah, of course," he said.

"I almost feel sorry for the Tigenans."

"Why?" he wanted to know.

"Well, at first I was really skeptical. Like, who would want to live here?" I said. "And when I asked Koolae if I could become a sister of Tigenan, it was for the Starkiller hull, not because I felt a deep affection for the Tigenans."

"I'm sure Koolae was fully aware of that," Marco assured me.

"I know," I said. "But it is pretty obvious that I was getting more than I was giving. I wanted the hull, and Koolae wanted the Order's attention. I'm just not sure if Tigenan will benefit by being recognized in the Order. Their children are going to leave them and become starcrawlers like us, without a home. The Tigenans will see more outsiders come in, some of whom will not respect them. Some of whom will corrupt them and change them. And all because I had a mission to retrieve an artifact that the Order really, really wants."

Marco sighed.

"You can't take that burden onto yourself, Alyvia," he said. He reached out and smacked my arm. "I mean, you can never guess how you will influence others. You don't know if the Tigenans will have their lives ruined, or bettered by all of this."

I shrugged.

"I hear how you talk about them," he said. "You envy having a community like theirs. A family. But you're being pessimistic. The Tigenans could have all their dreams come true thanks to you. We just need to hope that is the case."

"I guess you're right," I conceded. "I don't have to look for the doom and gloom of the situation just yet."

"Exactly," Marco said.

"It's just that I feel responsible for them now," I admitted. "It's not every day that you become an adopted member of a foreign race."

Marco laughed.

"What was it like? The ritual, I mean. It seemed rather intense."

I remembered the cave where Koolae and his women had performed the ceremony.

"They drugged you with something?" Marco prompted.

"That's what AJ said when he was taking my readings and calling me a fool," I said. "It was one of those drugs that heightens the intensity of your senses. I was out of it and yet more aware at the same time, if that's possible."

"We heard you talking to Sen," Marco said.

"I know," I replied, surprised that no welling of uncomfortable panic rose in my chest. I tapped the side of my head. "He's still there, sitting in a rowboat with me, out on the lake near our home."

"That's amazing," Marco said. I paused to see if he was going to try and dig deeper but he smiled at me and shook his head.

"Come on, I think it's dinner time," he said. He got up and offered me a hand. I took it and let him help me to my feet. We left my room, and compared other tribes in the Order and whether they'd been negatively socialized. We found the others already seated at the table and waiting for us.

"Finally decided to join us, did you?" AJ asked when we came in.

"What's for sup?" Marco asked.

"Soup," AJ answered.

"We always have soup when you feed us," Gig grumbled at him. "How about taking out a cookbook and trying something new?"

"You don't have to eat it," AJ assured him.

"Boys, let's have a meal in peace, can we?" the Captain asked, sounding like a haggard mother.

AJ got up and served the table from his cook station. I watched as everyone received a bowl of soup and piece of bread.

Except me.

"What?" I asked. I glanced around at the food in front of everyone else, and then looked at my own plate dumbly, not sure what was happening. Instead of soup and bread, AJ had served me a meal replacement tablet.

"What the hell, Cason?" Gig said in his grumbly voice.

"I'm helping you," AJ said to me. "After all that rich food the Tigenans were pouring down your throat, you wouldn't want to gain too much weight, would you?"

My jaw dropped. I waited for him to say he was kidding but he didn't. He smirked at me and raised his eyebrows.

"You're disgusting," I told him. I was shocked at his nerve, and about to lose my temper.

"AJ!" the Captain scolded. "I can't believe you just did that."

"Alyvia, don't listen to him," Marco said. "He's just jealous that you're skinnier than he is."

AJ laughed.

"In fact, you're a little too thin," Marco continued. "You could use some extra meat on your bones."

"Hardly," AJ said with a snicker. "It's just a joke. Alyvia, give me your plate back, I have soup for you right here."

He nonchalantly picked up his ladle by the soup dish and stared at me. I was so mortified, I had no idea what to say. I knew my face was flushed with embarrassment. I don't think anyone else knew what to say either, the attack was so unexpected. I stared at my plate, suddenly far from hungry and unable to meet anyone's eyes.

"I think it's best if I went back to my room before I embarrass myself in front of the Captain," I heard myself say in a strained voice. Then I got up and left.

"Alyvia," Marco protested.

"She's really not good at taking a joke," I heard AJ say behind me. "Does the Academy train them out of having a sense of humor these days?"

I felt like turning back to strangle him, but I forced myself to hightail it back to my quarters. My heart wouldn't stop pounding in my chest.

I guess there was just no escaping my childhood. Fit or fat; women did not have a choice. We were expected to be fit for our husbands—at any cost. As a child, I had been put on a diet shortly after birth. On a few occasions I had been starved if my mother noticed extra fat around my tummy when I changed my clothes.

By contrast, the freedom I'd been given at the Academy to eat what I wanted had been confusing. I'd never lost that self-consciousness about my body but Stryker had helped me redefine my perceptions of "fat" versus "healthy." He had been extremely patient with his lessons, until I'd learned not to obsess over my weight so much. It had been a difficult belief to break.

Nonetheless, as soon as I got to my room I went straight to the mirror that hung in the hall between my bedroom and shower, and examined myself closely. I was wearing a simple undershirt that hugged my curves. Turning sideways the way AJ would see me, I squatted down as if I were sitting in a chair and analyzed myself again – trying to see my body from his point of view.

"I'm not getting fat," I muttered. I didn't sound convinced so I said it again more firmly. I was angry that he'd gotten to me.

I didn't think I looked different than the first day on board with the Merry Maids. I'd lost a ton of weight while I recovered from my poisoned knife wound, but it was starting to come back. I guess that's why AJ said I was fat?

What a jerk!

A knock sounded at my door. I whirled to look at it in surprise, then turned back to check my reflection in the mirror. My face was still a little flushed, but I looked okay. Figuring it was probably Marco coming back to check on me, I was shocked to open my door and see AJ standing there. He leaned against the door frame with his arms crossed.

"They made me come and fetch you back to the table," he said in a bored voice.

"Don't worry about it," I replied as my anger rose again. I clenched my hands into fists and stepped away from him. "I'll eat in my room tonight."

"That's what I told them, but they made me come anyway."

I narrowed my eyes at him.

"I guess you wasted your time."

He looked up at the ceiling.

"I don't know why," AJ agreed. "Can't you take a joke? Why does everyone jump to protect you the instant you pout about something?"

"They don't!" I said. My face grow hotter. "Why are you such a jerk?"

AJ stood upright and took a long look at me. He pretended he was hurt by what I'd said.

"Why do you dislike me so much?" he asked.

"You're an ass," I said immediately. "How dare you try to cut me down because of my body. You seriously rub me the wrong way."

Something changed in AJ's pale blue eyes. He grinned in what he must have thought was a seductive way.

"Well," he said, "I can rub you the right way, if you like."

He reached out to touch my right shoulder, so close I could feel his breath on my face.

"No!"

I jerked away from his touch so violently he froze where he was, his arm still outstretched as he stared at me in surprise.

"Get out!" I shouted, the panic obvious in my voice. I stared at him with wide eyes and heard my breath ratchet faster. A wave of nausea rose in my belly and swept up into my throat. I grabbed onto my desk to keep me steady.

AJ looked at me strangely, his expression replaced by puzzled seriousness.

"Alyvia," he said quietly. He threw his hands up to show me he meant no harm but he took another step closer, and started to say, "I was just..."

I felt his presence loom over me and panicked.

"Don't come near me," I begged. I stumbled away from him until the entire room was between us. I didn't stop until the far wall pressed against my back and held me up.

I didn't see AJ for a moment. I saw someone else—back when I was just a little girl with no one to protect me. Hot tears fell on my cheeks. I pressed my fingers over my eyes to hide them from AJ's gaze. I could hear my shallow breathing in the silence of the room, but I knew he was still there.

"Alyvia, I would never hurt you," he said. He sounded upset. "I was just..."

I shook my head. I knew it was him but I couldn't shake the need to run.

"Can you just go away?" I asked miserably. "The last thing I want to do is let you see me cry. Please?"

My voice broke, so I didn't say more.

"Okay, I'm going," he said. "I'm sorry. I didn't know."

He closed the door and left.

I let my wobbly legs give out. I slid to the floor, pulled my knees to my chest and rested my forehead on my knees.

Ugly sobs shook me for a minute as I felt shame and anger rush through me.

Out of all the people in the world—out of all the people on this ship—
why did I have a meltdown in front of AJ? Why couldn't it have been
someone, anyone, else? Marco, or Gig, or even my commanding officer, the
Captain. I would rather the Captain see my appalling dramatics than AJ. But
of course, none of those people could push my buttons the way AJ did.
This was the second time he'd riled me up until I broke. I hated myself for
letting him do it, and I hated him for doing it.

Why couldn't he just leave me alone?

It was hard enough for me to leave the comfort of the Academy, where
I had my friends and the structure of my training regime. I'd been forced to
chuck that comfort for the unknown of being a Merry Maid. My forehead
started to hurt from the strain of crying. I tried to get myself under control
as my brain started to remind me of Master Omin's threat. A sliver of fear
shot through me when I realized any of the crew could come to my room
right now and find me in pieces, and emotionally unfit. I wondered if AJ
would say something.

I wished there was someone I could talk and help calm my nerves. The
Captain would toss me from the ship if she saw me like this. Marco was
kind but he would probably share with the Captain if he thought she
needed to know I was a mess. And Gig was a little less weary of me but I'm
sure he was still more attached to Maddy than whether I could fit in with
the crew.

I needed a friend.

Not that it mattered. This was my job. I came here to work, not worry
about making friends. Still. I wished there was someone on the Merry
Maids team who understood me just now. I needed Cutter. He always made
me feel like I was in a safe place, and if there was something upsetting me, I
could come to him about it. He would give me a hug and some peace of
mind.

I wiped my face and sat up. I did some exercises in my room to loosen
tense muscles and keep myself limber. Then I did some telekinesis with
objects in my room, like the Tigenan gifts and my pillows and chairs.

Gig found me later, balanced upside down on both hands, feet pointed
straight up into the air while objects revolved around me.

"Come in," I'd called when he knocked and asked to come in. He saw
me and shook his head.

"I feel like I'm at the circus," he said.

"What's a circus?" I asked.

Gig made a face.

"You've never heard of the circus?" he asked. "Serious?"

"Serious," I said. "What is it?

"Ask me that the next time we go back to see my dad," he said. "I'll take you to see one."

"Okay," I said. I tried not to lose my concentration. I balanced on one arm, and shifted my other arm so I could stretch it up into the air. Then I separated my legs into the splits, still keeping every object balanced in the air and rotating around me.

Gig went to sit on the bed and watch.

"I came to talk to you," he said.

"About what?"

"AJ," Gig said.

I paused. All of the objects around me dipped mid-air. It took an amazing strength of will, but somehow I kept everything from crashing to the floor at the mention of AJ's name.

"Do we have to?" I asked. "I'd just forgotten all about him."

Gig's face looked dark.

"I want to know what happened," he said.

I looked at him upside down and saw that he wasn't going anywhere. I sighed in resignation, and sent all of the hovering objects back where they belonged. Then I straightened my body out and flipped over so that I was standing facing Gig. A second later, the blood rushed back out of my head and I dropped to the ground.

Gig shook his head at me.

"Alright, what do you want?" I said when I could. I held my head pressed between my hands.

"I just want to know what happened."

I stared up at my ceiling and massaged my temples.

"AJ came and said you guys had forced him to come after me," I said, unable to meet Gig's eyes. "I told him to buzz off."

"Well, I think you told him more than that," Gig said. "He came back to the table looking troubled, and wouldn't tell us what happened. He picked at his food for a minute, and then gave up and left. He told the Captain he was tired and wanted to go to his room."

Relief washed over me. AJ didn't tell them.

Gig paused and tried to catch my eye. I gave in and met his gaze. I tried to make my face blank so he couldn't read me but Gig didn't seem to buy it.

"I'm thinking you two exchanged words again, am I right?"

I shrugged.

Gig sighed.

"Can you just tell me what happened?" he asked patiently.

I swallowed.

"Why do you need to know?" I asked.

"I need to know so I can find out if AJ and I need to have another talk," Gig said flatly.

I stared at Gig in surprise. He looked dangerous and ready for a fight. His expression actually reminded me of a look I'd seen on Cutter's face a few times. It was a look that meant Cutter was about to get into a fight on my behalf—that protective older-brother look I hated to see because it meant I couldn't handle my own business.

I sat up and faced Gig squarely.

"No, I don't want you to get involved," I said firmly. "AJ and I had a small meltdown today, but I've realized that I just need to remove myself from his influence. He pushes all my buttons, and I let him manipulate me into feeling like I did when I was a kid. It has nothing to do with AJ at all. I appreciate that you're willing to step up for me, but it's not necessary. Okay?"

"If that's what you want," Gig said. "AJ is just about due for a good lesson on manners, but I can wait for a little while longer."

"Thanks, Gig," I said. I meant it. "You're stellar."

Gig didn't respond to my compliment.

"Have you two always had such a close relationship?" I asked.

I raised my eyebrows so he could see I was kidding. Gig looked like he wanted to say something truthful, but his frown smoothed out and the corners of his lips turned up a little.

"We're like brothers," he said. He almost managed to keep the sarcasm out of his voice. Almost.

I laughed and scooted across the floor so I could lean my back against the window. Gig shifted off the bed and sat on the floor so he could lean against my bed frame. I was surprised that he was interested in hanging out but I appreciated it.

"You know, there has only been one time since I've known AJ that he has actually acted like a human being," Gig said. "We'd been deployed to a backwater pisshole in the Outer Line, and he'd gone to land with us to offer Medical. We were cleaning up after a rebellion that had erupted near an orphanage. The way AJ acted with those little kids would make you do a one-eighty on how you feel about him, I promise you."

"Really?" I said. I tried to picture it.

"Honestly," Gig assured me. "He irritates me just about as much as he irritates you but I've found a way to live with him. He's on my squad; it's my duty to protect him."

I nodded.

"I came to a similar conclusion when I realized I need AJ for my health care," I admitted.

Gig's laughter rumbled in the room.

150

I stretched out my legs like Gig and looked down at my feet.

"So is that what being a Gunner boils down to?" I asked. "Protecting your squad?"

A corner of Gig's mouth lifted.

"Something like that," he said.

"Is that why you're trying to ease up any conflict with AJ?" I asked. "To protect your squad?"

Gig didn't laugh. He thought about it and stared out at the stars behind my head. I stared at his face, able to see there was more in his thoughts than just me and AJ.

My voice softened.

"Is that why you hated Maddy leaving?" I asked. "Because you couldn't keep your squad together?"

The question was out there and floating over our heads. I immediately regretted it but didn't take it back. Gig looked at me sharply. My face reflected in his eyes while he tried to find the words he was looking for.

He exhaled sharply, and shrugged.

"Maybe," he admitted finally. "That's probably the best way to describe it. It's not like she and I were ever…anything," he said. "But I thought…"

His voice trailed off.

"You thought she knew how you felt," I guessed.

Gig shut his mouth. He looked uncomfortable as he nodded slowly.

"But you never said anything," I said.

Gig shook his head no.

"And she never said anything when she left," I continued.

Gig said no.

"If she had said something, would you have gone with her?"

Gig looked away.

"Sorry, that was too personal," I said. "I shouldn't have asked it."

"No," Gig said, his brow furrowed. "No…"

His thoughts drifted away until he was lost in the stars. I kept silent and let him sort out his answer in peace.

I shifted uncomfortably; my rear was numb. I got up on my knees and grabbed the pillows from my bed. I handed him one to prop up his back. I rolled the second pillow and laid down on it so I could prop up my head and stare out at the stars from between my knees.

"I think that because I was so used to protecting her and watching out for her, that I started to feel like there was a deeper connection than there really was," he said. "But if she'd asked me? No, I wouldn't have gone with her."

"Unless she needed you," I said, only half teasing.

"She didn't need me," Gig agreed. "But the Captain, AJ and Marco needed me, and I knew the new Courier would need me, so I had to stay."

"I guess I proved that when I found a knife in my gut on the first mission," I said ruefully.

"Well, I couldn't protect you from that and it kills me to admit it," he said. "Then you ran off and started an earthquake in the second mission."

"An earthquake!" I craned my head to look up at him.

"That's why I came tearing into that cave where Koolae had you talking to your brother," he said.

I swallowed.

"The whole place was bucking and rumbling," he continued. "Rocks were dislodging overhead. We're lucky no one got hurt."

"I don't remember that part," I said faintly.

"Well, it was quite a show," he said, "and it figured you'd be right in the middle of it where I wasn't keeping an eye on you."

"I knew you'd be there if I needed you," I assured him.

"Yeah well, maybe you should learn not to count on me so much," he said. "Then maybe you'd wait until I was by your side before you jumped in feet first like that."

I smiled. Gig's protective nature reminded me an awful lot of Cutter. I was having inappropriate feelings of fondness for Gig that had nothing to do with him. Although Cutter and I had spent many nights sitting up and talking the way Gig and I were now.

"Gig," I said. "You spend all this time protecting us. Who protects you?"

Gig glanced down at me with an odd look on his face. He probably thought it was a weird question.

"I'm serious," I said. "Who do you rely on? We all rely on you now. Before I came here, I relied on Cutter and Stryker. Who do you rely on?"

The words were slow.

"The Captain, I guess," he said. "My dad. But mostly me."

I nodded.

"Your dad was nice," I said.

"He liked you, too," Gig assured me.

"What did he say?"

"If you want to know, you'll have to get him to tell you," he said. "I won't repeat it."

I laughed.

"If it's vulgar, I've heard it before," I said reasonably. "You don't have to be shy."

He didn't budge.

"I'm not shy," he said.

We sat in silence for a while, and just enjoyed the view.

Much later, Gig shook me awake and told me to get in my bed.

"Sorry, I dozed off," I said, half awake. I blinked at him in the quiet darkness and saw him grin.

"I did too," he said.

He picked up my pillows and tossed them on the bed for me. I followed the pillows and climbed under the covers. I was asleep again before he got out the door.

After that night, Gig and I were tighter. Also, I avoided AJ with such skill that I felt it deserved its own master's robes. If he came into the gym while I was working, I'd turn my back to him and finish up without acknowledging him. I didn't talk to him at meals, and he obliged by not speaking to me either. If we found each other in the same hallway, I passed him quickly, and ducked my head so our eyes wouldn't meet. Usually I just kept tabs on where I thought he would be and slipped through the halls to avoid his daily routine.

If Cutter could see me now, he'd raise his eyebrows and ask if I was playing the avoidance game. What he didn't seem to understand is that the avoidance game made it very easy to deal with my problems.

The only problem is that I think my avoidance game was beginning to trouble the rest of the crew.

"Are you okay?" Marco asked.

I glanced at him from where I sat on the Pilot's deck, snuggled up in my favorite chair.

"Yeah, why?" I asked.

"You seem like you've been tense lately," he said. "You know, since the other night at dinner."

I pretended like I didn't know what he was talking about.

"I can see Gig's talk with you about AJ didn't do anything to change your mind."

I remembered my scene with AJ and tried to keep the heat from my face. I looked everywhere but at Marco.

"About AJ?" I asked. "I just made a decision, that's all. I'll talk to AJ when I need a Medic."

Marco paused.

"Did he put his foot in it that bad when he came to your room to apologize?" he asked.

"When you *made* him come and apologize?" I corrected him. "Yes."

"I didn't make him do anything," Marco protested.

I gave him a look that said I didn't believe him.

"I didn't!" Marco said. "I simply encouraged him to quit being such an ass. And then the Captain ordered him to quit being such an ass. So he tried. Or…he was supposed to try."

He tried something, alright, I thought to myself.

"But what happened?" Marco asked. "He must have tried something on you again. Did he?"

I put my head in my hands and groaned.

"This isn't what I want to talk about," I said.

"Give it up, she wouldn't spill to me either," Gig said from the entranceway.

I knew they were both looking at me, but I refused to meet their eyes. I lifted my head and glanced at the dash.

"So, how much longer until we're back with Master Ignoracius?" I asked in an elegant attempt to change the subject.

Marco sighed, obviously wishing he could wring the truth from me.

"We'll be there in a few hours," he said.

I nodded, and resolutely stared out ahead at the stars. Gig gave up and found a chair.

"So what are we talking about?" he asked.

I darted my eyes toward Marco and tried to think up an interesting answer.

"The Drawer," he supplied. "Alyvia was just telling me she wanted another history lesson on the greatest band of all time."

I groaned and sunk low in my chair. I almost caved and dropped the charade. Marco grinned at me with a mischievous twinkle in his eye.

"Gig, weren't you saying something about doing another gym lesson today?" I asked hopefully.

I turned to look at him for the first time and saw that he was smiling, trying to decide whether to save me.

"Well…" he said. "It's actually getting close to arrival time. You shouldn't work *too* hard."

I made a betrayed face, and tried to think my way out of this one. If I was going down though, Gig was going with me.

"In that case, you shouldn't work out either," I said. "So we would love a lesson on the Drawer, Marco. Tell us how the Drawer can influence us even after all these years."

To our disbelief, Marco gave us a full debrief on how the Drawer could influence us for generations to come. It was such a long and drawn out oratory that I eventually tuned out and closed my eyes just to escape. The Captain saved us at about the time when I wanted to crawl back to my room.

"Hey, sorry to break up the fun," she said. "Marco and I have some system checks to do."

Gig and I were out of that room so fast, you would have thought there was a fire.

"Next time, I'll recommend working out," Gig assured me with a tortured expression.

"Thank you," I said, and breathed my own sigh of relief.

"Where are you going?" he asked. He had followed me through the door into the hallway.

"Gym," I said. "I feel like stretching."

"Need a partner?" he asked.

"Sure, if you want," I said. "I could use the help."

"Okay," he said. He followed me to the gym and we kicked off our shoes before going to the mat. Gig took a seat while I did some basic stretches and watched me move from stretch to stretch.

"How old were you when you realized you were good at movement?" he asked.

I glanced at him and saw he was asking seriously, so I paused to think.

Stryker had me training in everything before he found out what my strengths were. Movement was one of them. But...

"Seven," I said. "I was always running around climbing and tumbling, but I began formally training when I was seven."

"I think I was still learning to spell at seven," he joked. "I didn't have the discipline to begin formal training in anything."

"It wasn't my choice," I assured him. "I was just a party trick in training. I'm ready for you now."

Gig got up and came over. I lay down on my back and lifted my legs straight up with my arms stretched out from my sides. Kneeling down, Gig pushed my legs so that I was bent in half, my legs touching my chest. I relaxed into the stretch, and took deep breaths while I let my muscles re-accustom to their flexibility. After a nod from me, Gig took my right ankle and pushed it out to the side so I was doing a half split. I grunted as my hip flexors protested, but I eventually relaxed into this stretch as well.

Stretching with a partner looked awkward, and everyone in the Academy's gym who studied body movement had been embarrassed by the whistles and hoots. I had gotten used to it and it didn't really faze me anymore.

Of course, right when I thought that, AJ walked in. Gig saw me catch sight of him, and turned his head to look. I waited for AJ to say, "oh, am I interrupting something" in that sleazy way he was so good at. Even Gig tensed and shot AJ a glare. As we waited, AJ snapped his mouth shut, turned on his heel and walked out.

I frowned at AJ's weird behavior and saw that Gig's eyebrows were raised. Gig turned his head and stared at me, completely amazed. I gave him a look.

While Gig continued to stretch me out, I thought about AJ, and wondered if I'd gotten through to him or if he was just putting on a show while he cooked up a new way to torture me. Gig seemed to take AJ in stride. He shifted both my legs into splits, and pressed my inner thighs down toward the mat. My muscles stretched, aching back into the familiar pattern, and it felt so good.

"I've been missing these stretches," I said. "Without a trainer, I'm getting lazy."

"It's easy to forget the basics," he said. "Even for me. Neither of us are Masters, so we have to be disciplined about continuing our training."

"I wish Stryker could have come with me," I said. "He was ready to leave the Academy anyway. He could have been our trainer."

"But would he want to?" Gig asked.

"I don't know, it just occurred to me."

Gig was very close. I could smell his scent, all other thoughts suddenly floated away. I examined his full lips, straight nose and the darkness of his eyes. There was a little laugh line on the right side of his lips that I'd never noticed before. It was kind of sexy.

Gig noticed my stillness and paused to let up a bit.

"Am I hurting you?" he asked.

"No," I said a bit too quickly.

Gig did a few more stretches for me, then stood up.

"Are we done?" he asked.

"Yeah," I said, sitting up. "Thanks."

"You're welcome," he said, and left.

12

Hector Ignoracius waited at his door when we arrived.

"So, you got it," he said to me.

"Yes," the Captain answered for us. "Alyvia and Gig retrieved the hull from the Tigenans."

He didn't look pleased we'd found it, but I thought he might be impressed that we'd solved the puzzle on how.

"Then I have a new Sister to greet and welcome," he said. He stepped out of the doorway and motioned me forward. "The rest of you can wait on the ship."

I stopped in my tracks, one foot in and one foot outside his doorway. The rest of the Merry Maids, especially the Captain who was one of his friends, were obviously surprised.

"We have rituals to share," he said apologetically to the Captain.

She glanced from me to her friend and frowned.

"Fine," Captain Orvobedes said. "We'll wait for her return."

Gig opened his mouth to protest but the Captain took his arm and led him away. He glanced back and shot a dark look at Master Ignoracius. I didn't want to be left alone with him but if the Captain was okay with it, I figured I should suck it up.

I went into the hut and found a seat on his couch. Master Ignoracius came in and left the door open so sunlight could filter in pleasantly. It brought in with it the salty scent of the water.

I could hear the waves lap against the hut's framework below my feet.

"Care for something to drink?" he asked. He took a seat on the couch across from mine and gestured to a pitcher of lemonade and two glasses that sat on a low table between us. He'd obviously been waiting for me.

157

"Sure, that would be great," I said.

He poured my drink and handed it to me before pouring one for himself.

"Tell me what happened with Koolae," he said.

I began with our arrival on Tigenan and meeting Koolae, and ended with our celebratory farewell.

"Even now, the Order is flying some of the youngsters to the Academy," I said.

"So he finally took my advice and gave his list of demands," he said. "Glad to hear it."

"Why didn't you warn me before I went there that I would need to become one of them?" I asked, letting my irritation show.

"It was just a test," he said with a shrug. "I knew Koolae would never accept you unless he felt your spirit was strong. If he'd denied you, I would have known you were not meant to retrieve the Starkiller pieces."

"So am I going to find more missing information on my other trips?" I asked.

"The rest of the pieces aren't guarded, they're just hidden."

"Uh-huh," I said politely, because he was friends with the Captain.

He smiled at me crookedly.

"You got through it okay," he said. "You're a Tigenan now. The tools Koolae gave you in that cave can serve you for the rest of your life if you remember them. Do you remember what he showed you?"

I nodded and took a sip of my lemonade. It stung and I coughed.

"This isn't lemonade," I said as I choked.

"I didn't say it was," he reminded me. "Show me what Koolae taught you, I want to make sure."

I put the drink back on the table and then leaned back to close my eyes. I took several deep breaths. Then I relaxed and found my way back to Sen and our boat. He sat across from me and smiled. I relaxed even more as a feeling of peace and happiness stole over me. I looked up and saw an enormous globe of power above us. If I wanted to, I could summon it closer and touch it.

Cool fingers touched my cheek, and also the nape of my neck.

I looked down from the ball of power and saw that Master Ignoracius now sat next to me. He looked around with a pleasant look on his face. His presence crowded our little boat.

He saw me staring.

"I'm just taking a look," his voice said in my ear. "It's beautiful here."

I debated kicking him out but he smiled at Sen and it distracted me.

"This is where I grew up," I said. "That's my brother, Sen."

Master Ignoracius looked at Sen, but his eyes were drawn back to me.

"You were a beautiful child," he said. "You look to be eight or nine."

"I was ten," I said. "A very small ten."

"Your parents should have fed you more."

I made a face, like *I know.*

"Girls aren't supposed to get fat," I said. "I was put on a diet from birth to ensure marriageability. In reality my parents just didn't care much about me, so you're seeing the neglect."

He frowned, as they all do when I speak of my childhood.

"Sounds like Cayberra," he said.

"It was," I agreed. "If it weren't for the Order I'd probably be ready to birth my sixtieth kid or so by now."

Master Ignoracius' fingers loosed my skin, and he disappeared from my vision of the lake.

I opened my eyes and lifted my head to look at him now beside me. He put an arm around my shoulder and squeezed. It was a pity display of comfort.

"What were you afraid of, Master Ignoracius?" I asked quietly. "Why did you hide Starkiller all over space, like a treasure hunt?"

His eyes dropped but I saw the haunted look my question sparked.

"You're young, but you seem like you've seen much in your years," he said. "So I tell you this not to convince you I was right in doing what I did, but to perhaps make you understand.

"When I was a Captain, I obeyed everything the Order told me to do. Sometimes we were on the right side of the law, and sometimes we weren't. When I had concerns though, the Order would not hear me out or allay my fears at all. They were more interested in gathering power to them. They cared not at all that their people were doing things they did not want to do. They expected total surrender to their will. And if you go after power with no thought to whether you're doing right or wrong in the process, you cannot be trusted to use that power in the first place."

I thought about what he said. I was barely navigating the Order myself now.

"How do you know that you're the right person to make that decision?" I asked, my mouth dry.

Hector's face was bare of emotion.

"Because I wouldn't even trust myself with that much power," he said.

I looked down at my hands and uncomfortably thought of my childhood.

"I guess I know what you mean," I said. "I've seen a man with unchecked powers murder the people he was supposed to protect. He had men, women and children killed while they slept in their beds. And no one could stop him."

Hector looked very sad.

"Alyvia," he said. "I wish I could tell you the Order would be any different than that, but I cannot."

I looked at him and saw the weariness in his eyes. He was tired, and ill, and he didn't have the strength to fight anymore. He would not be able to fight the Order if they decided to take Starkiller and use it against enemies.

Could I?

I leaned forward and snagged my drink from the table. He watched as I took a long drink and stared at the fire. I wondered if Master Ignoracius wasn't right to keep Starkiller hidden from the Order after all these years. I just knew that the decision wasn't mine.

"So what else did he say?" the Captain asked.

We sat in her quarters, while I gave her a debrief from my time with Master Ignoracius. I leaned back and relaxed my head against the back of the couch. I was feeling sleepy from the alcohol he'd given me, and was looking forward to going to my bed as soon as possible.

"He told me that the more I practice the techniques that Koolae taught me, the better I'll become at them," I said. "Then he asked me to champion the Tigenans' re-introduction into the Order."

"He's quite attached to their people, isn't he?" the Captain remarked. She set down her tablet and leaned back in her chair too.

"There isn't much to dislike except the location," I said. "The Tigenans seemed like one big family."

"Maybe they are," she said.

"People who don't have one tend to like that," I said.

The Captain tilted her head in acknowledgement.

"Tell me again about the next assignment," she said.

"Corleu Minor," I said. "Mostly ocean with a few patches of land. Master Ignoracius said we'd never land a ship there where he hid the artifact because it's too rocky. So we have to swim or use a small water sit."

She looked up like her ceiling could tell her the answer to what she wondered about.

"We don't have any water sits," she said.

"Do we have any prop packs?" I asked.

"We might," she said. "Have Gig check for us."

"Aye."

"Hopefully there won't be any surprises this time," she said. "Although with Hector, you never know."

The Captain looked sad thinking about Master Ignoracius. She excused me to find Gig and have him check our inventory logs.

"I'll give Marco the new destination," she said, and followed me out.

I watched her leave, then tapped the hallway's nearest screen and found out Gig was in his room, a few steps away.

I rang at his door, and waited for him to answer but he didn't come until my second knock. When he opened the door, I realized why. He had his eyes half open and wore nothing but black briefs.

I stared at his muscles and tried to remember what I'd come for.

"I am so sorry, Gig," I managed. "I didn't realize it was so late. I didn't mean to wake you."

Gig rubbed at his eyes and grunted something.

"Go back to sleep," I said. "We can talk in the morning."

I tried to make my escape, but Gig caught my arm and made me stop.

"Don't be ridiculous," he grumbled. "Get in here."

Then he melted back into the darkness of his room. I hesitated for a second and wondered if I could still wander off but I took a breath and went in, then closed the door behind me.

Gig flipped on a low light by his bed and crawled back under his covers with a tablet in hand. He propped himself against the wall and wiped his eyes. I took a look around, and realized I'd never been in here before. His room reminded me of his dad's weapon closet. Gig had an entire wall full of weaponry to the right of the doorway. Some of it looked like it was for show, but other pieces looked like they'd been used recently.

It also looked like part of the gym had been moved in here. He didn't have a desk like I did. There was no place for me to sit except on the foot of Gig's bed, so that's where I perched.

"How'd it go with Master Ignoracius?" he asked. He leaned against his pillow, with his bare chest still in view. I forced my eyes to his but he wasn't looking at me.

"Great," I said. "We have our next destination, which Marco is probably plotting right now. The Captain wanted me to ask you if we have the supplies we'll need."

"Where are we going?"

"Corleu Minor," I said.

"Never heard of it."

"That's probably why Hector hid something there," I said. "We'll have to research the area like we did with Tigenan."

Gig nodded.

"So what's the problem?" he asked.

"It's all water," I said. "Rocky water. Hector said we would need to swim or ride a water sit."

Gig frowned.

"We don't have any water sits," he said.

"I know, that's why Cap wanted me to ask you about it."

Gig tapped at the inventory list on his tablet. I waited while he yawned and surveyed the list.

"Do we have any prop packs?" I asked.

"Yes, but they aren't long range," he said. "If we have to go far we'll probably end up swimming and unable to get back quickly."

I thought about it.

"Well, we could save them until the return trip and swim first," I said. "I'm not a strong swimmer but if the water is mild I could probably do it."

"Or we could convince the Captain to stop and pick up a water sit," he said.

I shrugged. A whiff of the alcohol from Hector's hut hit my nose. I glanced at Gig to see if he smelled it too but he didn't say anything. I needed to escape and take a shower before he noticed. I didn't want his opinion of me to go back to my first day on the ship.

"If she'll do that then we don't have a problem," I said, "but she didn't suggest it."

"She probably doesn't want to stop in a little port where we'd be remembered."

"I'll ask her," I offered and got up to leave. I would ask her in the morning, after I showered.

"Hang on," Gig said. I turned back to face him, caught.

"What?"

"Sit down," he said.

I obeyed and tried to keep my face neutral.

"Tell me what happened with Master Ignoracius. Or 'Hector' as you're now calling him."

"Why?" I asked, wary of his tone.

"I want to know what happened and why he couldn't talk to you in front of the rest of us," Gig said.

"Oh," I said, and adjusted my mental gears. "Well, he really wanted to talk about Koolae, and my initiation into the Tigenan world. He'd been through it before, you know? And I guess he was actually a good friend of Koolae's before he left."

"That would explain why Koolae was so loyal to him," Gig said.

"*Hector* also told me that Koolae was a test," I said. "Koolae would have denied my request to become a Tigenan sister if he didn't think I was strong enough in spirit. The fact that I passed this test means Hector feels he can trust me to find the Starkiller's other missing pieces."

"*He* is testing *us?*" Gig said. "Who does he think he is?"

I looked down at his hands and saw they were clenched around the tablet. I frowned at him and tried to figure out why he was so tightly wound.

"I would say a disenfranchised individual with fears of what Starkiller might become when the Order has it," I said. "Hector doesn't trust putting that much power in their already powerful hands."

Gig's eyes flicked to mine.

"He fears the Order would use Starkiller to harm?"

"Why not?" I asked seriously. "What would stop them *if* they are corrupt?"

Gig frowned.

"We elect a team of leaders so that their powers will balance for the good of all," he said.

I shrugged, thinking of Master Omin's threats.

"Alyvia," Gig said. His deep voice rolled over me. He sat up and leaned closer. "Do you know how dangerous it is to follow in Hector's footsteps? Look where he ended up."

"Are you worried I'll turn anarchist?" I asked. "Relax, Gig. I owe more to the Order than that."

I left him there, and told him to go back to sleep. As I let myself out of his room, I heard a noise to my left. AJ stared at me from a few paces away. He'd obviously just come from the Medlab, and paused when he saw me. His face was unreadable.

I turned away from him quickly and went to my own room without saying a word. He was another person I didn't want to smell the alcohol in my pores. I hightailed it to my shower immediately.

Crawling into bed later, I thought of Master Omin and Master Ignoracius. Two sides of the same coin. Their faces followed me into my dreams.

"We found a station where they are selling water sits," the Captain said. "If we're fast about it, we can stop and pick up two."

"Great, I'll go," Gig said.

"Yes, and take Alyvia with you, please," the Captain said. "I don't want you to look like a Gunner picking up supplies. I want you go look like a couple heading off on a holiday. The rest of us will stay aboard ship."

I looked at Gig, one eyebrow raised and caught the ghost of a smile.

We were sitting at breakfast, munching on eggs and toast. Only Marco was missing; he was docking us to the station, I learned.

"That should make our mission on Corleu Minor easier," I said.

"Just don't go crazy and bring back things we don't need, like skis and rafts," the Captain said. "Alyvia, I expect you to keep Gig in check. He's been known to veer from the list."

163

I gave her a mock salute.

"Aye," I said.

"I thought you said Corleu Minor was a water planet," AJ said. "We could use those skis and rafts for a mini-vacation. I need a tan."

"You certainly do," the Captain said, "but the Order won't be giving us vacations until we find all of the missing Starkiller pieces."

AJ groaned.

"We're docking," Marco announced over the intercom.

"Okay you two," the Captain said to Gig and I. "You have ten minutes to look less formal, and more civilian."

I got up immediately and went straight to my quarters, Gig right behind on the way to his own. In a flurry I pulled off my clothes and tossed them on my bed. I dug through my drawers and pulled out clothes from my casual days at the Academy when jeans and a simple black tunic were my daily wear. I also had a pair of pink flip flops that Cutter had given me for some reason.

Gig was faster. He knocked at my door as I was sliding my feet into the sandals. I opened the door and examined his clothes while his eyes skimmed over me. He had put on a pair of dark blue warm-up pants and a sleeveless blue shirt that bared his muscular arms.

"Take down your hair," he said.

I turned away from him and went to my mirror to tug out the pins and barrettes that held my hair up in a bun. Once my hair was loose, I brushed it quickly until it fell in waves down my back.

"Do you have any other shoes?" I asked his reflection in the mirror. Gig looked down at his regulation black boots and made a face.

"What's wrong with them?" he asked.

"They look like something you'd wear on Tigenan, not on Corleu Minor," I said.

He considered my sandals.

"Actually, Marco has some shoes I can borrow," he said. He left my room to find them.

Meeting up again in the dock, I saw that he had indeed found a pair of black flip flops.

"Perfect," I said. If I were going to the beach with my boyfriend, I wouldn't mind if he looked like Gig.

"Good, let's go."

He opened the hatch doorway that was connected to the docking station. It led through a narrow hallway that accessed the transporter. I closed the hatch behind us and followed Gig through.

"Let me do all the haggling," he said, his tone reminding me of Cutter. "You can just stare at me adoringly."

I rolled my eyes and stepped onto the transporter after him. Gig tapped at the main menu and searched for the station's supply shop. Around us, the station's engines hummed through the walls.

"You're going on vacation with *me*," I said in a sassy voice. "So you should be staring at *me* adoringly."

"What is our story? Honeymoon trip?"

"I don't have a ring," I said. "Maybe just a holiday. All we have to do is hold hands and they probably won't ask any questions."

Gig nodded, then hit a short series of buttons and pressed enter. We lurched up immediately. The platform practically flew as we whistled higher and higher on our transporter. I looked up as we went, and watched an endless row of levels flash by in blinks of light. My hair streamed in my face from the wind, so I wrapped my hand around it, pulled it over my shoulder and held it there.

"How did we meet?" Gig asked as our transporter slowed slightly, then shifted sideways to arc around the station until we reached the correct section.

I thought about it.

"We met shipboard," I said. "If anyone asks what our stations are, I've forbidden us from talking about work, so we just won't talk about it."

Gig grinned.

"You've forbidden it? What are you, the one that wears the pants in this relationship?"

"Well, obviously," I said, and smiled.

Gig's face changed. He moved closer, so that he was directly in front of me. He leaned forward and rested his hands on the handholds at either side of my hips so that his face was very, very close to mine. My heart started beating a triple time in my chest, and I felt my breath come faster. I tilted my head up and saw the sudden mischief in his eyes.

"Put your arms around my neck if you want this to look real," he said.

I obeyed. I understood what he was doing—and did not mind at all. My fingers started a trail through his hair and I let my nails work lightly over his scalp. He closed his eyes and hummed, and leaned closer.

Gig's breath was hot on my neck. I breathed in his scent, and rested my forehead on his shoulder. Then we waited.

"Sometimes, I have the best job," I heard him murmur softly in my ear.

I grinned foolishly.

Our transporter lurched to a sudden stop, nearly toppling us to the floor. Gig stood up straighter and shifted to look around, in the perfect imitation of bewilderment.

"Let me guess, newlyweds?" a male voice said from over his shoulder.

I released Gig from my arms and made a show of tugging my tunic lower, as Gig turned to face the shopkeeper.

"Not yet," Gig said, and glanced back at me with a huge grin.

I smiled at him, and ran a hand through my hair, as if it was mussed. Then I glanced at our shopkeeper.

"Hi," I said, pushing embarrassment into my voice.

The shopkeeper smiled at us with hands buried in the pockets of his apron. He was probably in his thirties or so, with super-blond hair, sparkling eyes and extraordinarily white teeth.

"Well come on in, and let me see if I can't help you find what you need," he said smoothly. "The sooner we get you two out of here, the sooner you can...go about your business."

He winked at me.

Gig took my hand, and helped me step off the transporter and into the shop. I held onto it tightly, and felt the roughness of his skin against my palm. I pressed myself against his side, and kept my head ducked as if I were a shy young woman in love. I wanted to laugh.

"So what are you looking for, friend?" the shopkeeper asked Gig.

"Well, we're heading for a place with lots of beaches and water," Gig said. "I told my girl, here, that if we took water sits out into the ocean, we could anchor them together and dive down to see the water animals."

"Water sits?" the shopkeeper said. "Wouldn't you rather have a prop boat or something?"

"No, we need something small and easily transportable for our...small steerage," Gig said. "Do you have any sits available?"

"Just one, I'm afraid," the shopkeeper said. "If you want it, I can give you a bargain for it. Sits just aren't popular anymore. And you can ride it out on the water together, like a piggyback. Much more romantic."

"That sounds great," Gig said. "Don't you think, darling?"

I looked up at Gig and nodded happily.

"Now I don't have to learn how to drive one of those thingies," I said. I twirled the ends of my hair around my fingers. Gig raised an eyebrow as he watched my act. "Can we get it?"

"Well, we need to discuss this bargain price," Gig said, and looked back to the shopkeeper. "What kind of bargain are we talking about?"

"Come with me," the shopkeeper said. "Let's take a look at what I've got."

We followed him to the back corner of his shop, where he kept his watersport equipment. The water sit he had in stock was mounted from the ceiling.

"It's got a beautiful new paint job," the shopkeeper said. "Do you like it?

"How much power does it have?" Gig asked.

"Why is that important?" I asked. "We aren't going to be racing anyone, are we?"

"No, but we have to make sure it can carry two of us," Gig reasoned patiently.

I remembered my fight with AJ and pulled away from him with an outraged gasp.

"What are you saying," I demanded. "That I'm too heavy for this thing to carry me?"

Gig blinked at me in surprise.

The shopkeeper chuckled.

I had a hard time keeping a straight face.

"Of course he's not implying that, sweetie," he said. "What your man is trying to say, is that he doesn't want to risk your lovely skin in case this water sit breaks down and leaves you both stranded on the water."

"But it won't break down, will it?" I asked the shopkeeper. "You're like the best shop in this part of the galaxy. No one has ever complained about your products. I asked *all* my friends."

The shopkeeper shrugged, but looked pleased.

"Well," he said, and smiled at me.

I smiled back and tilted my head to the side.

Gig was not smiling.

"Ahem," he said. "Why don't you go back and wait by the counter, darling? You're probably exhausted from our trip so far. Let me take care of this for us."

I threw my arms around his neck and kissed cheek. A second later, the blood rushed to my face as I realized what I'd just done. I felt the surprise ripple through his shoulders.

"I'll be waiting," I managed. Then I let him go, and made my escape back to the main part of the shop. I glanced back once at the shopkeeper, and saw him wink at me brazenly.

I wanted to laugh, but I managed to keep quiet. Did I just kiss Gig's face?

I shook my head. I must be crazy.

They found me perched on the counter when they were done haggling, and came to find me.

"It was good doing business with you two," the shopkeeper said, and smiled at me again. "I hope you'll come back and find me again after your vacation if you find that you won't be needing a water sit anymore."

"Well isn't that sweet of you?" I asked, and pressed a hand to my heart.

Gig came over and lifted me down from the counter by my waist. I put my arm around him as he settled his arm around my shoulder.

"Let's go back to the ship and...plot our course," Gig suggested. I stared up at him adoringly, and hoped that I wasn't overdoing it. He looked down into my eyes and then his gaze traveled lower to my lips. I felt a flush come over my face that was not faked. All thoughts suddenly shut up as I held his gaze with mine.

"We'll deliver your water sit there in a few moments," the shopkeeper interrupted. "Discreetly. You won't even know we're there."

Gig nodded at him. As soon as his gaze left mine I was able to think again.

"Thanks," he said.

"Thanks!" I chirped.

We turned away and stepped onto the transporter. I smiled and waved to the shopkeeper as Gig pressed the keys on the touchpad and sent us skidding away.

I grinned at him as we flew back to the ship.

"I can't believe that worked," Gig grumbled, shaking his head at me. "The guy *winked* at you. He practically gave us that sit for free."

I shrugged.

"He wanted to make us happy," I said reasonably. "When he saw I was temperamental, he *had* to give you a good deal on the water sit, or else your vacation might have been a nightmare."

The corners of his lips turned up.

"You are something else," he said.

I took that as a compliment, and said thanks.

As we approached Corleu Minor, I sat beside Marco in the Pilot's deck, and watched the planet dwarf our little ship.

"I love water," I said. "Swimming makes me happy."

"Did you grow up where there's a lot of water?" he asked.

"No, not really," I said. "There was a lake nearby, but that's it. I didn't see the ocean until Stryker took me to competitions. I didn't want to leave the water."

"And now you'll be spending all day in the water," he said. "We're going to have to drag you out, aren't we?"

"Yup," I said. I played with the zipper to my water suit as I slouched in my chair. I liked the sound as I unzipped it from my neck to my waist, and then zipped it back up again. I was wearing a bikini underneath, but no water socks. I would be going barefoot on this mission.

"I hate the water," Marco said. "I can never stay above the surface."

"You don't know how to swim?" I asked, amazed. "Marco, it's so fun."

"I guess I'll never know," he said. "Pools are more my thing. And...tubs."

I rolled my eyes.

"You need to get out more, man," I teased.

"That's probably true," he agreed.

"Where are we?" Gig asked. He came in to stand between our chairs. I looked up at him to say hi, and realized he too was dressed in his water suit but his wasn't fully on. He hadn't put his arms into the sleeves yet, so the top half of his suit hung around his waist, and left his muscular bare chest available for viewing.

I smiled at him and then turned back to the viewer so he wouldn't think I was ogling his body. The skin on my arms had goose bumps though, and I fought the urge to turn back and look.

"Gig, you're naked," Marco said dryly.

"And?" Gig said.

"Just thought you should know," Marco said. "Anyway, we're pretty close. I'll notify the Captain so she can see you off. You two should begin preparing yourselves."

"Alright," I said. "Thanks."

Gig and I left him to bring the ship into Corleu Minor's atmosphere. We found the Captain sitting at the dining table, reviewing records on a tablet. She waved us over when she saw us come in and set aside her tablet.

"Both of you are clear on this mission?" she asked.

"Yes, Captain," Gig said. "We know what we have to do."

"Good," she said. "Let's make this an uneventful mission, shall we?"

I nodded, and saw that Gig did the same.

The Captain got up and went with us out to the dock, where we'd left the water sit tethered. A pack sat on the floor next to the sit, already zipped and ready to go.

"What did you pack?" the Captain asked.

"Flashlights, flares, breathers, explosives, water and an inflatable raft," Gig said. "Oh, and a cask for the device."

"Hector said today's item is the power supply," I said. "So Gig and I built something makeshift to hold it until you pick us up again."

"Good," the Captain said. She crossed her arms over her chest and looked at the water sit critically.

"You checked this thing from top to bottom?" she asked Gig. "It looks a little too clean if you know what I mean."

"It doesn't have any mechanical problems," Gig said. "I checked everything. She'll get us there and back."

"It had better," she said, and winked at me.

We shifted as the ship bucked a little under our feet.

"Oh good, we're in atmo," she said.

I followed her to the windows of the bay doors, where we could see that

Marco had begun steering us lower and lower. Corleu Minor's waters spread out below us, like a shifting blue blanket of light. I grinned in excitement.

According to the research I'd done with Gig, Corleu Minor had never been settled, because there weren't enough places for ships to land. The climate was very dangerous during the rainy season, when tsunamis were common and had such strength they could travel the entire length of the globe. And rainy season, it turned out, was the majority of the time.

But the water would be warm, I'd learned, and there wouldn't be any scary sea monsters where we would be.

"Try not to enjoy yourself too much," the Captain said when she saw my face. "You ARE working, remember?"

I laughed and shrugged.

"Come on Gig, get that thing over here," she said over her shoulder as Marco announced over the comm our arrival at the drop-off point.

I went and grabbed the pack while the Captain opened the bay door and Gig started pushing the water sit to the edge. The salty scent of ocean immediately filled the room, along with the sound of the water moving below. I took in a deep breath until the smell filled my lungs to capacity.

As I walked the lip of the ship, I watched as the water below us came into diving distance. I slid my arms through the pack and snapped its belt around my waist. I stepped right up to the edge and took a couple deep breaths.

"Alyvia," I heard Gig begin to say.

It was too late. I dipped a little, and leapt. Air streamed over my face and hair as I fell. I tucked and rotated, and then my body sliced into the water with hardly a splash. The perfect dive.

The water felt good against my skin. I paused for a second underwater when my momentum gave out, and savored the feeling of peace. Then I kicked to the surface to see if Gig was coming.

When my head popped up above the water, I looked around and saw Gig and the Captain still standing on the ship's deck. They watched to see where I'd surface. As soon as they sighted me, the captain shook her head.

"Show off," Gig called out.

He pushed the water sit over the edge, so that it landed in the water nearby. Then he jumped in the water after it, purposefully splashing me.

I laughed and glanced back at the captain. When Gig surfaced next to the sit, she said, "try to stay out of trouble, okay? Comm us when you're ready for pickup."

I waved to her as she closed the bay door, and Gig and I treaded water as we watched the ship fly away.

Gig used the sit to pull himself out of the water. I paddled over and took his hand so he could pull me up behind him. Once I was settled with my body tucked up against his, he revved the sit into life. I put on my sun goggles and saw Gig already wore his. Then we were off, speeding through the water at breakneck speed. I wrapped my arms around Gig's waist to hold on, and tilted my head away so I could feel the full force of the wind against my face as we whipped over the water. With the sun pounding down on us from a cloudless blue sky, the water on my arms and legs dried quickly.

Gig had accessed the water sit's navigation system and projected it ahead of us. It glowed transparently so that he could still see where he was going, but it guided us with Hector's directions. I glanced at it occasionally, to see our progress as we zipped across the water. We quickly fled the drop-off point, and one of only a few places on Corleu Minor where there was an open stretch of sea. Ahead of us was the real Corleu Minor; rocky outcroppings stretched up from the water like bony fingers. Gig slowed as we approached them. We would have to weave around them carefully and not scrape our sit against any of the rocks. Some of the rocky towers we passed peaked in jagged points. Others were more rounded, and funneled open to emit steam. When we passed these, the water and air around us felt warmer.

"It's hotter here," Gig shouted over his shoulder so I could hear him. "I hope Ignoracius isn't trying to send us up one of those."

I nodded in agreement. With Hector we had no assurances.

I breathed in the smell of ocean, and snuggled closer to Gig to rest my head against his back. I closed my eyes against the sun and let it warm my face.

There wasn't much time to relax before Gig slowed the sit to a stop. We bobbed on the water in silence as the sit's engine grumbled below us. I opened my eyes and looked around.

"Look over there," Gig said, and pointed to our left.

My eyes scanned the rocks around us before I sighted something moving in the water a distance away. I squinted at it and stood up on the sit, holding Gig's shoulders for balance.

Silvery bodies were surging just under the surface of the water, probably six or seven in all. They rounded an outcropping of rock, disappeared from view for a second, and then appeared on the other side.

In a flash, I remembered an entry in the research I'd done on Corleu Minor.

"Cleos!" I said in delight. "They're kind of like dolphins."

"Are they friendly?"

"I think so," I said. "I read that no one has ever had any problems with them because they tend to shy from visitors."

"Good," Gig said. "Let's keep going."

I sat down and put my arms around Gig's waist as he sped off again, and tried to watch the cleos as they swam. The cleos didn't seem interested in us, but I hoped to catch a better look before we left.

When I checked the navigation over Gig's shoulder, I saw that we were approaching Hector's coordinates. Gig slowed the water sit as we came closer, until we were faced with a monstrous rock outcropping that dwarfed all of the others we'd seen so far.

"This is it," he said. He stopped the sit and shut down the engine. I pulled off the pack and unzipped it to search for the two breathers we'd brought along. I handed him one and put the other in my mouth. Then I zipped the pack again and kicked away from the sit to land in the water with a splash. Gig stood up on the sit, and then stepped into the water with no preamble. He surfaced nearby and began to kick toward the rocks. I looped the pack around my shoulders again and followed him.

When we were close enough, Gig stopped and motioned downward. He ducked down below the surface and kicked himself lower. I dove underwater too, and felt the pack resist as I swam lower. My goggles were tight against my face but I didn't bother to adjust them. We followed the rocks as they curved down toward the ocean floor. Gig had a water light that he used to scan for openings. As we swam lower, the light from above dimmed. I focused on the light Gig was using, and kept swimming lower and lower.

We found the entrance finally, a jagged crevice in the wall the width of a man. Gig paused there, and waited for me. Face to face, he made quick motions with his hands. I nodded. He wanted me to wait while he went in. He would flash his light when it was my turn to come up. He squeezed into the hole and kicked upward into the spire of rock. I peered in after him so I could watch his light retreat higher and higher inside the rock wall. The darkness of the ocean closed in around me the further he went. I glanced behind me and saw some sunlight still filter through the water far above. I turned back to the rocks and peered up at Gig. He was still swimming.

I sighed and tried to stay patient.

Finally, I saw the sign from Gig. I kicked my way up quickly and aimed straight for the light he shown down for me. The tunnel up wasn't very wide. Every now and then my kicking feet accidentally came into contact with the rock. When I neared the surface, I felt Gig's hand pull at mine and help me the rest of the way to the surface.

As my head came up above water, and I cleared my eyes, I realized what a tight fit it was. With both of us trying to tread water our hands and feet would occasionally collide. Gig had pushed his goggles up to rest on his head.

"Look," he said. He pointed his light straight up. I followed its beam and groaned aloud. I pulled my goggles down around my neck and stared. There was a rock shelf above us, still ten meters above, and nothing but the rocks to climb in order to get there.

"So Hector got us again," Gig grumbled, looking annoyed.

"He said..." I began, but stopped. My disappointment choked the words back.

Gig looked down at my face when he heard my voice drop away. The space between us was nonexistent as I bumped into him again.

He touched my chin.

"Don't frown," he said gently. His foot accidentally kicked mine.

I looked away, unable to hide how unhappy I was that Hector had let me down. Gig looped an arm my waist and pulled me closer.

"This isn't working," he said as I accidentally kicked him this time. "Hold on to me."

I wrapped my arms around his neck, and circled my legs around his waist to let him tread water for the both of us. His body was deliciously warm against mine.

"Well, once again, Hector fails to mention an important part of getting an artifact," I said. "I thought we'd be able to trust him this time."

"We need to find a way up there," Gig said. "I'm not sure I'm flexible enough to shimmy up those rocks."

I sighed.

"Let me see again," I said.

Gig lifted the water light and let me see the rocks that led up to the shelf where the artifact was probably hidden. I judged the distance up and the quality of the rocks.

"I can do it," I said after a second. "I can use my tele to help."

Gig didn't reply right away. I looked away from the rocks to see his face, which was only a few inches from mine. There was something unreadable in his eyes that I didn't recognize.

"What?" I asked. A shiver ran down my spine. Gig felt my body quake against his. His eyes were molten as he ran a hand down my side in a caress.

He swallowed so hard I could see his adam's apple bob. He loosed a breath, then said, "go ahead. When you're up there, light the flares and tell me what you see."

Unsettled, but not sure how to ask what I wanted to know, I nodded. Gig loosed me to find my way up the wall. He backed away to give me some space.

With the pack still on my back, I reached out and grabbed hold of the rocks nearest to us. I focused on what I needed to do, and bobbed in the water for a second while I planned. Once I figured it out, I kicked up and away from the wall with a surge of effort and used my tele to pull myself higher and higher. I grabbed on to rocks on one side of the wall and used my tele to propel my body across the divide, then kicked away and pushed off from the other wall. The momentum helped me shimmy my way higher and higher until I made it all the way up.

Once I reached the ledge at the top, I collapsed to my hands and knees to try and catch my breath from the exertion. I flopped over onto my back and allowed myself to catch my breath and relax.

"You okay?" Gig asked from below. The sound of his treading water paused as he waited for my answer.

"Yeah," I said. I tried to ignore the sound of blood pounding through my head. My hands ached and shook, and so did my bare feet. I lifted my hands up to my face so I could take a look, and realized they were scratched and bleeding. The rocks were sharper than I'd realized, and I'd flayed myself pretty good.

I dropped my arms at my sides again and turned my head to look around for the first time. What I saw made me sit up and utter the most heartfelt curse I'd ever thought up. I ripped my goggles off from around my neck and pelted them at the nearby wall.

"Now what?" Gig wanted to know. His voice sounded edgy.

I groaned, and turned away in disgust so I could peer over the ledge. Gig still tread water below, his face turned up to mine. I snagged the pack and pulled it open so I could take out a length of rope.

"You are not going to believe this," I said.

"It's another one of Ignoracius' tricks," he guessed immediately.

I sighed. I found a place to secure the rope on my end, and then tossed the free end down to him.

"Come on up and take a look for yourself," I said. "Take your time, we'll probably be here for a while."

Despite my warning, Gig practically flew up the rope. He pulled himself up onto the ledge just a few moments later. I stared at him with an impressed look on my face. That had to have been some type of rope climbing record. I sat on the ledge with my legs dangling over the edge, as he took one look and repeated the curse he'd heard me use.

He dropped into a crouch and shook his head.

"Unbelievable," he muttered. "This is just unbelievable."

"We should comm the Captain and tell her to get comfortable," I said.

Gig took the pack and rummaged through it to find our waterproof case that had the commlink in it. He pulled it out and explained the situation to the Captain, who seemed disappointed at our news. When they closed the communication, Gig sat down on the ledge beside me. He looked pretty peeved.

"So what do we do now?" I asked.

"Keep each other company," he said. "Get comfortable."

I examined my hands again. Jagged crisscrossed ribbons of red lined my palms and fingers. The blood was dotting up in places where the cut refused to close. The cuts stung but they weren't painful.

Gig leaned over to take a look.

"We'll have AJ fix you up when we get back to the ship," he said.

I nodded, even though I had no intention of going to AJ. I planned to hit up the Medlab when he wasn't there.

I was really thinking about Hector and how annoying it was to be duped. There had been something genuine about Hector that I had trusted. I glanced back behind me, still feeling disbelief.

The ledge we were sitting on extended above us like an upside down cone. In the dead center of the ledge, a perfect circle had been cut that descended straight down into the rock.

Hector had told us that this "well" was where he'd hidden Starkiller's power supply. He said it would be floating in the center of this well, encased by a box of Cyline metal. The Cyline could be detonated off of the power supply, but it was extremely flammable, so the entire thing needed to be dunked immediately back into the water.

What Hector did NOT tell us was that the well could only be visited at certain times of day, when the tide was high enough to reach the top of the well. Gig and I had come too early, and now had to wait until the water rose. It was just another frustrating omission that we were beginning to expect from him.

Gig pushed my arm playfully.

"Don't be mad at yourself," he said. "Wanting to trust someone is not a fault. We both just have to keep in mind that this man is not happy about letting Starkiller's pieces be found. We may have to deal with these stupid delays, but at least he's not leading us on a wild chase."

"Which doesn't mean he *couldn't* lead us on a wild chase," I reminded him. "I don't know why I trusted him this time, I really don't."

"It's okay," Gig said. He hooked an arm around my neck and dragged me into a half-hug. "We can just relax for a while, or go swimming and come back. What do you want to do?"

I thought about it, and tried to let the frustration go. There was no use in pouting. The corners of my mouth turned up as I thought of an idea.

"Let's go out and swim," I said lighting up. "I get to drive the sit this time."

Gig let go of me, and went to get the rope.

"First one down," he joked, and dropped onto the rope to let himself down.

I grinned and stared straight down into the water, I judged the distance and the amount of room Gig took up as he went. Then I pushed off the ledge and plummeted down to the water with my arms tucked tight against my body and my toes pointed.

"Hey!" I heard Gig shout as I flew past him.

Then I was in the water. It was a tight fit, but I resisted the pull back to the surface of the water and swung around so that I was pointed down. Then I popped my breather into my mouth for air and swam lower to the access hole.

I was already out and into the ocean before Gig made it into the water. I kicked my way up to the sky and aimed for the sit I spotted bobbing nearby. As soon as I surfaced, I paused for a second to get used to not being underwater. I felt the air and sun on my face and glanced around at how the water shimmered in the sunlight, and the ocean pulsed against the rock towers.

"Good choice," I said aloud. Then I hoisted myself up and sat on the sit's wing with my feet still in the water.

When Gig surfaced a few moments later, he looked really annoyed.

"What are you thinking when you do stuff like that?" he demanded. "Are you *trying* to get yourself hurt?"

"Of course not," I said. "Don't be a poor loser. I won the race."

"I'm not being a poor loser," he said. "I'm worrying for your health and safety."

"That's not necessary," I said in a gentle tone. "I'm fine, and you're...slow."

He shook his head and swam closer to buoy himself by grabbing onto the sit. He was obviously not happy with me.

"You can trust me, Gig," I said. "I measured the fall and the margin of error. I hit the water cleanly. I executed a flawless dive. I'm not stupid."

"I'm not saying you're stupid," he argued. "I'm..."

"You're implying it," I interrupted. "You think I'm some idiot kid that doesn't know better than to do something stupid. I may make mistakes sometimes, but can you give me some credit?"

Gig's eyes met mine as I stared at him in defiance.

"What if you'd made a mistake?" he asked, his tone softer. "What if you accidentally cracked your head open, or misjudged and broke your back when you hit the water?"

"What if I second-guessed everything I did, and worried about what didn't happen?" I threw back at him.

"Can I help it if I worry?" he asked. "I don't want to see you hurt."

I paused, and the fight suddenly went out of me.

"Gig," I said. "We'll have to face getting hurt if the time comes. Until then, just trust me, and I will trust you."

The water near his head rippled when he exhaled air slowly from his nose.

"Okay," he said. "Okay. I will try and work with that."

"Okay," I agreed. "Now get up here so I can fire this thing up."

I moved up and into the seat, and grabbed the steering column. The cuts on my hand protested as I held it, but I ignored the pain.

The sit tilted as Gig hoisted himself to straddle the seat behind me. When he put his arms around my waist the water dripping from his hair fell on the back of my neck and made me squeal. It felt like bits of ice on my warm skin. Gig laughed at my reaction and ran his hands over his hair so that more water fell on me. I squirmed and pushed back into him. His arms tightened around me for a second and then let go.

When I got control of my pounding heart, I kicked the sit into life and released it from its stand-still.

"Ready?" I asked Gig over my shoulder.

His answer was lost as I hit the accelerator and we sped away like lightening ripping over the water. Gig had clutched on to me tighter when we started. I felt the tension in his arms as we zigzagged around the stony towers. I felt playful and took some time to loop our sit around one of the towers six times until we were nice and dizzy. Then I snapped us out of it and went tearing in the other direction.

There were times when we hit a patch of water and bounced up and down as we went. We skimmed the surface like a pebble before the sit found traction again. I laughed, and could feel Gig's laughter rumble in his chest behind me. Eventually we came to an open field of water that was ringed by the rocky towers. I slowed the sit to a crawl as we came into the center.

"This is a weird formation," I said. "What do you think made them ring like this?"

"I don't know," Gig said. "Maybe there was another tower in the center, but it crumbled to pieces?"

"Or ashes," I suggested, thinking of the towers that steamed with open-ended tops. I drove the sit in a circuit along the inner ring, to check out each stony tower as we passed.

"Look, that one has a beach," Gig said as we neared one of them.

"Let's take a break," I suggested. I drove the sit straight to the beach, and let the front end meet the black-colored sand. Gig got off from behind me and helped me follow.

"It's weird to be on land again," he said. I watched him walk off-balance across the sand.

I took a few steps and realized he was right. My legs tried to shift with the un-shifting ground below my feet. I followed him up the beach a little until he found the spot where he wanted to sit down and relax. We were about halfway between the water and the rocky tower that jutted up behind us.

I dropped beside Gig and felt the warmth of the sand below me seep through my water suit. I dropped to my back and stretched luxuriously. Gig squinted out at the water, and looked pleased.

"Maybe I was wrong," he said.

"Wrong about what?"

"Maybe we should have thanked Ignoracius for not telling us all of the info. Now we can stay on the beach all day while we wait."

I smiled.

"Good point!" I said. "AJ will be jealous."

The sand seemed to shift just enough so I was cradled and comfortable. I closed my eyes against the sun and fully relaxed. After a while, the fabric of my water suit felt dry and parched against my skin. It was uncomfortable to nap in, so I sat up again and unzipped it so that I could shrug my arms out of it and push it down to my waist.

Gig watched while I bared my upper torso to the sun. I adjusted my bikini top to make sure it was still tied tightly, and caught him looking.

"What?" I asked.

Gig dragged his eyes up to meet mine, and the corner of his mouth lifted.

"Well, I have eyes don't I," he said.

I burst out laughing. So he remembered my line from the gym.

I lay back again, and was pleased to find that I was much more comfortable. I threw an arm over my eyes and relaxed again. I could feel Gig shift beside me to lie down in the sand too. A moment later he sighed, and I could hear the sound of his watersuit unzipping.

I looked, and saw Gig baring his chest to the sun like I had. I grinned and covered my eyes again before he could catch me looking.

"Your hand," Gig hissed. His fingers grabbed the arm I had flung over my eyes.

I didn't move.

"The rocks tore them up when I climbed up the ledge," I said. "Are they bleeding?"

"Yes, let me put something on them," he said.

I heard the pack unzip, and the sound of him rummaging for the med case. He must have found an ointment in there because I felt him rubbing it onto both my hands a moment later. He also put some on my feet while I forced myself not to squirm away from him.

When he was done, I heard him settle down next to me again.

I snoozed. The sound of the water crashing against the beach lulled me into sleep. At some point my skin felt warm enough, and my back felt cold in comparison, so I rolled over onto my stomach with my head on my arms, and fell back to sleep.

"Alyvia?" I heard Gig say some time later.

"Hmm?"

"Are you asleep?" he asked.

"No," I said, but kept my eyes shut.

"I have a question," he said quietly. "When you kissed me in that watersport shop, was that part of the ruse, or did you do it on impulse?"

What?

I blinked my eyes open at him and saw that he was on his side facing me with his head propped up on his hand.

"Why?" I asked.

"I was thinking about it," he said. "Tell me seriously."

I squinted my eyes at him but started to laugh.

"It was a surprise to you *and* me," I said. "Could you tell?"

He grinned in response to my laughter.

"You did look surprised," he said. "We both probably did."

"Why are you asking?"

"I've seen you do several impulsive things now," he said. "I'm starting to realize it's a pattern."

I groaned.

"Do you have to analyze me right now?" I asked. "Can't we just enjoy the sun and the sand and the water?"

He sighed.

"Yes," he said, and rolled onto his back.

I looked at him like he was crazy, but he didn't see me. I tried to close my eyes and fall back to sleep, but I couldn't now. I sat up and faced the water to see the sun shimmer on the horizon.

"Is being impulsive a good thing, or a bad thing?" I asked.

Gig didn't say anything. I was offended.

"You think it's bad!" I said. "I don't sit back and analyze everything like you but even if I wanted to, I couldn't. I've been trained to react. The second something feels wrong, I have to be able to switch tactics. Stryker taught me to follow my instincts."

"I'm not saying it is bad," Gig assured me, and finally looked me in the eye. "I just don't want to see your impulsive actions hurt you. As your Gunner, it's hard to protect you from yourself. The time may come when you're on your own and I won't be there to watch out for you. You should learn to take a second and figure out the best course of action."

I wasn't sure how to put my annoyance into words.

"I mean, I did manage to live this long," I muttered grumpily, irritated that I had to explain myself.

I realized I was frowning at my feet. Why was I getting all worked up? What Gig said was ridiculous. I didn't want him to think I had faults, though. I had been determined to earn his respect and this felt like the opposite of that.

I looked at him sideways, and met his eyes.

"Maybe *you* should learn to be a little more impulsive, instead of sitting back and letting life happen around you while you think about it," I suggested. I saw his eyes flash when he realized I was talking about Maddy.

I got up from beside him and looked down at him. The surprise on Gig's face, and maybe the hurt that I saw there, made me pause.

"OR," I said, and met his eyes seriously, "maybe our differences are good, because we balance each other out. As two, we are stronger than one of us on our own. I would like for you to think of me as an asset some day and not an idiot."

I left him there, and walked straight into the water as I zipped up my suit again.

"Alyvia," he said.

I dove into the waves and swam long strokes away from the beach. The water had cooled as the sun sank lower into the afternoon. My arms and breath synched as I swam steadily. I paused after some time, and began to tread water. I glanced back to see how far from shore I was. Gig, and the water sit, were quite a distance away. Gig stood at the edge of the water and watched my progress with a hand shading his eyes.

I took several breaths in and out in two quick successions, and on the third breath I sucked in air and held it. Then I dove straight down into the water, with my eyes wide open as I looked around and kicked lower and lower.

I was positioned approximately dead center in the ring of rock towers. If something had once been in the center, I was there now. I swam down deep into the ocean, and put my water breather into my mouth when I couldn't hold my breath any longer. The ocean floor wasn't much further here. As I approached the bottom, I squinted around at everything in sight.

I don't know why it interested me so much to see if there were any rock tower remains in the center of the ring where we relaxed. Cutter used to get annoyed when I'd find something to wonder about, because it would distract me until I found the answers I looked for. Now this ring mystery had caught my attention, and I just had to see what was below.

I swam in a tight circle around the area, and then slowly swam in wider and wider circles. Below me was the sandy ocean floor. It stretched out with no hint of anything that could have been there before.

I kept swimming around and around until I finally noticed something different. In a circular pattern, the ocean floor had sprouted algae. As I swam back and forth over the ring, I realized something else: the temperature on the inside of the ring was warmer than the temperature away from the ring. It was like a hotspot in the water.

Something touched my shoulder and gripped it firmly. I jumped and turned my head to see Gig. With his other hand he showed me the light he'd brought with him. Excited, I grabbed it and powered it on. I motioned for him to follow, swam closer to the algae and showed him how it ringed in a circle. Then I made him swim from the center of the ring to the outside. Gig gamely did as he was asked, then swam back to the center. He made a quizzical gesture with his hands, so I made the hand sign for warm. Gig gave me a thumbs up and swam it again. I swam over to him and grinned. I gave him his light back.

Gig took the light, and then took my arm and pulled me closer. I let him wrap an arm around my waist so that we were pressed against each other. I wondered if he could feel my heart suddenly begin to pound harder. I looked up into his face, and realized he was looking at something over my shoulder. He pointed at it, and motioned for me to look.

I turned my head, and saw something shimmer in the distance, a large silver fish-like body swam toward us. I stared at it as it moved closer, and felt my breath come faster. Then the animal made a noise; its call sounding like a high-pitched song. It was a cleo!

I circled Gig's shoulders with my left arm, and slowly reached out toward the cleo with my right. It swam over slowly and cautiously, until it was inches from my fingertips. I didn't move. I stared into the cleo's shining black eyes, and could see the intelligence there. One flick of the cleo's long tail sent it swimming past us. Its body slid against the palm of my hand. When it arced around us, the water it displaced bounced us around a little. Gig reached out himself so that he could touch the cleo too. I saw the look on his face as his hand made contact. He stared at the cleo in amazement.

I laughed, and could feel Gig laugh too. We both patted the cleo as it circled us several more times, once upside down so we could touch its belly.

Then a high-pitched song called out in the distance, and the cleo swam away to join its friends. We watched it until we couldn't make out its shape in the dark water anymore.

I turned to look at Gig and saw him smile like a little kid. My heart was bursting in wonder. I put my other arm around his shoulders and hugged him tightly. He squeezed me against the sharp planes of his chest. One hand moved up my back to brace the back of my neck. I pulled away from him a little to look at him. Gig looked very serious now. I could just make out his eyes in the growing darkness and saw that he searched my eyes for something.

I tilted my head to the side, and waited for him to make a move. It occurred to me that he wanted to kiss me, but he held himself back. I wondered if he was thinking about Maddy and it made my eyes narrow. My pulse pounded through my entire body as I gripped Gig in a tighter hug and let my legs wrap around his waist again. His eyes sharpened and stayed locked on mine as I reached up and took my water breather from my mouth. I touched my lips to his left cheek, close to his ear. His grip on the back of my neck tightened a little and started to massage my skin there. I kissed him again, closer to his lips, and he pressed me tighter to his body. I had never wanted to kiss someone the way I wanted to kiss Gig now. Shocked at the feelings of heat that spread from my belly, I took a quick pop of air from my breather and then grasped Gig's breather in my fingers. He let me remove it from his mouth. One of his hands caressed down the length of my back, and made me shiver against him.

I pressed my lips to his in a soft, lingering kiss. Then I sucked his lower lip into my mouth.

Gig exhaled a little. The air bubbles tickled my cheek. He crushed me against him and took over the kiss. His lips moved against mine with an intensity that made my insides throb until neither of us had much air left. Heat radiated through my entire body as I lost myself in the kiss and forgot about everything else.

Eventually his kiss softened as we realized we needed to breathe. I gave him his water breather and popped mine into my mouth. I sucked at its air until I could catch my breath but I was seeing stars. Gig's arms loosened their hold around me. The temperature of the water cooled me off a little. I grinned and swam in a tight circle around him, then kicked away until I was swimming toward our sit. Gig had parked it above us. I knew he followed, and giddily swam harder. I popped up next to the sit a moment before he did. I took my breather out and grabbed the sit to let it keep me afloat as I caught my breath. Gig did the same, his black hair was slicked back and dripped on his shoulders. I wanted to reach out and run my fingers through it.

I glanced at the setting sun, and looked back at Gig, who watched me now with hungry eyes. I smiled, and felt my cheeks get warm.

"Wanna go back?" I asked. My voice came out throatier than I expected.

Gig shook his head no, and used the sit to edge closer. I realized he was coming back for another kiss. The water dropped from his head like shimmering crystals. He leaned closer, and I leaned forward to meet him. My breath paused as my lids dropped closed.

Our lips touched at the same moment the sit bleeped loudly. The noise startled me. Gig's body got stiff. He pulled away, and climbed up onto the sit to press a blinking control button.

"Aye?" he said.

"Gig, Alyvia, why aren't you two at the site?" the Captain asked over the comm. "Our sensors show you twenty minutes away."

Gig's eyes went to mine and he gave me a secret smile.

"We decided to kill some time by exploring the area," he said. "We're waiting for the water levels to rise, which should be happening shortly."

"Good," the Captain said. "Comm us when you're ready for pick-up."

"Aye Captain," Gig said. He pressed the comm button again to turn it off. He looked down at me ruefully and offered a hand. I took it and let him help me up into the seat behind him.

"So much for our vacation, and back to work," I said. I saw the pack on the sit's handlebars and pulled it over my shoulders.

Gig powered the sit into life and pulled my arms around his waist. He drove us back to the rock tower with the Starkiller's power supply in it. On the trip, I stared at the sunset and reveled at the way the light turned the sky into a beautiful rosy-purple. I leaned my head against Gig's back and enjoyed the feel of wind on my face.

If Cutter could see me now, he would be shocked, I thought. The boys I'd been interested in at the Academy had been few and far between. It had taken me a very long time to trust *him*, let alone people I wanted to go out with. I thought back to those early days when I'd first come to the Academy. I had been so raw and emotional and messed up. I had not understood that a haven like the Academy could even exist. It was a testament to Cutter and Stryker's love and unending support for me that I could learn to live a normal life free of the past I'd left behind.

I sent a silent prayer to the stars to watch over them.

What would I have become if they hadn't crossed my path?

My mind went back to Gig. I'd secretly wondered what it was like to kiss him several times over the past few weeks. I was attracted to his body but there was something even more attractive about him in general. He was steady under pressure, like a calm in the storm. It wasn't just a cocky Gunner persona, it was more. Whenever he was in the room I felt like my frayed edges were a little smoother. He was a balm to my kinetic energy.

I felt his hand squeeze mine. He was thinking about me too.

When we arrived at our rock tower, we didn't say anything. I followed Gig into the water. He led the way as we dived down to the entrance and back up into the center of the tower. When we surfaced, we didn't need the rope to get up onto the shelf. The tide had risen high enough that we could pull ourselves up out of the water. Which was good because my hands were bleeding again. I balled them into fists and pressed them close to my chest.

I looked over the hole of the well and saw that the metal-encased power supply was floating up closer to the lip where we could get to it. Gig unzipped the pack on my back and pulled out the explosives.

"Let me do it," I said.

Gig held out the explosives and kept the detonator for himself. I used my tele to float the explosives into the well and carefully attached them to the Cyline metal.

"We should get back in the water," Gig said.

"Okay, let me get a hold of the power supply first," I said. I concentrated on it to make sure I knew where it would be when it was out of sight.

Gig must have found my goggles. I felt him pull them over my head and rest them on the top of my head before he dropped back into the water by the way we'd come. I focused my will on the power supply encased by metal, and got it locked with my tele before I followed him into the water. He had has goggles over his eyes again. I pulled mine on and turned toward him.

"Duck down," he said.

We both pushed ourselves down in the water and faced each other so I could see the detonator in his hands. He looked at me when he raised it. I nodded. His thumb pressed the button.

Immediately I heard an explosion of rock above us and objects pinged into the water above our heads. With my tele, I immediately dropped the power supply into the water. I dunked it down deep in case the flammable metal around it had caught fire. Gig helped pull me to the surface quickly. I ignored the way my hands stung as I pulled myself out of the water and got close to the well. Pieces of metal were on fire here and there in the water. I dropped to my belly and made the power supply come up higher in the water with my tele. When I saw that it looked intact, I breathed a sigh of relief and grabbed it carefully with my hands. It was a dull shade of silver with veins of wires sticking out from one end, and a flat smooth surface on the other. The center was a fat tube that had three twistable sections.

Gig came to my side and opened the case we'd brought. He put it under the water and waited as I placed the power supply inside, then he snapped the lid shut and locked it in place.

I got to my knees and pulled our pack out and opened it for him. As he stuffed the case inside, something tickled my knees. I dropped my head to stare at the rock beneath me. Water gushed around me from the well and moved toward the way we'd come. It started to flood our shelf quickly like water filling a bath. I stood up in alarm and saw it was up past my ankles and growing higher. The water was warm, unpleasantly warm, and getting warmer. I looked up at Gig. He zipped the pack closed quickly. He saw it too.

"Let's get out of here," he said. He snagged my wrist and urgently pulled me back to our exit. I glanced back at the well and saw water fountain up from it. The water at my legs was uncomfortably hot now and close to scalding. I popped my water breather into my mouth and immediately dove down into our tunnel and swam down to the exit hole. I felt Gig churning water behind me. I didn't see a telltale light to tell me when we'd reached the end but I supposed if it was darker outside with the setting sun, the light might be too weak to reach this far. I swam lower and searched but it wasn't there. Gig found his light and shone the beam on the rock wall, searching up and down in confusion. When we pointed it down, we realized what was wrong. A pile of rubble blocked our way. It must have crashed loose when we ignited the explosives, or it had shifted when we weren't paying attention. I felt a stream of hot water at my back and turned my head toward it. A fissure in the internal rock wall was leaking water quickly, the pressure behind it causing the water to stream at me and warm the water around me quickly. I realized the other side of the wall must have been where the well dropped low. I grabbed Gig's arm and pulled him closer to make him feel the water.

His face was hard to see in the dimness of his flashlight, but I could tell he was troubled. He kicked lower and tried pushing aside rocks to get to the exit. We would have to dig our way out and we needed to do it fast.

I swam down to him and tapped his foot. He looked up toward me and adjusted the light in his hand to see the quick hand motions I made.

"Anchor me," I signed to him. "I'll move the rocks."

He righted his body and moved behind me to grab hold of me around the arms and waist. I tried to concentrate even though I knew the hot water was now streaming against his back. I used my tele to reach down below my feet and gather a bundle of rocks. It was a strain to lift their weight, and I felt the pressure in my lower back, but I did it and pushed the rocks past us and up the tunnel to settle on the shelf where the well sprouted. I dropped them about where I guessed the well was, in case that could stop it up, if possible.

As soon as I loosed them I grabbed more rocks from below us. The heaviness weighed down on me, but I surged them up past us too and onto the shelf. I did it again and again, lifting the rocks up and out of the way until my body shook with fatigue. Gig noticed that I had to dig my thumb into my lower back. He adjusted our positioning and swatted my hand away so that he could massage my lower back with his thumbs while holding me in place at my waist.

I couldn't keep doing this. My breath was whooshing in and out from the labor, and I felt my lungs contract. It felt like my breather couldn't accommodate how much air I needed. I started to get dizzy, and my body felt like it was roasting. I trembled in Gig's arms but I kept going. The rocks moved slower as I lifted them out of the way, much more sluggishly than when I'd first started.

After dropping another pile of rocks on the shelf above us, I looked down to start the next pile and almost shouted in joy when I saw that our exit to the ocean was in sight. I just had to clear a few more piles. I took two quick breaths, gathered more strength, and pushed the remaining rocks away, out of our escape hole.

Gig helped me dive down toward the hole and out into the cooler water of the ocean. I kicked up to the surface tiredly, with Gig at my side the entire way up. He took my hand when we surfaced and helped me grab the sit to keep me floating above the water. My arms felt like weak noodles but I made myself hold on. He pulled the breather from my mouth and pushed my goggles up onto the top of my head. I saw the concern in his eyes as they raked over me.

"Are you okay?" he asked.

"I'm fine, just tired," I gasped. "Go ahead and comm the Captain."

He cupped the side of my face and nodded.

I waited while he climbed up onto the water sit and sent a message to the ship. Then he reached down and grabbed me from out of the water. He lifted me up easily to sit in front of him on the seat. I didn't have the energy to throw my leg over the seat, so I sat there almost side saddle, and leaned heavily against the sit.

Gig's hands started to massage from my shoulders to my lower back. I closed my eyes and groaned loudly as his fingers and palms worked to loosen my overused muscles. When he'd worked at my back for a while and I felt like I could breathe again, I slumped backward and dropped my head against his shoulder with my eyes still closed.

"Thank you," I said gratefully.

"Thank *you*," he replied, "for getting us out of there."

His lips and hot breath touched the skin at my exposed neck. I shivered, and lifted a hand to twine my fingers in his wet hair. His teeth nibbled at my shoulder and made me gasp. I felt his fingers roam up from my waist to my rib cage and turned my head to catch his lips with mine.

A low hum approached us over the water. Gig's head lifted to see what it was.

"They're here," he murmured.

I nodded but didn't open my eyes or move away from him. My stomach grumbled angrily.

"Do you have any snacks?" I asked. "I'm starving."

"No but I'll get you something as soon as we board."

I sighed.

Gig let go of me, and stood up in the sit to wave his arms. I pressed my hands against the sit to keep myself upright. I cracked my eyes open a little to see where the ship was. We watched as Marco positioned the ship as low to the water as he could. The bay doors opened at the docks to reveal the Captain and AJ there waiting for us.

"Leave the sit here," the Captain shouted as she and AJ lowered a rope ladder down to us.

"Do you need help up?" Gig asked.

"No, I can do it," I said stubbornly. He helped me stand up on the sit and take hold of the ladder. I wobbled on my feet but managed to stay up. Then I stepped onto the ladder and felt it sway precariously. My hands protested, so I forced myself to climb as quickly as I could, and used a little tele to help make it easier.

"Alyvia," I heard Gig say from below me.

I paused and looked down. Gig stared at the ladder in dismay.

"Your hands," he said. "They're bleeding again."

I looked, and he was right. The scratches on my hands were open and bleeding all over the rope but there was nothing I could do about them now.

"They're fine," I called down to him, and started the climb again.

At the top, the Captain and AJ helped pull me over the lip into the dock, and did the same for Gig. I stumbled to a workbench and sat down, then swayed there like I was drunk. I wiped at the sweat on my brow and leaned forward to rest my elbows on my legs.

When Gig appeared at the top of the ladder and climbed up, the Captain closed the bay doors and commed Marco that we could leave. Gig came over to where I sat and extended an arm. He helped me stand, and held on to my wrist.

"Show AJ your hands," he said.

I pulled away from him and crossed my arms. Gig looked at me in surprise but I didn't meet his eyes. My back muscles twinged and pulsed from the tension.

I bit back a groan.

"It's not that bad, it looks worse than it really is," I mumbled. A chill rippled along my spine and for a second I felt like I might vomit. I stared at the ground and tried to will away the dizziness. I wanted to close my eyes and lay down.

"Nonsense," I heard the Captain say, "your hands have been sliced up. There's blood all over the ladder. Have AJ look at them before you lose them all together."

I knew a command when I heard one. I bit my lip and loosened my hands so AJ could see them.

"Let's get to the lab," AJ said immediately. "Come on."

I hesitated, unable to follow him as he turned and headed for the door. I tried to think of a convenient excuse, but my brain was muddled and I couldn't force it to focus. I needed something to eat.

"Hey, you're looking a little too pale," Gig murmured. He stepped closer and put a hand on my shoulder. "Go with AJ, okay?"

"We'll be there in a minute to check on you," the Captain added.

"Hang on, I think she's going to faint," AJ said.

His boots came into my field of vision. I tried to concentrate but my vision was graying and I toppled forward. Arms caught me and lifted me up.

"I've got her," AJ said. "I need someone to get her juice and crackers."

My head lolled against his chest. AJ rushed from the dock all the way to his Medlab. When we passed the Pilot's deck I saw Marco at his controls and wished I could sit with him.

In the Medlab, AJ gently settled me onto the examining table. My heart was beating a little too fast, and my breathing felt shallow and rushed. AJ flashed a light in my eyes and asked me something that sounded like gibberish. I winced when he pricked my arm with something. I was still feeling nauseous but he looped an arm under my head and lifted me a little. I felt a tube of water at my lips and opened my mouth to drink it. It felt good to my parched mouth and tongue. When he set me back down, I realized color was coming back to the room.

I felt him turn over my wrists so that I my palms faced up on the table. He sat beside me and began to swab at my palms. I sucked in a breath when it started to sting, and tried to jerk my hands away, but AJ stopped me.

"Hey!" I said. I tried to jerk my hand away from him again but I was too weak and his determination to hold my hands still was making me panic.

"Alyvia, stop!" AJ said. "I need you to stay still so I can mend you."

"Let me go!" I shouted and tried to tug away from him.

AJ got up and leaned over me so I could see his eyes. He put a hand against my shoulder and pressed it flat against the table. I tried to squirm from him and push his hand away but there was no power behind my movements. I must have looked pathetic but I was one snap decision away from smacking him with a wall of tele energy.

"Wait a minute, wait a minute," he said gently. "Just hold on one minute."

I saw the seriousness in his pale blue eyes and forced myself to pause.

"I'm trying to mend your palms," he said quietly. "I can't do that if you're jerking them away from me. Alyvia, I'm the Medic on this ship. I need to do my job. Can you relax and let me do my job?"

I opened my mouth to say something, but closed it again. My eyes drifted away from his and to the computer screen on the wall behind him.

"Alyvia."

His voice was quiet. I looked him in the eye hesitantly.

"That day, in your room," he said, then faltered. He cleared his throat and tried again. "That day, in your room. I don't know what happened there, but I did not intend to frighten you. I would never *hurt* you or try to *harm* you in any way. I know I can come on strong but I'm not that guy. I'm not a -."

"I know," I interrupted him. "*I'm* sorry. I was scared."

"You don't have anything to apologize for," he said. "I'm the one who scared you. I'm sorry. I'd never…"

He sighed when the words didn't come out right. I watched him while he grasped for the right thing to say.

"I'd never hurt you," he said finally. "I'm not like that man who…"

My breath caught in my throat.

"What guy?" I asked. It felt like the world had stopped to listen.

AJ looked down at the floor.

"I read your file," he said. "After what happened between us."

"What file?" I choked out.

"Your private med file from when you were first tested and admitted into the Academy," he said. "The one only your health caretaker can access."

I tried to swallow a lump in my throat, and this time I was the one who looked away when AJ lifted his eyes to mine. Hot tears started to prick at my eyes.

"Anyway, I am sorry. Please tell me you believe me when I say that."

I couldn't look him in the eye and see the hurt there without believing him. I nodded, and saw his relief.

"Thank you," he said.

I waited and tried to pull my emotions back into check as AJ gathered more tools from his cabinets and drawers for my hands. He came back with a tray of items and wiped at my eyes, then continued working on my hands. That was a sweet gesture.

Gig came in with a plate of crackers and a cup filled with juice. He and AJ helped me to sit up, and then Gig had to hand feed me while AJ finished up. My palms felt numb. I was vaguely aware that he was touching them, but I couldn't really feel it.

When Gig finished tilting the last of the juice into my mouth, I sighed. I felt stronger but still lethargic. Gig looked concerned for me but he smiled when I said thanks. He rubbed my back and let me lean against him. I felt my heavy eyelids droop closed.

I drifted on a cloud for a while, until I felt AJ tap me. He showed me a blue wafer and told me to open my mouth but not to bike it. The tablet tasted bitter, but I sucked on it and felt it start to dissolve on my tongue.

"That's to stimulate your body to produce more blood," he said. "You lost too much in the water."

I nodded. Gig helped me settle back on the table and told me he'd be back. I don't know where AJ had wandered off to so I closed my eyes and napped.

"Is she okay?" I heard the Captain say a bit later. I hadn't heard her come in but in my drowsy state nothing bothered me.

"She'll be fine," AJ said. "Her hands are starting to heal nicely. She lost too much blood, so once her body produces more to make up for it she'll be up and around immediately."

"Gig said they were trapped in that rock," the Captain said. "Alyvia had to use her telekinesis to clear the way. Gig said some of those rocks were too large, and that she was overextending her muscles."

AJ sighed.

"Okay, I'd better make sure she didn't tear any," he said. "Thanks for telling me. I'll run a full body scan in case there's anything else she managed to do to herself down there."

"Why so disapproving?" the Captain asked. I'd noticed it too.

AJ grumbled something in response.

"What?" the Captain asked.

"I said she's doing too much," AJ said. "We never had Maddy doing some of these things."

"We had Maddy doing some tricky things, you just don't remember," the Captain said. "Alyvia is doing an exceptional job for us. She's young, and untested, but she's shown us so far that she can handle it."

"I just don't want her to work herself into the ground," AJ said. "As her doctor, her health and safety are my responsibility."

"No, her health and safety are *my* responsibility," the Captain said. "Treating her when I fail is your responsibility."

AJ didn't reply.

The Captain told him to report my progress to her when he was done. I heard her leave. A few moments later, AJ shook me lightly and asked me to roll over so he could scan my back. I grunted and slowly turned over on the rock he called an examining table. I used one of my arms as a pillow and closed my eyes again.

I heard Gig and Marco's voices come into the Medlab.

"Aren't we popular tonight," AJ muttered.

"Hey AJ," Marco said quietly, "how is she doing?"

"Recovering nicely," AJ said brusquely. "I was just about to check and see if she had any muscle damage."

"You should have seen the rocks she was moving," Gig said. "Some of them were bigger than the two of us put together, and she was moving them like this."

I heard the clatter of something light hit the floor, and Marco chuckled. I opened my eyes at the noise and lifted my head to look around.

"Alyvia, you impresses me every day," Marco said. He squatted down so I could see his blue eyes. "I can't imagine having that much talent at such a young age."

I murmured something to him in response.

"You were flying fighter planes at that age," Gig reminded him.

"Yeah, but that doesn't take any skill. You just point and shoot—any idiot can do that."

Gig and Marco laughed. I smiled at their exchange but was having trouble keeping my eyes open. I put my head back on my arm and relaxed to the sound of their voices.

"So you didn't have any problems?" Gig asked AJ quietly.

"No," AJ said. "We talked."

"About what?" Gig wanted to know.

"About things between us," AJ said. "We're fine."

"What did you say?"

"That's between us," AJ said. I could tell he enjoyed Gig's irritation.

"Well that's good," Marco cut in. "No one should be having difficulties on our team. I'm glad you cleared the air."

"Me too," AJ said.

I murmured something too but my eyes had closed again.

Gig said nothing.

He and Marco left me in AJ's care and returned to their duties. I fell into a deep sleep in the silence, too tired to crawl to my bed but still extremely hungry.

13

"We won't be going back to see Hector after this mission," the Captain said. She had just finished the debrief with Gig and me and now leaned back in her chair. We sat in her room at her guest chairs while she sat at her desk. "He's agreed to send us the instructions for the next piece of Starkiller so that we don't have to keep going back to him."

The Captain met my gaze.

"He asked me to congratulate you on another successful mission."

I nodded, and glanced at Gig. We knew Hector hadn't made it easy for us to complete the mission. I was still a little too upset with him to see him right now anyway.

"So where are we off to next?" Gig asked.

"Caro," the Captain said.

I had heard of Caro but never been there. It was the home to Jubilee, one of the largest known cities in all the 'verse. Jubilee was known for having the greatest disparity between wealth and poverty among all the cities of men. Many of my classmates at the Academy had been there, or were from there. It was on my list of places I wanted to go.

"We should be there in about sixteen days," the Captain said. "Master Omin intends to meet us there, to retrieve the pieces we've found so far. He wants to begin studying the Starkiller."

I sucked in a breath and tensed, all thoughts pushed aside.

"Do I have to be there when he meets us?" I asked.

The Captain gave me a look of sympathy.

"I'll try to keep you out of it," she said. That was all she could promise.

I slumped in my chair and tried not to say anything to embarrass myself.

"Alyvia," the Captain said, "did something happen between you and

Master Omin that you can tell us about?"

I remembered his cold hand on the back of my neck and shivered.

"Yes," I whispered. I wrapped my arms around myself.

The Captain slipped from her seat and came to me. I watched her with wide eyes as she perched on the arm of my chair and bent closer. Like we had a secret to share. Gig stayed silent. I felt the comfort of his presence but I could also feel the cold of that railing outside the Council chambers. I had gripped it so tightly when Master Omin whispered dangerous words in my ear.

I looked down at my hands and stared at the bandages AJ made me wear.

"He's a strong 'path," the Captain said. She touched my shoulder gently. "He could have augmented a feeling you were having and used it to get what he wanted from you."

"Crippling fear?" I suggested.

"Terror," she nodded. "I have heard unverified reports that he used Terror to secure his position on the Council."

I swallowed. When I lifted my gaze to her hazel eyes, I saw the sympathy there, and it made me feel a little relieved.

A little.

"He made me so afraid," I murmured. "He knew about all the terrible things I'd done as a kid, and threatened to tell you and the team. I was afraid that if you knew, you wouldn't want me on your team in the first place."

She hugged me to her and made noises of sympathy.

"He played on your fear until it felt more real than it ever would have been before," she said.

I shook my head. The fear was justified. I opened my mouth to tell her so but she pulled away and moved to answer her chiming comm from Marco.

"I'm reading another Order ship passing nearby," he said to the Captain. "It's the Regal."

"Hail them," the Captain said. "I'm on my way."

"Aye."

The Captain turned back to us.

"I'm sorry, I need to talk to the Regal's Captain," she said.

I saw Gig get up, so I got up too.

"We will log our mission, and then work on supper," he said.

"Thanks you two," the Captain said. She rubbed my arm as she passed me. "Don't fear, Alyvia. Your team will not abandon you."

I nodded but didn't meet her gaze this time. She didn't know what I knew.

"How are your cooking skills?" Gig asked. I saw him pull out some pans from the commissary cabinet and place them on the counter.

"I can make some things," I offered. I'd spent the last hour staring at the tablet in front of me, pretending to thumb through my report. I was really thinking about the Governor of Cayberra, and whether he was still alive. I did not want to search for the information in case it could be tracked back to me. I needed to figure out how to do it discreetly.

I pushed the tablet away and got up from the table.

Gig waited until I was at his side, then offered me a packet of noodles.

"Are you okay?" he asked. He put an arm around my shoulders and pulled me closer. I nodded but the smile I gave him was weak.

"I still feel tired," I said. "Am I still pale looking?"

He looked at my face and nodded.

"A bit but not as bad as when we first got back," he said. "Maybe I should do the cooking and you should go take a nap."

"I heard it was my turn," I argued. "Many times. AJ won't stop harping on how unfair it is for the rookie not to take a turn in the kitchen."

Gig shrugged.

"I could not care less what AJ thinks about anything," he said.

"Well," I started to say, but AJ's voice from the doorway interrupted me.

"That much is obvious," AJ said. He came and pulled himself up on the counter next to me. "Discussing me, are we?"

I stared up at him and tilted my head. Gig's hand fell away from my shoulder.

"Do you appear when people say your name?" I teased him. "You're like the bogeyman."

He smiled. He liked that description.

"I guess it comes in handy to skulk around," Gig grumbled behind me.

"I don't have to," AJ said. "I can hear you talking from almost everywhere on the ship. Have you ever considered the other people who have to live with you?"

"No," Gig said. He resumed his rummaging around the kitchen.

AJ looked pleased to get under Gig's skin.

I raised an eyebrow at him.

"Did you want to help us?" I asked.

"No," AJ said. He pulled something from his back pocket. I looked and saw they were his medical shears.

I held up my bandaged hands.

"You came to take these off?" I asked.

"Yep, the ointment I gave you should be dry and absorbed by now," he said. "Are you ready for them to come off?"

I bounced.

"Yes, please!"

AJ smirked but he cut away the bandages for me. I had marks on my palms and a couple fingers but the skin looked healthy. AJ pulled out a tube and showed it to me.

"This is a medicinal lotion that I want you to use until it's gone," he said. "Apply it every morning when you wake up, and before you go to bed, or whenever your skin feels itchy."

"Can I put some on now?" I asked.

"Yeah, let me do it," he said.

I dutifully held my hands out for him and waited while he massaged the lotion into my skin. When he was done, he handed me the tube. Gig moved about in silence. He quietly worked on his recipe while AJ tended to me.

"Thanks, AJ," I said.

"You're welcome."

He dropped down from the counter, collected my discarded wraps, and left the commissary to head back to his lab.

Congratulations to me, AJ and I had just had an interaction that didn't go wrong.

I turned with raised eyebrows to look at Gig.

"Don't get used to it," he said. "I'm sure he'll be back to the old AJ in no time."

I made a face.

"I hope not," I said.

I came to peer at what he was doing. I watched for a minute as he rolled items together in his bare hands. My eyes widened.

"Are you making meatballs?" I asked.

"Meatballs, and spaghetti," he confirmed.

I did a happy dance around the table. Gig laughed at me and watched while I completed my circuit.

"What should I work on?"

"Why don't you check the pasta," he said with a grin.

He looked very handsome.

I sidled up next to him, put both arms around his waist, and hugged him tightly with his arm between us.

"All that for spaghetti and meatballs?" he asked.

I shrugged.

"I am a simple girl, Gig," I said. "A simple girl."

He laughed again. His hands were covered in his meatball mixture but he looped his left arm over my head so that he could pull me closer. He kissed my forehead before he released me again.

"Seriously, please check the pasta," he said. He winked at me.

I knew my cheeks were pink so I turned and happily checked the pasta. The water was boiling but getting low. I grabbed the stirring fork from the counter and nabbed a string of spaghetti. When I chewed it, it was soft, so I turned off the cooker and looked around for the strainer.

"It's in the cabinet on your left," Gig said.

I used tele to bring it into my hand.

"You're cheating," he said.

"Not at all," I said. "I'm being efficient."

I watched as he finished making his meatballs, and then I cut bread slices, buttered them, and added garlic and cheese.

By the time we called the rest of the team for sup, the commissary smelled delicious. When Marco found out what we were having he did the same dance I had, except his included spinning me around and dipping me. I laughed with him and saw everyone in the room seemed to be in a very good mood.

Even AJ laughed when Marco tried to spin him.

"Go back to that one," he said, and pointed at me.

Marco was about to but the Captain walked in and allowed herself to be twirled as well.

"I guess Gig and Alyvia are cooking for the rest of the week if this is how we're going to react," she said.

She gave me a high five. It stung my newly healed hands but I didn't let it show.

"Gig's smiling," Marco said. "Wow, I didn't realize you had teeth, brother."

Gig showed Marco his teeth to prove it.

AJ leaned closer to me.

"I see you managed to get a tan on Corleu Minor," he said.

"I sure did," I agreed. I looked at my tanned arms and smiled. "Now that we have a water sit on Corleu Minor, we can all go back there whenever we need a break, and nap on the beach we found."

AJ snorted.

"You got lucky," he said.

"Why?"

"We haven't had a break in three years," the Captain said. She put some meatballs on my plate for me. "Sorry, Lyv, you'll get used to it."

I made a disappointed face but I was happy she called me Lyv.

"Does that mean I shouldn't hold too much hope of exploring Jubilee?"

I asked.

"Probably not," she said, "we should get there at least a full day before Master Omin does. If we find the piece quickly, it's possible you could spend the rest of that time exploring."

"Did Hector give us the exact coordinates for the piece, or are we on a goose chase?" I asked.

"He gave us the coordinates," the Captain said. "I need to scan Caro to see where they point."

"I can do that for you," Gig offered.

The Captain looked pleased.

"Well alright, then," she said.

"Marco and I can plan out our entrance and exit plans," he added.

Marco nodded at him to show he would help. His mouth was too full of food to reply.

"Thanks, team," the Captain said, "and good work on dinner. I nominate you to do it again tomorrow."

Marco seconded that motion.

"Well that's easy," Gig replied, "because we're having leftovers."

Later, when Marco and I were sitting on the Pilot's deck, I noticed him looking around to see if any of the others were nearby.

"Hey, kid, can I be nosy for a second?"

My walls instantly went up but I looked at him sideways.

"I dunno," I said. "What do you want to be nosy about?"

He looked around once more. I did too, in case whatever he asked me was embarrassing.

"Mmm," he grunted. "I feel so old."

I raised an eyebrow at him.

"What's the deal, Marco?"

He sighed.

"Are you and Gig…flirting?" he asked.

I blew out air, grateful that was all he wanted to know. My imagination had been whirring to all the horrific things he could possibly ask me. For now, Gig wasn't one of them.

"Maybe a little," I said.

I thought of the kissing on Corleu Minor and couldn't help the sudden smile.

"That's all it is right now," I said. "Just flirting."

Marco stared at me with wide eyes. I glanced at his console to make sure it was on autopilot, and relaxed when I saw it was. I looked at him again and made an expectant face.

"Why are you looking at me like that?"

"I just haven't seen this side of Gig before," Marco said. "He seems all happy and…do I dare say *friendly*?"

I laughed at how confused Marco looked. I wasn't sure what else I should say. I knew that officers were free to do what they wished when they weren't on duty, so Gig and I weren't breaking any rules. Although we were technically on duty when I kissed him under the water. I didn't know if Gig was interested in kissing again, but if he was, I was all for it.

"Okay, I'm just going to say one last thing, and then we can drop it," he said. He looked at me seriously and gave me his paternal tone of voice. "Be careful. If things don't work out, being on this small of a ship can be extremely awkward. I would hate to see one of you transfer because you couldn't stand working with the other."

My gushy feelings fell away at Marco's words. I looked him in the eye and nodded my head. I couldn't picture where I could go if things didn't work out with the Merry Maids. I might be assigned to a new team that I would have to start over with, or, I would be sent back to the Academy to wait for another assignment. I could miss out on all the adventures in store for the Merry Maids.

"Okay," I said. "I will be very careful."

He gave me a pat on the shoulder.

"See me in the Medlab before your next workout," AJ said the next morning when I stumbled into the kitchen. "I want to examine your muscles and make sure they've recovered from their strain."

I mumbled something in agreement. He looked like he had just been for a jog. I saw him nab a tube of water from the chiller and head out.

"Is it just me, or did you and AJ become friendlier?" Marco asked. He handed me a cup of black coffee and turned back to the machine to make another one.

"I think he stopped being skeevy," I said. "At last."

Marco snickered but did not disagree.

"For some reason, I was dreaming about spaghetti and meatballs," he said. He left to check his nav system and I wandered back to my room.

"Workout today?" I heard Gig ask before I could close my door. I saw him standing in his own doorway. He looked like he'd been dreaming about spaghetti and meatballs too. He wiped at his eyes and yawned lethargically.

"Yeah, I think we need it to shake off last night's dinner," I said. "Want to meet up in…"

I didn't know how long it was going to take AJ to scan me.

"…maybe an hour?" I finished.

He nodded and went back to his room.

I went into mine and closed the door. I brought my coffee with me into the washroom and spent the next few minutes washing up and braiding my hair. When I had changed into some practice gear, I sat on the floor of my room and did some morning stretches while I sipped the last of my coffee and stared out at the stars.

It was Cutter's birthday today.

Last year, I had traded in some of my stuff for Units so I could buy the items I needed to make Cutter a cake. It had taken a lot of determination to keep the other students away from it before I could present it to Cutter. I knew he loved it because no one was offered a piece until he was full. I think he had at least two or three pieces that day.

I wondered if anyone was helping Cutter celebrate his birthday today.

"Happy birthday, my friend," I said to the stars.

When I found AJ in the Medic's lab, he was in the middle of cleaning and polishing his supplies.

"Is this what you do in here all day?" I joked.

AJ half-frowned at me but he seemed to know I was kidding.

"Do you mind lying on this table so I can scan your back?"

I went to the nearest table and lay my head on the pillow.

"Will this take long?" I asked.

"Why, do you have somewhere you need to be?" he asked.

"No, I just hate your tables," I said. "As the person who has probably been here the most these past few weeks, I can tell you that they're not very comfortable."

"I will notate that," he said. He came closer with a Medical wand in his hand. "Please hold still for a moment."

I closed my eyes and regulated my breathing while he scanned me. I could hear him quietly circulate the table for a few moments.

"You probably need to wait at least two more days before carrying anything heavier than half your body weight," he said.

I opened my eyes and looked at him.

"No problem," I said. "Anything else?"

He looked like he wanted to say something more. His weight shifted so he could lean his hip against the table. I sat up and waited.

"How are you adjusting to life away from the Academy?" he asked.

I frowned at him.

"Are you psych eval-ing me, now?" I asked.

He rolled his eyes. He obviously didn't like my tone of voice.

"As the Medic, I am responsible for physical and mental health of all on this team," he said.

I pushed myself off the table so I could face him with the table between us.

"If you were concerned about my mental health, you wouldn't have made it so uncomfortable for me to be around you," I said. "Of everyone on this team, you have been the one I've avoided most."

"I wasn't trying to torture you," he said, "I just didn't realize…"

"That's the problem, AJ," I said. "You didn't stop until you read my private med file."

He closed his mouth and nodded.

"You now know more about me than anyone else on this ship," I said. "But it should not have taken *that* for you to treat me better."

He had the class to look ashamed.

I turned to leave but thought of something before I got to the door. When I looked back at him, AJ was in his desk chair looking pained.

Probably from the horror of having to admit he was wrong.

"Thanks, by the way," I said. His clear blue eyes met mine. "For keeping my file private. I appreciate that."

He nodded.

14

"Keep up!"

I stumbled from my gawking at everything around me and tried to find Gig in the swarm of people we waded through. He was on the opposite side of the street, waving me down. With this many people all heading in the same direction, it was almost impossible to change directions. Even using my tele to gently push people out of the way, it took me an impossible amount of time to go what should have taken me ten steps to accomplish.

Gig himself was not immovable. The swarming people jostled even him, and caused him to move away as I drew nearer. When I got to his side, I could tell he was about to scold me to stay close but he had to push a man away who was about to walk into me.

The noise didn't help. The sound of these people talking, shouting and laughing, was deafening. I wanted to clap my hands over my ears but I didn't think it would help. I didn't think it was possible but just the sound of human voices was a distraction to overcome. I was grateful for our comm links, so at least Gig could hear me without having to lose my voice shouting.

"Can you put me on your shoulders, like a little kid?" I joked. I had seen kids being carried that way at a fair that Stryker had once taken me to explore. Gig's lips curled a little but he didn't fully smile.

"We're supposed to blend in, not stand out, remember?"

"Piggyback?"

He shook his head.

"Come on," he grumbled. He looped his right arm around my shoulder and hustled me along with the tide of people. When needed, he used his left arm to block people from separating us. I tried not to stare at everything like a greenie but it was difficult. Jubilee was the most visually stunning place I had ever seen. All of the buildings that towered on either side of the street we were traveling seemed to be made of a metallic white phosphorescent material that I struggled to identify. They all had flashing signs, advertisements or interesting lettering that I wanted to stop and study. Gig was relentless, and kept me moving despite myself.

Prior to this mission, Gig had explained why using local transport wasn't an option. He didn't want anyone to scan our carrier and identify us as ever having been to Jubilee. At the rate we were going though, and the colorfulness of his cursing, I wondered if Gig had changed his mind.

"You're almost there," I heard the Captain say in my ear. "Stay together."

Gig grunted.

It took us an hour but I finally spotted the warehouse we needed to get into.

"There she is," I said. I glanced at Gig and saw he'd spotted the building too.

We'd spent hours poring over the warehouse's specs when we weren't training. It turns out AJ was better at research than either of us, so I had convinced Gig to let AJ help us. We learned our destination was a secured warehouse run by the city, with thousands of public workers who came in and out each day to work there. Gig and I had created fake credentials to pose as employees for the day. We were dressed in the best semblance of warehouse uniforms we could find but Gig was determined that we not stick around long enough for anyone to look at them.

"We just need to get in, secure the piece, and avoid the roaming security bots," Gig had said before we leapt off ship. Marco had deposited us on the outskirts of Jubilee where fly-ins were common and he could mix with passenger and cargo ships. We shadowed a passenger ship that brought workers up to Jubilee from another city, and then blended ourselves into their queue as they made their way down the congested streets leading to the warehouse district.

I tried to picture Hector making this trip years before, and wondered if the city had changed at all since he walked this path. It seemed so far removed from his prison on the beach.

"Security check," Gig muttered.

I looked up and saw we had made it to the check-in gate at the warehouse. The workers around us were pressed even tighter together, so they could file past the check-in, single file. Gig put me in front of him, and kept close even though there was a lot less jostling. The noise had also reduced to tolerable levels at last. I took several breaths to keep my heart rate low and watched what people did ahead of us. Everyone seemed to take their ID cards and hold them up as they passed the main gate. The gate was built to scan them as they passed. It lit green with each successful scan.

I stared at the person in front of me as I shuffled through the gate with my fake credential held over my head. It scanned green.

Next was Gig. My breath stopped when he tried to pass the gate. There was an angry sounding bleep that drew everyone's attention. I glanced back and saw the gate had flashed a red color. I felt Gig's tension at my back but didn't dare to look at his face.

"Stupid 'chinery," he groused loudly.

"Backup," a guard's voice called out. "Everyone back up so he can scan it again."

I paused, not sure if I should wait.

"Move," Gig said loudly. I knew it was for my benefit. "Everyone back up."

My limbs felt like static pulses were going through them.

"Keep going, Alyvia," the Captain said in my ear. "Wait for Gig in your first backup meeting place."

Gig and I had agreed on five places to meet if we should get separated for any reason. I took a deep breath and forced myself to move forward again. To keep myself from worrying, I counted every step that took me away from Gig.

"C'mere, man," I could hear the guard say to Gig.

"This is the third time I've had to be hand scanned," Gig grumbled. What he said could be true. Caro was a member of the Order. We had been given special access to satellite records of this warehouse, so we knew this particular gate was buggy.

"Yeah, yeah, just give me your badge," the guard said.

I tried to move away slowly but the crowd around me had picked up speed again. I felt like a lost leaf on their current. I couldn't hear the conversation Gig was having behind me, so I gave up and walked normally. I was up the steps that lead into the warehouse and about to walk through the main doors when I felt more than saw that someone watched me.

"Hey, Sweetheart," a man called.

I frowned and looked for the voice. Who would call someone Sweetheart in this day and age? When I spotted who it was, I saw a pair of bushy brown eyebrows first. The man who sported them was probably about Marco's age. He wore the warehouse uniform and was only about three people to my right but he stared right at me.

"Did you just call me Sweetheart?" I asked him. The men between us snickered but when they saw who I was talking to, they changed directions to get out of our way.

"You're supposed to remain out of sight," the Captain reminded me in my ear. *Too late*, I thought.

"Yeah, I did," the man said. "This your first day?"

"Why do you ask?"

"Because everyone knows they got to put this on before walking through these doors," he said, and pointed at the helmet perched on his head. The commanding tone of his voice told me this guy was used to bossing people around. He was probably one of the foremen and I'd caught his attention.

Great.

I reached down and unclipped my helmet from my belt.

"What are you, the helmet police?" I mumbled. I donned my helmet and noticed that, sure enough, everyone else already had their helmets on too. I was annoyed we had missed this detail.

"Thanks, boss," I said to the man. I turned and kept walking through the entrance.

I intended to part ways with him but the man seemed intent to keep pace with me. I changed course and angled to the opposite side wall away from him but the man made his way to my side anyway. His hands were slightly gnarled, and would be too arthritic to use within a few years. Nevertheless, they were fisted at his sides when he got close.

"Do we have a problem here?" the Captain asked in my ear.

I met the man's eyes as he neared. They were trained on me, and he did not look amused.

"Yep," I said in a low voice. When he finally made it through the mob of workers to stand in front of me, I asked, "can I help you?"

"What are you doing?" the man asked. "You're supposed to report to your shift."

"I know that," I said. "I'm early for my shift. Please leave me alone."

The man huffed.

"You don't look like you belong with these warehouse girls, Sweetheart," he said. "You're too soft and pretty."

I raised an eyebrow at him.

"Thank you?"

He frowned at me.

"Rumors floatin' around that the Order been sending spies to these warehouses, looking for something to steal," he said. "You know anything about that?"

I did because I was there to steal something. I raised both my eyebrows now and tried to look eager as I stepped a little closer to him. I caught a whiff of sweat from his shirt and tried not to breathe it in too deeply.

"Wait, the Order's here?" I asked. "You know where?"

The man suddenly looked very disgusted with me.

"Oh I see," he said, and backed up.

"What?" I didn't think my question would work this well. The man was finally interested in leaving me alone. He was about two seconds from walking off.

"No loyalty to yer family, eh," he said. "You want to jump planet and run off to the Order. Probably got some dumb hulking boyfriend who wants to make a name for himself."

I shrugged. And like magic, Gig was suddenly there at my side.

"Hey baby," he said, and put an arm around me. "Thanks for waiting for me to get here."

I saw the stranger's eyes flash in anger at Gig. He stomped away, barely blending into the herd of people around him. Gig watched him leave too. He dropped his arm as soon as the man was out of sight.

"Oh good, my dumb boyfriend is here," I joked. I could hear Marco laugh in my ear and a snicker from the Captain.

There was a ghost of a smile on his face.

"Shut up," he said. "Let's get out of here."

"How could he have known that the Order was here," we heard the Captain muse.

I followed Gig further into the warehouse until we came to an oversized metal stairwell that run up the left wall. Gig and I needed to get to the fifth level, and we knew from our scouting that this stairwell could take us there. The only awkward part was that most workers didn't stop at five, they were mostly on floors eight and above. Gig had contrived a lame way for us to try and sneak into the floor five stairwell. As soon as we got to the fifth floor, he grabbed me by the waist and hauled me toward the door that would grant us access. I was ready. I had sighted some lights on the level across from us and used my tele to make their stairwell suddenly flash on and off like a kid playing with the switch. The workers around us all swiveled their heads to look, and the workers on that level who were in the stairwell looked frightened for a moment. That was all the distraction we needed before Gig quietly zipped me through the doorway and closed the door behind us.

"Nicely done," he said.

"You too."

Gig and I were now in a poorly lit hallway. There were four metal doors on the left and two on the right, then the hallway made a right turn and disappeared from sight.

"We want that one," Gig said. He pointed at the second door on the right. "You're up, Marco."

"Standby," Marco said in our ears.

Gig and I walked slowly toward the door. We saw an access panel on the right side of the doorway. It suddenly lit up and seemed to start cycling letters and numbers across its face. After a few moments, it lit a solid green.

"Go," Marco said.

Gig pulled open the door and peered inside.

"It's dark," he said quietly. "Put on your night eyes."

I adjusted my nightvision over my eyes and followed him through the door. Gig slid his into place as well and led the way. When we heard the door click shut behind us we relaxed a bit.

I scanned the room and saw towers of bins from the floor to the ceiling pushed up against the walls. There were bins stacked in haphazard piles around the middle of the room too, though not as high. There were empty walkways around them, just wide enough for a drone to maneuver through them and retrieve cargo as needed.

"Do you remember where to go?" Gig asked me.

I nodded.

"Follow me," I said. We rounded a pile of cargo ahead of us and followed it on the left side. Hector had provided specific instructions for where to go. I knew the prize was near the far back left wall. We had a climb ahead of us, but this was a straightforward mission.

Gig and I had only made it about 200 steps before the lights suddenly flooded our night eyes. I had time to suck in a breath before Gig covered my mouth with his hand and hustled me toward a nook in the wall. I pulled off my night eyes and blinked at the suddenly lit-up warehouse around us.

"I told you they wouldn't make it here before we did," we heard a male gloat from near the entrance.

"Shut up, idiot," a woman hissed.

Gig was a wall of tension beside me. I pulled his hand off my mouth and looked around at the towers around us. Across the aisle, I could see a break in the cargo where I could climb and hide, if needed.

"Do we even know what we're looking for?" a third voice asked. Another male.

"We need cargo from marker thirteen twelve," the woman said. "Let's hurry up and find it."

I looked at Gig and saw that he was staring toward the entrance with his eyes narrowed. The voices of our intruders were heading to the right, away from the path we'd taken.

"That's our bin," I whispered. "They're here for the Starkiller piece."

Gig's eyes met mine. He looked like he was in pain.

"What's wrong?" I asked.

Gig closed his eyes and pinched his nose.

"That woman is Maddy," he said. "I recognize her voice."

"Maddy?" we heard Marco exclaim in our ear pieces.

"What the hell is she doing there?" the Captain wanted to know. "How did she find out about the Starkiller?"

"We have a mole," I suggested.

"Impossible," Gig said.

"The Order, then," I said. I thought of Master Omin and Master Maranda. They didn't seem to trust the Captain. I wouldn't put it past them to try and circumvent the Merry Maids if they could. This time, we hadn't gone to Hector directly. He had told me the whereabouts of the Starkiller in a series of encrypted messages. Maddy could have been given part of the information but she obviously hadn't been given the map.

"We're supposed to turn our pieces over to Master Omin tomorrow," the Captain said over the comm. "So it doesn't make sense for him to try and slide in before our job is done."

Gig opened his mouth to reply but another voice interrupted.

"This is the fifth room we've looked in," we heard one of the men say. His voice came from the aisle next to ours. "If we don't find it soon, we're going to run into your friends."

"Shut *up*, I said," Maddy told him. She sounded pissed.

"I wonder what they'll say when they see you," the man continued. He obviously didn't care that Maddy wanted him to be quiet. "I hope I'm there to see their faces when they realize you're working against them now."

Gig's face was like a storm cloud. I elbowed him gently. He looked down at me with questions in his eyes that I couldn't answer. If Maddy and the two men made a loop around our wall, they would see us immediately. We needed to decide if we were going to hide, fight, or talk. Gig saw my hand gestures and shook his head no when I made a motion to fight. He nodded when I said hide or talk.

Which? I asked him.

The intruders' voices moved on. We waited and watched but they did not turn the corner in our direction. Gig turned back to me and made some hand signals of his own. He motioned for me to go on and get the Starkiller piece. He was going to follow Maddy.

I frowned at him. Why would he want to follow Maddy? His duty was to me, and our mission.

It's okay, he signaled. *Go ahead.*

I made a face but did as he suggested. Maddy and her team were angling from where we were in a horizontal line. They had gone right when they walked in, turned left to come back toward where we were, and were now angling right again. By the time they made lined circuits of the entire warehouse, the location of the Starkiller would be one of the last areas they reached. If I made a beeline to the piece and stayed out of their sight, I could potentially grab the piece and be back to the front entrance before they ever got there.

It felt weird to walk away from Gig but I knew what I had to do. I didn't look back to see him trail Maddy. I was peeved at this whole thing but we could talk about it later.

I quietly jogged around the cargo piles to the back of the room. I tried to take as little time as possible. At first, the labels for each tower were confusing when I read them. It didn't seem like the piles made sense except that the numbers seemed to generally go down the further back into the room I pushed.

As soon as I sighted the tower I wanted, I looked up to confirm that cargo bin thirteen twelve was the fourth bin from the bottom. There it was, with two bins piled on top. Normally, a drone would be able to lift and maneuver the bins out of the way to get to the one I wanted but we didn't want any record of activity in this warehouse. That meant I had to move the bin myself without Gig's help. I couldn't hear Maddy and the others from wherever they were, so I got started and hoped they wouldn't notice the movement. I used my tele to slowly lift the topmost bin and set it on the pile beside it. The bin was light, and it was easy to move without much noise. The second bin was heavier but I was able to lift it as well. I pushed it over to the pile behind it and settled it quietly. Now I was able to get to the bin I wanted. I shifted it forward carefully, with the intent to set it on the ground at my feet.

"Stop," Gig whispered in my earpiece. I immediately stopped the bin. It peeked out about a quarter of the way. "I think they saw you."

"What do I do?" I whispered back.

"Standby," he said. "I'm going to make a distraction. Grab the bin and then meet me at the door."

"A distraction?" I wanted to say but I bit my lip. My eyes were trained on the bin I needed and I didn't want the distraction to force me to lose it.

The Captain didn't have the same problem.

"What kind of distraction?" she said in our ears. "Too much noise from this quadrant will attract security drones."

Gig didn't reply. Instead, I heard a sudden thunderous crash from the other side of the warehouse, followed by confused shouting. I didn't wait for Gig to call an order. I swooped the bin off the shelf and let it settle at my feet. I had the lid off a heartbeat later. It revealed canvas tarps and metal rods. I heard the sound of a drone and turned to look over my shoulder. A security drone hovered near the entrance. It looked like it was scanning the room. I slid quietly around a tower of bins so that I was out of its sight. Then I turned and peered as far back as I could to the far right side of the room.

"Gig, I hope you're making your way to the exit," I said quietly. "A security drone just flew in."

Then I used my tele to topple another tower of bins. They made a satisfying crash and a plume of dust grew from the pile.

The security drone sounded a short bleep and sailed straight for the ruckus. I watched it go, and then turned back to my work. Below the canvas bags, I found a pack with the numbers 1312 stamped on the outside. This is what I'd come for. I snatched it up and pulled the straps over my shoulders. Gig came running around a corner the moment I turned toward the door.

"Come on," he whisper shouted, and gestured for me to move, move, move. I ran to him, and then past him, leading the way to the exit. Gig was swiveling his head to see if anyone followed us. We were about to make it to the exit doors when they suddenly whooshed open and two more security drones flew in. I didn't think, I just reacted. I *pushed* and the drones went up high, close to the ceiling, with no control of their gyrometrics. Gig and I sailed out the door before I let them go.

"Lock the door, Marco," Gig called out.

"Already done," Marco said.

"Open the opposite door."

We watched the control panel come to life, and then whir green. When Gig and I stepped inside, this warehouse was pitch black, just like the one we'd just been inside.

"What are we doing?" I asked him when the door was shut. According to plan, we were supposed to exit back to the staircase, follow the other men up a few more floors, and then join the queue of crew who were leaving, and blend in with them as they left for the day.

"I want to see if they come out," Gig said.

"You're waiting for Maddy," I said.

"I want to know if they get arrested, or if they walk out," he said. I pulled on my nightvision again, and saw him peer through the window that led into the hallway.

"Why?" I asked.

"Because if the Order is working against us, and hired Maddy to do it, then we have bigger problems," he said.

"I tend to agree but I don't like that you're still in that bay," the Captain said. "We could figure out if Maddy gets arrested by linking in to the security cameras again."

"We don't want our signatures in the security system too long," Marco said. "I already wiped them arriving and I need to wipe them leaving. If I also snoop for other things, we may trigger a red flag and we don't want that kind of attention."

"I think we should get out of here, but I'm willing to stay if you want to see what happens to your friend," I said.

Gig looked my way and nodded.

While he went back to peering through the window, I turned to scan the room behind us. Like the other warehouse, this room was stacked with bins in columns from side to side. There was more order to this warehouse than there was in the last. The columns were arranged neatly and evenly on all sides and their labels made order in how they were arranged along the line.

"I see them," Gig whispered.

There was a long pause. Then he stood up slowly, with a rigidity to his back.

"Well I guess that answers that," he said.

I edged toward Gig.

"What happened?" I asked him.

"They walked out," Gig said. "Maddy was working for the Order."

I nodded. I was not surprised. Being at the Academy was different than being in the field on assignment. No one at the Academy taught double-dealing and trickery as part of the coursework. I had learned that from growing up on a planet where the people in charge were all snakes.

"Come back to the ship," the Captain said. She sounded furious.

"I need to call some meetings."

Gig and I were in the gym when the Captain walked in. She stopped when she realized all of the practice balls were paused mid-air around the room.

"Do you mind?" she asked me.

With a quick pull, the balls all lurched back to the container where they belonged. They pinged into place with multiple thunks as they hit the bin and settled in place.

"What news, Captain?" Gig asked.

"I've been getting the runaround from the Order," she said. "They deny sending Maddy with a team to steal the Starkiller piece from us. Master Omin wants us to stay put until he arrives and then the rest of the Council wants us to return to Master Ignoracius. They believe if our communications are compromised, we have to go back to speaking with Hector in person."

"That's ridiculous," Gig said. "Going back and forth between Hector and each mission will extend this mission for weeks."

"There was never a timeline on this mission," the Captain said. "We are at the mercy of the Council."

"So what are they doing about Maddy?" I asked. "If they're not claiming her, are they going to look for her?"

"Yes," the Captain said. Her eyes went to Gig to gauge his reaction. "They plan to find her to see who she works for and find out why she's involved."

Gig frowned but nodded his head.

"Stay on your guards," she said. "If Maddy is still out there, I don't want to risk a run-in that we're not prepared to handle."

I looked between her and Gig and assumed she meant a run-in that Gig was not prepared to handle. When the Captain left, Gig went in search of the punching bag. I pulled the tape off my hands and feet since it looked like we were done here. I left him alone and made my way to my room. I could see the lights of Jubilee from my window. It was stunning even from this distance. I sat at my desk, stared at the city, and daydreamed about what it must be like to live in such a crowded but beautiful city.

I eventually hauled my butt to the shower when I realized the rumbling sound I kept hearing was my stomach announcing that it was empty.

"The Captain is meeting Master Omin in the city, and Gig is escorting her," Marco explained when I came for dinner that night.

I nodded and sat next to AJ. I had spent the past few hours anxiously dreading the call that Master Omin had arrived and that I needed to come greet him. I sighed in relief and spooned some salad and meat on my plate. The weight of worry lifted from my gut.

I paused.

"Do you think Master Omin will return with the Captain?"

Marco made a face and shook his head.

"Master Omin has never set foot on our ship, I'm sure he doesn't intend to do so now, either."

"Don't worry," AJ said to me. "He doesn't have to come near you if you don't want him to."

I looked at AJ in surprise.

"I'm not sure that's how the Order works but…thanks," I said.

I glanced at Marco. He was making a scared face at AJ. It caught me off guard, and I laughed. When AJ glanced from me to Marco, Marco's face was back to normal. He put a piece of meat in his mouth and chewed with an innocent look on his face.

"Are you guys making fun of me?" AJ asked.

I didn't know what to say.

"No," Marco said when he swallowed. "However we are laughing *because* of you."

AJ frowned at him but didn't say anything.

"Marco's like your big brother," I said. "He has to keep you humble."

"I already have a brother," AJ said. "He doesn't try to keep me humble."

I glanced at him to see if we hurt his feelings but he was looking at his food while he cut up his meat.

"What is he like?" I asked.

"He's more messed up than me," AJ said. He shrugged. "It's fine."

I frowned at him. He seemed uncomfortable and…maybe a little lost.

I glanced at Marco, and saw he was kind of frowning at AJ too. We were both trying to figure out if AJ was messing with us, or if a wall had come down. I decided to go ahead and be the sucker.

"Did you guys have crappy parents or something?" I asked AJ. I knew a lot about that subject.

AJ gave a short laugh.

"They're perfectionists," he said, and stabbed at his food. "Except no matter how perfect we are, we still can't seem to be perfect enough. I graduated as the earliest field doctor in Academy history and my parents still had nothing positive to say."

"Nothing?" Marco asked. "I didn't know that, man."

AJ shrugged again and kept eating.

"I mean, I wasn't raised under traditional circumstances but even I know that is not the way to treat your kid," Marco said.

I hadn't asked Marco about his life before the Academy.

"Did you have crappy parents too?" I asked him. AJ seemed to relax when I took the focus off of him. I hadn't realized he was tense until that moment.

"My parents didn't even stick around," Marco said. "I was abandoned at a transfer station where Pilots fuel up for their routes."

My heart went out to him. AJ said sorry. We were quiet for a moment.

Marco glanced at me and so did AJ. I felt dread creep across my gut. I knew it was my turn to share and I really didn't want to. There were two Alyvias, Alyvia before the Academy and Alyvia after the Academy. Every day since the moment I'd come to the Academy, I had built up a wall between who I am now and who I used to be.

A monster.

I was stronger now. Tougher.

And yet, I was still afraid to peek over that wall. I didn't want to remind myself of how things were before. I was terrified, actually. I spent so long trying to erase the past that I didn't even know what would happen if I stopped. The only regret to burying everything away was that it also meant I was burying memories of my brother too.

I cleared my throat. My vision swam a little but I blinked it away.

"If it's any consolation," I rasped. "My parents were shit too."

AJ and Marco nodded. They knew I was going to say that but they didn't know why.

"We're the shit parents club," Marco said.

"Actually, we are," AJ agreed. "Cap's parents are supportive as hell and Gig's dad adores him for some reason."

"The asshole," Marco offered.

AJ nodded but he was smirking.

"To the shit parents club," Marco said. He lifted his cup.

"To the shit parents club," AJ repeated. He reached for his own cup and lifted it up to clink against Marco's.

I looked for my cup and saw I'd set it by my left hand. As I reached for it, I sighed a little. I had once asked Stryker why my parents didn't like me. He had told me it wasn't my fault but I had a nagging feeling that part of it was my fault. I had wasted time wishing that I wasn't in the shit parents club but as I grew up and saw how parents came to visit their kids at the Academy, and how they doted on them and gassed them up, I slowly realized that my experience was unnatural. I was the admiral of the shit parents club. When I came to the Merry Maids, I was terrified that Master Omin was going to alienate me from the team because of it.

I lifted my glass and smiled at Marco and AJ.

We were actually bonding over this.

I moved my glass to clink it with theirs, and opened my mouth to say the toast. Before the first word left my lips, the nearest comm panel suddenly lit up red and an alarm began to chirp through the entire ship.

Marco dropped his glass and lit over to the wall. His chair tumbled over in his wake. AJ jumped up and grabbed Marco's glass to right it but the red wine spread across the table and dripped to the floor. I saw Marco hit the comm link.

"Code red," Gig's voice shouted over the speaker. "Immediate extraction."

Marco cursed and hit two more buttons on the comm control.

"What happened?" he yelled. "Send coordinates."

He bolted from the wall out of the room, in the direction of his Pilot's chair. Gig's voice echoed through the entire ship so we could hear him and move about as necessary. The sound of yelling and shattering glass broadcast from wherever Gig and the Captain were. It sounded like he was in the middle of a riot.

They were just supposed to be at dinner.

Gig relayed their coordinates and told Marco NTW. I raised my eyebrows. No Time Wasted?

"We were attacked," Gig said. "The Captain and Omin are down. They both need immediate medical attention."

AJ stopped fussing over the spilled drink and ran from the room, headed toward his lab.

"Prepping medkits now," he yelled. "Marco, ETA?"

213

"Three minutes," Marco answered. I could hear him over the comm line as he smacked at his toggles and cursed under his breath.

There was a pause. I heard our ship's engines roar to life and felt the shift as it lifted into the air.

"Tippin," Gig said over the comm. I heard the sound of gunfire and then he grunted.

"Aye," I called out immediately. I hadn't moved except to put my glass back down on the table. I stared at the spreading stain of Marco's wine and listened.

"I don't want to do this, but I need you as backup," Gig said. "Go to my room and grab a gun from my wall called Azrael. It's on the left-hand side, about waist level. Pick one for you too from the top shelf. Get your gear on and as soon as Marco is above us, get your ass here immediately. Marco, as soon as she's down prep two baskets for Omin and the Cap. We need to hightail before the authorities arrive."

I jumped up and ran to Gig's room. I turned on his lights so I wouldn't walk into any of his workout gear and went to inspect his arsenal. I had seen it before but hadn't inspected it like I did now. Gig's weapons were lovingly polished and neatly labeled. I scanned them for the one he wanted. Azrael was right where he mentioned, except it was at his waist level, not mine. The thing was a beast with quick clips and two sighters. It looked like the kind of weapon you would use if you wanted to get multiple rounds off as quickly as possible but still only take up one hand.

I looked at the top shelf and saw a selection of simple guns that were small and semi-dainty. They had cutesy names like Nyx and Shini. I made a face. Why couldn't he have told me to grab a gun with a little more meat? As I looked for one that appealed to me, I listened as Gig and Marco relayed messages. The sound of gunfire still raged where Gig was but his tone never changed. If he sounded upset, I might have been scared or nervous but he didn't. He was calm and matter of fact. It made me feel like I was just heading to the Academy's shooting range for some practice with Cutter and his Gunner friends.

Every so often we heard the murmur of a woman's voice. I wondered how bad the Captain's injuries were. Gig was probably furious that he hadn't been able to keep her from an injury.

"Two minutes," Marco announced. We were close to arrival.

I sighed and grabbed the biggest gun I saw on the top shelf. It was labeled Seth, which sounded like an unassuming name for a gun. I had to tuck Seth into my belt when I grabbed Azrael – Azrael was just as much of a monster as I assumed it would be, and it felt uncomfortable in my hands. I cradled it to my chest awkwardly and ran to my room. I dropped Gig's toy on my bed so I could dump my feet into boots and pull on gear over my lounging clothes. I strapped on my knives, snagged a tie for my hair and then grabbed Azrael again.

I almost knocked AJ over as I ran from my room.

"I'll help you get strapped in your jump harness," he said. "Give me that."

He took Azrael from my hands and propped the weight on his shoulder.

"You don't have to make that look so easy," I grumbled.

I ran after him as he led the way to the dock.

"What?" AJ called over his shoulder.

"Nothing."

"Thirty seconds," we heard Marco say over the comm.

"She's strapping in now," AJ said. He helped me step into the line. While he worked on my connections, I belted a comm link to my wrist and then tied up my hair. When I was ready, he handed me Azrael.

"Marco, she's a go," AJ called out. He backed away from me.

"Thanks," I said to him. The lights by the bay doors started to flash, and a blip later the doors began to open.

"Be careful," AJ said.

I nodded that I heard him and turned to watch the night sky yawn open in front of me. As soon as the doors stopped, I stepped to the lip and peered over. Marco had navigated us to a part of Jubilee that was quiet. Or should have been. Whoever was trying to get to Gig and our Cap had numbers. I saw them swarming the lower levels of the warehouse that we hovered above.

"Go when ready," Marco's voice called out.

I pressed Azrael close and leapt into the night.

215

15

As soon my feet touched the roof, I put Azrael on the ground and then slipped myself out of the line. When I was free and had Azrael's weight crushed against my chest again, I sprinted toward the nearest stairwell. I had tried to take in as much of the area as I could while I dropped. The building Gig had led us to was three stories, with very few windows and surrounded by a ten-foot fence. It reminded me of the warehouse Gig and I had looted earlier except much smaller in comparison and on the unpopulated outskirts of Jubilee. Dozens of similar buildings littered the neighborhood but only a handful of the other buildings were still lit up.

This area was either used for long-term storage or it was abandoned.

Whoever wanted to get to Gig and the Cap crawled the first floor like ants. As soon as they sighted our ship I heard them yell and curse but none of them opened fire. Adrenaline pumped my heart faster than normal. I twisted the handle to the stairwell door and flung it open, then as it started to swing shut, I peeked at the last minute to see if anyone was on the other side.

Empty.

I pulled Seth from my waistband and cautiously opened the door again. It looked like the stairwell was open from my floor to the bottom. I heard shouting and breaking glass down below me but I didn't take the chance of peering over the railing.

"I'm in," I said quietly. "Where are you, Gig?"

"Third floor," he answered immediately. "I triggered a flood on the second floor that's slowing them down but some of them just made it to this floor. I need you to help me get Omin and the Captain to where you are and then up to the roof. I can't carry them both AND return fire."

I hugged the wall and ran down the stairs until I saw the door to the third floor. I could feel heat now in the stairwell with me.

"Is there a fire below me?" I asked.

"Probably," Gig said. "I left some explosives for them to trigger if they tried to use the stairwell where you would be."

A loud boom directly beneath my feet announced another explosive triggered. I immediately regretted not getting any earplugs before jumping. I hadn't even thought about it.

"What was that?" Marco shouted over the ringing in my ear.

"One of Gig's bombs," I said quickly. Smoke wafted up and swirled in the air around me. I coughed as the acrid smell choked up my nose.

"That sounded too close," Marco replied.

"Gig, I'm at the door," I said. "Are they coming in the opposite side?"

"Yes," he said. "When you open the door, they will see you. Is there anything you can use to prop it?"

I looked around but the stairwell was empty. Azrael's weight might work, though.

"Yeah, I think I've got something," I said to the massive gun. "Where are you in the room?"

"When you step in, we're about fifteen paces to the right tucked behind a cement pony wall."

"How many are of these guys are in the room too?"

"Seven," he said. "Take out the two by the door across from you. I'll cover you. Then get back into the stairwell and wait for me. I'm going to come get my gun from you and then clear the rest of the room. I want you to use your tele to close the opposite door and barricade it. Once we're clear, I can grab Omin if you can grab the Captain. We need to get out of here ten minutes ago."

"Copy," I said. I set down Azrael against the wall right next to where the door would end up when it swung open. Then I grabbed one of my knives from my belt and held Seth at the ready again. "On your signal."

Time slowed as I sucked in slow, steady breaths and bounced a little on the balls of my feet.

"Go!" Gig called out.

I used my telekinesis to turn the handle and throw my door open. As an afterthought, I used my tele to slide Azrael over to keep it open. When I stepped forward, I spotted two men in warehouse bibs and work boots at the opposite door, at about the same time they saw me. I whipped my wrist and flung my knife at the man I saw first. I fired my gun at the second man and stepped back. I was out of the way before they could get their shots off. The wall was pelted with a few bullets but I knew I'd hit them both. In my hand, Seth made a weird hissing sound that made me stare. It sounded like a snake was trapped in the barrel.

The rap of a gun sounded from the room and quickly moved toward my position, followed by the sound of returned fire. I peered around the edge of the door to the opposite doorway and saw the men were no longer standing there. One of them had a knife protruding from his neck as he lay still on his back. I pulled with my tele and watched the knife snatch back into my waiting hand.

The other man was also on the ground but he rolled around in pain. I'd managed to shoot him in the shoulder or chest but it wasn't a fatal shot. Yet.

I *pushed* away from me with my tele, and shoved the bodies of both men through the open doorway. I slammed their door shut and slid the bolt closed that would lock out anyone else coming from that way. I looked around at the path between our doors to find something I could use to build up a blockade in case they managed to tear the door down. I saw drafting tables, brown boxes and shipping cartons. While I listened for Gig, I turned two drafting tables over and shoved them against the door lengthwise. They were metal concoctions, and *heavy*. For safe measure, I slid the shipping cartons over too. They were also heavy, and did a nice job of bracing the tables against the doorway.

"They got us trapped!" a voice yelled from the back of the room. "We need b—."

I flung a heavy brown box toward where I estimated the voice was, and heard the satisfying sound of a thump.

"Nice one," Gig's voice said in my ear.

He suddenly appeared in the doorway and almost barreled into me but I sidestepped him quickly. He had the Captain tucked under one arm.

"I thought you were going to go back for them," I said.

"Change of plans," Gig said. "She insists she's fine."

The Captain lifted her head blearily.

"It's just blood lossss," she slurred. "My arm."

She clutched her right arm tight to her chest. Gig had tied it with a handkerchief but the handkerchief wept dark red blood. Too much blood. Her hair was in shambles around her head, and her clothing was bloodied and torn.

Gig bent close so that I had to meet his eyes directly. His tone was firm but his hand on my chin was a whisper.

"Take her up and get her to AJ," he said. "I'll be right behind you after I collect Omin."

I took a steadying breath and nodded. He watched me as I quickly wiped the blood off my knife and put it back in the sheath.

"Aye," I said. I stepped in to take on the weight of the Captain from him. Seth stayed in my hand in case I needed him again.

"Oh, Gig, grab that doorstop, will you?"

Gig turned with a frown to see what I meant. I started to coax the Captain up the stairs but she almost tripped over them several times as we went up one step, swayed, and then tried to go up the next step. It was like trying to get a drunk to walk normally. I still heard Gig gasp.

"You used my baby as a door stop?"

He sounded so offended. It wasn't the time to laugh but I wanted to.

"What'd you do?" The Captain asked me. Her arm was over my shoulder and I held up most of her weight. I glanced back and saw that Gig had gone back into the warehouse. The sound of gunfire was louder and more frightening now with the addition of Azrael.

I tried to smile at her even though her eyes were unfocused.

"I used his gun as the doorstop," I said.

Her lips lifted in a half smile. I saw her right leg lift to step up onto the next step and she almost fell over. I caught her and dragged her back to her feet with some effort. We had only gotten to the fourth step. I was never going to get her out of here and make it to AJ before she bled out.

"This isn't going to work," I said. I paused and squatted down to grab at the Captain's legs. She toppled over my right shoulder easily. I caught her carefully, and then stood up with a grunt and balanced her weight.

"Do NOT drop me," she commanded. It was a weak command but I heard it anyway. I felt her hands clutch at the gear on my back.

"Aye, Captain," I said. "Hang on!"

I went up the stairs, trying not to jostle her too much or fall backward from her weight on my shoulder. She groaned but didn't say another word. I made it up to the roof and flung the door open.

The night was alive with yelling and the sound of the ship's engine.

"AJ, is that bucket down?" I yelled. "I've got the Captain."

"It's down," he said through the comm link. "I'm ready! You guys need to hurry. Reinforcements just showed up and I can see the Order's cruisers making their way here too. They're going to be on us in less than two minutes."

I scrambled across the roof to where the buckets were waiting. As I got closer I saw AJ inside the ship's dock watching our progress. As soon as I crossed to where the bucket was, I carefully leaned down and put the Captain in a bucket. She groaned but let me strap her into it.

"Well done, Tippin," she said tiredly.

"Get her up," I said to AJ. "I'm heading back for Omin."

"No need," Gig grunted over the comm. "We're coming up the steps now. Get yourself up."

AJ had started the Captain's line, and she was already halfway up to the ship. I picked up my line from earlier and strapped myself into it. I still had Seth clutched in my hand but I didn't want to put him away until we were all safe.

"Bring me up," I said to AJ. He hit the button for my line, and I started to rise. I used my weight to shift my body around so I could watch for Gig. He appeared a breath later. His body slammed through the door from the stairwell and onto the roof. His precious gun was in one hand and Master Omin was over his other shoulder. Omin looked like he was unconscious. I was grateful for that. A chill ran down my spine as soon as I spotted his robes and the top of his head.

It suddenly dawned on me that I was going to be trapped on a small ship with him. Anxiety started to flow through my veins as I watched Gig make it to the bucket and get Omin settled inside.

"Clear," AJ said close by. I'd reached the top. He grabbed my arm and helped me step up onto the lip of the dock, and then turned back to the Captain when he saw I was okay. His medical supplies were laid out beside them, and he reached for one that looked like a needle.

"I'm fine, AJ," the Captain was trying to say, "attend Omin first."

"He's not up yet," AJ said. "Stop talking, Captain."

The Cap looked like she'd been trapped in a smoky oven. I got a better look at her clothing, face and hair all covered in soot. She looked like she had broken a blood vessel in her eye and a bruise had started to form on her chin.

"Omin's in," Gig said. "Drop me a line."

"I'll do it," I said to AJ.

I pulled off my line and dropped it over for Gig, and then ran to the control station to hit the button to bring up Omin. I glanced over the lip of the dock and saw that Omin's bucket had started to raise. Gig had started to strap himself into his line.

Flashing lights caught my eye. I lifted my head to see what was happening.

"The Order's here," I called out. Their cruisers were in front of the building. They lit up all of the neighboring buildings, especially ours.

"Going dark," I heard Marco say.

All of the lights on the ship went into night mode. We could still see, but the lowlights made me squint.

"I can't work like this," AJ said. "I'm going to take the Captain to my lab. Bring Omin as soon as he's in."

"Copy," I said. I didn't watch AJ pack up and leave with the Captain's budget. Gig called out that he was ready to come up, so I hit the button that would lift his line. Omin's bucket had just reached the lip of the dock. I ran to him and slid his bucket into the dock. His eyes were closed and his breathing sounded shallow. I looked around for the bump attachment that would allow me to make his bucket gravitate so we could push him to the med lab when I heard Marco shout in my ear.

"Incoming!"

My head snapped up and I saw a man had emerged from the roof stairwell with a gun in his hand. The light from the stairs lit up his face. His warehouse bibs. His work boots. The familiar sight of his beard.

I sucked in a breath when I saw him lift his gun at Gig. Gig was a sitting duck dangling from his line. I didn't hesitate. I took a step, and my hands slammed together in front of me like a door slamming shut. The force of telekinesis that I shot at the man barreled into him and through him. The ship lurched backward under my feet as I watched the wave of tele lift him up and hurtle end over end, over the other edge of the roof. A look of perfect shock was on his face before he disappeared.

"What—," Marco's voice sounded surprised and I could hear an urgent alert start beeping on his console. Gig was up and over the lip of the dock a heartbeat later. I shook off my dread and ran to smack the button that would close the bay.

"Gig's inside," I said. "Go, Marco!"

"Copy," Marco said. I felt the ship shift and the view of the warehouse through the dock's windows fell away. "I'm turning off the AO comms."

The dock grew silent.

Gig had set Azrael down on a work bench so he could free himself from is line. I brought over Seth and set it down beside Azrael.

"You just saved my ass," Gig murmured to me.

I went back to looking for the gravity bump. It was next to one of AJ's medical boxes. I'd missed it in the low light. I snagged it, and brought it over to Omin so I could try to figure out which side of the bucket had the attachment.

"That was the man who questioned me earlier," I said. I remembered how he had dogged me at the warehouse when I got separated from Gig, and then the way his face had changed when my tele flung him off the roof. He was dead now.

Gig took the gravity bump from me and tapped the angled side. It lit up, and he crouched to slide it under Omin's bucket. In the lowlight of the dock I couldn't see Omin's face.

I shivered.

"I know," Gig said. "He led the first wave that shot the Captain's arm and almost took out Omin."

I glanced down at Omin's body in the shadows. Gig stood and pressed a button on Omin's bucket. The whole thing lifted and floated mid-air.

"I'll take him to AJ if you want to grab all this shit AJ left behind."

I clasped my hands together to stop their shaking.

"Fine with me," I agreed.

"Are you okay?" he asked.

"Of course I am," I said. I stepped toward AJ's stuff. "Let's…"

"No," Gig said. His hand stopped me and turned me to face him. "You're not."

I opened my mouth to protest but he leaned down and wrapped his arms around me in a tight hug that pressed me against his chest. I was surprised for a second and stood there dumbly. Then my mind finally cleared and my shoulders relaxed from where they were crowding my ears. I lifted my arms to hug him around the waist. I guess he was right. As soon as the tension left my body, it was obvious how much of it there had been, and I had been trying to ignore it.

Gig's tight hug loosened after a moment and he peered down at my face.

"Okay?" he asked again.

I nodded.

"Thank you," I said. I frowned at him. "How did you know?"

"I know you by now," he said. His hands slid up to palm the sides of my face. "I didn't want to drag you into that fight but when I saw you in action, I was impressed as hell. You didn't hesitate. You did what you had to do, and you saved my ass more than when I was dangling like target practice from that line. I needed backup in there and you took care of it."

I took a shaky breath.

"Thank you," I murmured.

Gig kissed me lightly on the lips. He looked like he was going to do it again, but he sighed and ducked his head. I let him give me another tight hug, and then he let me go.

"I'm going to take Omin to the Medlab now," he said with a groan. "Bring AJ's things?"

I smiled but I don't know if he could see it in the darkness.

"Okay," I said.

Gig gathered his guns and left with Omin's bucket. I turned and methodically packed up the medical supplies strewn around the floor.

I paused to tap at my wrist.

"Hey, Marco, do we still need it dark around here?"

"No," Marco said. The ship lit up again. "We weren't followed and just left atmo."

"Thank you."

Now that I could see, I neatly organized AJ's medical supplies onto one of the trolleys AJ had rolled into the hanger. Then I decided to re-loop all the tethers we'd used to jump ship and drop the buckets. I even did a quick walk up and down the dock with a broom, followed by a lazy mopping job that would have shamed my mother and sent me to punishment.

My stomach grumbled angrily. A wave of dizziness caused my skin to prickle. I took a deep breath and then grabbed AJ's trolley. I wanted to get it to him and then go find a snack. I turned on the follow feature on the trolley and then led it from the hanger to his lab. I was curious how the Captain was doing but I dreaded the moment I had to face Omin again.

When I came into the Medlab, the Captain was sitting up at one of the tables and talking with Gig. AJ was next to Master Omin, who was still unconscious. I breathed a sigh of relief and quietly tucked the trolley next to AJ's desk.

"Alyvia," the Captain said, "nice work. You and Gig make a decent extraction team."

I turned and stepped closer to her so I could peer at her arm.

"How are you?" I asked. AJ had strapped some kind of band to her injured arm, and it was lit up. The sleeve of her tunic had been cut away and dried blood tracked down to her elbow.

"I'll be fine within the hour," she said, and patted my shoulder.

"That's not what I said," AJ argued from where he worked.

The Captain glared at his back.

"Doctor Cason assured me I would be out of here in an hour," she said firmly.

AJ shook his head.

"No."

I smirked.

"Suddenly realize how crap these beds are?" I asked her. Her eyes twinkled in mischief, and probably painkillers.

"Why didn't you say something sooner?" she demanded.

I dropped my jaw in feigned offense.

"Maybe you'll start listening to me," I teased.

Gig tried to hide his grin.

"It's hard to work when you all are being loud," AJ complained.

The Captain laughed but tried to keep it quiet.

"Sorry," she whispered, but didn't sound sorry at all.

I didn't feel that sorry for AJ either but I went to his side anyway.

"Do you need help?" I asked him.

AJ glanced up at me in surprise but then quickly dropped his eyes back to what he was doing. It looked like his medical gloves were covered with Omin's blood.

"Do you know how to set up an IV?" he asked.

"No," I admitted.

Gig came over to join us.

"I do," he said. "I can do it."

My stomach grumbled again, louder this time.

AJ smirked but didn't look at me.

"Did you use your tele recently, Alyvia?"

My head snapped up to look at his face. I remembered how the ship had pitched below me and the man's face as he was sent flying over the edge of the roof.

"Um, yes," I admitted. "How did you know?"

AJ shook his head.

"Go fuel up, and try to eat some greens," he said.

I lifted an eyebrow at him even though he couldn't see my expression. Gig stared at him too.

"Okay," I said. He didn't have to tell me twice.

"Bring me something too," the Captain called after me.

I told her I would and excused myself to the kitchen. It was still a disaster area from our aborted dinner earlier. I noted our cold plates on the table and wondered if Marco was still hungry. He appeared in the doorway as if I had summoned him.

"Hey," he said. "Our course is set to Thredenar so we can get Omin back to the Council."

I nodded and blinked at the table. My vision was blurry.

"So much for dinner," I said. "Are you still hungry?"

"Yeah, I came to heat up my food again," he said. "Is that what you're doing?"

"AJ ordered me to eat something."

Marco gave me a funny half-bow that had me smiling.

"After you," he said.

I looked at my abandoned plate and heard my stomach grumble again. A wave of exhaustion rolled over me and I leaned on the tabletop to keep from falling over.

"Whoa," Marco said. He rushed over to help steady me. I felt his warm hand on my arm and let him help me sit in his chair.

"You go ahead with your food," I said. "I don't think I have the energy to wait for it to heat up."

The room spun dangerously.

"I'm going to go get AJ," Marco said. He sounded worried.

"No, no, no," I said. "AJ's busy. I just need to eat something. Can you hand me my plate?"

It was on the other side of the table, but it seemed so much further. I couldn't bring myself to stand up and reach for it. Marco helped slide it in front of me with a concerned frown on his face.

"Eat the salad while I heat up the meat," he ordered me. I saw his hand snag the meat off my plate and heard the sounds of him warming it.

I blearily picked up the fork and started to funnel salad into my mouth. I finished it before the meat was done heating, so Marco pushed his leftover salad onto my plate. I crunched on it gratefully.

"I was supposed to bring the Cap some food too," I remembered out loud.

"I'll take care of that in a minute," Marco promised.

I tried to nod but I swayed in my chair, and had to grip the table again to keep myself in my seat.

Marco came over and dropped two pieces of tender meat onto my plate and told me not to burn my tongue. I tried to use the fork to cut into it but the fork wasn't sharp enough to slice through. I put down the fork and grabbed the meat with my fingers with the intention of eating it like a caveman.

"Here, let me help you," Marco said from my side.

I put my arm on the table and used my hand to prop up my head while I waited for him to cut my meat for me.

"I'm like a child," I mumbled as I watched him.

Marco pat my head and then pinched my cheek. I laughed but I pushed his hand away. He used the opportunity to put the fork back in my grasp.

"I'm not chewing this for you first, that's where I draw the line," he said. I eyed him as he sat next to me and watched me chew the food he'd cut up. His face was concerned but he tried to make it look normal when he saw me looking.

"Should I get you coffee or something?" he asked.

"I don't know," I said with my mouth full. "I think I just used up too much energy earlier when I—."

When I killed him, I was about to say but I choked on the words. Marco thought I was choking on my food, and he gave my back a sharp swat.

"Ow!"

The sound of his hand hitting my back made me start laughing uncontrollably with my fork clutched to my chest. Marco's bewildered face made me laugh harder until I hiccupped and cried at the same time. I laughed as I watched him get up and go to the comm on the wall. I tried to shake my hand at him not to go but he didn't see me.

"What the hell did you guys do to Alyvia?" he asked into the comm unit.

I could hear Gig and the Captain's voices go silent on the other end.

"What do you mean?" the Captain asked.

"She's over here sitting like a limp noodle, choking on her steak," Marco said. "She can barely lift her head and I think she might be a little delirious."

I tried to catch my breath.

"I'm just tired," I called out.

"She needs to eat," I heard AJ say over the line. "Whenever she uses large amounts of telekinetic energy, her metabolism goes off the charts."

"Limp noodle," I repeated to myself. I started to giggle again.

"She can sleep it off here in the lab," AJ said. "I've got some energy restoring cocktails that will help."

"Cocktails?" I asked quizzically.

"In an IV," AJ clarified. "It helps restore your metabolism after big tele uses."

I shook my head. I was *not* spending the night in his lab, especially with Omin there.

"She caused the ship to lilt earlier," Gig spoke up. "I was coming up the line and one of the men from the warehouse got through the traps. Tippin saw him and sent a wave of tele that pushed him away before he could get a shot off at me. The force of her tele made our ship pitch."

Marco turned to stare at me with a mixture of awe and pride.

"I was wondering what the hell that was," he said.

"Have you ever known anyone to have tele strong enough to move a spacecraft?" I heard the Captain ask. I don't know who she was asking but no one replied.

I looked up at Marco and tried to keep my face impassive but my eyes watered.

"I killed him," I said. "The man from the warehouse. The one who wouldn't leave me alone. That was him I killed."

Marco's mouth opened and his eyes filled with sudden understanding.

I heard Gig curse.

Marco came and sat down next to me. He pulled me into his arms and cocooned me there like Cutter used to. I clutched his arm like a pathetic child.

"Aw, kid," he said sympathetically. "It's always hard the first time..."

I shook my head and tried to pull away but I didn't have any strength left. I rested my head in the crook of his neck.

"It wasn't my first time," I admitted. "My first kill was when I was seven, I think? Or eight? I just...I didn't mean to this time. I saw the man aim for Gig and I just *reacted*."

Hot tears suddenly pricked at my eyes and dropped onto my cheeks in guilty waves.

"Now I *know* that information is not in her file," the Captain said. She sounded concerned.

I shook my head. No, it wouldn't be, would it? That was from before my life at the Academy. If they knew back then, the Academy never admitted it. My reputation was known, though, to the ambassadors and recruiters who visited my home planet. I just didn't know if that information made it to any of the others who set me up with Stryker and let me join the Academy when I was eleven. Master Omin seemed to know what I'd done but it had never been acknowledged before him.

The Governor's Pet, some called me.

Or, the Dark Wife. I remembered how a man spat the name at me before I killed him. He had died screaming. I'd stared in horror at his lifeless body for a long time after he was gone and everyone else had lost interest. Eventually someone had collected me and taken me away.

"You were just a little girl," Marco said. Had I spoken aloud?

I shuddered. Marco's arms tightened around me.

Fatigue finally caught up with me. I yawned and closed my eyes, and enjoyed the way that Marco was gently rocking me. I wanted to ask him if he could help me get to my own bed but the energy it would take to open my mouth and choose words seemed insurmountable.

I heard him murmur my name. I think I dropped the fork I'd been holding because it clanked against the ground close to my ear. I smelled the faint scent of cigar in Marco's clothes, and wondered if he smoked on the ship.

He stroked my hair, and that was it for me. My body lost all tension.

I slept.

"Who did they send us?" the Captain asked over the comm line.

No one answered.

ABOUT THE AUTHOR

Stefanie Contreras was born and raised in Phoenix, Arizona and graduated with an M.S. in Communications from the University of Oregon and a B.S. in Journalism and Advertising from Northern Arizona University. As a native Phoenician she likes to escape the desert heat by writing in air-conditioned coffee shops. A self-proclaimed #geekgirl, she loves coffee, comicon, Geek Girl Brunch Phoenix, and amassing a ridiculous collection of cosplay accessories. Growing up as an avid life-long reader and fan of sci-fi, fantasy, and YA, Stefanie self-published her first fantasy book, Untested, in 2017. Follow Stef @latinageekgirl on Instagram and Twitter, or visit www.latinageekgirl.com.

63333647R00128

Made in the USA
Columbia, SC
10 July 2019